"ENCHANTING . . .

With subtlety and grace, Obejas depicts Alejandra's intensifying awareness of her own identity, as a Cuban, a Jew, and a woman."

—*Los Angeles Times Book Review*

"Obejas relates the compelling and disquieting history of Judaism and anti-Semitism in Cuba amidst evocative musings on exile, oppression, inheritance, the unexpected consequences of actions both weak and heroic, and the unruliness of desire and love."

—*Booklist* (starred review)

"Achy Obejas trains her poet's eye and her journalist's zeal on the ambiguities of exile, the disappointments of passionate love, and the fascinating 500-year story of Cuba's hidden Jews. We won't get anything as pat as a happy ending for our heroine, Alejandra, born with the Revolution, but the reader is guaranteed a magnificent journey."

—RAY SUAREZ
The NewsHour with Jim Lehrer
Author of *The Old Neighborhood*

"Unforgettable . . . Obejas combines the best elements of her writing into a novel of contemporary epic proportions."

—*Windy City Times*

"Lyrical . . . Obejas invests her characters with passions and peculiarities, making them and the details of their days luscious."

—*Girlfriends*

Please turn the page for more reviews. . . .

DAYS OF AWE

ACHY OBEJAS

BALLANTINE BOOKS · NEW YORK

A Ballantine Book
Published by The Ballantine Publishing Group

Copyright © 2001 by Achy Obejas
Reader's Guide copyright © 2002 by Achy Obejas and
The Ballantine Publishing Group, a division of Random House, Inc.
"A Conversation with Achy Obejas," copyright © 2002 by Ilan Stavans

www.ballantinebooks.com/BRC/

Library of Congress Catalog Control Number: 2002092022

ISBN 0-345-44154-0

Cover illustration © Gary Kelly
Photo of palm trees © Hillary Younglove/Graphistock

Manufactured in the United States of America

First Hardcover Edition: August 2001
First Trade Paperback Edition: August 2002

10 9 8 7 6 5 4 3 2 1

Para Tania,
siempre

Son los hombres los que inventan los dioses a sus semejan-
zas, y cada pueblo imagina un cielo diferente, con divi-
nidades que viven y piensan lo mismo que el pueblo que las
ha creado. Siempre fue el cielo copia de los hombres, se
poblo de imágenes serenas, regocijadas o vengativas, según
viviesen en paz, en gozo de sentido, o en esclavitud y tor-
mento las poblaciones que las crearon; cada sacudida en la
historia de un pueblo altera su Olimpo.

—JOSÉ MARTÍ

It's humankind who invents gods in our image, and so each
nation imagines a different heaven, with divinities who live
and think in the same way as the people who create them.
Heaven has always been a reflection of humanity, populated
by images that are serene, joyful, or vengeful, depending on
whether their creators live in peace, in the fullness of our
senses, or in slavery and torment; each shake-up of history
alters the nation's Olympus.

—JOSÉ MARTÍ (TRANSLATION BY ACHY OBEJAS)

ACKNOWLEDGMENTS

This novel began in 1994 at New Words Books in Boston, when Judith Wachs and some of her friends came up to me and asked, "Are you Jewish?" They had recognized in my surname ravages of an ancestry to which I had only vaguely paid attention. The next day, Judith invited me to her home and played me the music of the Sephardim. I will always be grateful to her for that special day.

Since then I've had the good fortune to have at my side during the journey to this book some pretty amazing people. My agent, Charlotte Sheedy, for whom I have the deepest love and respect, has been my steady copilot. In the last year, Leona Nevler at Ballantine Books has been a gracious guardian angel—all writers should feel this lucky with their editor.

I'm grateful to Howard Tyner, Geoff Brown, Tim McNulty, Tim Bannon, Kevin Moore, Linda Bergstrom, Jeff Lyon, Marcia Borucki, Margaret Patterson, Larry Kart, Itasca Wiggins, Mo Ryan, Monica Eng, Pat Kampert, Marsha Peters, Tom Heinz, and the Tempo copy desk at the *Chicago Tribune*. Without their indulgence and good humor, I would never have had the time and space to write this novel. I am most obliged to Gerry Kern, who has never, ever hesitated in his support and has made everything possible.

For his special guidance, thanks go to Moisés Asís. His wisdom and kindness were invaluable.

For assisting with research, I'm obliged to Natalia Bolívar, Maritza Corrales Compestany, Schulamith Halevy, Esther Pérez, Spertus Museum of Judaica (Chicago), Michael Terry, Rallis Wisenthal, and the good people on the anusim list-serve. My parents, José and Alicia, and my cousin, Tony Milera, were free with their memories and insights.

Particular appreciation goes to "Chichi" Fresneda and Juanito González.

In addition, I'm indebted to María Eugenia Alegría, Carlos Augusto Alfonso, Uva de Aragón, Jorge Luis Arcos, Tom Asch and Strong Coffee (Chicago), Ruth Behar, Lourdes Benigni and Casa de Las Américas (Havana), Deborah Bruguera, Linda Bubon and Anne Christophersen at Women & Children First Books (Chicago), Adriana Busot, Suzanne Cohan-Lange, Norberto Codina, Josefina de Diego, Gary Dretzka, Catherine Edelman, Argelia Fernández, David Forrer, Ambrosio Fórnet, Victor Fowler, María Josefa Gómez and Sonia Jiménez, Shannon Greene Robb, Ron Grossman, Charles Halevi, Instituto Cervantes (Chicago), Maria Kostas, Jenny Magnus and Beau O'Reilly at the Lunar Cabaret (Chicago), Mal and Sandra at the Broadway/Montrose Currency Exchange (Chicago), Félix and María Masud, Chris Mazza, Louis Mendez, Ana E. Obejas, Ofra Obejas, Maria Carmen Ovejas ("Manem"), Patricia Peláez, Don Rattner and Nirmala Daiya, Albita Rodríguez and Miriam Wong, Francisco López "Sacha" and the Union of Writers and Artists of Cuba (Havana), Lucía Sardiñas, Lawrence Schimel, Brendan and Brenda Shiller, Helen Shiller, Paul Sierra, Gini Sorrentini, Art and Pauline Tarvardian, Elizabeth Taylor, Kaarin Tisue, Nena Torres and Matt Piers, James Warren, Teresa Wiltz, Owen Youngman, and my students over the years at the University of Chicago, DePaul University, the School of the Art Institute of Chicago, and Columbia College.

And, of course, mil gracias, mil besos to Tania Bruguera.

AUTHOR'S NOTE

Though I use many different sources throughout, including *Tanakh: The Holy Scriptures* (Philadelphia/Jerusalem: Jewish Publication Society, 1985), most of the biblical quotes are from The Holy Bible, Revised Standard Version (New York: Thomas Nelson & Sons, 1952).

DAYS OF AWE

Revolutions happen, I'm convinced, because intuition tells us we're meant for a greater world. If this one were good enough, we'd settle, happy as hens, and never rise up. But we know better: We feel the urge, ardent and fallible as it may be, for a kind of continual transcendence.

Even Eve—or was it Lilith?—felt the pang of desire for something else well before she was officially bestowed the mortal right to yearn. It wasn't sweet talk that drove her out of paradise but a longing for the kind of exultation only rebellion can bring. In my book, she traded up: placid immortality for the anarchy of emotions.

In a word, revolution.

Sure, revolts are inevitably messy and bloody, no matter how just; sometimes the cataclysms they bring only provoke a wish for more and more uprisings. Revolutions can be so unstable, so heartwrenching, that they can make yesterday's lethargy seem heavenly.

Revolutions, however, are as human as the instinct to breathe. The word itself is imbedded with a kind of circular logic that has at its core a contradiction. Revolutions are, after all, for the moment. The minute they cease to be the outside challenge, the moment they become the power inside, they shift more than their balance. They demand another upheaval, another ensanguined engagement.

And they're as regular as the seasons.

Indeed, we measure time by the constant and sluggish turn of our own watery orb; nothing could be steadier and more predictable than these collective, planetary revolutions. Constant insurrection is in our system, in our programming, our cranial codes.

And me, I've got my own revolution.

I was born New Year's Day 1959, at one in the afternoon in Havana, with church bells clanging raucously under baroque spires and congregations purring with prayer. Along the Malecón, the stone lip around the city's coastline, people are drunk with happiness, insomnia, and the pungent aroma of sex. They throw lilies, carnations, and white roses to the ragged coral off the shore for Yemayá, goddess of fertility, the moon, and the ocean.

At Maternidad de Línea clinic in the Vedado neighborhood, the windows rattle from a plane zooming by, crucifixes quiver on the walls. The aircraft glides eerily close to the surface of the seaboard, casting raven shadows across the petal-covered waters. At the hospital, every radio is tuned to the same screaming news.

Everyone's in the streets, red and black armbands and beaded bracelets hang from their wrists, gold crosses against the moist skin and shiny hair of their chests. The radio announcers play carnival music, military anthems, and, finally, patriotic songs.

Up and down the clinic's halls there are intermittent cries of joy and despair. Beautiful women faint from the rapture and heat, or erupt suddenly into inconsolable sobs. When they hear the bulletins, several patients lapse into comas from which they will never recover.

"For the love of god," says an old man, "but this kind of thing happens here all the time!"

I am only minutes old and already dying, my tiny heart pumping in a struggle with the incompatible Rh factors my parents have bequeathed me. I'm hooked up to tubes and electric machines. A glass cylinder of blood is strung up, then another, but my insolent soul refuses every new dose. Each time, the machines rattle and beep with diminished hope.

A doctor whispers to my father: "It's a new day, a new day—and your daughter will live because she is the first new life of this new day!" (A lie, of course, but a persistent one.)

In the meantime, my mother is splayed on an operating table, exhausted. She is so white and soft she looks like she's made of soap. She has a bluish mole on her right cheek; the sign, some say, of those who confuse pain and bliss. Her arms dangle over the sides, her legs akimbo and use-less, barely covered by the sheet the nurse has tossed over her.

My father, his blue-black beard glistening from tears, gathers my mother in his arms. In spite of the horrible humidity and the pallor of her skin, she is ravishing. He caresses her forehead, squints, and gnashes his teeth.

"She is cursed, your daughter," says a bitter nurse, "for she has ar-rived on the darkest day in the history of the world!"

The doctor shoos her away and my father nervously wipes his brow with a handkerchief that's already soaked with my mother's sweat. On the wall behind my parents is a picture of Christ offering his vain and hal-lowed core.

But my mother has a singular plan. She makes the sign of the cross and pulls a tin box from a bag my father has reluctantly but respectfully brought her. She carefully extracts a small ball sheathed in fragrant mint and basil leaves. She unwraps it, revealing a mauve rooster's heart with purple veins, a thin sash of fat at the crown. Then she drops the heart un-ceremoniously in her mouth, chewing purposefully.

My father's grip on her loosens. He promises to light a blue candle when he gets home, to let the gore from the slaughtered cock continue to drench the floor.

A janitor whispers: "Congratulations, congratulations!" He sweeps in a circle around and away from my parents.

All the while, hoses from a new bottle of blood drip into my veins, uninterrupted and without solace. My mother's eyes are shut, her hand on my father's, her fingers circling the bone of a hairless knuckle.

In the distance, there's the staccato of sniper fire. It will take the rebel leader Fidel Castro one week and one day to traverse the whole of the is-land, from Santiago de Cuba to Havana, marking each stop along the way with a fusillade of words.

Before this day is over, I will have eight tumultuous interludes of my own. The first and the last blood transfusion will be from my father, the swelling vein on his arm a verdant river flooding the tributaries of my cir-culatory system. He will insist on standing, insist on cradling me in the nest formed by his long, elegant fingers. An astigmatic priest will be by, one of his hands on my father's head, the other on my burning torso, his lips moving in Catholic prayer.

Then my father will slowly close his eyes and offer his own quiet but defiant benediction.

"Ner Adonai nishmat adam," he will whisper, "my dear Alejandra, ner Adonai nishmat adam."

I

Well before dawn on Sunday, the fifteenth of April 1961, the day we left Cuba—a dreaded day, an ashen day without a single blush of blue in the skies over Havana—my mother ensconced herself in a back room of our apartment, arranging a series of clear glasses of water under a small effigy of Saint Jude, the patron saint of impossible causes.

"This will help purify us," she said carrying in the tumblers, filled not with tap water but with the sanitized kind that came in huge blue bottles.

If my mother's Saint Jude looked a little shiny compared with the other saints on her altar, that's because he was fairly new to her pantheon. My mother's prayers usually went to the Virgin of Charity, Cuba's patron, to whom she'd entrusted my mortal soul if I survived those delicate first hours of transfusions and gunfire.

Even as she lit a white candle to Saint Jude to help us on our journey, which seemed impossible enough, her preferred icon was carefully wrapped in newspapers, plastic sheets, and a double-folded yellow cotton blanket. It was then tucked into a box to which my father had fashioned a handle from thin rope and the inside of a toilet paper roll. Regardless of Saint Jude's divine jurisdictions and whatever seemingly untenable situations we might encounter, it was the Virgin who was traveling with us, the Virgin who would be settled at the pinnacle of whatever new altar my mother constructed wherever we might wind up.

I've always thought of the Virgin of Charity as the perfect mentor for Cuba: Cradling her child in her arms, she floats above a turbulent sea in which a boat with three men is being tossed about. One of the men is black and he is in the center of the boat, kneeling in prayer while the other two, who are white, row furiously and helplessly. (It's unspoken but understood that it's the entreaties of the black man, not the labor of the white rowers, that provides their deliverance.)

I've always found it poignant, if not tragic, that Cuba, whose people are constantly seeking escape and entrusting their fortunes to the sea in the most rickety of vessels, should have early on foreseen this fate and projected it onto its sacred benefactor. When her feast day rolls around each eighth of September, devotees like my mother dress in bumblebee yellow and wink knowingly at each other in church. Also known as Ochún, this particularly Cuban madonna is the Yoruba goddess of love, patron saint of sweet water. She's a beauty, the pearl of paradise, a flirtatious but faithful lover to Changó, the capricious god of thunder.

It's these very elements, I think, that make my mother's choice of this vision of Mary—la Virgen de la Caridad del Cobre—as my patron a perfect guardian: I am a child not just of revolution but also of exile, both of which have so much to do with love and faith.

Even then, on that gloomy gray dawn in 1961, as my father waited for my mother and paced on the third-floor balcony of our home, there were Cubans leaving the island on anything that would float and looking to the skies for signs of salvation. The Cuban Revolution was two years old then, and already defying expectations.

What fueled those who were leaving was less fear of communism, which Fidel had only hinted at at that point, or shortages of any kind, because the U.S. embargo was still a distant concern, but the persistent rumors of invasions and imminent combat that were sweeping Havana. From the countryside came reports that cane fields were being torched, the flames like red waves. What were thought to be American planes constantly buzzed the city. Weeks before, El Encanto—Havana's most exquisite department store and perhaps its most conspicuous link to the United States—had burned to the ground. Its destruction had traumatized the city no less than the break of diplomatic relations between Cuba and Washington, D.C., back in January. Not an hour went by without the breathless dispatch: "The yanquis are coming, the yanquis are coming."

Perhaps no one would admit it now, generations later, but until that spring, when Fidel's police began to sweep out its enemies, real and perceived, and to make chants of "¡Paredón! ¡Paredón!" a part of every Cuban nightmare, few people aside from Fulgencio Batista's operatives had left Cuba because of political persecution or economic opportunity. Though sugar prices were flat, no one believed they'd stay that way. What was actually propelling people off the island was a sense that things were beginning to look more and more like another one of those bloody skirmishes the United States periodically undertook in Latin America.

We knew, through my mother's cousin José Carlos, who'd call us surreptitiously from Guatemala City, where he was engaged in a training mission with American military and CIA advisers, that there were Cuban exiles amassing in Nicaragua, waiting to assault the island. José Carlos's voice was always anxious, almost giddy, on the scratchy line from Central America—surely, had anyone known about the calls, they would have been sufficient grounds to kick him off the invading refugee-composed Brigade 2506.

"Peru is very beautiful, yes, and we've met Indians from all the tribes," he'd say in his own convoluted code in case the lines were tapped, meaning that there were Cubans from all over involved. "Some are a little savage," he'd add, and my parents would imagine that the men were simply more rugged than José Carlos, a gentle soul who'd been a second-grade teacher in Sagua La Grande before the revolution.

It was only later that they learned that José Carlos, who'd worked arduously for Fidel in the early days of the revolution, was finding among the ranks of the 2506 men who'd served in Batista's secret police, murderers and torturers who had personally abused him during his short stint in jail just before Fidel triumphed.

"They have no shame about what they may have done in the past," he wrote in a letter to his wife, Eliana, which she received much later, when a friend who'd also been in the 2506 tracked her down and delivered it for José Carlos, who died without firing a shot, drowned in the warm coastal waters just off Cuba. "Orejón Ramos, the man who slashed my throat in jail, just laughed when he saw me. 'You? Here? But weren't you one of Fidel's best friends?' he taunted. He pointed me out to everybody: 'See this guy here, this skinny hero of the 2506? If it weren't for him and his friends, none of us would be risking our lives here today!' "

It was because of José Carlos's letters and calls just before the invasion of Playa Girón that my parents came to the conclusion that we had to leave Cuba, at least for a while.

The first thing my mother did was sign me up for a foster child program sponsored by the Catholic Church, which would have placed me with an American family in, say, Iowa or Indiana. In her thinking, at least one of us—me, the baby, the important one, the hope for the future—would be passed over, spared whatever was going to happen in Cuba and sent off with the hope of finding a modern pharaoh's daughter.

It never occurred to my mother that I'd disappear, become an American, perhaps not too outwardly, but in those small imperceptible ways in which people don't even realize that they've made irreversible changes. She never considered that, away from them, I might learn to slouch, that I could feel cocky enough to hurry people along when they tried to tell me a story, or that, in the golden fields of Iowa or Indiana, I might pick up a fear of the dark, a revulsion for the predicaments of faith.

That something happened anyway; that I eventually lost some of my equilibrium, even with the two of them present, didn't matter. In the end, my mother didn't have to think about those possibilities—not about the wheat and corn of the American Midwest (with which we would become familiar later, but by our own choice), or about whether they'd lose me for a month or a lifetime.

Certainly my father didn't want us—and especially me—to be anything but Cuban. "It's better for you to be Cuban," he'd say, as if I had a choice then, as if I understood any of it enough to have any input in the matter.

To my father the island was as much the caiman-shaped rock that's Cuba, with its breathless beaches and poverty, as wherever the three of us might be living. He could manage with an imagined isle, but not without the substance of us. We—my mother and I, the weight of us—were the necessary elements to anchor my father in the physical world. As soon as he heard about my mother's plan to send me off to the United States without them, he immediately and without discussion canceled my trip.

"We will not be separated," he said gravely, "*never*. The act of separation itself is what's evil." And he tore the application forms in half very carefully in front of an unnerved priest, who told him in no uncertain terms what a selfish man he was to deny me safe passage to a good Catholic home in the United States.

"This program is run by the church—what could be safer, Señor San José?" the priest implored.

My father just smiled. "Yes, yes," he said, his hands trembling, "I'm very familiar with your programs. And, no, thank you."

As my parents explored their options, there was never any question about where we would go. (By the mid-1960s, Cubans would be welcomed with open arms in the United States, enrolled in special welfare programs, eventually even given unique financial aid packages to help us get through college.) We were prized, frisky, and smart, and, perhaps most important, we would surely return to our sunny island once the United States had toppled Fidel. This is what had always happened: Nobody who displeased Uncle Sam stayed in power very long. A few months, maybe a year or two, and then the dictator himself would be in exile somewhere—usually Miami— and we'd be back to our normal lives, our real lives, the lives we were destined for in Cuba.

After the foster parent program fiasco, my mother signed us up—all three of us—to leave Cuba through one of the regular flights to the United States. She took me to a local photographer, who snapped me all giggly for my passport photo, and had us all vaccinated, fingerprinted, and examined by the government authorities who would decide whether we could get a visa. All the while, she saved her pesos—which had had, until just a few months before, an even exchange with the U.S. dollar—for three round-trip tickets on Pan American Airlines: Havana-Miami, Miami-Havana.

At my mother's insistence, both she and my father began to learn English during this time, practicing by reading to each other every night and inadvertently starting my father off on his life's work. For textbooks, they used an old English-language Bible, the revised standard version with the more contemporary approach, and compared its verses to the old Bilbao Spanish-language Bible my mother had inherited from her father. My mother would read entire English sentences in a rush, barely flirting with each word, waiting for their purpose to emerge through banter and play.

"For everything there is a season," she would say, but it was all as cryptic to her as the original Hebrew and Aramaic. All her life, my mother would decipher messages as much from facial expression and posture, tone and attitude, as from any etymological knowledge.

My father, who would go on to become one of the most sought-after literary translators in the United States, would read aloud slowly, savoring each word on his tongue as if it were an essential oil, a delicate spice, or water for the garden.

". . . and a time for every matter under heaven," he would

breathe, each consonant crisp, each vowel like a musical note through his peony lips.

He'd write down the English words believing each letter contained the formula for happiness and, after he and my mother were through reading for the night, look them up in his gold-leaf Oxford English/Spanish dictionary. After he found the Spanish translations, he'd cross-reference them back into English, discovering synonyms, searching for the new words in prayers of deliverance to see how they stood in context, if he could tell by the company they kept if these were helpful words, if they were friend or foe. He was fascinated by the pursuit of meaning, by corralling significance in a word or phrase from the vast array the universe offered.

As time went by and I began to share some of his curiosities, he would tell me about his frustrations with heaven, how he searched in vain for a Spanish equivalent. "The dictionary said cielo, but that's sky," he explained. "I looked up paradise—paraíso—I looked up nirvana, Valhalla, Eden. But still the closest thing was cielo, as if, in Spanish, the enigma of the sky could never be penetrated, as if the stars were just the stars, the moon just the moon."

Over the years he would compile a catalog of words that refused to convert from one language to the other. Heaven was at the top of his list of stubborn English; in Spanish, it was escampar, which is what happens when it stops raining.

For my father, these were fascinating dialectic conundrums: What was the purpose of any one word? What came first: the concept or the sound? How do words mean?

But for me there was something much more crucial at stake: If it is true that speech reflects the realities of life, that it is, for example, precisely the everyday abundance and diversity of snow that feeds the dozens of Eskimoan terms, or the handful of Taíno words for tobacco, what does it say about us—Cubans, Hispanics—that we can't even imagine heaven enough to name it?

Most of the time I like to think that our inability to express heaven is simply a measure of our respect for a higher power; that, like certain Orthodox Jews who insist on never pronouncing or writing the word for god, we have a deeper understanding, a profound humility about our role in the cosmos. I hold fast to this notion, always praying that it is not just a fatal lack of imagination.

The rest of the time I remember escampar, with its promise that the rain will cease, and that the skies will once more be clear and full of heavenly light.

II

During the time my mother was trying to get us passage out of the country, my father was wondering how long he would be able to keep his job at the floral shop on Muralla Street in Old Havana under the current conditions. He'd travel there every day by foot, a circuitous route north from the Vedado to the Malecón so he could see the ocean and feel its breeze, then east to the colonial district, through the labyrinth of dusty narrow lanes.

For my father, the walk was a meditation. He'd gaze at the plate of shimmering water—at the promise of its coolness in the winter, the tepid embrace of the waves in summer when Havana was smothered in humidity—and review the miracle of his life. It had had such a long and seemingly aimless trajectory before finally finding some direction when he met my mother. Each day, once in the morning, once in mid-afternoon during his lunch break, and again on his way home in the early evening, he gave thanks over and over, sometimes more than a hundred times a day, right there at the altar that was, for him, the Malecón.

During the early months of 1961, however, he often found himself distracted. He'd look out from the shore and see shadows under the surface of the water, black phantoms slithering around the reefs off the seawall. Every day, he'd pick up endless cigarette butts, paper cups, and discarded mamey or mango seeds, their pulp dried and dirty. He'd arrive at the floral shop and make a beeline for the sink, where he'd scrub his hands and try to erase the refuse from his mind, using all his might to focus back on the beauty of his young wife at the seawall, the smell of talcum and violet water on baby me, and the comfort of the lamplight next to his favorite rocking chair for reading.

Regardless of his efforts, it was hard to stay focused. Up and down Muralla, where Jewish immigrants had established a flourishing enclave, fear of nationalization plagued every business, whether a warehouse with a large-mouthed metal door or a general store or textile factory. For months now, the shopkeepers would sometimes find their business day disrupted with the sudden appearance of soldiers at a neighbor's front door, their guns heavy and menacing. Then they'd see the deposed owner, pale and weeping, as he handed his keys over to the imposing commander. The businessman would be shooed away as the embarrassed employees heard from the military men how the enterprise was theirs now, part of the national patrimony.

Most of the time the takeovers were peaceful, even if tense; sometimes the owner would resist but always lose in the scuffle that followed. A few times the soldiers would be a little overenthusiastic and rough up the merchant unnecessarily, or break a window or two just to prove they could. In nearly every case, the entrepreneur and his family would vanish, reappearing in Miami Beach via a postcard or phone call within weeks.

The owner of the floral shop where my father worked, an elderly Polish Jew named Olinsky, had heard that Fidel was planning to take over his modest little store as well, and he, too, had begun to make noises about fleeing.

"The only reason they think they're going to get this place is because they don't know me!" the old man would say. He was short, bent over, his hair bursts of thick white that shot up like Albert Einstein's. He had wide blue eyes that seemed in perpetual shock. "I've been through this before, there's nothing these amateurs can teach me! I'll have it shuttered and burned before those bastards will have the pleasure of a single one of my roses!"

Olinsky did not believe in planes—he'd come to Cuba on a Spanish freighter during World War II—nor in asking permission to

leave, and was aghast at my father when he told him we were waiting for our chance to get visas and plane tickets.

"Hrrrmmmph," Olinsky muttered, his hand waving my father
away as if he were a fly. "Why are you so stupid, Enrich, eh?"

My father's name is Enrique—Enrique Elías San José—but Gregor Olinsky, branded survivor of Auschwitz and hater of Germans, a
man who loved my father like a son, never called him anything but
Enrich, to my father's constant amusement.

"Enrich, how can you be Ytzak's grandson and be so stupid?"
Olinsky asked. "What does Ytzak say about all this, eh?"

Ytzak Garazi, an imposing military veteran who'd lost the lower
half of his left leg in Cuba's struggle for independence, was my
great-grandfather. It was through Ytzak, an active member of many
of Old Havana's civic organizations, that the job had landed in my
father's lap, a plum, really, with flexible hours and surprisingly good
pay. My father, whose green thumb was legendary in our family,
could work there while he went to the University of Havana, where
he studied pedagogy and dreamt of someday becoming a literature
professor. He was already forty-one years old, a late bloomer if ever
there was one, and genuinely happy for the first time in his life.
Even the revolution and the possibility of exile had failed to affect
his first flush of satisfaction.

"Señor Olinsky—" my father began in explanation, but Olinsky
cut him off.

"What if they don't let you go, huh?" the old man asked. "What
are you going to do then? Because you can't suddenly pretend you
want to stay here—you can't, they'll know you once tried to
leave—and what kind of job do you think you'll get after I leave,
huh? Because you know, even if they take over what's left of this
store after I'm gone, nobody—not even you and your beautiful
hands, Enrich—can run this place without me. I am the soul of this
shop!"

Whenever Olinsky got going, my father kept busy so as not to upset him. That day he took a handful of red roses and baby's breath and arranged them into a long-stem vase to be taken over to the beautiful young Italian woman who was currently staying at the Ambos Mundos Hotel. She was a correspondent for a Communist newspaper back in Rome and she'd chosen to lodge at the Ambos Mundos because that had once been Ernest Hemingway's hotel, and she was sure, U.S. invasion or no U.S. invasion, there was a story in Hemingway's haunts, no matter what.

In spite of the tension in the air, the beautiful Italian journalist's brisk walks through Havana had caught the eye of a local doctor, a young fellow named Paco Tacón, who was sending her a fortune in roses every day for weeks, all of which she accepted, none of which she answered.

According to the bellboys at the Ambos Mundos, though the beautiful Italian gave away many of the radiant roses, she kept enough that their scent trailed all the way down the halls and into the elevators, causing the few tourists still willing to come to Havana under the threat of an American attack to think that this distinct fragrance was a signature of the hotel, which they remarked upon in their calls and cables back home to Barcelona and New York, Cairo and Caracas.

For Olinsky, who was making an unexpected bonanza from this unrequited love, Paco Tacón's roses were a sure sign that his plan to leave was the correct one, certainly not Enrique's passive waiting game: The profit from the yearning doctor was going to bribe a local playboy—one Johnny Suro, with his thin movie star mustache and sparkly eyes—into sailing his yacht to Miami and taking Olinsky into a cheery exile.

Olinsky knew nothing about boats, except that Johnny's was spacious and could surely accommodate him. He also knew that Johnny, in spite of his aristocratic and very rich forefathers, was flat broke: His family money had been illusionary for about a generation already, and Johnny's real source of income—hustling American tourist women, especially divorcées—had dried up since tensions had escalated between the United States and Fidel. (As it was, Johnny already owed Olinsky a nice chunk of change from past courtships.)

More important, through some bit of snobbery, Johnny Suro's yacht—even though Johnny himself, with his easygoing manner and the long cigar in his mouth, couldn't have been more criollo—sailed under a Spanish flag. Aside from comforting Olinsky because it echoed his first arrival in Cuba, it also meant that there was hope it could slip through both the American and Cuban Coast Guards, an enemy of neither.

"Señor Olinsky," Enrique announced one day as he ran into the shop, his face aglow, his avian hands fluttering, "I have the best news!"

"Hrrrmmmph," said the old man, barely looking up from some leafy poincianas he was watering. Though he had lived in Cuba for nearly twenty years now, the old Pole was still perplexed by the natives, whom he regarded as too easily excited. Even Enrique, who was generally mild-mannered, could get red-faced during a domino game, swoon over a particular bit of poetry, or do unspeakable things with his shoulders and hips at the sound of a drum.

Yet my father—who wanted so much for me to be Cuban—was always cautious about identifying himself as Cuban, as if he knew that, in spite of his passport and all other appearances, there was a mark somewhere on his heart that would give away his imperfection. He admitted, always, to a Cuban birth, but what he celebrated, perversely enough, was his Spanish heritage. In his later years in particular, he loved to tell others how certainly Cervantes was better than Shakespeare, how the Spanish armadas had crossed the Atlantic as if it were nothing more than a glistening pond.

"What I speak is pure castellano," he would say proudly, anchoring himself solidly in Iberia, "from Castilla, the land of castles."

The only sure thing that pleased him about being Cuban was directly derived from Spain: an adaptability that he saw in the

Cuban sense of joy. That it arose as an answer to the Spanish attitude toward inevitability—a corrupt and funereal surrender, neither
godly nor bright—never occurred to him.

If I suggested that black Africa was the real source of Cuba's
vitality, my father, who was not a racist by any means, would
retort: What kind of propaganda could have led you to such a conclusion? There was certainly good from that dark continent, but in
Cuba it all manifested in music, all else was Spanish, all else was by
the grace of god. As adults, we'd argue about this many times, a debate with no end or winners, each of us defending what we perceived to be the island's honor while my mother silently suffered
our stubbornness.

What has taken me a lifetime to understand is that my father
reached back for his spiritual inheritance to Spain, as if Cuba almost didn't exist, because Spain was scar tissue, whereas Cuba was a
gaping historical wound.

"Señor Olinsky, please listen to me," my father insisted that April
morning in 1961, grabbing him by the shoulders. It was the first
time he'd ever touched the elderly Polish man and the sudden
warmth and strength of my father's hands startled him. Instinctively, Olinsky recoiled. Flustered now, Enrique reached out again
for the old man, which only caused him to back away even more.

"What? What?" Olinsky snapped, slapping my father's fingers
away, leaving a red slash across his right hand.

"I didn't mean any disrespect," a shocked Enrique said, his
folded hand stinging from Olinsky's hard clap. It had been more than
twenty years—since his grandmother Leah's funeral in Oriente—
that anybody had hit him for any reason. "I have news," he finally
said, but the words were dull now.

Enrique watched as Olinsky stood before him, this curved-back
little man, shaking, huffing with anger.

"I . . . I'm really sorry, Señor Olinsky . . . I . . ."

"What is your news, you stupid man?" Olinsky raged, and as he shouted, a shower of unintended spittle hit Enrique's cheek.

My father did not move his hands, he did not cover or wipe his face. Instead he took a breath and closed his eyes in this peculiarly languid way of his. After a pause, he opened them, just as slowly, and looked down at the ground, speaking as gently and evenly as he could: "We got our visas for the United States, we got our permissions to leave, and my wife, Nena, is buying the airline tickets right now, today. We leave in two weeks."

"Hrrrmmmph," said an unimpressed Olinsky.

"Señor Olinsky, I . . . I'm quitting the floral shop," Enrique said. "I know you understand, because you're planning on leaving yourself. You have been very good to me, and to Nena and my daughter, Alejandra, too, and I wanted to thank you—we wanted to thank you, my grandfather Ytzak especially—by perhaps having you to dinner at our house one last time before we leave. I mean, we don't know when we'll meet again, if ever. Tomorrow night, Señor Olinsky?"

But the old Jew just shook his head and frowned. "You're not getting on that plane," he said. "Trust me. You're not flying out of Cuba."

III

On the morning of that spring day in 1961, while my mother prayed at her altar, my father paced anxiously out on the balcony. Below, police sirens howled. Women walked briskly through the streets, babies clinging to their shoulders while older children clutched their hands. Men shouted at one another, their usually robust voices inflected a little higher.

Up on the balcony, my father rubbed his immaculate palms and stepped deliberately from one end to the other, his face grim. He had a clear view of the city's confusion, of the way people were beginning to trickle out of their homes in the wake of the bombings, dazed and unsteady. Later, a few avid antirevolutionaries, convinced American forces were about to topple Fidel, jostled with his supporters, screaming epithets and promises of revenge. Fidel's milicianos—volunteers to defend the nation precisely from foreign attacks—screamed back their own insults and threats. My father knew it was just a matter of time before the hysteria bubbled up to our balcony.

He stepped inside and dialed the phone, as he had been doing periodically since he first heard the commotion. There was no answer at Olinsky's apartment or at the floral shop. He'd already called his grandfather Ytzak, the old soldier, who was apparently out in the streets hobbling about on his peg leg and rabble-rousing. At eighty years of age, Ytzak, the family's most ardent fan of the United States, still felt intimately connected to every ripple and quiver of the island's political storms. The bombings, thought Enrique, would be breaking his heart.

Suddenly, there was another boom. I felt it like a hard clap against my child's flat chest, like something monstrous and mean. My father rushed to the veranda and scanned the Havana skyline. The sound was a heavy, crackling convulsion. Just then, a swarm of crows fluttered past our balcony, their flight path arching upward, even as one of them flapped and struggled, then reluctantly dropped from sight.

"My god, what now?" my mother asked, nervously emerging from her seclusion. She was wearing an emerald-colored business suit, prudent flats, and an American-made Timex watch, but her hair, with its lush locks, was coiled and waved like a benevolent Medusa. The mole on her cheek gave her a certain exoticism, as if a native off the pages of *National Geographic* had been dressed for a job in a law office but couldn't quite hide her more sensuous and precarious origins. Fourteen years younger than my father, she was twenty-seven then, her beauty at its prime.

"It sounds as if it's next door," Enrique said of the bombing. He was surprisingly confident, as if the mere presence of my mother instantly lent him both comfort and credibility. "It's actually quite far, though, across the water somewhere. The air bases, maybe the airport. But it reverberates, it shakes everything."

I was standing between them, a two-year-old without a notion of the weight of moment, aware only of the tangible terror in the air, of the way my parents stared across the room at each other, bewildered.

Instinctively, my mother bent down to straighten my travel dress, a lacy pink-and-white farewell gift from Ytzak, as if there were still some hope of being received in a modern, northern airport, its fluorescent lights illuminating national airlines to faraway vacation spots like the French Riviera or Singapore. But we weren't going anywhere; all flights in and out of Cuba had been canceled.

My mother kissed me, her lips cool against my cheek. "Enrique, what are we going to do?" she asked, standing up again, breathless.

Before my father could answer, we heard a loud, urgent rapping on the apartment door. For an instant, all the noise spilling in from the balcony seemed to vanish. There was a suffocating emptiness into which each knock exploded, garbled, as if in slow motion. Through the door to the balcony we could see black clouds swelling in the skies.

My father signaled us to hide in the bedroom. As my mother gathered me to her and inched away, he strode tentatively, bravely, toward the door. I could feel my mother's heartbeat through the emerald-colored business suit, through the layers of lace, and the skin and bone of both our bodies—a rushed, critical pulse that matched each of my father's stealthy steps. Then, before his fingers reached the latch, we heard the sharp cry of a familiar voice.

"Enrich, Enrich," called Olinsky from the hallway. "Open up, open up!"

He popped into my parents' apartment like a lurid jack-in-the-box, his limbs and middle jiggling in his white four-pocket guayabera. His hair stood on end as if he'd stuck his finger in a socket. "We've got to go now," he said, standing in the center of the living room like a crazy person, his big blue eyes even bigger, looking everywhere and at nothing all at once.

"Go where?" asked my father, quickly closing the door behind the nervous old man. "We're under attack. Señor Olinsky, are you all right?"

He was afraid the bombings might have triggered nightmarish memories for the displaced European, that Olinsky might have fallen back twenty years to when the earth shifted under him for the first time.

"Are you all right?" Enrique repeated, cautiously placing his hands on Olinsky's shoulders to steady him. It was okay this time, he knew.

"All right? Yes, of course I'm all right," snapped the old man, his eyes dazzling azure disks. "But none of us will be if we stay here. Listen to me: They're not bombing Havana, not yet, but they're getting closer and the police are out of control. Castro has given orders to arrest anybody and everybody who's ever looked at him funny.

The jails are already full. There are rumors that they've started holding people at the Blanquita Theater."

(Later, we would learn that Eliana, José Carlos's wife, had gotten snared in one of the raids and was dragged off to a sports stadium in Matanzas, where she spent the invasion nervously wondering if her husband would be able to rescue her, princelike, and fill in the outlines of their beautiful story for the rest of their lives.)

"But where will we go?" asked my mother, our bodies still fused together at the door of the bedroom. Standing there inside the frame—the safest place in the house in the unlikely case of an earthquake—my mother could not imagine any other refuge.

"Where?" Olinsky looked at her, confounded. These Cubans, he thought, so smart but so weak—it all seemed so obvious to him! "Where? By god, Nena, where else? To the United States!"

"Señor Olinsky, we're being bombed by the United States!" my father exclaimed in frustration.

"That's why we must leave now," Olinsky repeated, pulling at my mother's hand. "I have it all figured out. . . ."

And he did, although if he'd laid out his plan a day, an hour, perhaps even a minute earlier, Olinsky could have been certified insane, he could have spent the invasion of Playa Girón locked up under psychiatric observation, not allowed to mingle even with common criminals—that's how deranged his reasoning was.

His strategy was so simple as to seem impossible: With the American-backed exiles poised to attack, probably in Cienfuegos, every available Cuban military ship, aircraft, and officer would be making its way south to the battle site. The northern coasts of Havana would be virtually deserted. (It would later turn out that this wasn't true, that in fact the beaches off the capital were heavily patrolled that night and throughout the week of the U.S.-backed attack.)

It wasn't because of any inherent faith in Olinsky's plan that we left that night. It was only because a bomb exploded, killing several people somewhere near an airfield, and the delirium caused by those deaths was just rolling into Havana when Olinsky's fingers curled around my mother's wrist. It was in that instant that my mother and father made the decision that would forever change my life.

"Let's go," Enrique said, taking me from my mother's arms, molding me to his shoulder as if I were rubber or clay while she ran to grab the carefully wrapped box with the Virgin of Charity.

"Aren't we cheating . . . ? I mean, we were supposed to be on a plane. . . ." Nena said, hesitating. All her prayers had concerned images of flight, of a huge silver bird that would carry us like nestlings in its beak; all her efforts had been aimed at speed and resolution. Now her husband and his imprudent employer were pushing her out the door toward water, not the sweet, drinkable kind, whose patron was wrapped in a box in her arms, but to the paradox of salt, curative and curse.

"I don't know, I don't know," Enrique replied, flustered. His hair and beard were damp, his face as red as Olinsky's.

"Goral," said the old man impatiently, his hands waving in the air in his usual frustrated manner.

"What?" asked my mother.

"It's inevitable," said my father, carefully closing the apartment door behind him while balancing me—I was hot and fidgety—in his arms. "It's fate."

What else could it be? What else could explain the manner in which we left Cuba that day?

After hours of battling our way through Havana's chaotic streets, and even more hours in a strange hearselike car out of the city, we arrived via skinny, dusty roads at what is today known as Hemingway's marina. We had a dinner of soda crackers and guava paste in the car. Then, as night fell, Olinsky, my parents, and I slipped into suave Johnny Suro's small-keeled yacht—*La Marilyn*—

and cruised out of Cuba and into the inky black as if we hadn't a care in the world.

We left without revving the motor, with Johnny and Enrique using long paddles to guide the boat through the long reeds on the shore and into the path of a northbound current that would take us out of Cuban territorial waters.

My mother and I watched from the steps to the cabin, unsure about whether to stay outside in support of their efforts, or inside, where it was murky but safer. My mother's hair danced in the air, forming a halo not unlike the Virgin of Charity's, whose wrapped figure was resting in the yacht's cabin. The emerald-colored suit made her seem like a mermaid poised uneasily out of her element.

As Johnny and my father navigated the silent sloop, Olinsky sat in the bolted chair from which Johnny and his playboy friends normally hauled in giant swordfish, tenacious mackerel, and even the occasional dolphin or shark. When Johnny, an accomplished sailor, was sure we were on the right path, he grinned from ear to ear with satisfaction, the ashes from his cigar sprinkling his bare chest.

"Nena, please come help me," he said all of a sudden. As he rushed past us on the steps, he whistled a merry little tune.

To my astonishment, my mother followed him below deck, handing me to my father who quickly scooped me up to the warm curve of his shoulder. In a minute, we could hear a rattling from the unlit cabin and Johnny's relaxed, easy laugh.

But Enrique, who was always cautiously jealous of others (he had no reason whatsoever to be this way, but always twitched when other men noticed my mother, which was, unfortunately for him, often) simply gazed out past the shadowy waves, past the moonlight to the shivering lights of Havana.

Olinsky, too, was in his own world, his arms at his sides, but instead of staring back at the irreclaimable island like Enrique, he fixed his enormous eyes on the nothingness off the front of the boat.

"Alejandra," my father finally whispered, turning me so I could see what he was seeing. There was a catch in his voice as he rearranged my weight in his arms. "Look, look at the city with me," he said, although he surely knew that I was too little to understand.

The breeze was cool, the ocean splashed gently against *La Marilyn*. As the sloop slid through the water, a triangle of fog hovered just before us. From it emerged a gauzy figure, almost human, holding a bundle in its ghostly arms. Olinsky, oblivious until that moment, turned around and blinked.

Just then there was a fluttering above the surface: a series of thin white stripes lifted off the water, like spirits dancing back to Havana. The two men glanced at each other nervously. (Years later, when my father would tell the story of our escape from Cuba, this apparition was considerably less sensational. It was, he said, just a herd of clearwing butterflies, nothing more, their white-lined transparent wings vibrating as they made their way to shore.)

It was at that moment that my father choked from the truth of what we were doing. "When I found Havana, I thought I'd never leave," he confided with a crack in his voice to Olinsky, whose eyes were glassy and round in the night.

"Hrrrmmmph," muttered the old man, who'd had to run from many places: from Warsaw, Prague, Marseilles, and all the little towns in between that he'd seen only from beneath a blanket in the back of a cart, the cracked door of a railroad car, or the deck of a ship.

"Perhaps she'll come back someday," my father whispered, patting my back with his hand as I began to drift off to sleep. He had already resigned himself to his own displacement, as if he'd been waiting all his life for this moment, the fulfillment of prophesy. He thought he could see me many years later, a young woman in American-brand sneakers, hopping to the tarmac at Havana's airport. But when he tried to conjure my mother and himself behind me—telling me to be careful, or to calm down—the image faded. "Maybe she'll return, a grown woman, and remember something about this moment. I will tell her . . . I will tell her this story so she remembers it, always."

Olinsky snapped out of his stupor, spit into the sea, and wiped his mouth with the sleeve of his guayabera. "Enrich, do not be such a romantic," the old Pole said. He had just saved the lives of this man and his family and here he was, already nostalgic, already full of regrets! "What matters is to go forward. Stop dwelling on your lost city. Look ahead, man."

"There's nothing ahead, it's pitch black, a wilderness," Enrique said listlessly.

"Then look up, look at the stars," said Olinsky. He thought if he gave Enrique a task, it might absorb him; he was that kind of man, serious always, and that could perhaps be exploited in a moment like this, before he allowed his sentiments to sweep them all back to Havana. "Find our way north, tell us how long it'll take us to get there."

Enrique shrugged. "The stars are good for distance, not for time," he said.

"What?" asked a confused Olinsky.

"Time measured by the stars is about four minutes less a day than when measured by the sun," my father said. "It's called sidereal time. I don't know, I read it somewhere." He sighed. Olinsky shook his head, dismayed.

Just then a festive Johnny Suro came bounding up the steps from the cabin, my mother behind him. She was carrying a short stack of plastic glasses, laughing, although it was obvious her heart wasn't in it.

Johnny did an impromptu dance while vigorously agitating a martini shaker. "Gentlemen," he said in his hopeful, easy voice as my mother served drinks for everyone, "I am pleased to announce that we are now out of Cuban waters and on an official pleasure cruise."

It was the closest Johnny would get to a political speech. It was clear his buoyancy came from the adventure, from knowing the events that were unfolding would make a good tale. For Johnny, Havana and Miami, where he'd vacationed often, were interchangeable because in both places he was essentially the same person: a bon vivant, an athletic and privileged young man with charm and smarts to spare.

As my father sipped the medicinal drink and my mother put me to sleep below deck, a whistling Johnny kicked the yacht's motor into gear, turned on its lights, and directed us north.

Olinsky's perennially startled eyes stared straight ahead.

The next day, as we drifted in the measureless blue of the sea—*La Marilyn*'s motor having developed a problem that had Johnny elbow deep in grease but still whistling—I sat on my mother's lap, drinking a Coca-Cola from the yacht's well-stocked icebox. An occasional seagull wafted above us as a sunburned, crack-lipped Olinsky walked the deck, circles of sweat darkening the armpits of his guayabera. All the while, he refused to push up his sleeves, refused to display the blue-green number on his arm.

"Nenita," my father said, taking a seat next to my mother on one of the boat's little padded benches. He had been scrutinizing the uninterrupted water, its sumptuous curve along the horizon, thinking that now he understood how men might have believed that the world could just drop off there, into some infinite abyss. "Every one of those men who came with Columbus must have been utterly desperate. What miserable lives they must have had if this terrible, silent unknown was preferable!"

There was no one else but us then, no one to call to, no one who might find us should anything happen. It was all a blue, blue void. "I was just thinking, how it's so immense out here," my father whispered to my mother. "I was thinking how it's such a terrible beauty, and a return trip, if they don't let us in. . . ."

"We'll be fine," my mother said. She knew to let him talk out his fears, to let him examine all the awful possibilities aloud. "There's no reason in the world we won't be fine."

Then, in the moment my father leaned over to kiss my mother's forehead, we heard the ocean's gentle silence broken by the blare of airplanes above us. One, two, three tubular Cuban B-26s flew directly overhead, their noses pockmarked with bullet holes.

"They're headed for Havana!" my father shouted, horrified. "They're going in the wrong direction!"

Alarmed, Olinsky grabbed oil-drenched Johnny and threw him against the railing. This carefree young man—had he betrayed them? Had this rich man's son turned the boat around in the middle of the night so skillfully that no one had noticed? Was he fiddling with the motor as a trick to kill time until Cuban security could haul them back?

"Tell me, is it us who are going in the wrong direction?" Olinsky demanded of a very startled Johnny.

The young man squinted in the harsh light. Suddenly, the question for him was not about the compass, about matters of north and south, but about the substance of his soul. He thought about the haphazard summer houses that dotted the beaches of Varadero, how their garish colors seemed not gaudy at all but an organic extension of the surrounding Caribbean bounty. As he looked at us—at the flaming halo around my mother's head, my father's expression of constant melancholia, and the innocence in my eyes—he tried to imagine us in austere Miami, a city always looking south for its thrills, where, until recently, for a $10 ferry ride the common streets of Havana became paradise.

It would be this incident, when Olinsky's doubts about Johnny's intentions rushed forth, that would cause the handsome playboy to turn around once we reached Florida. He would keep his promise to take us safely there, to let us disembark as refugees, but he would never touch U.S. soil himself. Instead, he sailed back to Cuba, refusing exile with people who could think him a traitor. He arrived on the island just in time to grab one of his grandfather's sacred guns from the wars of independence, and dash to the Australia sugar mill, where the fighting had already begun just off Bahía de Cochinos. (How he got through all those blocked roads remains a mystery, one of the few stories Johnny refuses to tell.)

In later years, Johnny, a decorated civilian veteran of Playa Girón, would rise steadily through Cuba's government ranks. In

1995, he was named the head of a special task force in the Ministry of Tourism assigned to rehabilitate women who'd turned to prostitution during the desperate early days of the Special Period in Times of Peace, a job for which he proved remarkably empathetic and well-suited.

It would be some time before we knew exactly what had happened that spring day while we were floating in the sea: how the CIA had dressed some U.S. planes to look like the Cuban air force in an effort to fool Fidel and the media; that while we drifted under the Caribbean sun until Johnny fixed our motor, Fidel was center-stage in Havana. The hundreds of thousands gathered to hear him in the scorching heat chanted: "Somos socialistas . . . pa'lante y pa'lante . . . y al que no le guste . . . que tome purgante!"

The next morning, as the CIA-backed Brigade 2506 landed at Playa Girón and my mother's cousin José Carlos drowned, we made our way past the U.S. Coast Guard (whose job then was to be helpful, not to arrest and deport Cubans, as happened later) and sailed into the waterfront at 14th Street and Ocean Drive in Miami Beach, much to the amazement of the Jewish retirees who were wading in the tub-warm waters.

Olinsky, seeing the handful of white-haired old Jews in their colorful beach trunks, started laughing uncontrollably. "This is Babylon?" he asked. "This?"

When my mother tried to calm him by putting her arm around him, the trembling old Pole surprised everyone: He climbed over the side of the yacht and dove into the ocean, paddling madly toward his brethren, his body a ghostly blur through the clear water.

"Mir sind pleitim!" he shouted between breaths. Although it was not deep where he swam, an exhausted Olinsky had to struggle against the mild currents.

"Refugees? From where?" asked one of the retirees, incredulous.

"From Poland—via Cuba!" shouted Olinsky, still in Yiddish, as two other old men grabbed him by the arms and pulled him to shore, where he collapsed on the sand, still laughing hysterically. My father, on the deck of *La Marilyn*, looked on in a near panic.

"And them? They're Polish, too?" the retiree asked, his finger pointing at the rest of *La Marilyn's* passengers—cigar-smoking Johnny, my mother and her wild hair, my frightened father, and me—all of us watching the rescue of Olinsky from the deck of *La Marilyn* with utter fascination.

"Oh my god," my father whispered hoarsely to my mother.

She squeezed his hand.

"All Cubans," Olinsky said about us as we waited anxiously, "except for him." And he singled out my father. "He's Spanish, a Jew," he said, grinning, "marrano"—but he caught himself and, in an attempt to soften the pejorative, switched quickly to Hebrew—"anusim."

My father, shocked by the only word he understood—marrano—covered his face, humiliated and angry.

At the time, I was too young to appreciate any of this, to have a sense of what it meant to my father, or to me. And in the years to come, I would forget everything about this episode except its broadest strokes: that we escaped from Cuba by boat the night of the invasion of Bay of Pigs, that we were protected by the Virgin of Charity and landed in Miami Beach among the tourists, that my mother wore an emerald-colored suit and her hair frolicked in the air as Havana sank into the sea.

IV

My father's a Jew, a real Jew, but it's complicated. It's a long story, technically a little more than five hundred years old. It is, in many ways, a select history, even though its effects are global, its traditions of mystery and concealment a painful legacy.

If the story could be dated, it might be to 1480, when King Ferdinand and Queen Isabella issued an order that established tribunals throughout Spain to deal with cases of "heretical depravity." The point of what would become the Spanish Inquisition was to punish converts to Christianity who continued secretly performing Jewish rites and ceremonies—to condemn them, really, for circumcising their male children, or simple acts like lighting candles on Friday nights.

Jews who refused to convert to Christianity were strewn on torture racks, had water pushed up their noses, or were buried up to their heads in dirt and left to die. Thousands were publicly flogged and burned alive in huge public displays called autos-de-fé. Both royalty and clergy would attend these spectacles as entertainments, drinking ices and teas as Jews and other blasphemers were consumed by flames. The Spanish priests in charge of this murderous apostasy were so frenzied that, on at least one occasion, they had the bones of one hundred already dead crypto-Jews exhumed and publicly cremated in a ceremony meant to serve as a warning to those still living. (All this madness was considered "necessary cruelty" by a Catholic Church that, in 1992, on the five hundredth anniversary of both the Inquisition and the European arrival in the Americas, seriously considered canonizing the queen.)

Twelve years after Ferdinand and Isabella's decree, when Christopher Columbus went looking for India, he took with him a trio of caravels staffed in great part by Jews fleeing Spain under an order of expulsion that displaced more than two hundred thousand people. (Rather than lift the order—still technically in place if not in force five hundred years later—the Spanish king offered an acknowledgment of this suffering and an apology of sorts, finally, in 1992.) Among Columbus's crew were many marranos—Spanish for pigs— or conversos, as the forcibly Christianized Jews were more gently referred to, including his ship's physician and lookout, Rodrigo de Triana, said to be the first European to lay eyes on Cuba.

Other Jews and marranos were not as lucky as those with Columbus: Hearing that many of them had swallowed gold and gems in order to smuggle their wealth out of Spain, ship captains took them on as passengers and as soon as they were out to sea, sliced their bellies open looking for treasure. Back in Spain, Ferdinand and Isabella confiscated all the property and worldly goods of those who were expelled or "relaxed" by the Inquisition, using these monies to underwrite their lavish lifestyles, constant war, and the conquistadors' adventures in the New World.

Had Columbus found India instead of Cuba, his fugitive marranos might have been able to make their way to what is now Maharashtra, where Jews had settled since the second century before the common era, descendants of refugees from Galilee fleeing yet another persecution. What no one could know in Columbus's day was that by 1510, thousands of anusim would settle in Goa, the seat of the Portuguese viceroy in India, nor that in fifty years that same city would welcome its own terrorizing version of the Inquisition.

But in 1492, there was no lack of desire for India on the *Pinta*, *Niña*, and *Santa María*. Indeed, when Columbus (who was Italian but often said to be himself a Jew) was told by Cuba's aboriginal people that he'd landed in Cuba-na-can, he willfully heard instead Kublai

Khan, the Mongol conqueror of China. He went to his grave fourteen years later, penniless and stubbornly convinced Cuba was the southern coast of Asia, mythical India still waiting to reveal itself.

The exact spot in Cuba where Columbus and his secret Jews first disembarked is still somewhat in dispute, but it is generally agreed that it was on the northeastern coast, around Bariay Bay, on the unyielding earth of the province hopefully named Oriente—the east—with its hidden harbors and impossibly long lizards that look like wingless dragons.

Perhaps some of the Jews who came with Columbus climbed to the summit of the nearby mountains and saw the possibilities in the surrounding countryside: the little towns with native names—Banes just off the bay, and Mayarí along the river—that would arise from the bones of the indigenous people the Spaniards insisted on calling Indians and whom they killed with disease and slavery. Or maybe they had visions of the great sugar plantations with English appellations, like Boston and Preston, where a few centuries later the buzz of machetes slicing through the air would rival the sucking sounds of mosquitos during the zafra. Possibly, like the ship's Jewish interpreter, Luis de Torres, they saw the fortunes to be made in the rolled tobacco leaves the small-boned, illiterate natives so enjoyed smoking.

Standing there, looking out at the lush jungle, they might have intuited the future American military base at Guantánamo in the far distance, a rusting chainlike fortress surrounded by a moat of land mines and strings of human blood. It is possible that, with a symphony of tree frogs behind them, these runaway Spanish Jews glimpsed the thousands of tents housing Cuban refugees living there in limbo during the latter part of the twentieth century—sallow-skinned men, bony and desperate, waiting for somebody to claim them.

But no power of divination would have scared off Columbus's marranos: exile and diaspora are like genetic markers for Jews, as normal as hair or teeth. They would have accepted their destiny no matter how clearly any tragedy may have appeared to them.

Centuries later, that early view from the mountainous peaks would be enshrined by a hotel with a sweeping veranda, erected to house visitors to nearby American-owned corporations, including the ubiquitous United Fruit Company, about which Pablo Neruda, the great Chilean poet and sympathizer of Fidel's revolution, would write scornful verses. That view would certainly have been welcomed by Columbus's hidden Jews: Their descendants, most of them baptized and confirmed Catholics by then, would be alive, making a living from the very panorama offered by that veranda, prosperous in Cuba at last for a brief, golden era.

My family—according to my father, according to the few yellowed papers in Havana and Santiago de Cuba that still bear our names—has been on the island from the very beginning, although it is just as impossible to pinpoint our exact moment of arrival as it is Columbus's first footsteps. The family Bibles that bore that information are lost in the currents of the Mayarí River, victims of a family struggle for our Jewish souls.

But it is entirely conceivable that it happened right there on a patch of sand with Columbus, that the first of the San Josés of Cuba put his foot down in Oriente, ran off through the hibiscus and cedars, and planted his own roots right then. No one knows for sure, including the remnants of our family back in Spain; what documentation exists there is as scarce as it is dubious.

Yet there's little doubt in my own mind about my father's family—that is, that we're direct descendants of fifteenth-century Jews from Seville, where there was a particularly vibrant Hebraic community prior to Ferdinand and Isabella's orders, who spoke Ladino and judeo-español (a mix of Spanish and Hebrew that works out like a Sephardic version of Yiddish) and enjoyed the privileges that came to Jews during their Spanish arcadia: advising kings, establishing universities and synagogues, and flourishing as a cultural and religious community.

It was these long-dead predecessors who, when the Inquisition demanded that Jews convert, were asked for proof of their new religion. Wanting desperately to fit in and survive, the first New Christians in our family, like so many of their neighbors and friends, baptized themselves with the most exaggerated Catholic names available, those of saints. This is why we're San José, instead of Bejar, Leyva, or Yarmus. Because we seemed to convert easily, we were spared the usual torments and the odious subterfuge of having to rechristen ourselves with the names of places, plants, or animals: Torres, Flores, Oveja.

The persecution by the Inquisition, which later extended to the colonies in the New World and remained active until 1834, may have been an assault on their very souls, but the Sephardim endured, accommodating each new demand, each new violation. In fact, many secret Jews managed, somehow, to reconcile the redemption offered by Jesus and the wait for the messiah; many converso and anusim families even had members in the Catholic clergy. Some, like Morell de Santa Cruz, an eighteenth-century bishop in Havana, infiltrated the highest ranks. (The man was so popular among the people that the path on which he used to take his daily stroll is still, even during revolutionary times, called Obispo, the bishop's street.)

Until his death, Morell's Catholic credentials seemed impeccable. But in his last few days it seemed the bishop lost his mind, speaking babble, engaging in odd-patterned gestures and bizarre ritualistic behaviors. In his final moment, Morell slowly rotated his countenance to the wall, his face figuratively turned east toward Jerusalem. When his will was opened to be read, his last testament seemed a deliberate defense against the Inquisition, a virtual admission of crypto-Judaism. On closer examination, the Inquisitors realized they'd been burning Santa Cruces at the stake for quite a while: one of Morell's ancestors had been executed in Spain in 1490, two in 1491, another in 1492, two others in 1501—all for "heretical depravity."

That these Santa Cruces were from a good family, connected

and even powerful, was irrelevant. Many of the Inquisition's victims were, in fact, magistrates, governors, prosecutors of the Inquisition itself. From its inception, the Inquisition had not been particularly discriminating in who it targeted—poor or rich, converted or not, repentant or defiant. Almost immediately, it had taken on a life of its own. In 1614, one particularly zealous Inquisitor General, Don Alonso Enríquez de Armendáriz, excommunicated the entire city of Havana, even then deemed Sin City of the Tropics.

In those days, Havana already had countless taverns and brothels along the docks, all jammed with swarthy men of varying nationalities and professions, including many English pirates, Dutch slave traders, African freemen, and—because their presence was not legal in the Spanish colonies—hidden Jews, each seeking their fortunes, enjoying sex with the locals, cutting quick deals and guarding their secrets.

The San Josés from whom I'm descended weren't among them. They were in Oriente, many assimilating into the weird, hallucinogenic paradise that Cuba can be; others holding on, pairing within the ever-dwindling community of clandestine Jews in the mountains and countryside, praying in seclusion. It would be nearly three hundred years before one of us—my great-grandfather Ytzak—made it out of that impossible verdancy and to Cuba's capital, where he discovered there were other, very different kinds of Jews in the world.

Whenever my father was asked if he was a Jew, he would slowly lower then lift his eyes, with all the vanity of royalty.

"All people of Spanish descent have some Jewish blood in them, of course," he would say.

If he was asked if he practiced Judaism, he would sigh, exasperated.

"Who doesn't? Don't all the great religions owe something to Judaism?" His manner would be brusque, as if he were bored by something so terribly, and painfully, obvious.

Asked what he did on Friday nights, he would fix his eyes on a faraway point for a small eternity then turn all their fury on the questioner.

"That depends on the season," he would say, pushing the moment to its crisis.

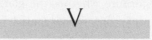

V

If my father's lineage is obscured by necessary deceptions and veiled secrets, my mother's is as clear as stitches, as irrefutable as forensic bands of DNA. Her family story reads like the biblical begots, one name following logically from another, each a stop on a train line that covers a map of the earth.

Not that my mother has ever known much about her ancestors, or cared. She has always been especially adept at living in the moment, at understanding that she is the axis of her own world. Unlike my father and me, who are afflicted with a feverish kind of racial memory that compels us to constantly glance backward, my mother shares Olinsky's stubborn optimism: she stares dead ahead, free of any burden, free to reinvent herself as necessary, free to reinterpret pain as karmic jet fuel, propelling her—and us—toward the next level of the journey.

Perhaps this all makes sense within the vicissitudes of my mother's life. She is, like my father and me, an only child, but unlike us, who grew up surrounded by firewalls of love, she was raised as if on a winded plain, always exposed.

Nena never knew her mother, who died giving birth to her in a Havana hospital in 1934. Her father, a taxi driver, never recovered from the shock. He would gape at Nena, his eyes red and bulging, unsure if she was the demon who'd killed his wife or a divine scrap offered to him by the gods, a little piece of her he could keep as a souvenir. As a result, he never knew what to do, whether to cradle Nena or ignore her. He would study for hours on end the bluish mole on her cheek, unsure whether the glaring imperfection was the print of a cloven hoof or just a trademark of mortality.

By the time Nena was walking, my maternal grandfather was long dead. He was discovered without breath one morning, his inert fingers clamped to a sepia-toned photograph from his wedding day. After his funeral (the photograph still in his hands, even in the family crypt), Nena went to live with relatives who'd take her in by seasons.

She'd spend fall and winter in Havana with her aunt Graciela and her uncle Frank, going to school with her cousins José Carlos and Gladys, who were just a few years older than she and who would turn out to be friends for life. Her aunt and her family had a modern apartment in the Vedado filled with new American appliances. By the time Nena married my father in 1958 and moved out, her aunt was on the absolute cutting edge of domestic technology: There, in the kitchen, was a fully automatic Whirlpool dishwasher.

In the spring Nena would be shuttled to Santiago de Cuba, where her grandmother had moved after widowhood and remarriage, and where Nena spent her days hanging out with the black women who worked as servants in the steamy kitchen or doing laundry in the expansive back courtyard—anything to avoid her grandmother's new husband, a spidery Spaniard who, to the day he died at a sickly ninety-seven, continued to think he was irresistible to women.

Back then, the Spaniard amused himself by grabbing the help behind my great-grandmother's back, pinching their buttocks and weighing their breasts as if they were ripe melons. He'd stand in front of Nena, smacking his lips, and tell her he knew how much she longed for him, but that they'd have to wait until she was a little older, because right now, it would hurt too much, and his love for her was too strong to let him cause her pain. But as soon as she was old enough—and they'd know, by the width of her hips, by the color of her aureoles—he'd initiate her into the rites of love, because it should be done by an older man, one with experience and tenderness.

When Nena shared with the women in her grandmother's kitchen the old man's desire, they became her personal spiritual army. They anointed her with herbs, blew cigar smoke at different parts of her body (which gave Nena a dizzying, vertiginous sensation), lit candles, and seemingly emptied every neighboring creek and ravine to provide the fresh, pure water needed to cleanse and redeem her.

One night, one of the women took one of the Spaniard's fattest, most glorious white roosters and, holding it by the feet, swept its feathers from Nena's head to her toes. She felt its heat, the rush of its wings on her skin. Then with one quick snap, the woman twisted the bird's head off, tossing it on the ground for the lizards and garden snakes. Blood gushed from the bird's neck, warm and sweet.

The spring she turned twelve, Nena got her period and watched her body curve and lengthen. That year, she came down with an illness so mysterious that even her aunt Graciela couldn't find a modern machine to diagnose her. The doctors determined that only the quiet of the seaside, the powers of salt water, could save her. From then on, Nena went early to her summer getaway in Varadero, where her late mother's cousin, Barbarita, offered refuge as well as splendor.

Everyone believed flaming-haired, beautiful Barbarita was a spinster, but, in fact, she had a passionate, lifelong relationship with a Chinese-Cuban man named Wang Francisco Le, who worked as a chef for the American-owned International Hotel in Varadero.

Because neither's family would have approved, marriage was inconceivable to them. But for more than forty years, the lovers shared a home with an ocean view. Wang Francisco kept a separate hotel room the entire time, for appearances only, in case any of our many relatives should come to Varadero and question their propriety.

Every now and then Nena would catch glimpses of the gentle devotion between them, the way lanky Wang Francisco would bring sticky rice balls from Chinatown in Havana for Barbarita's pleasure, offering them to her with his fingers; or how, when they thought Nena fast asleep, they'd curl into the hammock together out in the backyard where Barbarita, a translator by trade, would read to him her attempts to bring poets such as Li Po and Tu Fu alive in Spanish. (The challenge, beyond the obvious, was that these were poets from roughly after the T'ang dynasty, who wrote in an archaic Chinese that Barbarita managed, somehow, to render in modern Latin American Spanish.)

As the years went by, Barbarita became so adept at written Chinese that, by 1989, when Wang Francisco was long dead, a group of young Chinese-Cubans came in from Havana looking expressly for her. They'd brought with them the original poems by Bei Dao that had been read in Tiananmen Square as tanks rolled and all the world watched, except Cuba.

"La época del hielo terminó / ¿por qué está todo helado?"* she recited to them in Spanish, hers and their native language, so that they finally understood and went back to Havana's Chinatown talking about the red-haired lady in Varadero who had fed them the tastiest fried rice. (Barbarita's translations later appeared in an underground newspaper the young Chinese-Cubans published, which was promptly confiscated by government authorities.)

Curiously, Barbarita encouraged my mother to pursue translation as a career, not from Chinese but from English. The future, she said, was American (in spite of the millions and millions of Chinese people), and she brought home Ernest Hemingway and William Faulkner for Nena to convert to Spanish, but my mother got bored

---

* "The Ice Age is over now / why is there ice everywhere?" From Bei Dao's "The Answer," translated into English from the original Chinese by Bonnie S. McDougall in *Against Forgetting: Twentieth Century Poetry of Witness*, edited by Carolyn Forché (New York: W. W. Norton, 1954). Subsequent Spanish translation by A.O.

fast with Hemingway's macho exploits and Faulkner's wry pities—a good thing in the end, because it may well have been her disinterest that helped my father find his calling. When my parents arrived penniless in the United States, they were saved by one of Barbarita's clients who, in a gesture to her, offered my mother a quick translating job. She passed it off to my father without a second thought, inauspiciously launching his career.

For Nena, that became even greater proof that her destiny had always been not to be anybody's daughter, not to have a particular career, not to hold forth on the noble Spanish lineage in her chromosomes, but to be the life partner of Enrique Elías San José, the shy man from Oriente with the blue-black beard and sad eyes who would love her with all his strength and intelligence.

When they first met she felt no fire, no burning desire at all, nothing more or less than a sense of complete satisfaction. From their first encounter, Nena understood their fate together, intertwining her fingers with his as if they'd been lovers forever, unable to imagine falling asleep at the end of her days in the arms of anyone else. And if he was constantly pulled back to some other time, if voices from centuries before echoed in the chambers of his heart, she was there, in the here and now, which she knew was what really mattered.

My mother can talk at length about her father, the forlorn taxi driver, her aunt Graciela and her love of gadgetry, and about Barbarita and her Chinese paramour. She can spin charming, funny stories about the myriad relatives she lived with in so many different places, her gangly cousins' birthday parties and first communions.

But she can't say much about her grandmother Marta, the youngest daughter of Haitian slaves, who saved her grandfather's life with a powerful healing spell when he was injured during Cuba's war of independence in 1898 and whom he rewarded with true love and marriage; or the American confederate veteran who fled to the island after the U.S. civil war, a barrel-chested hunk of man named Charlie Madigan, who entered our bloodstream in the mid-nineteenth century (through a strong-willed mulata ex-slave); or Logan, the aged British pirate, who retired to Havana in the late 1700s, shortly after the British invasion of Cuba, gardening in the profuse wilderness of what is now courtly Miramar, and bred dozens of children with his island-born wife, keeping our legacy alive.

My mother cannot dip back in her genetic pool and claim anything or anyone, because it is all marvelously distant to her, as fanciful and irrelevant as Athena bursting from the head of Zeus. When I sat her down one day and spread before her long columns of dates and names of people who had collaborated over time to create her and me, she laughed nervously, asking questions about why the Mormon church should happen to have so much genealogical information about Cubans—"Isn't that odd? Do you trust it?"—rather than expressing interest in any of the characters that popped up like massive buds on her extensive and complicated family tree.

Perhaps the biggest surprise of all was the quiet revelation that my mother's family, like my father's, came from Seville, and that like them, they were Jewish, too.

I would like very much to affirm that, to shout it out, because it would give me the matrilineal stamp I'm missing. But the truth is that I've never formally staked a claim, or ever will—not only because of my own adverse reaction to organized religions and the concept of legitimacy, but because it would be untrue: My mother's family was Jewish once, but it's been hundreds and hundreds of years since they made a conscious decision to convert.

Years before the Inquisition, in the church records of Spain, these Abravanels were baptized, had communion, confirmed their souls to a Christian god, and married with vows that evoked the blessings of Jesus. When they died, it was not a haham—a rabbi—but a priest who stood over them in their final moments.

Perhaps at some point their conversion was coerced, like that of my father's family. Maybe after the passing of some particularly anti-Semitic law—legal codes that prohibited Jews from owning property, or that banned them from emigrating—it was more a conversion of convenience. They would observe Christian laws, eat fish on Fridays, and rest on Sundays. They would attend church and learn Latin prayers.

But at some point, these Abravanels not only took on Christian rites, they began to drop Jewish ceremony. They had to work Fridays, so the lighting of kabalat shabat candles went by the wayside. To avoid pork elicited suspicion, so why not a little bite? If Pesaj was forbidden in its Jewish form, why not Christianize it? Surely, if they had to, thirty-six Jewish saints could fit snugly into one Christian archangel. The greater evil would be to perish from the earth.

Who knows what generation it was that could no longer intone Sh'ma Ysra'el, Adonai eloheinu, Adonai ehad—never mind understand that those six words carried the essential credo of Judaism. At some point Jews like these Abravanels were no longer anusim, but real converts. Their zeal for Jesus, Joseph, and Mary, for Saint Paul and the Apostles, would give them a chance at entry to the professions, betrothals to nobility, the reward of knowing whatever riots were spawning in Seville and Toledo had nothing to do with them. Eventually, they were no longer anusim—coerced—but Catholics as morbid and prim as Ferdinand and Isabella.

At the point that the first Abravanel landed in Cuba in 1620—in Havana, the seat of the Spanish Viceroy—he was not running from Spain, but commissioned as a counselor to the new Captain General. That same year, as the *Mayflower* was sailing into history, Havana was already more than two hundred years old.

Anton Abravanel arrived in the Cuban capital after several hundred houses had been leveled by fire, and where prostitution, gambling, and graft were as common as rain. The city was in a constant state of alarm, the lookout on the bay signaling the highest state of alert every time a ship with a British, French, or Dutch flag sailed into view. Because news traveled slowly to the colonies, the habaneros never knew with whom they might be at war, a condition, I'm sure, that has been genetically encoded into our brains.

For the first few years, Anton Abravanel experienced heat, mosquitos, and a sugary sexual exhaustion with Cuban women of many hues, always making it a little breathlessly to his meetings with the Captain General. Then one late summer day in 1626, thirty Dutch ships appeared at the mouth of Havana harbor. That's when Anton was forced to focus, to consider the advice he had to give to his employer. For a week, the Dutch hovered, setting off spectacular fireworks of artillery every time a ship tried to nose its way into Havana.

Knowing that the Spanish silver fleet was due at any moment, the Captain General, one Don Lorenzo de Cabrera—corregidor of Cádiz, field marshal of Spain, and knight of the order of Santiago—sent word to warn them. The strategy had been devised by his counselor, Anton Abravanel, who proudly whispered it to his mulata of choice for the evening, not knowing her true love was an Italian sailor under the command of the Dutch sailing legend Piet Hein, sitting in his ship just outside Havana harbor. The tip proved fruitful for the Dutch, who chased the Spanish flotilla into Matanzas Bay and seized more than eighteen thousand pounds of silver, valued at more than twelve million Dutch guilders, one of the biggest prizes ever captured in the Caribbean.

A troubled and remorseful Anton Abravanel never revealed his sin to his superior, of course, but he knew: If his mistake were found out, it would be attributed not just to stupidity but to his latent Jewishness, still visible to all in his otherwise illustrious surname (he kept it because, in business, it still had a certain weight, Inquisition or no Inquisition). To make up for his miscalculation, Anton spent the rest of his days repenting and confessing to brown-robed friars. He stopped dallying and married a proper Spanish girl, a niece of the Captain General imported from Spain just for him. He went to mass daily, took communion, and instructed his children in the strictest adherence to Catholic belief, all in the hope of erasing the awful smudge on his soul.

But as Anton's children and grandchildren grew up in Cuba, their Catholicism eventually became as corrupted as the Abravanels' initial Judaism. The Church of England was a passing fancy with a lasting effect. Freemasonry established a foothold in Havana and sucked in almost all the prominent families, including the male Abravanels. Santería and voodoo thrived in secrecy, and shrines to the Virgin of Charity began sporting glasses of water, dead chickens, bottles of rum and firewater.

By the time my mother met my father, her religious legacy had come full circle: When he worriedly, and in his own convoluted and roundabout way, confessed to her that he was not really a Christian in spite of appearances, she had a dim memory, a sense of what he was talking about as something long renounced.

There was no question that for their union to work, my father had to be at ease. He was not a man who found comfort in faith but who felt its burden, its constant imbroglio. A converso or anusim girl—virtually impossible to find in Cuba anyway—might have inadvertently fueled resentment, an out-in-the-world Jew would have posed a crisis of identity, and a devout Christian would have suffocated him. But a lax Catholic, a girl who prayed while arranging glasses of water, who knew there were mysteries in life that could not always be explained and who could accept them and his often fruitless efforts to comprehend them . . . she was perfect.

Surely Enrique knew from my mother's name—the distinctly Sephardic Abravanel—that there must have been a Jewish part of her somewhere. Maybe he imagined their bloodlines going back, long ago kin meeting in a Seville market over a bin of mangoes imported from the New World, feeling a powerful affinity for each other, not understanding that their future was to produce them, to rescue him.

When I explained my mother's genealogical charts to my father in the basement of our Chicago home, closed off from the world as if I were about to decipher kabalistic secrets, he smiled and slowly lowered his lids, his face red from nothing but joy, then leaned back, humming, humming, as if he were praying in Jerusalem, swaying there ecstatically before the Western Wall.

VI

To this day, nearly forty years later, I don't know how my parents did it, how they were able to turn their backs and say good-bye to their home, to Havana, to that strange island of orchids bursting red and hummingbirds the size of bees.

I know there was a panic swirling in the streets that I will never be able to fully comprehend. But that act of departure—tucking into pockets birth certificates, a handful of American dollars, a particularly poignant letter from a loving friend; deciding to bring along a delicate plaster goddess, as plain as any; and never knowing whether they'd ever be able to return—all that still escapes me. I can't imagine standing before the mirror with that knowledge, freezing that terrible image of myself at that moment.

I consider my parents' flight and wonder what I would have done. Perhaps I might have gone to say farewell to my great-grandfather Ytzak, or at least tried to convince the old man to join us—not necessarily for his sake but for ours. Maybe, in their place, I would have grabbed a napkin from a favorite cafe, for the pure feel of it, for its coffee stains, for the pungent smell of its fresh oysters from Sagua.

I certainly would have taken a moment to look out from the Malecón, to measure the emptiness from the rough shore to the horizon. I would have wanted the time to consider how many darkening butterfly lilies, how many revolutionary triumphs and drowned balseros it would take to fill the gap.

I have heard from many, many people that on a clear night in Havana, you can stand on the Malecón, look north, and see the lights of Key West shining like a beacon. And I've strained, I've rolled up my jeans and leaned over the salty rocks at low tide—red and olive seaweed clinging to the dead coral—and stared ahead into the tenebrous night until orange and amber flashed in front of my eyes. But I've never had a glimpse of that tiny torch that others see, only blackness, only the same wilderness, the same phantoms that my father saw the night he left Cuba.

I know it's peculiar, because when I step on the pier at Key West, on the southernmost tip of the United States and where Cuba is closest, I don't need help spotting Havana. Without the benefit of binoculars, without stars or moon to light the way, even with a mist of clouds, I can always discern through the abyss of the sea the sprinkle of lights on the other side.

The first time I set foot in Cuba as an adult was in 1987, two years before the crumbling of the Berlin Wall and, eventually, the vast wasteland of the Special Period and Zero Option, the economic disaster that came to the island after the fall of the Soviet Union.

On arrival in the wee hours of the morning during that first trip, Havana's suffocating José Martí International felt more like a bus terminal than an airport, except for the spooky green-uniformed soldiers from the Ministry of the Interior. They watched stone-faced as we waited in interminable lines to get our visas and passports stamped, even though we were government guests arriving on a private plane. It's not that there were that many people in the lines with us, but rather that the process itself was obscure and required signatures and stamps from a vast number of functionaries—none of whom seemed immediately available.

At the end of the miserably hot and stuffy line, a nurse asked each and every passenger how we were feeling and if we wanted our blood pressure taken. Nearly everyone declined, a few with looks of terror, instantly paranoid about what message they might be inadvertently transmitting about their fears or vulnerabilities. High up on a wall, there was a faded advertisement for Johnny Walker Black that looked like a leftover from the Mafia party days of 1959.

On that first visit to Cuba, I didn't go as a tourist or a displaced person looking for roots. For me, it was a professional visit: I was interpreting for a group of progressive Chicago politicians and activists.

I'm an interpreter, an oral translator, my father's daughter but I'm nowhere near his rank and order. I'm not sought after by Mario Vargas Llosa and Carlos Fuentes. I'm not really trained in literature, nor do I teach language to eager graduate students the way my father did, deciphering not only the corresponding grammatical structures but also the layers underneath, the histories of the cultures. I don't have his patience, so I rarely do written work.

Unlike my father, who loved rhetoric in an intimate and rigorous way, I'm an interpreter of the broad and mundane sort: I stand up in courts and let myself be used like a hand puppet by the witness, usually an impoverished and undocumented Mexican immigrant whose leg was sliced in an industrial accident. (Wrapped in her dirty gray scarf, she looks to me for a moment like a war casualty, a refugee breathing momentary relief in spite of her injuries at a Red Cross camp.) Or I sit in meetings in public aid offices, as if I were Charlie McCarthy on some bureaucrat's knee, untangling rules and regulations for an unwed mother from Puerto Rico who is about to lose all her welfare assistance because she's chosen to go to college instead of taking a job at the local Burger King. ("Does she un-der-stand?" the bureaucrat inevitably asks, each syllable monstrously loud.)

I'm the mouthpiece for whom I'm paid to speak, whether it's the victim or the victimizer. I prefer the victim, of course, but I don't always have a choice. And sometimes— when the witness is clearly lying, or the bureaucrat is a second-generation Colombian who took the job with public aid thinking she could make a difference—it's hard to tell which is which.

"¿Es tu primera vez en Cuba?" asked the soldier who processed my papers at the Havana airport. He was young, with just a touch of fuzz on his chin. His Spanish was lazy and familiar.

"Sí," I said weakly, wondering if I sounded like a foreigner to him. I have no accent when I speak in Spanish; I'm never perceived to be anything but a native speaker. But I knew even then my rhythm was different from his: more neutral, yes, but also more reserved. I knew that simple *sí* had already betrayed me.

Even before accepting the job, it had become clear to me this would be no ordinary assignment. To begin with, I had to tell my parents it involved going to Cuba.

In the twenty-six years they'd been in the United States, they'd never once considered returning for a visit. When they discussed going back, it was always in the revolution's aftermath, during the kind of apocalypse that would break their hearts so forcibly that they'd have to resign themselves to life in the United States after all.

My parents are not fanatical refugees, they do not assume everything about the revolution is hideous. As much as they may be alienated in the United States, they've made peace with the difficult decision to leave Cuba. Yet when I said I was going back to the island, they paused as if they needed a moment to adjust their antennas, to rearrange their sense of disbelief into something coherent and civil. Then they kicked into exile-style paranoia.

"Be careful—don't talk to just anyone," my mother warned me about my upcoming visit. "You will get them in trouble if you talk to them."

"You could get yourself in trouble," my father said. "You could wind up in jail."

They were comfortably settled in Chicago by then, my father a literature professor at Loyola University who walked to work each day along the park trail that runs parallel to the lake, dreamily gazing at the water, whether shimmering or frozen white. He had become a large man, with a bear's chest and well-padded fingers, a long way from the bony boy from Oriente. He was sixty-seven years old, still vigorous, his hair as white as Ytzak's when we'd last seen him.

My mother had changed, too. Still resplendent with her hair loose, she'd comb it back and up, always constraining it, pretending to hide the abundance of new gray, reining it in with combs and pins and bands. She had remained thin, but what had appeared as tanned and silken in Havana was now pale, with blue ropes up and down her arms. The mole on her cheek had grown so that doctors suggested she have it surgically removed, but my mother demurred, saying it was her good-luck charm.

She'd chosen to remain a housewife, managing my father's affairs and growing roses and sunflowers in the springtime. As a child, there was nothing I loved more than to watch her tear into the dirt in our backyard with her bare hands, bending her back into the work until sweat drew a huge Rorschach on the back of her blouse. She was strong, sexy, I thought.

"Don't think you'll see anything real," she said. "You'll only be allowed to go where they want you to go. You won't get to see or hear anything they don't want you to see or hear."

"If you get in trouble, get a message to Moisés Menach—my old friend from Oriente—you can always find him through the Sephardic Center," said my father. "He's a party member, the head of his CDR, that should come in handy."

He suggested Johnny Suro as a backup in case of emergency, but then they both realized that Johnny, then a vice minister, was probably too high up in the government's bureaucracy to be so easily accessible to somebody like me.

"Carry your American passport at all times," said my mother. "If they try to keep you from coming back, tell them you're an American citizen, that you gave up being Cuban a long time ago—tell them you have nothing whatsoever to do with Cuba."

As she spoke, I could hear my father's nervous breathing, as if someone had just given him a swift kick in the gut.

———

The night before I left for Cuba, I picked up the ringing telephone and heard my father's timid voice on the other end. I knew instantly my mother wasn't on the other extension, that this was something private, a concern he wanted to share with me alone. He sighed as if he were an overwrought lover preparing to deliver an unfortunate list of clichés that were, nonetheless, his only recourse.

"Sometimes, it is better to imagine a place than to see the reality," he said, swallowing hard. "Sometimes, I think, it is better to have that ideal, that hope." His words flew like stones into a deep, dark well.

My bags sat gaping on the floor of my chaotic apartment, my boyfriend, Seth, who was staying behind, lay exhausted and asleep in our bed, his body exposed like a centerfold. "Honestly, Papi, I could care less about Cuba," I said, at the time believing every word. "It's no different to me than if I were going to Bolivia or Senegal or Spain." On the bed, Seth turned away, irritated by my whispers.

"Well, Spain, yes, that would be different," said my father, distracted now, off into his own world of doubts and preoccupations.

Standing in the airless airport in Havana, waiting for the fuzzy-chinned soldier to finish with my papers, I realized I hadn't been completely honest: It wasn't really my first trip to Cuba, but my first return to the Land of Oz I'd conjured in my dreams.

As a child—my English still fractured, my soul yearning for a place of safety in the brutal playground of U.S. adolescence—I imagined a Havana in which everyone moved with my mother's sensual grace, talked like my father, and looked like me: I'm olive-skinned, with almond-shaped eyes the same blue-gray as Ytzak's, chestnut-haired and slender but with hips. (There are moments, I know, when I can be as dazzling as my mother, but I have to work at them, I have to want them to make them happen.)

Havana was where I was supposed to have lived, where I should have emerged like Aphrodite from the foam—where my destiny had been denied. Now, here I was, in the city where I belonged, the city that should, would, be mine—especially when American horizons seemed bleak or cruel. As a child, I held Havana out to myself like a secret hiding place, a trump card, the Zion where I'd be welcomed after all my endless, unplanned travels in the diaspora.

At the time, I had no idea my rapturous imaginings about the city were a family tradition, that Ytzak had been in love with an imaginary metropolis, and that my father's obsessions with Spain gushed from the same fountain.

As a child, I once found a weathered street map of Havana among my parents' things and began to slowly, methodically, memorize the city. I started with Old Havana, the historic quarter, the cobblestoned, cramped lanes that spoke to me through photographs old and new about a constant cadence, about doors too close together, about a strangely comforting and untidy intimacy. I imagined being there, sitting on a grimy stoop, watching the human parade like a native.

I could, at the age of fourteen or fifteen, talk knowledgeably about how Compostela and Habana streets ran the full length of the district. I could place their intersections with Luz and Sol and inject just the right irony when mentioning Porvenir—a tiny, block-long street whose name means "a hopeful future."

I didn't know the landmarks. I couldn't say where something as grand and imposing as the cathedral was outside of its postal moorings; nor could I say what kind of landmark rested on any corner if it didn't bump up against the Malecón. But I could do the math in my head and declare exactly when Tejadillo became Trocadero (right after the intersection with Prado Boulevard, with all its decrepit luster), I could talk about how the Malecón stretched all the way from Old Havana past the glamorous Hotel Nacional, how it curved and hugged the city of my birth.

Curiously, I never imagined my parents there, our apartment or the floral shop. I pictured only me, a Cuban me, wild and free.

And then, as I grew older, as the years went by and I blithely came and went from our house in Chicago, slamming the screen door behind me—off to drama club, to swimming practice, to a meeting at the school newspaper, to smoke pot, to rock concerts in the Loop, to rendezvous with long-haired boys or willowy blonde girls—as the need for refuge became less and less, Havana faded, and my Cuban self vanished, like clearwings in early morning mist.

VII

At José Martí airport in 1987, our entourage was gathered up and bundled into private cars, all boxy Russian-made Ladas. We emerged onto a slender street that cut through a residential neighborhood of faded flat-roofed homes. Everything was gray. It was just after dawn and raining in long, hard sheets, but I pressed my face up against the car window anyway, trying to make sense of the swashes of dull colors on the other side. A crowded bus went huffing by, people spilling out of it every which way. There were young girls wearing faded reds, boys in white T-shirts that turned transparent when wet. I could make out the dark circles of their nipples, the penciled lines across their firm bellies.

Cuba had been receiving regular visitors from the United States, particularly exiles, for about eight years then, but as we passed, people stared. The gusanos, or worms, as those who'd left had been called, had become mariposas, butterflies, and just as fleetingly welcomed. There were no smiles among those sleepy faces that morning, only a cool defiance.

Ours was, ostensibly, a fact-finding mission: We traveled to hospitals and factories, saw firsthand how Cuban doctors treated Angolan war veterans, how workers processed rules and regulations in orderly workplace meetings that seemed the very antithesis of Cubans' natural playfulness. We met writers and artists who were paraded before us as evidence of the revolution's inclusiveness, its tolerance of the inexplicable. We watched a seniors' circle doing its breathless morning calisthenics. Several times, we were serenaded by scrub-faced young Pioneros who then presented us with color-crazy bouquets of distended buds.

We were put up at the Habana Libre Hotel, the former Hilton, which was empty but for a few Canadians and Russians. I identified the tourists instantly: They were red-skinned, like lobsters after boiling, and too curious and happy about everything. To my surprise, I was given a private room, for which I was grateful. I wasn't in the mood to listen to my tour group members talk about the wonders of Cuba anymore than I had to during the regular workday. Whatever Fidel's real achievements, their revolutionary zeal struck me as touristic, even kitschy.

Everywhere we went there were billboards exhorting solidarity with people all over the world and praising the revolution. In front of the U.S. Interests Section—the same inviolable glass and steel building that had housed the American embassy back before diplomatic relations were severed—a sign decried the U.S. embargo: ¡SEÑORES IMPERIALISTAS, NO LES TENEMOS ABSOLUTAMENTE NINGÚN MIEDO!

Back then, there was construction all over Havana—at every corner, metal spikes poked out of stacks of concrete blocks like long, stubborn blades of grass. Cuban men in loose undershirts milled about the building sites, perking up whenever a woman walked by. They called out with outrageous rhymes full of innuendo or performed long, dramatic monologues about how beauty made their hearts ache.

The women didn't reject the attention. To the contrary, the saucy strut, the pendulum swing of their hips all indicated it was well-practiced, absolutely meant to be provocative. And I responded: I envied the cubanas' easy strolls, the confidence with which they answered every salty flirtation.

"Me muero por ti," said one guy watching a particularly curvaceous local in a skin-tight green pantsuit strut by. "¡Me muero, me muero!"

As if to make his point, he pointed the tip of his drill at his heart and pressed the trigger. The instrument whirred, just centimeters from his chest, but the woman kept going. When it became clear she wasn't going to turn around, the construction guy smiled broadly, pointed the drill triumphantly at the sky and started laughing, turning his defeat into a symbolic victory of sorts. The workers in his unit howled, high-fiving him.

Just when the noise had subsided and the men were beginning to make as if they might be getting back to business, the blinding green vision reappeared. She stood on the opposite corner, hands on hips, legs spread apart. Her curves were like the slopes of a vital mountain.

"Oye," she shouted to her admirer, "so how come you're not dead already?"

And the men at the site, including the original guy who'd threatened to kill himself over her, broke out in applause and hilarity all over again, this time celebrating her audacity. When she swaggered away this time, it was her victory that was total.

All that week I dreaded the moment when some Cuban man would fix his sights on me, my heart in my throat as he decided whether I was due the complicated mix of flattery and possession that came with being island-born, or the courtesy of silence afforded foreigners. There was no way I could answer, and that had nothing to do with my fluency in Spanish. All week I trembled and crossed the street whenever I saw a group of construction workers, their watery eyes just beginning to focus on me.

In spite of all the revolutionary fervor, there was a somber undercurrent in Havana even then, as if it knew what was coming, as if it understood that soon the Soviet Union would be history, the country would be in tatters, and many of its most talented artists, the very people who were introduced to us as products of the revolution, would soon be living abroad.

A little more than a year after my first visit to Cuba, Arnaldo Ochoa, a hero of the revolution, found himself accused of drug trafficking and treason in a television trial watched by millions of

Cubans on the island and abroad. He was found guilty and shot to death before a firing squad—¡paredón!—an event that shook Cubans everywhere to the core.

In 1987, I strolled through the city breathing something like burning sulfur in the air. Whether on the majestic boulevards of Miramar or the tight alleys of the historic district, I would run into discarded animal parts: an empty crab shell, chicken bones with the marrow sucked out of them, a fish skeleton so complete and white it looked like an ivory comb. At first I considered these might be offerings to gods I didn't know, but they seemed much too random, too ordinary and blunt. There was never a red ribbon, a piece of paper folded with spells, or any kind of rock or amulet. Once, I saw a dead rat with its feet inexplicably cut off swelling in the midday sun by the curb.

There were loose dogs everywhere, yelping excitedly, yet curiously without bite. None ever came up to me, not one ever felt threatening. Invariably mutts, they trailed clouds of fleas, registered whole patches of baldness on their rumps. They would look up through rheumy eyes, gnaw at some terrible itch on their backside, and run along.

One day, at a meeting with educators, one of the members of our delegation got up to speak. The sensitive child of Cuban exiles and the founder of various well-meaning leftist groups in the United States, he'd named his only son after the disappeared revolutionary leader Camilo Cienfuegos.

"The day the blockade is lifted—and it will be lifted . . . lifted soon—it will bring many things," he proclaimed in halting Spanish without an interpreter. His voice rose and fell, complete with dramatic pauses just like Fidel. "New appliances and timely magazines . . . technological wonders and abundance, yes . . . but . . . it will also bring disasters . . . like greed . . . and racism."

He became quite emotional then, recounting his own terrible

stories at the hands of American prejudice. Even though he was still taking his public speaking cues from Fidel, the personal woes he was recounting were alien to anything Fidel, who speaks only of glories and threats, would have ever talked about. I was embarrassed for him, for all of us.

Then I looked around the room, at the varied colors of the members of our foreign-based delegation, and at the white-skinned, hazel-eyed descendants of northern Spain wearing official Cuban government name tags. The only island Cubans without them were the two charcoal-toned women in the room, one who walked like a shadow behind us, reaching over to pour fresh bottled water from a pitcher into our sweating tumblers, while the other sat stolidly just off a small hallway, ready to hand a few sheets of tissue paper to anyone going to the rest room.

Suddenly, rich red blood gushed out of the speaker's nose, splattering all over his white guayabera. He looked down at himself, at the way the blood was soaking through the fabric to his breast. It was as if the blood were sprouting from a wound there instead.

"Dios mío, what's happening to me?" he cried, plummeting.

I was closest to him so I slipped my arms around his body as soon as he began to drop, feeling the warm stickiness of his chest. He was wearing a slender gold chain with a crucifix that snapped the instant I touched him and clanged on the floor as loud as a church bell fallen loose from a tower. As he leaned on me, I heard his heart pounding, the blood beating senselessly against the walls that confined it. His pulse matched my own irregular rhythms.

"¿Qué, me está pasando?" he cried as we plunged, his body completely covering mine.

"It's just a nosebleed, just a nosebleed," the woman who'd been refilling our glasses said as she dunked her hand in the pitcher's coolness and sprayed the man's face with a quick snap of her fingers.

She laid him out next to me and began running her hand from his forehead to his thigh in quick, practiced gestures. I watched, hypnotized like everyone else, until she finished with him and turned to me, her hand like a bird fluttering, closing my eyelids, tracing my neck, around my breasts, and down to the tender place just inside my hip.

Then the other woman came toward us, the single sheets of tissue paper now crumpled into a white rose in her hand, and quietly wiped the blood away.

VIII

Anytime a Cuban returns to the island, we become couriers for those who do not. No matter how obstinate those who remain abroad may be about their exile, how partisan to the U.S. embargo, there is no blockade of emotion.

From the moment flights were first allowed between the United States and Cuba, the return has been something of a spectacle. Peek at the waiting area in Miami International and the Cubans who are going back are easy to spot. They're the ones in the special holding pen who, in order to get around the weight limits imposed on baggage, wear three and four gaudily colored shirts at a time, boots as big as clown's feet over sandals or sneakers, belts made from strings of sausages. Women don hats whose brims are dotted with earrings, pins, and other bangles that relatives in Cuba can resell to tourists. Men carry American-brand cigarettes in every pocket, and practical Italian handbags stuffed with medicines they'd normally mock as effeminate in their everyday lives.

Because of shortages in Cuba, those who return also tend to carry extraordinary quantities of foods. When the customs officers open the human-sized duffel bags of the returning exiles, cans of Spam and tuna, bottles of baby food and meat sauce spill from their bellies. I once witnessed a customs inspection in Miami that netted more than fifty pounds of frozen beef, each slab of red flesh chilled solid inside frosty freezer bags. When the customs officer, a dismayed Nicaraguan, objected, the Cuban passenger claimed the meat was not for consumption but for religious practices.

"An offering to Changó," she said, adjusting the can of sardines she was wearing like an amulet around her neck. "It's the only way the gods will let my sister out of Cuba!" The crowd of other Cubans who had gathered around her nodded approval (despite the fact that her claim was obviously fraudulent). They looked at the Nicaraguan officer as if he were some poor slob destined for tragedy.

Not all the freight back to Cuba is so perverse or dramatic. Every Cuban carries at least the U.S. allowed limit of $100 a day. Nearly everybody carries thousands more, usually stuffed in their pockets, suitcase linings, and tampon cartons, as if the customs officials could possibly be unaware. Because Cuba's is a cash economy, credit cards and traveler's checks are generally worthless, souvenirs from capitalism as alien as the Dow or a drive-up.

Curiously, returning exiles are seldom bodily searched in Miami, seldom asked about the peculiar bulges in their bosoms or thighs. It's an honor system to which everyone seems to silently subscribe. Even the Cubans who refuse to go to Cuba, who claim they wouldn't give Fidel a single dollar to prop up his Communist dictatorship, play along: They slip a $100 bill or two for their aunts or cousins into the pockets of some other Cuban who's going to the island to visit his dying mother. Money's never trusted to traveling Americans or other Latin Americans, only to Cubans, who, regardless of politics, are the only ones who really understand.

In 1987, it was still illegal for Cubans on the island to have dollars, and there were still enough Soviet subsidies available (and only a nascent black market) that most people weren't focused on currency. Our most precious cargo wasn't money or meat, but letters. Because there is no direct mail service between Cuba and the United States as a consequence of the embargo, correspondence can sometimes take months while the envelopes bounce around third countries—sometimes Mexico, sometimes Canada, even as far away as Italy—often showing up in Havana opened, missing pages, more the idea of a letter than a letter itself. As a result, exiles have developed an informal system of sending mail with those who return, who hand-deliver the missives or leave them with a relative or friend for later pickup.

Back in 1987, we were required to be at the airport by nine o'clock at night even though the flights to Cuba didn't leave Miami until one in the morning, a departure time designed, we were sure, to exhaust us, to have us arrive in Havana at an awful, weary dawn, unbathed and surly.

We killed the time by organizing our mail pouches. The non-Cubans, including the group of politicos for whom I was working, looked on with a mixture of amusement and confusion as a woman with a bottle of milk of magnesium stuffed into a cheese basket on her head claimed to be going to Holguín, on the eastern side of the island, and volunteered to carry all the correspondence for Oriente except for Santiago de Cuba, which an older gentleman with a razor-thin mustache and ten T-shirts bracing his torso took and carefully folded into his Italian handbag. A young, nervous fellow who hadn't seen his father in ten years took all the letters addressed to folks in Santa Clara, at the central crossroads of the island.

Those of us who were Havana-bound were more inclined to hold on to our own mail, although everyone seemed pleased that a young woman from Marianao volunteered to take those letters, sparing us all trips to that distant neighborhood.

"Is anybody going anywhere special in Havana?" asked a man wearing many trousers, all of them bunched up on his crotch when he sat down, revealing their many layers like a rainbow at his waist. The non-Cuban members of my travel group stared at him unabashed.

"I'm going to the Arab society, over in Old Havana," said an elderly grandmother with a plastic shopping bag for a purse. A man with various suit jackets and perspiration dripping off his chin in spite of the airport's efficient air-conditioning handed her two letters to take to relatives who lived two doors down and who, apparently, he didn't want to have to see.

I looked down at the correspondence that had been entrusted to me: one letter from my father to his childhood pal, Moisés Menach. I'd heard about him all my life, a supporting character in all my father's stories about growing up. "I'm going to the Sephardic Hebrew Center, at Seventeen and E, wherever that is," I volunteered (no one took me up on my offer). My father had suggested dropping the letter there rather than trying to find him; he was unsure of Moisés's whereabouts after so many years.

My mother had declined to send anything, offering a surprisingly reactionary response: "When I left Cuba, I left everything. This life—the people here—this is what matters to me now."

"You still have people in Cuba?" asked one of the Americans on my tour group, focusing on the envelope in my hand.

"No," I said flatly. "This is a favor I'm doing for somebody. I don't have anyone in Cuba."

I knew—from the stories of Cuban acquaintances—that there were certain similarities to all first return trips to Cuba. I knew, for example, that at some point I would go looking for our home in Havana, that I would break down and cry at an unexpected moment, that it was assumed I would call the relatives who'd stayed on the island, buy them presents, have an emotional reunion, and promise to stay in touch.

But the only kin who'd stayed that I was really curious about was Ytzak, who was long dead (with an irresolvable mystery), buried outside of Havana in Guanabacoa. I had already calculated that I wouldn't have time with my heavy interpreting schedule to get out of the city. I told myself I'd pay my respects to him on some other trip, or never. It didn't matter then. The only other person that vaguely registered was Barbarita, somewhere in Varadero, but my mother had failed to give me an address or a phone number, and I had even less time for that kind of detective work.

On my last Sunday in Cuba, I still hadn't delivered the letter for Moisés Menach. I had struck up a fairly friendly relationship with one of the government interpreters, a gracious young woman named Estrella Rodríguez, and I was considering simply leaving it to her for delivery. I hadn't read my father's letter but I wasn't worried about its contents. My father is careful with words in his most unguarded moments so I knew this dispatch was simply a page of pleasantries for his friend, nothing the strictest censors could possibly find offensive. It didn't matter who gave it to Moisés, whether a janitor at the temple or the highest ranking officer in the Ministry of the Interior.

When I approached Estrella before breakfast, before I could even say a word, she surprised me by telling me I could take the day off, that she'd realized I'd had no time for myself and that I, as someone born in Cuba—and on the very day the revolution triumphed!— should have a moment to ponder the consequences.

"Everyone born here, no matter where they live in the world, is cursed," she said. Estrella was slender but, like me, with hips. If not for her black skin, we could have been sisters, illegitimate relations from a suspicious family tree.

"Not me," I said. "I'm free. I mean, Havana's a beautiful city, I grant you that, but no more than Paris, no more than Venice or Prague."

She laughed. "Everybody who comes to Cuba, especially Cubans from abroad, in spite of everything, they fall in love—with the island, with another Cuban, or with our little tragedies," she said. "But you, Ale—you, of all people—you think you're immune, you think nothing can happen to you."

I laughed, too, at her romantic notions, at her twisted nationalism. "I've told you, my being Cuban is an accident of timing and geography," I said. "And everything's already happened to me."

Estrella became agitated. "Don't say that, Alejandra, don't say that. There are many things, you'll see, for which you're still destined. Just be patient."

This is the oddity of Cuba as a godless society: Everywhere I went, people mentioned their deities, by name or by implication: through barely concealed bead necklaces that signaled by their color combinations to whom the wearer was devoted, or via shell-eyed Elegguás behind doors, glasses of water, or cigars left to burn on their own. It seemed everybody, like Estrella, thought they had a touch of clairvoyance and was constantly reading signs into the most ordinary words and gestures.

"Respect," said Estrella, her skin like a starless night, "even if you don't understand, respect."

With Estrella to cover for me, I snuck away from the tour group, determined to walk the city by myself in the cacophonous late morning. Havana, it turns out, is the noisiest place in the world. In spite of the lack of automobile traffic, each car on the street made its own thunderous racket: metal squealing, motors coughing, bumpers dangling from the chassis and throwing off sparks as they scraped against the city's craterous streets. Not to be outdone, buses struggled to the corners, overloaded and spitting black smoke in tiny explosions. In the meantime, radios competed with each other, family dramas played out on the streets as Cubans accused each other of infidelity before their neighbors, then begged forgiveness with theatrical flourishes.

By this time, I had a rough idea of where the Sephardic temple was and I figured I'd make my way there later, drop off the letter for Moisés Menach, and get back to the Habana Libre in time for the big farewell bash. It was rumored that Fidel himself might show and I was intrigued with the idea of seeing him in the flesh.

As I left the hotel that morning, the light was golden but dusty. The low-energy piropos that came my way had a sham Iberian accent, as if I were a Spanish tourist the lazy Havana boys were trying to impress. At first, I was pleased I wasn't being identified as American. Since I knew I wasn't quite the carnal comrade of the island, I liked the idea of being perceived as a European sophisticate, a woman of mystery and means.

Later, though, I found myself uncomfortable with my new mistaken identity: The fact is, I like American women, they have always been much more my models of choice than Latin American or European women. So why was I so pleased to have avoided my real relationship to them? I decided that it wasn't that I was being slowly brainwashed by anti-American Cubans but that it was my very American-ness, the depth of my privilege, that allowed me to feel embarrassed by the possibility of association; that it was precisely because I knew Americans, that for me they weren't exalted creatures but neighbors, friends, and lovers, that I saw their humanity with all its glorious imperfections.

For the same reason, I told myself, being mistaken for a Spaniard could be appealing—the distance from Spain made the association exotic and cool, and I could picture myself as a Mediterranean Mrs. Peel, sleek and imperturbable.

I smiled to myself. My father, as worried as he was about my being in Cuba, would have been so pleased.

Stepping out of the Habana Libre, I was instantly situated. The exercise of years ago, of trying to memorize the street map of Havana, had come in handy throughout my stay. I found myself anticipating streets and intersections. I knew the order of things, even if I didn't always know where I was going.

I walked on, past fences choked with bougainvillea, marble mansions as ostentatious as Rome, and soldiers in crisp uniforms with taciturn faces. Everywhere I went, there was laundry flapping on lines hung from balconies and windows. It was all light colors, pastels rippling in the wind.

A few adolescent boys approached me, asked for chewing gum, then leapt back, prize in hand, to the walls from which they seemed to emerge like miniature golems. The Malecón, with its salty spray and cracked facade, was grayer than I'd imagined, bleaker than the photos I'd seen. The few people out seemed pasty and hungover, all staring north across the water. An old man leaned against the seawall with his peculiar litany: "Por el amor de dios, por el amor de dios."

At some point, as if by magic, I looked up and saw my old apartment building sitting ashen on a residential street in the Vedado. I had remembered it palatial, but here it was, only three stories high, square and barren. There were no Greek columns to hold up the balconies, though I could have sworn I'd run around them as a small child. The windows were boarded up, the terrace from which my father and I had watched the panic during the bombings was chipped and lifeless. The front gate to the building, now slightly unhinged, bore the green and red traces of mold and rust that would paint all of Havana just a few years later.

I took my Instamatic out of my purse and snapped a few photos, thinking that, as much as it would pain her to see this scene, my mother would appreciate it. (It never occurred to me what my father, stuck in his imaginary Spain, might think, or that he'd even miss Cuba.) After a series of shots of the building itself, I turned a few inches and framed the house next door. Surely my mother would remember her neighbors, would want to see what had happened to our old home in comparison to all the others on the street. As I focused, I noticed a man at a whitewashed window, shirtless and sure. He waved. I ignored him and clicked the shutter, then turned my attention to the house on the other side.

I wanted to shoot the whole neighborhood, to give my mother the entire picture, so I focused on the buildings across the street. This would have been my parents' view, these blue bunkers with balconies on each floor and bars on the windows. I remembered them vaguely, recalled that then—as now—children would race up and down those exposed concrete steps as if they were flying.

"Hey," the guy at the window yelled at me. "No one's going to remember those buildings. They're new."

But I remembered them, I was sure of it. My mother would remember them. I could picture the view through the bars of our terrace, the way they served as a frame for those other lives, always louder and more interesting than anyone else in the neighborhood. Didn't my father once save a cat trapped on the stairway across the street during a hurricane? Or were all these memories like those of the Greek columns, sweet but invented?

"Those buildings were built by the revolution," the guy at the window said. He sneered: "Long after you were gone, all of you."

I don't know how he knew, what he saw from his perch that gave away the truth of my origins and our subsequent escape. Why couldn't he think I was a Spanish tourist like everyone else? I stepped across the street and shot a picture of our apartment from my new vantage point.

"Hmm . . . these buildings were built in 1960," said a voice behind me.

I turned around fast. Sitting there on the steps and seemingly made of smoke was a wan old man in a red shirt, a small cup of coffee in hand. He had dark, dark rings around his eyes, so dramatic he looked like Theda Bara, the silent-movie queen. His eyes were huge, round, and his right pupil was misty, as if a cloud had permanently settled there. He was skinny, with long legs stretching out of baggy shorts.

"We left in sixty-one," I said. "I was sure I remembered them."

He nodded. "Yes, they were built by the government," he said. "But that building there"—he pointed to the one with the man at the window—"that one's prerevolution. That one's privately constructed, privately owned since 1932." He twisted a bit on the step, rearranging his bones. "Take a picture of it, okay?" he said.

"Yes," I said, measuring the distances. "I used to live there, next door, in the third-floor apartment." I pointed at our empty balcony, its crumbling ledge.

Suddenly, the old man brightened and grinned. He had white, white teeth, real shiners. For a moment, he looked black, mulato. "Then you must be . . . Alejandra, right? Enrique and Nena's daughter?" Before I had a chance to respond, he slapped his thigh with his free hand, almost spilling the coffee in the tiny cup he held in the other. "The revolution's own! You were the skinniest baby I ever saw. You looked like a slug, like something born by mistake—not unlike the scraggly rebels themselves! Look at you now!" He whistled appreciatively, snapping his loose hand in the air in one quick motion.

I laughed uneasily. I was unnerved by the fact that he knew me, knew my birthday, knew I shared the same life span as the island's most recent experiment. I felt ephemeral. "I'm afraid I don't remember you, I don't remember your name," I said.

"Not important, not important," he said, still fidgeting, his right eye rolling around in his head like spilled milk. "I used to own your building, too. I used to rent to your father and mother."

"Really? Then you're Moisés Menach, my father's friend from Oriente?" They were supposed to be the same age, yet this man looked so much more worn, so much older than my father.

Moisés nodded again, pleased with himself. The way he slowly closed, then barely lifted his eyes had a distinct, elegant arrogance I recognized from my father's own gestures. I bent down to kiss Moisés but he turned his head a bit, more out of embarrassment than anything else. He smelled of coffee and tobacco. His free hand wrapped around mine, tremulous but strong.

I knew from my father that Moisés Menach had come to Havana to take care of a house left by an uncle who'd waited forty years to get a visa to the United States. Even though the uncle's life in Cuba was settled—he was seventy years old, had a family and a small kosher cafeteria on Muralla Street—when the visa finally arrived he felt obliged to complete his journey, packing everything up and boarding a steamer straight for New York.

Moisés tried to keep the cafeteria going for a while but failed miserably. He was lucky, though: In his anxiety, he'd begun to play the lottery and one day unexpectedly won a small fortune. With that, he sold off what was left of the cafeteria and bought a building next to his uncle's house—where we eventually lived—and settled into a comfortable life as a private landlord.

"New people moved in after your parents left," Moisés said, picking up the conversation as if the comings and goings of previous tenants really mattered. "Then they left, too. I don't remember when I lost that building, not exactly. Somewhere around there. Early. They said I didn't need two places, I could only live in one. I said, okay. I mean, that made sense. The last family moved out a year ago, I think. Technically, their son, David, lives in your old place. But he's never around. You can see everything's boarded up. I think he's got a girlfriend in Trinidad, that's what I hear. But he tells people he lives here. He doesn't want to lose the apartment. I understand that, too."

He focused his blurry gaze on the house next door. "That house? The one I asked you to photograph? That's my house. I'm only sitting here because I'm visiting Olguita, my daughter-in-law—actually, my ex-daughter-in-law—I like her, she's family," said Moisés, shrugging. "But that house? That's mine. I have the papers for it in my name from 1950. I legally inherited it. Take a picture, okay? Take a picture and show everybody who used to live here and thinks they're going to come back and make false claims. These buildings are the revolution's, but that one there, that's mine."

On my return to Cuba a decade later, I ask Moisés about the wrinkled envelope I'd finally handed him in our last moments together that first time around. He grins, his nearly sightless eyes reeling back. Then he goes to a difficult, creaking drawer in a bureau in his unlit and crowded living room and pulls it out, smoothing the stationery with his fingers.

"Moisés," the letter reads, "this daughter of mine, Alejandra, is precious to me. She is my darling child. When the time comes, tell her everything." It's signed: "Your brother, Enrique."

IX

As the plane sailed into Havana on my first trip back in 1987, I looked out the window in anticipation but saw only black. Cuba doesn't light up until just before the actual landing: The fleeting illumination, which comes from posts situated far apart on the roads just outside the capital, spills enough of a yellowish glow to indicate a deserted countryside, single-lane routes, thick bush all around. As the plane descends, it's possible to glimpse the bulky outlines of a few bohios, those picturesque but miserable thatched huts from postcards and jaunty guajiras.

On my return to Cuba after twenty-six years, the plane stumbled on the landing, jerked us around, then groaned to a halt. All the while I felt strangely invulnerable, convinced nothing could happen to me, that in spite of the heart-rending cries from the other passengers, we'd all walk out safely into the warm Cuban rain.

As we stepped to the ground there was an overpowering smell of mildew in the air. Many of our fellow passengers became highly agitated. Most just stood there at first, disoriented, aware only that they were firmly in Cuba for the first time in so many years, their hands shaking, tears coursing down their cheeks. Some dropped to their knees and kissed the tarmac, wails of despair coming from them until other passengers yanked them back on their feet. The uniformed soldiers from the Ministry of the Interior looked on with a bland acceptance, as indifferent to them as to the precipitation.

I grabbed my carry-on bag and marched around the exile com-

motion, falling into lock-step with my party of activists and politicians, most of whom were Puerto Rican and American. There were
less than a handful of returning exiles in our group. I looked through
my purse for my passports, unsure which—U.S. or Cuban—to hand
to the customs official.

This was the incident I was thinking about later, when I told
Estrella everything had already happened to me: What could be
more dramatic than returning to the place of your birth and feeling
nothing, absolutely nothing, but the slightest shiver of an echo
from a bottomless pit?

There are two things I remember most about that trip. The first is
how I clung to every privilege and habit that separated me from the
islanders. I didn't claim to be American; I understood that to be impossible, and I didn't want it anyway.

But I took taxis everywhere, standing defiantly on any sun-
drenched street corner holding my arm out in the air to get their
attention. Cubans couldn't afford taxis then—still can't, really—
and I was haughty, impatient about the entire transaction. I'd yell
out taxi, in perfect English, instead of *tahk-see*, like the natives. I'd
wave one of my singularly illegal dollars if I had to, soaking in their
envy; they glared at me with just a little bit of hatred. I wore black
every single day, not out of mourning, not out of any fashion or political motive, but because black is not a color anybody wears in the
tropics; black absorbs the heat and attracts mosquitos but also sucks
up sweat and other stains without leaving a mark.

During all my interpreting in Havana, whenever I had to nego-
tiate between individuals, I'd always let them know I was partial to
the English-speaker. I'd indicate this with my body, by leaning or
standing closer to the American, by deferring or simply gazing at
him or her more intimately than the Spanish-speaker.

Even though I ignored the island Cubans, my message was for
them: I have nothing in common with you (who can't answer

simple questions without feeling compelled to spew forth frothy commentaries), but with them, with the taller, healthier northerners (the ones who communicate efficiently, who aren't ashamed to admit when they don't have an answer). Regardless of what language I was speaking, what words I was pronouncing, my mouth was filled with rocks and stones and broken glass.

Occasionally, I'd step out of the conversation with a comment or beneficial aside, but it was always for the sake of our tour group, never the hosts. If a local Cuban asked me a direct question, I'd quickly translate the words into English like an automaton, and if they protested that it was meant for me personally, I'd define the rules of my job: That I was invisible, that I had no opinion or judgment, that I was there simply to convert one language into another and that they should never address me as an individual but always focus their pronouncements on the other person.

"These are not my words," I explained. "I have no words of my own here."

The other memory is a scene at Moisés's home.

When I met him, I was curious, of course, about Moisés himself, about his survival in Cuba, how it might have intersected with what our lives would have been if we'd stayed. This is one of the inescapable things about being born in Cuba: the life that was somehow denied by revolution and exile, our lives in the subjunctive—contingent, emotionally conjured lives of doubt and passion. Everything is measured by what might have been, everything is wishful—if Fidel hadn't triumphed, if the exiles had won at Bay of Pigs, if we hadn't left. I have never questioned why the subjunctive exists in Spanish, with its cultures of yearning, but neither have I had reservations about its absence in English, with its cool confidence.

I was also curious about the experiences my parents had had before me. Who doesn't wonder about the people who brought them into existence, about who they were back when they were young, their dreams embryonic bursts of shapeless colors in their sleep?

I'd always imagined my mother as something of a marvel, as the object not so much of men's comments on the street but of an ache inside them. She would have been desired, not for the sake of possession but of union. My mother, I assumed, was the kind of woman men (and women, too) dream about, not as an adventure but for eternity. My mother, I thought, was the subjunctive personified.

"She took your breath away," Moisés said unembarrassed, his eyes looking off into the distance as if he could see her again through his milky screen, radiating. "She made you hurt all over."

And my father? Moisés had known him since they were only months old, two little soiled worms screaming for their mothers' breasts. I imagined my father awkward and pretty as a boy, good-hearted and easily embarrassed, not yet defensive and pompous about his intellect—a youngster capable of a hearty laugh, of climbing a tree just to see how high he could go, a child concerned more with wonder than with meaning.

"Your father, yes, well, he's a complicated man," Moisés said.

Upon our meeting, Moisés invited me home with him to the high-ceilinged house in which he lived with his wife, Ester; his divorced son, Ernesto (like a few others of that early generation in Cuba, prophetically named in honor of Che Guevara); his daughter, Angela, and her husband, Orlando (whom I realized immediately was the disagreeable man yelling at me from Moisés's upstairs window), and their three daughters—Deborah, Yosemí, baby Paulina—and teenage son, Rafa; and Ester's father, Rodolfo, an ancient mummy-like mass who sat before the TV all day, whether there was anything on the tube or not. Later I found out that he claims to have not slept since 1961, when the Americans bombed the air bases before invading Playa Girón.

Inside the large house, Ester—a warmly cushioned woman with large, comfortable breasts to which she held me as if I were a long-lost daughter—trembled and wiped away tears. "Alejandra, I've dreamt about you!" she said, although she has never described a single nocturnal vision to me.

A handsome fellow with the same lagoons under his eyes as his father, Ernesto immediately brought out a bottle of rum and poured glasses for everybody. He pulled ice trays without dividers from the freezer and ran them under water to loosen the large white rectangles. When they popped from the trays, he wrapped them in dish towels and banged them against the kitchen counter until they shattered into brittle spears. Then he undid the towels and carefully picked out the biggest chunks for me.

When we returned to the living room, Rafa and his sisters, all with large curious Menach eyes, stared at me from their perches on and around the heavy mahogany furniture. Raven-haired Yosemí held the slobbering Paulina to her shoulder.

"Were you really born on the same day the revolution triumphed?" she asked accusingly.

"Absolutely, absolutely!" Moisés said happily, not giving me a chance to answer. "She was—is!—our revolution's first new life!"

I cringed. We never talked about my birthday back in Chicago, just celebrated it on its own—not even in tandem with the new year—as if it stood alone. When I finally shared the coincidence of my nativity with my friends, it was always ironic, or embarrassing. Now here was Moisés patting me heartily on the back as if I'd had a choice.

The Menach front room served as the all-activity center of the house. The TV was there, as was Rodolfo, the patriarchal zombie, and the large family-size dining room table. There were several old wooden rockers, one with a broken arm, and a folding chair. On one wall hung a metal picture frame with the winning lottery ticket that had helped Moisés become a landlord in the fifties. The stub floated on plain white paper, its numbers, though large, obscured by wear and a layer of moisture under the glass. Its edges were orange, as if paper could rust. Next to it was a startlingly mature portrait of Orlando, also framed, which I would later learn was Deborah's handiwork.

Angela's surly husband, Orlando, an unshaven forty-year-old with a slight paunch, sat (still shirtless) on the ladder to an improvised second floor, a barbacoa, as the islanders call the rickety loft spaces. The kids slept up there, where the adults could barely stand. Bronze-skinned Orlando guzzled his rum noisily. Angela, thin as a bird and swarthy like her father, smiled as she strolled back to the kitchen, just off the dining area, in order to help Ester prepare a welcoming meal for me (I'd protested, to no avail).

"I thought you were Jewish," I said to Moisés, noting that at least one of his children had been named for someone who, at the time of his birth, had been very much alive. From what I understood, this fell outside of Jewish custom.

"Of course we're Jews!" Moisés Menach said proudly, pointing to the mezuzah tacked just inside his door. (I'd always thought these were displayed outside, but Moisés later explained that was just tradition, not law, and that many Sephardim kept theirs inside—a legacy, I quickly surmised, of the Inquisition.)

When I expressed my confusion with his children's names, he told me the Sephardim aren't very strict about naming children after living relatives. "Besides, in Cuba, we're Cubans," he said, smiling, even his misty eye twinkling. "And here, we are always naming our children for heroes, heroes who are very much alive and can serve as examples."

Ernesto puffed up his chest, jokingly trying to radiate a bit of his namesake. Then he gasped, comically faking one of Che's famous asthma attacks. The kids laughed. Angela, poking her head out of the kitchen, rolled her eyes and waved her hand in dismissal. Orlando looked on darkly.

As all this was going on, neighbors and friends came in and out of Moisés's house, some curious about the visitor he was entertaining, others simply continuing their routines. Moisés's door, I would later learn, was always open: People bounced in to borrow tools, to play or flirt with Rafa or one of the girls, to gossip and hang out, to watch TV. Whatever food was available was shared, whatever rum ran free.

Sometimes Rodolfo, the mummified grandfather, would startle everyone by leaping out of his chair and angrily draping a worn bed-sheet over himself and the TV set, which he then turned way down so only he could hear, and only if he was within inches of its speaker.

"But what happens," I asked Moisés, "if the heroes you name your children after disappoint you later, if their humanity is evi-denced through a horrible act, like cowardice or corruption?"

Moisés, who was helping set the table for dinner, stopped; he held a plate in midair, its chipped edge pointed at me. "That . . . would . . . never . . . happen," he said, spacing his words out, one by one, for emphasis. His eyes opened wide, revealing more and more of the whites, which only underscored the deep black patches underneath. "That would never happen," he said again, quickly.

"But it did, didn't it?" I insisted, as if arguing with my own fa-ther. "I mean, in the early days of the revolution, didn't some peo-ple name their kids Huber, after Huber Matos?"

Matos, a commander in the revolutionary army, had split with Fidel early on and ended up spending most of his adult life as a po-litical prisoner in Cuba. He is a fading figure, as much in the dias-pora as in Cuba itself, but for exile children like me he was often portrayed as the "good" revolutionary, particularly because of his break and imprisonment. Eventually Fidel released him to exile in Miami, where it was thought he'd spark a counterrevolutionary movement. But instead, Matos virtually disappeared into the com-fort of his family, preferring to spend his time catching up with his children and grandchildren and becoming a rich old man.

As I was making my case, the neighbors all seemed to be listen-ing through the windows. A round woman with avocado green curlers in her hair nodded approval from the warm dusk outside. An old man with no teeth stood at the door and shook his head, dismayed. Rodolfo, under a bedsheet now, rolled the TV's volume button from side to side, so that the sound came in muffled, cascading waves.

Just then, a beautiful girl waltzed into the house, unconcerned with the conversation. She was wearing a nearly transparent cotton dress that revealed white panties against her caramel-kissed skin. Because she looked thirteen or fourteen years of age, at first I assumed she was a friend of Deborah and Yosemí. They had the same smoothness of cheeks, the same early spring breasts, the same Cupid's bow lips. What distinguished her immediately was a certain coquettishness.

I speculated that Deborah, who had curly saffron hair, clear eyes, and brown skin like her father, and even the terribly serious and pale Yosemí, were probably suppressed in the company of their kin, that they would shine as brightly in a different setting. But to my surprise, they greeted the new girl with a vague indifference. Only an excited Rafa welcomed her, folding his teenage body into a corner of the room to create a sliver of space between himself and the wooden wardrobe so she could watch the debate that had ensued between Moisés and me. When the girl acquiesced to Rafa's silent offer, he turned a deep crimson.

I watched her as I spoke: the way she looked at me, wholly unimpressed, her limbs carelessly resting on the edge of the wardrobe, impervious but not unaware of Rafa's suffering behind her. She was, I realized immediately, an extraordinary girl.

It was not Moisés, though, who picked up the gauntlet I'd thrown about Huber Matos. "No one! Not one person is named after Huber!" said Orlando, Angela's husband, a black-haired gentile who, I learned later, had refused to convert to Judaism upon marriage but was accepted into the family anyway, in large part because his support for the revolution was as feverish as Moisés's. Indeed, Angela had met him when they were teens, during his turn at neighborhood watch following Moisés's, when he'd come early, out of enthusiasm both for the job and for the older man's conversation.

In the years since, Orlando had taken enthusiastic part in every revolutionary project that came his way. As an economist, he was in the vanguard of state planning for everything from combat supplies for Cuba's excursions to Angola and other far-flung places to nutritional calculations in order to ration foods in a healthy and equitable way.

Now Orlando poured himself, and me, another glass of rum. "You go out there and talk to everybody in Cuba—you'll find lots of people named Ernesto, Camilo, Vladimir—but no one is named Huber. Why? Because people knew." He sneered at me, lifted his glass in the air, and with an unexpected tip to the strange girl, gulped down the sweet drink.

"You have to choose your heroes very carefully," Ernesto said. "I lucked out—my namesake died before he had a chance to become an asshole!" As he spoke, he laughed, ducking his father's light slap. Nonetheless, the neighbors quickly scattered, the toothless man gumming furiously as he ran. "Kidding. Just kidding!" Ernesto protested, but they were gone. "It's one way to clear a room, isn't it?"

"You see, Ale, they have no respect, you know? No respect," said Moisés, but it was clear that, though it really bothered him that his children might feel differently about the revolution, this was all familiar territory, games played a thousand times before.

In the corner, the strange girl sighed, indicating her boredom. Within minutes, she had vanished. Rafa, with his beautiful angel's face, kicked the wall behind him with his heel, his hands useless, buried in his bottomless pockets.

Soon Angela and Ester emerged from the kitchen with a feast: a large kettle overflowing with arroz con pollo, plates of sliced icy cucumbers and ripe tomatoes, fried plantains and a long, warm loaf of bread. I wanted to thank them but I was speechless. Moisés had announced me as a dinner guest as we walked through the door, not giving his family much time to prepare for much of anything, and yet here was this banquet, this jubilee. Tears welled in my eyes.

"Oh no, no, don't get emotional now," said Ernesto in his warm, friendly way. I immediately wondered why Olguita, his ex-wife, had divorced him.

"You're family, mi vida," said Ester, patting my hand as she positioned herself at the head of the table.

I tried to compose myself as the kids dropped into their assigned seats: Serious Yosemí and cheery Deborah on either side of their mother, Rafa next to his grandfather. Rodolfo, the mummy, remained static in front of the noisy TV, the bedsheet over his head.

"Angela . . . por favor . . ." said a drunken, smiling Orlando as he teetered next to his chair with his empty glass. He must have been attractive once, I thought, but he was so clearly in decline now. "I need something to settle my stomach. A glass of milk."

There was a general protest at the table, even though this was years before milk rationing. Angela, who'd struck me as good-humored and confident all day long, angrily put her silverware down and got up. As she disappeared, defeated, into the kitchen, the agitation continued. Everyone was clearly upset, although Orlando just stood there, propped against the chair, smirking as he waited. When Angela returned, she handed him a half full glass of milk. He skeptically examined it in front of the entire family but did not taste it, just set it down at his place setting, then arranged himself in his chair.

"You're not going to drink it?" protested Angela.

"Enough, enough," demanded Moisés, waving his hands as if he were gathering something rare and beloved to him. He said something to Ester in French and she nodded. Everybody calmed down, at least enough to lower their heads for a moment. Ernesto winked at me and smiled.

"All right now . . ." Without much more fanfare, Moisés began the blessing: "Baruch attah Adonai, elohainu melach ha olam, ha motzi—"

"Blessed is the god who brought us arroz con pollo!" exclaimed a playful Ernesto, reaching across to serve himself from the steaming rice and chicken dish. Moisés groaned. Ester squeezed his shoulder for comfort, whispering again in a French I recognized as slightly fractured, put together with distinct Spanish and Turkish inflections.

An austere Yosemí took my plate and began to serve me heaps of the delicacy. "Tell me when it's enough," she said, her eyebrows linked together across her forehead.

Ester poured water from a tin into everybody's mismatched glasses, Angela plucked tomato slices and cucumbers into a plate for her grandfather. All the while, everyone talked, laughing and spilling things without regard. Ernesto had just begun to refill the rum when Orlando got up abruptly, glass of milk in hand, and withdrew to the back of the house.

"Enough," I said to Yosemí long after she'd scooped up more than I could eat, and more than anyone should get if the meal were to be evenly distributed. "In fact, too much—let's put some back," I said, but no one would hear of it, everyone loudly demanding that I eat what was on my plate.

"Are you disparaging my arroz con pollo?" asked Ester, pretending to be offended.

I know it shouldn't have hit me the way it did. It wasn't that big a deal. But suddenly, it was as if the force of the ocean had been contained in my chest. To my surprise, I was crying—huge, heaving sobs.

"Excuse me," I said, getting up from the table, unnerved. Everyone complained again, dismayed by my emotions. A gentle Deborah handed me a white handkerchief and I turned from the table and blew my nose.

"It's okay, it's okay," said Ernesto, taking hold of my arm.

I didn't realize how much rum I'd had until I began my journey toward the bathroom in the back of the house (they wouldn't let me at the one near the dining room, claiming plumbing problems). Everything swayed; I was wobbly. My eyes weren't used to the darkness yet and I kept seeing sparks.

Instinctively, I reached out for a wall to support me but found that the long corridor to the bathroom opened without doors along the family's three bedrooms, all in a row. The furniture was heavy and somewhat monstrous in its elegance. The partitions between the rooms didn't go all the way to the ceiling but left an open space of several feet of air. Everything was tidy but crowded, with too much bric-a-brac for my spare northern tastes.

I was horrified to realize Moisés and Ester, Orlando and Angela, and Ernesto and whomever he brought home (his must have been the smallest room, the one with the cot that took up all the space in what may have once been a utility area of some sort) heard every whisper and whimper, every creak in each other's bed. Apparently, it was true about the old man's insomnia, since there was no place for him to lie down and sleep. Maybe, I wondered, they just left him in front of the TV, like a set piece.

By the time I got to the far side of the house, I'd adjusted to the shadows. I stepped into the dimness of what must have once been the servants' bathroom without turning on the light and found the sink. I splashed heavy, icy water on my face and looked for my reflection in the mirror. Its surface was broken by veins of ruptured mercury. My hair danced, electrified by the humidity like my mother's when she lived in Cuba.

I'd just pulled my panties down at the seatless toilet when I heard a rustling outside in the patio. At first I thought it was a breeze playing with the trees, but then I heard footsteps, heavy and deliberate, followed by a lighter, friskier walk.

"Here, sit here," I heard a husky voice say. It was Orlando, not drunk at all but meekly instructive. He moved something from one place to another, breaking a twig under his foot.

I quickly tugged my panties up, without peeing, and looked around the room for a view of the outdoors. Sure enough, high up near the ceiling, a horizontal window was propped open to let the air circulate. I scrambled up, balancing myself on the lid of the toilet tank, and poised myself at the window.

I had to use both hands to hold on to the sill and, as it was, my eyes were just barely able to see through the small space between the ledge and the frosted pane. But there below me, amid the thick bushes and dozens of tub-sized flower pots from which large yellow leaf papaya trees waved, Orlando poured the milk from his glass into a small puddle on the seat of an old metal patio chair. He was now hidden from the back door of the house by a thick hedge. The milk glistened in the moonlight.

Then the girl—the same stunning girl who'd left so bored hours ago—parted the greenery and stepped in beside him. Her dark curls floated in the air. She lifted her white dress. Her underwear was missing and a plush patch of black appeared between her legs. Then slowly, regally, looking Orlando in the eye the entire time, the girl lowered herself to the milk, her pubic hairs catching drops of white.

Orlando knelt in front of her like a supplicant as she dipped again and again. She arched her body, grinding her pubic bone into the cream, then he spread the girls' legs and lowered his lips to her sex. She spasmed, tossed her head back and relaxed into his mouth.

Once, the girl looked up, as if to the star-filled sky, and found my blue-gray eyes instead, glistening, no doubt, like a wild animal's. She smiled with quiet surprise but did nothing more than stroke Orlando's hair with her hand. I smiled back, strangely calm, as I watched her caress her lover's stubbly cheek and play with the nappy hair on his head. He continued lapping until she wrapped her legs around him and trapped him there, immobile.

When I exited the bathroom, my face was flushed. As soon as Moisés and his family saw me, they assumed I'd gotten sick. They beseeched me to sit down, to drink water, to get some fresh air (I steered them outside through the front and away from the back patio, oddly protective of Orlando and the girl). They apologized profusely, thinking it was their meal that had affected me so. Standing beside me at the door of the house, Deborah gently stroked my hair to soothe me.

I told Moisés's family I was exhausted and strung out and just needed to get back to the hotel. But the entire clan seemed to moan in unison. I said I'd simply catch a cab but they wouldn't hear of it: Orlando, who had inherited a '57 Buick from his father (and was the only one who could drive it), would take me back.

I quickly declined, of course, terrified of the scandal that would break out if they went to find him and discovered what I knew would be his compromising position. I reminded them he hadn't been feeling well either.

"That's okay," said Orlando, suddenly at the front door of the house. He was draining the glass of milk, unhurried but without swagger; there was no mark of victory anywhere on him. "I'm better now."

Orlando's Buick was a sloping tank that jerked in the lower gears. We pulled out to the street with a series of neck-snapping lunges, for which Orlando apologized in a barely audible, embarrassed voice.

We were not far from the Habana Libre, this I knew. The hotel sits on a well-lit strip in the Vedado, near the University of Havana and surrounded by plenty of traffic. So I was a bit startled when I realized Orlando was driving away from the city, onto the forbidding roads I'd seen from the plane as we landed. There would be no farewell bash for me, no chance of meeting Fidel. As we drove on, there were fewer and fewer lights, a vast wasteland.

We traveled wordlessly for maybe ten, fifteen minutes. The wind whipped in through the open windows of the car, my hair nipping at my cheeks and neck. Orlando stared straight ahead, intent on the road. There were bluish shadows under his pale brown eyes. I noticed his nose was slightly crooked in profile.

The motor grunted when he pulled to the side of the road, hissing before its final surrender. Out in the night, crickets continued their racket, lightning bugs flared as they circled about. Somewhere water gushed, slapping the shore.

I closed my eyes when Orlando touched my lips with his fingers. These were unburdened by labor, silky and tapered as if shaped by a manicurist. They had a strong, pungent smell, like a river swollen in summer. His lips fell on mine and there, in the slightly sour aftertaste in his mouth, I savored the richness of the beautiful girl.

When Orlando parted my legs and tried to lower his head, I resisted: I licked the stubble on his chin, bit at his lips. In response, he plunged his fingers into me, as agile as any tongue.

X

There was a time perhaps when everyone spoke the same language, before the debate about whether it was the object or the sound that came first. Back then, no one cared if we imitated nature's noise in our own way, or whether we imposed ourselves on the world, reducing its mighty possibilities to our limited vocabulary.

When we were of one language, no one argued about whether tree or árbol best fit those leafy creatures wrapped in rough bark out in the woods. Everything was understood, there was unanimity in the universe. I've often imagined that we must have spoken a language of the senses, a speech strictly of vowels: ooooh-aaaah-iiiiii.

It is not so limiting to speak in these open-mouthed ways; there are a myriad subtleties. Think about newborns, about the sounds made by the dying, the howls of animals in heat, the babbling of the insane. It is, I think, a kind of glossolalia: ecstatic and pure and boundless.

Imagine for an instant the genuine sounds made by the deaf, before they're taught how to pop their lips specifically for Ps, or humming for Ms. Theirs is our sound, all of ours, before it's contaminated by the world and by each other. That trumpet blast, the murmuring, the shrieking like cats, the gorgeous stillness—that's our hearts, the atonal music of our holy selves. It has a rhythm that defies culture and class, defies time: What tones emerge from the throats of the deaf have nothing to do with grammar or any set of rules about propriety. In their most authentic, uninhibited form, they're about desire and need: the most direct, the most religious kind of communication.

As a child, I held on to that uninfected, primal language long after I had heard my mother say bottle or botella, after my father had pronounced moon and luna with his flawless lips. For me, these were simpler: uuuooo and ooo-eh.

It's not that I couldn't grasp consonants—I understood the essence of their brashness, the way they worked like sturdy beams in construction—but I believed, firmly and instinctively, that they should be used sparingly, that it was more natural to ponder the possibilities of forming my mouth in an O than in a T, to explore diphthongs instead of flashing those dramatic double Rs Spanish loves so much.

When I was a child, Mami was aaah-oooh, Papi was iiii-oh. My own name was quickly reduced from Alejandra—so imperious, so long!—to Alef, Aleh, Ale—the L a concession, a compromise worked out by my mother and me because my father was terrified by my resistance.

It is precisely in how we handle language that my father and I connected and diverged. We were both in a wrestling match with the gods but the rules were different: His, on the page, was as defined and classic as Greco-Roman competition; mine, in the air, is as messy and organic as a playground scuffle.

For his decoding, my father needed contemplation, the meticulousness afforded by time. He liked his subjects: poetry about nature and the human condition, philosophical tracts about history, literature. For him, the search for meaning was endless: After a job was officially finished, he collected and rearranged his notes by his own method, a compendium of reflections and ideas on each work and what it provoked. Sometimes, years later, he would return to these writings, adding new explanations, new questions that had occurred to him.

Although my father worked with many living Latin American

writers (except Gabriel García Márquez who, as one of Fidel's best friends, sent my father admiring notes but knew, as my father also knew, that hiring him, an exile, would be both controversial and unseemly), translation for him had little to do with the rough and tumble, the magic of the New World.

For my father, translation was a spiritual return to Spain— although he never went there in real life, never booked a tour, demurred every time he received an invitation to lecture or receive an award. It was his way of creating and preserving Spain, of explaining his otherness in the United States without the blatant trauma of racism. That travel ban was not extended anywhere else but to Cuba, so that he became a regular at Mexican and Argentinean universities instead, the gracious visiting scholar whose painstaking manners impressed everyone as old-fashioned and very Spanish.

Each night, after his paid work was completed, my father would pull out the writings of Pedro Salinas or Ramón José Sender, Elena Quiroga, Abraham de Toledo, or any other ancient Spaniard. Some of what he labored over was archaic, different kinds of Ladino and judeo-español in fact, but he would never admit it, or his fascination. His favorite was the Sephardic poet Judah Halevi, possibly the most eloquent voice ever on the subject of exile (in both Ladino and Hebrew).

As I watched him scribbling (always by hand) late at night, he struck me as a direct descendant of Maimonides, writing his own guide to the perplexed, trying to rationalize godly acts, as if there were mortal ways to reason with things that are both sacred and mundane, like language itself. He would spend hours staring at his own responsa, the letters losing meaning and becoming light.

I told him once that the rabbis quoted in the discussions in the Talmud are known as amora'im, Aramaic for translators, making his entire career an inadvertent but quintessentially Jewish act. I told him this as a dare, as bait, expecting him to at least wince.

Instead, he paused, then looked up at me quizzically. "What does that say about you?" he asked.

My father was unimpressed by my work. He saw it not as a part of what he did, but as something else entirely.

He was irritated by the inevitability of the lost word or phrase in oral interpretation, by the fact that in a minute or two he could have found a better, more exact expression. Without a dictionary, he didn't know what to do with his immaculate hands, and he despised paraphrases and approximations. "You're just running division," he would say, betraying the translator's oldest prejudice. Moreover, he was always flustered by the complicated ordinariness of most interpreting work, by the frequent drama of its concerns.

But me, I'm an empath. I slip my client's words through my mouth as if they were formed by the electrical impulses of my own brain. I don't think, I hook in, I mind-meld, I feel, and I articulate all the agony or joy or confusion the client is experiencing, no matter how horrible or banal the proceedings. When I'm in my reverie, I have no clue about what I'm actually saying. It's all aaaah-uh-eeeeeeeeeeeeee.

It's not that I don't appreciate exactitude. Indeed, my professional reputation is based on my precision, on my talent for harnessing it all, no matter how frantic the situation—say, a hospital emergency room—or the intricacies of the dialogue—consider, for example, the conversation between a Guatemalan immigrant, a Mayan whose own Spanish is spiced with Quiché and a doctor using English-language medical terms to explain why the immigrant's only son will be a vegetable for the rest of his life because of the random bullet lodged in his brain.

My father may have tortured himself looking for a Spanish heaven, but I simply pluck the best word, whether cielo or paraíso or porvenir and give it motion and meaning with my utterance. I talk and talk, negotiating between intention and message, and when we arrive at agreement, my voice falls silent, as fleeting as the spirit of the boy in the coma as it disappears into the sky.

My father may have been of the ages, but I relish the moment. It is one of the few ways in which I am inescapably Cuban.

According to the Bible, the universal language I've dreamt about existed once, in what was the nascent city of Babylon. Its people were the descendants of Noah, prosperous but much too ambitious. They thought they could build a stairway, a tower to heaven. The Bible doesn't mention any dissension, not a single voice that questioned the wisdom of such a crazy notion. And so the Babylonians set about their impossible labor.

God, of course, was unimpressed. The punishment inflicted on the early Babylonians for their presumption was not merely to level the Tower of Babel but to create babble itself: Language was fractured into a confusion of tongues, chaos ripe for misunderstanding, hatred, and revolution.

Years later, when the Jews were expelled from Zion by the Babylonian king, he took the best and the brightest of the Israelites back to his kingdom. The Jews lamented this forced separation from their land, family, and friends.

Yet, nostalgia aside, the Jews flourished in exile: married, built homes, had children, became known for their splendid handicraft and established themselves as merchants. In short, they built a community along the Babylonian shores.

Seventy years or so after the Jewish exile began, Babylon was conquered by King Cyrus of Persia, who offered the Jews an opportunity to return to their own land. Perhaps not surprisingly, most of the Jews decided to remain in Babylon, tending to their families and businesses, continuing to lead the only life they really knew, sending monies and goods back to those who had stayed behind in now mythical Israel.

XI

Havana and Miami are nothing alike.

In Havana, the blue of the sea winks between colonial columns and Jetsons-style 1950s high-rises. Rain falls in spurts, then clears to not uncommon double rainbows shimmering just off the horizon. Fried pork flanks sizzle in fat just inside open windows, sewers spill with regularity, and battalions of roses and the purple-red flowers of banana trees awe the senses. Along the Malecón stretches a necklace of twinkling black coral—an aphrodisiac said to strengthen the heart, cure gout and epilepsy.

Havana has an insolent majesty—the way the centuries unfold in the ornate architecture, the gently scalloped stone facade of the García Lorca theater, or the inadvertent postmodernism of the capitol building, a miniature of the one based in Washington, D.C., a reduction perhaps meant to reflect expectations about the island's democratic possibilities. (Built in 1929 at a cost of $20 million, more than half the budget was later discovered to be payola, a fact that doesn't ever come up in conversation because Cubans, for whatever reason, choose instead to insist that their dome—in fact, their capitol—is bigger than the original, the evidence of their eyes be damned.) These days, Havana may be the very portrait of a post-nuclear holocaust, but the city is, as always, a rock.

Miami, by contrast, is acrid and flat, floating on the uneasy foundation of the Everglades. Miami may boast of its shiny steel towers along Brickell Avenue (never mentioning that they're monuments to Colombian drug cartels and the 1980s art of money laundering), but their height is restricted by both law and nature: Those skyscrapers are built on a bog. Whatever their reach, they will sink like a stone into the muddy swamps if they should ever exceed their grasp.

When we arrived in Miami in 1961, it was a ghost town, the holding place for the black—mostly West Indian—and Latino domestics, gardeners, and chauffeurs who traveled across the Venetian and McArthur causeways every day to tend to the needs of the rich and touristic in glittery Miami Beach. Miami's downtown then had an even, horizontal quality, the parched feel of the desert on its too-hot-to-touch pavement.

When my parents—papers in hand certifying their new status as Cuban exiles—stepped out of the magnificent pink tower known then as Freedom Center and onto sovereign but empty Biscayne Boulevard, they were amazed. Not by Miami's abundance, the orderliness of its traffic, or its cloudless sky. What shocked them was the quiet. If you rolled a stone along any residential street in Miami, you could hear it sputtering along, then winding down like everything else, exhausted and finally still.

For the first few hours after our release, my parents walked around the heart of Miami, up Flagler, down S.W. 2nd Street, up to N.E. 1st Avenue, in and around stores that sold sundries, nurse and janitor uniforms, and lots of luggage. Even at the shop counters, where the normal bustle of commerce should have echoed, all sound was muffled by the constant whirl of fans and the occasional hum of air-conditioning. The store owners were white-haired and cranky, like Olinsky, who was already on his way to his sister's house in Detroit.

I rode my father's tired shoulders as we strolled in and out of shops selling beltless slacks, plastic-wrapped women's dresses, and those ubiquitous suitcases. There were whole sets of three and five pieces that fit compactly one into the other for storage, huge mortal-sized cargo boxes that would require moving men to transport them if they were ever filled.

Perhaps it was the pervasiveness of so much travel gear that suggested Miami as a way station, not a destination. What is certain is that my parents needed only that short walk through the heart of the city to decide that anyplace else, even sight unseen, would be better.

That first night, sitting in the splendorous Miami home of Irene Cohen, an American who had been José Carlos's lover during his college days at the University of Pennsylvania, my mother called her cousin Gladys, who was then living in Chicago, and accepted her offer to live there, at least for a while, with her and her American husband, a prosperous dentist named Mike Kauf who competed in body-building contests on the side.

To help my parents find out a little bit about where they were going, Irene lent them the C volume of her kids' *Encyclopaedia Britannica*, in which they located Chicago on the map and read about Al Capone and Carl Sandburg, Enrico Fermi and the misfortunes (erroneously) blamed on Mrs. O'Leary's cow. The encyclopedia did not say much about Jean Baptiste DuSable, the city's African-American founder, and nothing at all about the race riots of 1919. It would be years before Chicago's story would rightfully include the siren song of Mahalia Jackson, the nightmare of the 1968 Democratic National Convention, or the wild night in 1983 when a jubilant Harold Washington sang a raucous "My Kind of Town" to celebrate his election as the city's first black mayor.

But as my parents read about Chicago from the thick volume, they each found their reasons to like it.

"There's water," my father thought to himself, and imagining Lake Shore Drive and how it might curve around the shore, he added: "And a Malecón."

"Sweet water," my mother mused while conjuring an endless blue pool where Ochún might feel at home: "We'll be safe there."

It would be a few days before passage to Chicago could be arranged. In the meantime, my parents tried to bring some order to their lives by establishing whatever they could of their routines. Borrowing Irene's glasses, including some Waterfords, my mother improvised an altar in the utility room, right on top of the dryer. Because the machine hummed and vibrated when operational, my mother would remove her icon, glasses, and candles each time a load needed to be dried, setting everything but the Virgin on the cold tile floor for the time being. She'd carry la Virgencita around with her for the forty minutes it took the clothes to tumble dry, then put everything back in place as quickly as possible.

Actually, my mother's icon had arrived damaged on American shores. When she first opened the rumpled box in Irene's guest bedroom and fished it out from the damp newspapers, its left hand was dangling as if by a sinew, and a layer of plaster, like a wedge of white deli meat, had been sliced from her face. Here and there, mysterious holes dotted her body, as if something or someone had attacked her with a poker. My mother crumbled at the sight, just folded like a used tissue next to the bed where the Virgin lay wounded, and cried and cried.

But my father, who never believed in Christian or pagan votaries, gathered the figure in his hands and, shaking the box and the newspapers, salvaged as much of her bits and pieces as he could. With a bright lamp and a bottle of Elmer's glue provided by Irene from her husband's workshop out in the garage, my father stayed up the whole first night we were in the United States—this, after our travail at sea—and, with his magic hands, restored my mother's precious saint with such love and craftsmanship that it is virtually impossible to see the scars, even to this day.

During those few days in Miami, my father took walks every morning—exhausting sojourns in which the heat and humidity humiliated him with their power, never finding natural bodies of water but lots of sticky aloe everywhere. He'd come back home with his tongue hanging out like a dog, his chest wet from sweat, and a weariness that drove him right back to bed.

There were already a number of Cuban cafes throughout the city then—dime-sized cafeterias that served cafecitos and bulky

Cuban sandwiches of pork, ham, and cheese—blasting their radios and drawing crowds of cigar-smoking men to the sidewalks outside their counters. With the Bay of Pigs debacle unfolding, the announcers were perpetually excited, dramatic in their diction.

"Bomb them, bomb them!" shouted one enraged old man listening in—his Bs were sprays of saliva, his Os like the missiles themselves dropping through the air—as another news report talked about casualties and the ever-increasing number of prisoners of war. The group around him at the cafeteria cheered.

My father was horrified: Even if bombing was the only way, how could anyone be jubilant over this, especially in their own country? Cuba was so small, so intimate: Might they not bomb their own neighbors, kill their friends and relatives in the process?

The cafeteria owner—a bear-shaped fellow with a large, porous nose—shook his head in dismay. "This isn't going to get us anywhere," he predicted. "Things will only get worse, you'll see."

My father was relieved; a voice of reason had been lifted. But to his surprise, the men shouted him down. "Are you crazy?" said the angry old man. "You think the Americans are going to let Fidel beat them? When has that ever happened, eh, that the Americans lose? And to whom? To a ball of dirt in military fatigues? Are you out of your mind?"

"Look, do you hear anything you believe on these news reports about an uprising? Have you heard from any of your relatives in Cuba about anybody doing anything?" the cafe owner retorted.

The crowd drew back, aghast. "What are you, some sort of Communist? What radio station are you listening to? All the ones I hear talk about how the Cubans are in revolt!" said the old man. Disgusted, he poured out his cafecito and stepped back from the counter.

"No, look, use your—" the cafe owner began.

The old man cut him off, spreading his arms like a barricade. "This guy's a Communist. I don't support Communists." He slapped away some coins a dumbfounded kid was holding out to pay for a can of soda. "Don't give your money to a Communist!" The coins rattled on the sidewalk, rolled away like mercury. The kid and the cafe owner exchanged embarrassed looks. Then the cafe owner waved him away, as if to say it was okay.

"It's because of people like you that we're in this mess!" the old man shouted while pointing at the cafe owner with a trembling index finger. By now, he had a Roman rabble behind him: "¡Ñángara! ¡Ñángara!"

The disgusted cafe owner turned away, letting the crowd shout for a while until they tired of it and returned to gossiping and the radio news. Later, when no one was looking, my father slipped up to the counter and handed the owner some coins.

"It's for the boy, for whatever he bought," Enrique said apologetically.

The cafe owner stared at him. "Is this some sort of joke?" In his hand he held out my father's money: three glistening Cuban coins.

"I . . . I just arrived," my father said, flustered, "it's all I have."

"These are no good here, my friend, absolutely no good," the cafe owner said. He slapped the coins back in my father's hands, holding them together with his own rough palms.

When it was all said and done, the Bay of Pigs invasion was a disaster. The United States, which had devised the idea of the assault and recruited the exiles to man it, never provided air cover, essentially condemning the volunteers to death. There are many theories about why this happened, but what's clear is that the CIA, in its arrogance, never really studied the Cuban situation well enough to realize an attack was probably impossible, at least then and there.

The agency's bungling gave Fidel his greatest victory and a lifetime of excuses: He became the first Latin American leader to repel an American military strike, a distinction that, in a century when U.S. troops had forced themselves on others dozens of times, created a legend. From then on, whenever things went badly in Cuba,

Fidel pointed north: "The yanquis are coming!" And every Cuban would rise to the occasion, their honor at stake. In Havana, Moisés and Orlando would run to their posts.

Years later, a memorial was built in Miami to honor the men of the Brigade 2506, many of whom were ransomed from Cuba by American authorities after Bay of Pigs, some of whom died in battles and others who were shot before the paredón.

Many years after my first trip to Cuba, my mother and I found ourselves in the dewy mist of early light, staring at scattered pieces of coconut shell, a dead chicken with a red ribbon tied around its feet, and a small pile of pebbles carefully arranged under a gargantuan ceiba tree on S.W. 13th Avenue in Miami. Regarded as sacred by many Cubans who practice santería, the ceiba sits behind the memorial to the Cubans who lost their lives during the exile invasion. My mother and I had come to leave a small bouquet at the shrine in memory of José Carlos. But the monument itself was somewhat neglected—it sported graffiti and one of its posts was missing a top.

"Don't touch anything," my mother said, meaning the brujería around the ceiba. The tree's gnarled roots—sometimes three, nearly four feet above the ground—twisted like tentacles through the small patch of dirt accorded to it on the promenade, ceremonially known as Cuban Memorial Way. "You don't know what the spells are for. They could be for evil and you don't want that kind of energy to rub off on you."

I stepped back and watched as she lay the bundle of blossoms—open-faced sunflowers, birds of paradise, and yellow daffodils—in a crook created by the bulging roots. She squatted for a moment on the packed, hard earth.

"I don't want to be here," she said softly, choking as she stood up again, wiping her hands against her dress, "none of this belongs here."

XII

When forced to admit to his Cuban origins, my father always described himself as a habanero, perhaps because of the urban quality that, in his mind, linked Havana back to Seville, the Spain of his imagination. He didn't say that he was an oriental, only that he was born in Oriente, and only when pressed.

He never recognized himself as having any special knowledge of the earth, of the way it yields to human needs, yet my mother's gardens were hers because she worked them, not because she understood them. It was my father who would decipher the symptoms of any malady just by glancing at the flowers' colors, or by the tenderness of the stems. He did this by barely looking, barely touching them, as if they might leave an awful residue on his manicured nails.

It was, in fact, my father who advised my mother to cultivate Paul Neyron roses, hearty hybrid perennials that are remarkably resistant to both the heat and the cold. They're nineteenth-century roses, elegant and still, roses I always assumed—without evidence, I admit—my father grew to love because of my great-grandfather Ytzak. I imagine them together in Oriente (the old man leaning on his cane to relieve the weight on his peg leg), smelling the delicate perfume, snipping them in bunches.

In our garden in Chicago, up in Rogers Park where the houses are still hospitable single homes with large yards in front and back, my mother would scoop up the soil, water the thorny stalks, and prune the blooms, ultimately enjoying the huge white, pink, and red blossoms that opened to six inches. She would spend hours out there, massaging the ground around her flowers, examining the size of the buds. To the sides she'd plant sunflowers, like gatekeepers, golden and tall. Often, she'd share gardening secrets with Mrs. Choy next door, an ethnic Chinese exile from Vietnam who grew sweet potatoes and sugarcane in utter defiance of Chicago's climate.

Yet the minute that there was a scourge of insects, or an early browning of leaves, it was my father—his reading glasses on the tip of his nose—who my mother would trudge out to the garden to look at the problem, beads of perspiration immediately forming on his forehead. She'd hang by his side, waiting. He'd scratch his white beard, touch the plants and grunt not unlike Olinsky, muttering advice on herbal solutions, irrigation, and new ways to enhance the light.

My mother would nod, always nod, as if she were taking mental notes from a great philosopher. (Quite often Mrs. Choy would join her, the two of them in awe of my father's intuitive connections with the flora.) Then my father would hurry back in the house, away from the sun and the heat and the tiny bugs that crawled into his shoes or flew around the blossoms, and throw himself back into one of his Cuban-style rocking chairs, the reading light on, the poetry waiting.

My father said he liked the large houses in Rogers Park, the fact that it had its own commercial area like a downtown, that it was on the lake. My father wouldn't be caught dead in swimwear (I've looked and looked but I don't think there's a single photo of my father bare-chested), but he liked walking on the shore, especially in the cool morning hours in autumn. He loved the way the water froze in winter, how the waves curled like lacy fingers.

My mother cherished the vast sandy beaches, too, but it was different: What she appreciated most was precisely the near-tropical heat, the commotion during the summers. No matter how hot it got, my mother could be counted on to turn up the temperature a few more degrees with her bubbling pots of black beans, her own hand-shredded vaca frita, and the sticky sweet caramel she'd derive from melting sugar for flan.

As she traveled from her fragrant gardens of fresh roses and sturdy sunflowers to her kitchen filled with the aroma of garlic and cumin, she'd dance and dance to whatever suited her: Beny Moré, Celia Cruz, Olga Guillot, and Fernando Albuerne. She adored Roberto Ledesma's versions of Armando Manzanero's songs, and, after I came back from Cuba on my first trip, she learned to spin to Los Van Van as if she were thirty years younger. She would sometimes—especially when Celia was pumping—take a paper towel and sweep her body with it from head to toe while dancing, as in the cleansings in her own grandmother's kitchen so long ago. (Sometimes our other neighbors, Polish émigrés named Chmelowiecz, would come over and ask her to please turn down the volume.)

Each July and August—while my father worked on his translations in the quiet and air-conditioned comfort of his basement study in the afternoons or played dominoes with his Cuban friends, the slapping of the pieces on the table a percussive symphony—she'd walk down to the little secret beach just off Jarvis Avenue and stroll up the short pier. Then she'd sit and dangle her naked feet in the cool, cool water.

Whenever I picture my mother there, staring off into the blue nothingness of Lake Michigan, I always try to imagine what she saw on the horizon: a collection of memories, neatly wrapped and stacked away, categorized like my father's notes on translation.

There is a word in Spanish, olvido, which is usually interpreted as oblivion or forgetfulness. But this is one term on which my father and I agree: Olvido is not just a void; but, much like memory itself, it is a place, with dimensions and weight. Rather than holding all we want to remember, it's a repository for what we want to forget.

Other Latin Americans, and some Americans who've had contact with Cubans, call us the Jews of the Caribbean.

It is not a phrase much known in Cuba itself, but it has a familiar currency in exile. It's meant as an epithet, playing off negative stereotypes about Jews. It alludes to the Cuban transmutation of Miami and Miami Beach (which, ironically, displaced a good number of Jews), from little meaningless metropolises to world-class cities.

The allusion is not to hard work, however, but to greed and covetousness. Essentially anti-Semitic in nature, calling us the Jews of the Caribbean is supposed to deem us as untrustworthy partners in business, possessed of an ambition so unbridled that we will sell out to anyone, that we are concerned only with higher prices and acquisitions.

When we are called the Jews of the Caribbean, it's almost an accident that, like Jews, we are a people in diaspora and that, like Jews, we are a people concerned with questions and answers and the temperament of a god that could make us suffer, like Job, so inexplicably and capriciously.

Growing up in Rogers Park, where a great many doors sprouted mezuzahs and the local Jewish community center kept up a steady stream of activities, I found other commonalities: Cubans and Jews both had families in which people had peculiar accents, both cooked funny foods, both were obsessed with a country in the Third World, both lived lives in the subjunctive, and both, quite frankly, thought they were the chosen people. In Rogers Park—in spite of the pockets of Asians, recently arrived Africans, and miscellaneous refugees from Central America and Eastern Europe—I was so surrounded by Jewish culture and life that I grew to believe Thanksgiving was the fall equivalent of Pesaj.

When I was older, I discovered that Cubans have a Masada, too. Like the Jewish story—which is never mentioned in the Torah or Talmud—the Cuban legend is also outside the official history books. Just as the Jews of the Great Revolt found themselves surrounded by Roman soldiers and chose to commit suicide rather than surrender, the earliest inhabitants of Cuba woke up one day and realized they were being decimated by the Spanish conquistadores. Unable to imagine continuing to live in such misery, the Indians decided to kill themselves by eating dirt, poisoning their bodies with the very ashes and bones of their ancestors.

Among Jews, Masada is a shrine to Jewish honor and perseverance that is studied and revered. Among Cubans, the story of the Indians is a rumor, the Indians themselves erased from the earth.

In Miami, in New York, and in every Cuban enclave I've ever encountered outside of the island, Cubans have a singular approach to being called the Jews of the Caribbean: We wear it like a badge of honor.

For years, I heard that in palo monte, an Afro-Cuban spirituality more aggressive than santería, the most powerful talisman, or altar piece, is called the prenda judía. It's said it requires the skull of a Jew.

In Guanabacoa, a hamlet just east of Havana known for its magic and where my great-grandfather Ytzak is buried, there's a little cemetery founded by American Jews in the early years of the twentieth century. Up on an airy hill overlooking a vast green countryside, the cemetery sits on the corner of Independencia del Este (East Independence, or independence from the east, depending on your reading) and Avenida Mártires (Martyrs Avenue), but the street sign is upside down and has been that way ever since anyone can remember.

In a corner of the cemetery is a monument, a tomb, under which are buried bars of soap made from human fat that were recovered from Nazi concentration camps. The memorial is generally neglected but undisturbed. The rest of the cemetery is in ruins, its marble tombstones crumbling, the crypts pried open. Many of the graves lie empty, supplying the shrines of the local paleros.

My parents have always said we chose Rogers Park because Mike Kauf, the body-building dentist married to Gladys, my mother's cousin, had been raised there and was able to let us stay for a while at his family's house, which was vacant when we arrived in the United States.

But I have always wondered whether, at least in his heart, my father—the secret Jew—wasn't happy that he could surround me effortlessly with the things I know he cared about so deeply. Not, of course, that my father ever said anything. Not that he ever participated, except in the most private and most mysterious of ways.

I remember the first time I realized how different my father was. It was a Midwestern day, like any other in summer: sunny, warm, humid. Lake Michigan was a slate of innocent indigo just blocks away from our modest little home, all brick and perfect rosebushes, stairs up to my hideaway of books and playthings, stairs down to my father's refuge, with his curious, smoky smells, the humming of his electronic typewriter, and his own gentle murmuring.

It was a day in which we were a swarm of wasps, my friends and I, eleven years old, tearing around the pool table in our basement, the only cool place in the house, pricking each other with cue sticks across the pond of green felt. A bite here and there, red marks that lit up our skin, then faded with a hiccup, a giggle, a fantastic scream of delight.

We didn't notice my father coming down the stairs. It's hard to believe that a man that magnificent in size and build could pass so invisibly between and around a throng of children high on their own blood sugar, squealing at every quick move, poking dangerously at each other as if spearing for sharks. But he went by us as stealthily as a rain cloud.

When we finally saw him, he was all darkness, a majestic shadow on the door to what was always called his office but was really some kind of black hole where he would frequently seal himself, immune to us. His lesson plans, letters to friends and colleagues, translations of poems, and stacks of student papers always carefully laid next to the typewriter, each set of pages overlapping the other. My father was always so tidy.

We didn't pay attention, really, just continued with our merriment, our childish violence. Then Papi asked us, in his usual polite manner, to please leave, to go outside. "Por favor," he said, nodding toward a stream of light that spilled into the drab, cool basement through the slit of a window from the sunny outdoors, a place where, no matter how idyllic, he'd never been comfortable. This was not a man, we could see in that instant, who had ever felt happy while throwing a ball, or who wiped sweat from his brow with a grin. He turned around in slow-motion, closing the door behind him.

One of my friends, a recently arrived Latvian boy ginger-tinted from the millions of freckles all over his face and arms, lifted his cue stick like a hunter's rifle and pretended to aim at where my father had stood.

"Hey," I said, reaching across the pool table with my own stick, inadvertently shattering the lightbulb in the lamp above it—a crackle and sputter and a tiny lightning storm.

My mother was at the top of the stairs in a flash, just her feet and calves visible, voice booming. My father appeared only to hold the lamp in his delicate hands, quickly glancing at his watch as he inspected the damage. On the pool table, scalloped pieces of glass rested like discarded eggshells.

My mother threw us out of the house, literally grabbed us under our armpits and tossed us out as if we were wild young dogs. She flung us onto the back lawn, where we bounced on the grass all green and rubbery. We panted, yelped, and jumped. We pushed our tongues out at one another, grabbed each other's clothes so they'd stretch into wild triangles and rhomboids, then crumble into strangely wrinkled buds. We rolled on the dirt, all the while feeling the sun sizzling our skin, retelling the story of the exploding lightbulb, how it had detonated like a grenade.

"Hey . . ."

I turned around, a curtain of hair in my eyes. I used my earth-smudged fingers to part it.

"Come here . . ." It was the ginger-colored Latvian kid, whispering excitedly from his new vantage point at a window looking into our basement. He waved us over with his hand, eyes fixed, mouth agape.

I scrambled to where he was, moving so fast all I could see were my own blurred tennis shoes. I was a lanky girl, all limbs, all pickup sticks, just like my father had been as an adolescent. When I reached the boy, our heads bumped, something smelled of vomit, and I felt myself getting nauseous. One of the Choys' daughter pushed in under me, her head bumping my chin.

"Look, look at Mr. San José," said the ginger boy, his finger pointing inside.

I struggled to get a view. The sun's glare sliced the windowpane in half and all I could see was my father's lower body, swaying back and forth like a metronome. I inched up, pushed with my hands through the tangle of adolescent arms and loose sod around the window, finally pressing up against the glass.

"Ah, Ale, I can't see . . ." somebody said behind me.

But I could see: There he was, my father, with eyes hooded, a mess of black straps around his left arm, holding something onto his head, his huge hands around a frayed book with pages that stuck out at odd angles. He was draped in a white shawl, whispering airy, alien words, his body rocking more ardently now, rolling with a powerful light that made his ears, his eyelashes, his lips, the tips of his fingers, all glow. There was so much flickering on the windowpane, it was blinding.

"Ale!" insisted the voice behind me.

The ground crumbled under me, somebody lifted my legs by the ankles to the sky, and my elbows and hands went waving, slapping against the window as the ginger boy tried to pull me away and the mountain of kids fell on my head.

My eyes were closed when I heard the sound—my eyes were closed because my head was buried between children's bodies and pointy weeds and I was afraid I'd be blinded if I opened them too soon. The sound came from my father's throat: It was anguished and angry, low and guttural like a far-off train in a tunnel. But in seconds it was like the train itself roaring with all its flashing might above my head, as if I were trapped between its belly and the tracks, and all the bells were ringing. At its apogee, I heard glass shatter.

When it was all over, when I felt air again on the back of my neck, I moved my head up slightly, then my bruised chin, and slowly opened my eyes. There, past the frame of the splintered basement window, was my father, his face wet from tears, glass shavings twinkling on his bloody hand.

XIII

I had just returned from that first visit to Cuba when I met Karen Kilberg, a smart, neatly dressed young lawyer who impressed me foremost with her size: She was over six feet tall, a giant who moved with the ease and power of a leopard. She even had its coloring, with golden hair, wide dark eyes, and thin dark lips; her business suit was spotted with a surprisingly tasteful jungle motif.

I was with Seth then, a lanky tousled-haired secular Jew studying photography at the School of the Art Institute. Younger, sweeter than me by far, he was an exquisite lover, pliable, poetically moody, and silky to the touch. I wasn't in love with him but I thought that I could be. My parents treated him with warmth, though it was also clear that they perceived him as, if not a phase, a kind of temporary respite. He had none of the volatility of my earlier lovers, none of the danger I was usually attracted to. (By contrast, it was clear his family, while obviously fond of me, considered his time with me a kind of exotic adventure.)

I was clearly committed to Seth when I met Karen, but I still thought of all that was unthinkable the minute I walked into her office and introduced myself as the last-minute Spanish-language interpreter for her afternoon court hearing. She barely looked up, tossing a file at me and immediately dialing up the agency that had sent me and calmly informing them that, since she'd wasted her time the week before giving background on the case to someone who had failed to show up on the critical court date, she had no intention whatsoever of paying. I put the file down fast but she reached over and, while still arguing with my boss on the phone, squeezed my arm as if to tell me not to worry.

I can't say it helped. I was a wreck going into court, watching her surveying the scene from the plaintiff's table, coldly eyeing the defense—a short, pale hospital administrator and his egg-shaped lawyer, both wearing kippot and eating dried apricots from a plastic bag.

I fumbled on my interpreter's oath, standing there in her sky-scraper shadow. Then I bungled the amazingly simple last name of the poor man Karen was representing—a recently arrived Cuban named Levi, which I kept pronouncing like the denim manufac-turer instead of the Spanish variant, *lev-eee*. He was short but stocky, with a bushy patriot's mustache and a thick head of curls.

Levi, who looked to be about forty, had lost his right arm when an ambulance spun out of control and crashed through the doors of Cook County Hospital's emergency room, where he worked as an orderly. The industrial steel bucket he was using to help mop the place had somehow gotten in the ambulance's crush and whirl and been transformed into something of a rotary saw, a mighty machete that cut through Levi's flesh and bone as if his arm were a tender stalk of sugarcane during the harvest in his native Camagüey.

Karen was suing for several million dollars and Levi, who'd since acquired a fabulous, skin-colored and derma-textured pros-thetic that worked through some kind of magical patch with his own live neurons, sat with his new arm as lifeless as an empty sock, anxiously waiting for his fortune.

"Don't let this act fool you. I can do anything with this," he boasted to me before court, patting his new limb with his old hand. "I can play basketball if I want—can you imagine?—just like Mi-chael Jordan! But today, here, I have to be very careful. Miss Kilberg does not even want me to scratch my head with my new hand if it itches. No, I have to do it with my real hand, even if it's not as natural—you know, my new arm is totally a part of me now, I've just assumed it. But you come see me later, you come to my house if you like and we'll have a little mentirita—that's a rum and Coke, a Cuba Libre, but Cuba's not really free so that's why I call it a mentirita, because it's a big lie—and I'll show you all the things I can do with this arm. I tell you, it doesn't itch, it doesn't hurt—it is much better than my old one!"

I thought for sure Karen would ask for a continuance—an interpreter is a vital part of the proceedings and I knew nothing about her strategies, her client was obviously somewhat unreliable as well, and the defense seemed very confident, sitting there chewing on their dried apricots. But to my surprise Karen stood tall and went on as if nothing was wrong, as if every piece was in place.

After a series of experts attested to Levi's suffering, Levi himself testified for nearly two hours—long, convoluted discourses on everything from the plantation he'd lost after the Cuban revolution to the numb shock of seeing his own blood spraying out of his shoulder as if it were a showerhead.

Although as an interpreter I'm only supposed to repeat exactly what's said to me, it soon became clear from the way Levi talked to me—"Okay, so this is the part where I say about the mental trauma of bone breaking, right?"—that he'd rehearsed built-in clues with the originally scheduled interpreter. I kept looking up at Karen, who absolutely reigned over me, but she'd just stare back impassively, as if there was nothing particular in my gaze. That should have kept me on track professionally, but instead I shifted ever so subtly, so imperceptively, handling the interpretation in ways that could only help her case.

By the time Levi got off the stand for the afternoon, the two guys with the kippot and dried apricots had surrendered, calling for a recess and whispering madly with Karen while Levi and I sat and watched. Levi tapped his new, motorized fingers on his thighs, over and over, as if they were impatient to play basketball or make love.

"You were great!" Karen said later, after she and I waved off an excited Levi and went back to her office. "I want to work with you again, but let's skip the agency. They already know I'm mad so it's no big deal. I'll spend less, you'll make more. Here's my card."

It was white, with robin's-egg-blue raised lettering (like the Israeli flag), and read: "Sima Karen Kilberg."

"Sima?" I said, looking up at her again, all blond, all six feet of long, long legs and nonexistent hips. "That's Spanish. Are you Hispanic?" I felt like an idiot the minute I heard myself.

She blinked. "No, of course not. And it's not Spanish."

"Sure it is," I insisted. "*Si-ma*; it's phonetic."

She chuckled. "It's Hebrew."

"It's my grandmother's name."

"Are you Jewish?"

"I'm Cuban," I said.

"Levi's Jewish," she said. "There are lots of Cuban Jews."

"No, no, we're Catholic," I said. "I mean, c'mon, San José?"

"Aw . . . yes, of course," she said, looking at me as if for the first time. "Ask your grandmother about her name," Karen said. "Maybe you'll get an interesting family story out of it."

"She's dead," I said.

"I'm sorry," she said. "Was she your father's or your mother's mother?"

"My father's," I said.

"Ask him."

"Ask him what?"

"If you're Jewish," she said.

I never worked for Karen again—I don't know why, maybe because I felt so transparent, so like a terminal patient suddenly aware that all the medicine I'd been taking may have just been placebos administered to a control group in some macabre experiment. Karen called but I just erased the tape each time. Seth looked at me funny, a little jealous, but too genuinely threatened to ask any questions.

I might have forgotten all about her, except for two things: I began to have recurrent sexual dreams in which Levi would use his mechanical fingers to enter me like a flawless vibrator, then pull out, lick my juices, and nod at Karen, who would take her own licks then say "Yep, yep, yep." I would wake up in a panic, unable to tell a frightened Seth what was going on in my head, or why I was so unusually wet between my legs.

The other reason is that I raced from Karen's office that day, past the giant Picasso sculpture at Daley Plaza with all its ambiguity and into a nearby cab—one of those bubblelike yellow taxis that are getting rarer and rarer—and dashed home, where I ran up the stairs two and three steps at a time and breathlessly called my father.

"Are you okay?" he asked, hearing my winded voice.

"Are we Jews?" I demanded.

"Are we *what?*" he asked, horrified.

"Are we Jews?"

"You're Catholic; you've been baptized," he said, as if that was evidence.

"Was Abuela Sima a Jew?"

"Abuela Sima . . . ?" He was startled, his voice sank. "Why . . . why are you asking this, Ale?"

"I want to know," I said. "Sima's a Hebrew name."

"Well, and what if it is? What does that mean? Do you think everybody named David or Miriam is Jewish, too?" He was clearly angry now.

"That's precisely the point," I insisted. "I mean, Sima's not that common—I just met the second Sima of my life today, and she's Jewish, and she asked if I'm Jewish, and when I said no, she was rather adamant that I ask Abuela Sima, or you—I told her Abuela's dead—whether we're Jewish, and she said there might be an interesting family story here."

There was a hollow silence on the phone, as if the line had suddenly gone dead.

"Papi?" I said. I clicked the button a few times.

"She converted," he said matter-of-factly. I waited for him to elaborate. "She converted," he said again, as if I hadn't heard.

"Converted? From what to what?"

"To Catholicism," he said. "What else?"

"From Judaism? So we're Jewish, at least part Jewish?"

"We're Spaniards, we're Catholic," he insisted. "We're like everybody else in Cuba."

XIV

My father, Enrique, dropped from my grandmother Sima's womb on a cloudy August day in 1920 in a tiny house on a muddy acre near the one-lane town of Mayarí in Oriente. For good luck, a rooster's severed head hung from the door of the room like mistletoe. "Adim chanath chouts Lilith" was written in the animal's blood on the door frame.

It was a time of great prosperity in Cuba—the natives called it "the dance of the millions." No one could know that, less than a decade later, the country would be practically bankrupt and under one of the bloodiest dictatorships in its history.

Enrique's father was Luis San José, like Sima, a secret Jew, but unlike Sima, who held on to their inherited fear of discovery as if it were the breath of life itself, Luis was less sure of punishment, and, indeed, less sure of what, if anything, they might be punished for. Luis's family had been in Cuba so long, their worship hidden and passed on in such subterfuge that, like the distortions inherent in a child's game of whispers, by the time it was Luis's turn he had no real understanding of Hebrew, no concept that common words and expressions in the hills of Oriente—such as bizcocho, chinelas, facha—were all transparently judeo-español. He knew he was a Jew, but he wasn't altogether sure he really understood, or cared, what that meant.

According to what Moisés Menach has told me in letters that began arriving shortly after my first trip to Cuba, Luis and Sima were simple folk, common to the core. They made the torturous trek to church in Santiago de Cuba at Christmas every year but changed their linens and lit candles now and then on Friday nights. Because Luis and Sima lived deep in the woods, through nearly un-passable roads bristling with orchids and bromeliads and hung with vines, they felt safe enough to be somewhat careless about their faith.

Moisés Menach tells me my grandparents had braided home-made candles and a brass menorah in plain sight, right next to a small icon of the Virgin of Charity, who was said to have first ap-peared not far from where they lived. He tells me his family, re-cently arrived from Turkey, instantly recognized Luis and Sima as marranos, and that they were astonished that there were any anusim at all left in Cuba, since Jews, for so long banned from the Spanish colonies, had for years been emigrating from Cuba to Mexico, Venezuela, and Costa Rica as they each declared indepen-dence and dropped the anti-Semitic prohibitions of their colonial master.

"We couldn't imagine how Luis and Sima arrived at their situa-tion, if they were just so isolated that they never knew anyone but each other, or if their fear kept them from ever making more than cursory contact with others," Moisés wrote me. "They were to us, and perhaps to themselves, too, the last living marranos in the New World."

Still, other than to the trained eyes of the Menachs, Luis and Sima remained indistinguishable from the rest of the peasantry in the provinces. If their Christianity appeared perfunctory, it only matched that of their neighbors. With high illiteracy in the countryside, a large black population that relied on its own forms of venerations, and the near total absence of any sort of Catholic insti-tutional presence, Luis and Sima's lackadaisical approach didn't even draw curiosity, much less suspicion.

Indeed, there were times when the two of them inadvertently fit right in, such as in the days before Yom Kippur, when Luis would wake up before dawn and take two chickens—a white cock for him, usually a speckled hen for her—and swing them by their feet around his and her heads, the animals screeching and flapping, while the two of them chanted the necessary prayers of thanksgiving and atonement. To anyone who might have spied them performing the kaparot, it would have seemed like just another campesino family, infused by the fevers of santería, cleansing themselves of whatever evil had been afflicting them.

What might have horrified anyone peeking in later is that, after the chickens were properly slaughtered and their guts tossed on the roof for birds, Luis and Sima did not leave the animals to rot as sacrifices to the gods—according to santería, the dead birds were now the repositories of all the wickedness absorbed from the lives of the supplicants—but instead prepared them for a delicious and hearty feast.

But back then, hardly anyone was looking. In those days in Oriente, what mattered most was sugar, not god, and the most devout efforts were reserved for the hard work offered by the ubiquitous mills. Dark, silent Luis, who was stout and strong, made his living by working in the fields, wielding a machete like a swordsman. On his own time during the dead season, he'd work his own small acre, growing malanga and sweet potatoes, and even his own tiny tobacco vega.

A woman with the kind of plain beauty that unfolded as you got to know her, Sima knew how to handle her own sharp points, taking in sewing between her extensive and arduous duties with the black women in the mill's kitchen. During the months away from the refinery, she'd help in the garden, slipping into Luis's arms between the vines of tobacco, emerging hours later, intoxicated and freed from her fears for a little while, laughing, with earth and leaves in her hair.

My father wasn't baptized, but that was not so unusual in Oriente. Fidel, who was born nearby on his father's farm on the same steamy August day six years later, once talked about how the families in the

area had to wait for a priest from Santiago to visit in order to receive the sacraments. Sometimes it was months between visits. Inevitably, some of the children slipped through the cracks, always
busy or elsewhere when the priest arrived to douse them with holy
water. Their faces remained dirty, their souls stained.

"I remember that those who weren't baptized were called Jews,"
Fidel once told an interviewer. "I couldn't understand what the
term *Jew* meant—I'm referring to the time when I was four or five
years old. I knew it was a very noisy, dark-colored bird, and every
time somebody said, 'He's a Jew,' I thought they were talking about
that bird. . . ."*

Certainly Fidel, who wasn't baptized until he was about five
years old, might have been mistaken for a Jew in those early years,
but he'd surely shrugged it off. To be a Jew meant nothing to him,
except perhaps the possibility of a clamorous flight.

But my father knew that Jews were flightless birds—without the
keel on their breastbones, their leg bones and toe structures exactly
like his: big and heavy, thick and strong for running. That was how
they'd get away if someone came for them, not in a lyrical flight
above the tall mahogany forests.

For my father, who saw his parents scurry to hide the menorah
and candles whenever a stranger showed up, being a Jew was something tangible: It was the void between Cuba and Spain, between
him and everybody else.

The truth is that Luis and Sima, whom I met only as a child, only
when I was small enough to be carried in their arms, were not especially religious. From what I've heard, being Jewish to them was like
being left-handed, something innate that becomes problematic only
when others notice and whisper.

I confess I've often thought Luis and Sima were more secret

---

* From *Fidel and Religion* by Frei Betto (New York: Simon & Schuster, 1987).

assimilationists than clandestine Jews. They wanted their families, after more than four hundred years in Cuba, to take root, to blend into the vast garden of Cuba. It's not that they wanted to be Catholic—I've heard the story from Moisés Menach about the string of obscenities my otherwise gracious grandfather spewed while they ran around to prepare for a visit by the regional priest to meet me, the infant granddaughter just baptized in Havana.

What Luis and Sima wanted was to be like everyone else; to be, in effect, Cuban—to walk in and out of the shadows of the giant laurels on the plaza in Santiago (now gone) and order anything on the menu at the marble-floored Hotel Venus; to speak only Spanish, forget their slangy judeo-español, and both Ladino and Hebrew, which were too abstract and too much effort; to think about Havana, not a lost paradisiacal Seville; to feel connected to the verses of José Martí, resting right there in the cemetery in Santiago, instead of Judah Halevi, who wrote about how his body was in Spain and his heart in Jerusalem: "How can I find flavor in food? How shall it be sweet to me?"

But my grandparents lacked a clear enough vision of their own, and the strength to impose it. Besides, they lived a short trek from my great-grandfather Ytzak, Sima's father. He liked to say that he was more Cuban than the Indian chief Hatuey (apparently forgetting that Hatuey was born in Hispaniola, modern-day Haiti), but what he desired more than anything was to be openly Jewish. He thought it was possible to be both, and to be whole.

What Ytzak wanted was to sit in his rocker and tell stories in which Jews were the proper heroes, to invite friends—Jews and non-Jews—to his home for Pesaj, to be able to explain and have others understand why he wrapped tefillin around his head and arm each morning. Luis and, especially, Sima, who performed the rituals better than they understood them, were horrified: To them, to be a public Jew was to risk their lives. As much as they were alienated from the sources of their Jewishness, they were also trapped. This was the only way they knew how to be.

But Ytzak's desire was such that, though he was raised in the same double-life of crypto-Jews all over Europe and the Americas—publicly Catholic, privately Jewish—he eventually created his own version of Halevi's dilemma, spatial as well as spiritual: In Oriente, he respected his family's insularity and acted Catholic, keeping quiet, hiding his paraphernalia. But in Havana, he was a Jew, a public Jew, a shamelessly slap-happy Jew.

Unlike Luis and Sima, who were raised in the countryside betrothed to one another practically since birth, Ytzak had grown up in Santiago, a city that had throughout its long history mastered a certain urbanity. From Santiago's pink and turquoise houses spilled children who spoke French and English as well as Spanish. Ytzak noted that the Americans who came and went lived as though they were still in New York or Texas. The same Cuban Catholics he saw in church on Sunday morning drank blood from the severed jugulars of live goats at toques de santos in the dead of night. The Haitians in the city, scorned and often treated like animals, never ceased being African. Even if they wanted to escape their destiny, their skin color marked them—they couldn't be anything else. Everybody, it seemed to him, lived openly with their burdens and contradictions.

Yet he and the handful of other crypto-Jews he knew in Santiago all went about their lives pretending, fearful. Unlike their neighbors, they occupied a kind of netherworld: White enough, even the darker Sephardim, to separate themselves from the misery of the Africans, but never sure how long their passing would last, or what their fates would be if their lies were uncovered. Never officially allowed in the Spanish colonies, their misery came from both within and without: Essentially illegal, formally nonexistent, survival required compromising the most basic aspect of their souls—to survive as Jews they had to pretend to be otherwise. (Often this meant identifying via nationality, so that, generations later, they still told other Cubans they were Portuguese or Turks, and later Poles or Germans—even though they'd have been openly persecuted by most of those whose nationality they pretended to share.)

Most of the time, they were blessed with how well they could pull off the subterfuge. But their curse was that, quite often, the disguise became their lives in such a way that they no longer recognized who they really were.

In Cuba, Santiago was a particularly difficult place for Jews. It had been the only city besides Havana to have an official tribunal of the Inquisition; it was in the plaza before the city's grand cathedral that Jews and other nonbelievers had been publicly humiliated and "relaxed." Indeed, traditions lingered: When holy week came around, Catholic priests prepared effigies of Judas to burn—stuffed straw figures they called judíos. Ytzak and the other anusim kept quiet, sometimes even torching the figures themselves.

After the Easter eve burnings, a tradition in Santiago called for the stoning of Chinese businesses, an exercise no one—not even Moisés Menach, who claims to have witnessed it himself—could explain except to say the santiagueros were confused about who or what was really a Jew. But for Ytzak, the message was clear: Being a Jew in Cuba was dangerous, not at all like being American, French, English, or even the wretched Haitians.

In the years after the war of independence, during the U.S. occupation, Ytzak met a few American Jews in the hospital where he was rehabilitated for his war injury. He liked and envied them but they struck him as different, not at all Jewish in the way he understood himself to be. Years later, he met a traveling salesman from Havana who wore a thin gold Star of David around his neck the same way Ytzak himself had always worn a Christian cross (for protection not from evil spirits but from other Catholics). The peasants called the salesman El Moro—The Moor—but the man just laughed and said, "No, I'm a Jew."

An old woman who was becoming one of the man's regular customers—she had in fact introduced him to Ytzak—paled when she heard him admit it. "But you're human!" the old lady said, and the salesman laughed again.

To Ytzak's surprise, it made no difference in the end: The old woman bought some undergarments, a beautifully embroidered linen shirt for her husband, and a pair of leather shoes for her son. The salesman kept coming back, still called The Moor by the stubborn citizens of Oriente who were nonetheless happy to add to his profits.

One night, Ytzak approached The Moor at the boardinghouse where he always stayed and asked him how he dared be so bold. The young Lebanese man, whose family had survived generations of turmoil, couldn't fathom Jews like Ytzak and looked at him askance. "It's who I am," he said, shrugging his shoulders, counting his earnings. "At the end of the day, no matter what else has happened, I give thanks to a Jewish god." (He also explained to Ytzak that the Americans he'd met were most likely Ashkenazi, Jews indeed, but different from the two of them, who were Sephardim.)

A few years later, while Cuba was still struggling with being a republic and Ytzak could no longer bear his life in Oriente, he decided he'd be a Jew, a real Jew—even Ashkenazi if necessary. He left his wife, Leah, who refused to consider revealing herself, and his daughter, Sima (who was only eight then and as a result forever infused with the idea that desire for revelation meant tragedy), in the countryside, relocating them not far from the grounds of the sugar plantation where he'd once had a job running a grinder.

Ytzak headed for Havana, where he now knew it was possible to be both Cuban and Jewish out in the open, to let the light glint off his own gold Star of David. The Moor became a friend who, with a stirring letter of introduction, got him a job in one of the Jewish-owned shoe factories in the city. He also got him a room in the home of a well-to-do American Jewish family with the improbable Irish name of Corwen who were somehow connected with the American embassy.

For a short while, Ytzak lived his dream in Havana: His very first public service was the night before Simchas Torah. The loose, mostly American congregation was full of hilarity and light. And when the Torah was passed up to him for a kiss, Ytzak let free a torrent of happy tears. When he pronounced aloud the first few words of Genesis, he felt it was his very own life that was being renewed.

In the grainy black-and-white photos Moisés Menach gave me of the 1914 opening in Old Havana of Chevet Ahim, Cuba's first Sephardic society and synagogue, Ytzak's blue-gray eyes twinkle as he grins from ear to ear, proudly leaning on his peg leg in the middle of the group of founders, his white linen Dril 100 suit flapping in the wind, his right hand holding a stylish straw hat in place.

Many years later, when I found Chevet Ahim in the ancient city, I discovered it on a narrow street called Inquisidor, so-called because a commissary of the Inquisition once lived and menaced the populace from there.

According to Moisés Menach, the real reason my father was not baptized was not because Luis and Sima consciously decided against it, or because they took any kind of stand for Judaism. It didn't happen because Ytzak, who had moved back to Oriente the minute he heard Sima was pregnant, concocted a way to make sure it could never occur without revealing that they were, at least first, Jews.

As soon as Enrique emerged from between Sima's legs, Ytzak bundled him up and headed straight for Santiago on horseback (his dark, wooden peg leg dangerously tangled in the stirrups), then switched to the American-owned Cuba Railroad, which rammed its way through the bush with both efficiency and stubbornness. They traveled the length of the country in five days, through Oriente, past Camagüey, through the heart of Santa Clara's sugar district—right by Dos Hermanas, Andreíta, San Francisco, San Agustín, and Caracas, all splendorous mills whose output had the power to tip the global market. Everywhere there was lush tropical green, banana groves sprouting between scraggly rocks, and thickly wooded hills that opened up to expansive sea coasts blue as the sky.

I can see them: Ytzak holding on to my father, a feverish red slug who smelled of sour milk, drooling and crying, all his screaming swallowed by the huffing and snorting of the locomotive as they raced through the Cuban countryside.

Back in Oriente, Sima and Luis waited in anguish. Ytzak had left a note explaining his intention to give Enrique a brit milah, "to initiate him into the covenant of God and Abraham." He wanted to have it done at Chevet Ahim, surrounded by Jews who lived as Jews, something he'd discussed with Luis and Sima and which they'd roundly rejected as unnecessary and risky. Now they felt helpless and betrayed, Luis pacing in their tiny house, Sima cursing loudly in all the languages she knew. Leah, ashamed of her husband, condemned Judaism, blaming it for his obsessions and constant escapades.

There were, of course, no mohels in Oriente—there weren't any rabbis either—no one there dedicated to snipping the foreskin of the young converso and anusim boys. But crypto-Jews had managed somehow, from father to son, to do what was necessary, to jot down in their crumbling family Bibles the rituals, the methodology, the results of their efforts—right there on the inside pages next to the elaborate family trees, each dating back to 1492. Luis had had every intention of circumcising Enrique; it had never occurred to him to do otherwise. But he would baptize him first, and he would do it their way—not by removing the foreskin but by scarring it.

But that Ytzak had kidnapped the baby—that's what they called what he'd done—infuriated Luis. In a fit, he took the family Bibles—the one belonging to him as well as the one belonging to Ytzak—and, with Leah egging him on and Sima crying and pleading with him, hurled them into the gentle currents of the Mayarí River. The books spilled their rare ink into the waters, and with it our family history.

Back in Havana, on the eighth day of his life, my father was circumcised by a Portuguese mohel visiting Cuba from Panama. There was solemn song and joyful celebration as the baby boy was cradled in Ytzak's arms. He was given the Hebrew name Elfas, as chosen by

Ytzak, who surprised everyone by skipping right over Luis and Sima in the naming ceremony: Eliahu ben Ytzak.

According to Moisés Menach, who heard the story many times from Ytzak himself, my father stared straight ahead as the blade touched his foreskin. And even after the blood, he never, ever cried.

XV

When Americans first meet Cubans, they always ask: What do you think of Fidel? The question is invariably poised jovially, as if in anticipation of some terribly clever punch line.

For most Cubans, there is only one answer: Fidel is the devil. This is said both in hatred and love, in derision and admiration.

In Miami and other exile communities, he is called by his first name as if he were family: Fidel, the black sheep; Fidel, the bad seed; Fidel, that son of a bitch. In Miami, everybody wants to break his fingers.

In Havana and the rest of the island, he has no name. People indicate him by pulling at invisible beards or tapping make-believe epaulets. On TV, the announcers say El Comandante en Jefe Fidel Castro Ruz with an unnatural formality that suggests when the camera turns, they quickly glimpse behind them and breathe with relief. "Ay, Fidel," they sigh.

On both sides of the Straits of Florida there's a story about Fidel's first victory speech in Havana. Sometime shortly after he began, a white dove perched on his left shoulder, leaving everyone breathless. This is Fidel's voodoo: He does the impossible.

He gets that bird to pose with him, whether through strategy or sorcery doesn't matter. In one case, it's divine intervention; in the other, a stroke of theatrical genius; in both, he wins.

Fidel makes a joke out of the CIA and its poisonous shoe polish and explosive scuba gear. (According to his own count, the agency has tried to kill him 637 times, which is surely some sort of record.)

He survives—some even say thrives—long after Eastern Europe falls to history and chunks of the Berlin Wall are sold off by amateur capitalists. Fidel banters in Harlem, throws a mean pitch, gives up smoking cigars and Cuba's tobacco industry flourishes anyway.

As a dictator, he is peculiar. In Cuba, there are few photos of him on the thousands of political billboards all over the island. Nothing is named after him. No one knows exactly where he lives. When something goes wrong—and in Cuba everything goes wrong, from the belching buses to the collapsing bridges to the weightless peso—Cubans curse, then carefully reconsider.

"If Fidel only knew . . ." they say, as if then the buses would run, the bridges magically repair themselves, and their wages suddenly be enough. "This is so only because of his assistants, his corrupt associates, the people around him who want to protect him and empower themselves," they conjecture, spinning dark, ornate conspiracies. "He's not an economist!" they protest.

When Fidel speaks, his message has resonance because he absolutely believes every word he says. When he rants against the U.S. embargo, he feels the injustice in every twitching nerve. Even in a crowd of hundreds of thousands, he pierces every individual spirit, contaminates them with rage and rapture. When he talks about dignity and honor, he touches the optimism inherent in every human soul; he squeezes the possibility of hope out of the most cynical of hearts.

Indeed, Fidel's enemies are so vociferous, so rabid, precisely because he is so irresistible. Like former cult members, they know the kind of resolve it takes to undo his spell.

Fidel has educated entire generations of Cubans to believe they are entitled to more luminous, broader horizons, and that they will change the world—all the while seemingly unable to grasp that it is that same knowledge and ambition that hurls them out of his island purgatory, makes them dream of a life different from the one he offers.

Fidel likes to talk about history and, especially, the future, always the future. He cannot discuss the here and now with much comfort—the scarcities, the boredom, the silences—so he revels in revolutionary mythology and what will be: the advances of Cuban medicine, how it is close to discovering a cure for skin cancer and AIDS; how tourist dollars will build marvelous new schools and hospitals; and how socialism will, in spite of everything, triumph. Everything is absolute; there is nothing conditional. Every speech Fidel gives is a lesson, an exhortation to create utopia, to build a tower to heaven.

Fidel, like the devil himself, is an invention of necessity. He is the mirror onto which Cubans project their heroism and betrayals, their sense of righteousness and valor. Without Fidel, there would have been no golden age, no paradisiacal past, no lives in the subjunctive.

There was a time when, whenever Fidel talked, the island would turn to him as if he were the messiah. Every TV would feature his flickering image, every radio his cascading tones. A walk in Havana would reveal empty streets, entire families sitting before the TV or radio, clusters of citizens thoughtfully rubbing their chins or nodding their heads at the local CDR. Sometimes there would be a chat afterward in which Fidel's wisdom would be affirmed.

Today Fidel talks and no one much listens except the functionaries who have to meet with him and need to let the old man hear his words echoing, or the foreign businessmen who believe they get extra points if they can make one or two references to Fidel's latest speech in their dealings with the criollitos (Fidel's word), the second and third generation brats who are now in positions of authority throughout Cuba's nascent capitalist system and will undoubtedly, and without giving much of a damn, inherit it all—the transcendent history and the glittery new hotels, the untapped markets and the desperation.

There was a time when Fidel talked for hours and hours, waving his hands, using his index finger as a strategic pointer, leaning in and out of the podium. People stood through heat and downpours, through clouds of mosquitos and brain-numbing static from the enormous loudspeakers in the Plaza de la Revolución.

Now, when the tireless patriarch gets going, shirtless young boys sigh. "Is he still talking?" they ask, and then everybody starts complaining and the streets fill up with people on their way to the movies, the farmer's market, or the discotheque.

When I return to the island ten years later, in 1997, a weary Ester, Moisés's wife, and I decide to take in a movie one day. *The Madness of King George*, a British import, is playing at the Yara Theater and we take refuge in its meek air-conditioning, Ester dabbing at the slick crevice between her ample and very visible breasts with a threadbare white linen handkerchief.

At one point in the movie, when the king is at his most extreme senselessness, he lets himself go and sprouts a peppery beard that makes him look uncannily like Fidel, and which causes the entire theater to titter and murmur. Even Ester begins to look around, giggling nervously.

When he talks, Fidel says cuida'o, with that swing so particular to the island, not cuidado, like all the American-educated despots and dolts before him who spoke with precise diction and a quasi-Iberian airiness. Whatever else he may be, Fidel is quintessentially Cuban.

And as such, he is exactly what the movie Ester and I see suggests: stark, raving mad.

Fidel's insanity does not manifest in personal capriciousness, in palaces or affairs with movie stars, in whimsical flights to Madrid or Paris for quick shopping sprees, a chestful of bloodstained medals, or the ostentatiousness of celebrity parties with Chinese lanterns and security helicopters.

Fidel's insanity is collaborative, collective. He voices the wildest ambitions of the people, and because he has the unconditional power to manifest his will, brigades of Cubans set out to make his and their wishes come true.

Orlando, Moisés's son-in-law, calls this phenomenon los capri-chos. On my return to Cuba in 1997, we sit on the Malecón on an eerily cool, still night and he recites to me from an endless list of Fi-del's lunacies.

"Once upon a time," Orlando says, "there was something called 'the green belt of La Habana' . . . Fidel's master plan to increase cof-fee production by having everybody plant a moat of java beans around the city."

That was in the spring of 1968, when all sorts of regular citizens—teachers and lawyers and bus drivers who knew nothing about agriculture, and cared even less—trampled up and down the hills outside of the capital, aimlessly seeding the earth with ten mil-lion coffee beans.

"He"—Orlando signals with a quick tug at an invisible beard and a glance over his shoulders—"had plans for a rice belt, a dairy belt, and a vegetable belt, but when the coffee refused to sprout as planned, when the earth defied his best intentions, he focused back on sugarcane and never mentioned surrounding Havana with any-thing again."

Orlando then tells me about Fidel's promise to erect giant, ar-chitectural windbreakers all over the island that would tame the force of any gale so effectively that a citizen might calmly sit under a tree and read a newspaper during a hurricane.

And he tells me, too, about Fidel's idea for air-conditioned cat-tle ranches (with piped-in classical music), so that the animals would be spared the discomfort of the tropics and produce more milk and muscle, enriching Cuba's dairy and beef industries.

"Everybody was jealous of the cows," Orlando says. "Another time, he"—and again the unseen beard—"asked Cuban scientists to develop pork and poultry that tasted like seafood."

None of this, of course, ever materialized as anything more than one disaster after another, no matter how grandly announced and anticipated. And no disaster was greater than the proposed yield of ten million tons of sugar in 1970—a feat Cuba had never even been close to accomplishing.

But everyone was so committed to the ten million, so much had already been invested in money, human power, and propaganda, that the harvest had taken on a life of its own. On the streets, Cubans were actually asking each other, "What are you doing toward the ten million?"

In the end, the harvest produced only two things.

The first was the surreal postponing of Christmas Eve from December 1969 to July of the following year because Fidel deemed that every able-bodied Cuban needed to be in the fields cutting cane during the traditional holidays. (This switching of holidays for convenience's sake is apparently an old Cuban tradition: Though Havana was founded July 25, 1515, the celebrations take place on November 16 because there were other festivities already scheduled on the Catholic calendar for the real dates.)

The harvest's other legacy was bitterness.

"Want to hear the latest?" Orlando says to me as we listen to the waters gurgling below the Malecón. "You see, he"—but he doesn't comb at his chin this time, just looks around—"you know—el innombrable—had a brilliant idea, so he called in a group of scientists and told them, 'We can solve many problems—problems of milk production, problems of nutrition, even help teach people responsibility if we can make my idea a reality.' Well, the scientists all looked at each other—they're used to his ideas—and they say, 'Okay, what?' And he says, 'Let's breed a miniature cow. Just think, every family will have its own milk so we can use the state's production for export, the people will be better nourished, and the family can make a ritual out of taking care of its own vaquita.' Then one of the scientists—he's a wiseguy—he leans over to his colleague and says, 'Look at that, El Comandante has invented the goat!' "

When I tell Moisés Menach what I've heard about los caprichos (and even the mini-cow story), he shrugs. "They're crazy ideas, sure," he says, his milky eye drifting like freshly poured cream in coffee. "That's the benefit of hindsight. I don't deny, though, that some of those ideas sounded crazy even at the time. But why not?

People thought Leonardo's flying machines were crazy. Who knows who will be inspired by his ideas, the way the Wright Brothers were by Leonardo's . . . who knows?"

My father met Fidel only once. It was 1939 and Enrique was nineteen, by then a darkly somber young man, home from Havana for his grandmother's funeral. Leah, my great-grandmother, had drowned in the waters of the Mayarí.

When Enrique and a deeply distressed Ytzak (with whom my father was then living in Havana) arrived in Oriente to bury my grandmother, they first heard Fidel's name from my grandfather Luis, who had recently begun to work cutting cane on a modest estate called Manacas near the town of Birán.

"Some people swear he is the kindest man in all of Oriente," Luis said of the old Spaniard who was his new boss. "Others say he's a thief and a murderer. But the craziest thing is that the person who seems most angry with him—he has even come out to the fields and tried to organize us workers against him—is his son, Fidel. And he's only thirteen!"

His story was cut short when a weeping Sima emerged from the room where her mother lay. A black-robed priest from Santiago de Cuba followed her, trailing incense and blessings in Latin. Ytzak, red-faced and enraged, rended his fine linen guayabera right there, with one quick tear that seemed to blacken like flesh on fire. Sima went into hysterics, convinced nothing but evil would come to them now, sure that a report about Ytzak's brashness would go out to secret inquisitors who'd make their way to the hilly woods of Oriente and force them to repent.

Later, when Ytzak tried to recite the kaddish—at the top of his lungs, in full Jewish regalia—outside Leah's locked door, Luis and Enrique had to drag him away. Because Ytzak refused to contain himself—"We are yeudim, we are yeudim!" he kept shouting between Hebrew prayers—the locals had begun to talk, eventually refusing to help with the internment for fear of the devil himself. (It was Enrique and Moisés who dug Leah's grave, their young shoulders bending sadly into the task.) At the house, Ytzak covered all the mirrors with black and set a full meal out for the poor: beef stew and rice, bread and fruit, all of which went untouched by the campesinos, who wondered if the crazy old man was trying to poison somebody.

With all the gossip and tension in the air, Luis was forced to tell Haim, Moisés's father—the only person he thought he could possibly trust with this secret—the entire family story and enlist him in keeping Ytzak from the funeral until the priest was done and the simple pine box was sprinkled with dirt. But Haim, a lax Jew but a Jew who was nonetheless proud and open about his heritage, agreed to help only if Luis would let Ytzak say the kaddish at the grave later, alone, after everyone was gone. When Luis acceded, Haim, who was as big as a tower, sat Ytzak down and explained to him what was happening. To everyone's surprise, Ytzak stayed put, quietly weeping into his prayer book.

Out on the porch, Enrique pleaded with his father. "Let him go, the harm has already been done," he said, sweeping his arm to indicate the snooping neighbors. "It would have been bad enough if they'd thought we were Jews, but now they think we're satanists, for god's sake."

"No, no, no," Luis insisted.

"But Papá—"

A frustrated, angry Luis refused, his rough hands shaking.

"But—"

Without warning, Luis slapped his son hard across the face. "Do not defy me," he said. The veins on his head throbbed. "I am doing this for your mother, the only person who really cared about your grandmother. As it is, we already waited much too long to bury Leah so you could be here. You and Ytzak, you two wonderful Jews out in the world, are the cruelest, most selfish people on earth."

"Come on," a stunned Moisés Menach, who'd witnessed it all,

said to my father, who stood there like a statue, numb from shock, holding his stinging cheek in his hand.

He quickly took Enrique by the elbow and led him away from the stuffy family home. In the distance they could see the billowy stacks from the sugar mills. The air smelled of molasses. Moisés steered my distraught father into the tangled green of the countryside, into the thicket of cedars and flamboyants and wild hibiscus. In the blink of an eye, they found themselves by the river's edge, its currents laced with white as the foam rushed past the shores. Their shirts were pressed with sweat to their backs, their faces runny with red dust.

As they neared the gushing waters, my father stubbed his foot on a rock and grunted. But when he bent to nurse his hurt extremity, it was as if something inside him had broken instead. "I'm so sick of it," Enrique said, sobbing. "Being Jewish is a fucking curse. Everybody hates us! My god, look at what's happening in Europe— no one cares, no one even believes it!"

He sat down on the ground as Moisés put his arm around him, holding him silently. "My grandfather insists and insists, and in the meantime, everyone he loves turns against him," Enrique said. "In order to circumcise me the right way, to have his damned Jewish legacy, he lost his whole fucking Jewish history." He waved at the Mayarí, its waters curling on the shore, and Moisés remembered the story about Luis and the two family Bibles he'd thrown in the river.

After a moment, my father, still sniffling, reached down and unlaced the shoes bought wholesale on Muralla Street in Havana, stripped his drenched shirt and loose pants from his sturdy frame, and tiptoed to the very rim of the water, awkwardly making his way through gravel and rocks, weeds and discarded bits of rusted metal and glass.

Moisés stayed behind. As he watched my father's pallid body while he cautiously tested the river's temperature with his swollen left foot, he heard the unmistakable boo of a small owl, then a rustling of wings and the high-pitched scream of a warm-blooded creature caught by surprise in its fatal claws.

It was because Moisés had turned to the owl and its prey that he missed the exact moment when Fidel entered the picture. But there he was, a strapping adolescent, still covered with a layer of baby fat but clearly muscular underneath, standing wet and naked in front of my father. He was knee deep in the river and staring unabashedly at Enrique's penis.

"What happened to you?" the boy asked, unsure what to make of what he was seeing.

"What do you mean?" Enrique responded, blushing so much that Moisés, hurriedly approaching from behind him, could see the red in his ears.

"Your thing, it's been cut or something," said the young Fidel, who quickly glanced down at his own to make sure it was still intact.

"I'm . . . I'm a . . . Jew," said Enrique, the only time in his life he would ever volunteer that. Then he quickly hobbled back to his clothes and dressed, refusing to make eye contact with anyone.

"A Jew? Is he rich?" a grinning Fidel asked Moisés, who was now standing equidistant between the two, shocked but happy at my father's admission.

"No," Moisés said, annoyed and confused, remembering suddenly that this boy was the troublesome heir to the Manacas farm. "Are you?"

"Me? Heck no," said Fidel, smiling broadly. "I'm just lucky. You don't need money if you're lucky."

Then he laughed and threw himself back into the Mayarí, where his powerful arms and legs instantly propelled him out of sight.

XVI

After my father's circumcision, Ytzak and baby Enrique returned to Oriente and the puny plot of land where Luis and Sima lived. Banned by the angry parents for nearly an entire year from seeing his grandson, a dejected Ytzak went back to the small but tasteful house he'd once shared with Leah, the wife he'd left behind when he went off in search of a Jewish life. No one could have known then that her death years later would be so enigmatic, so emotional.

For her part, Leah, a gloomy woman whom Ytzak had once seen as both a challenge and beautiful, neither resisted nor encouraged his return. Whether they ever shared matrimonial intimacy again is anyone's guess, but what's certain is that they signed a new covenant, one in which their lives intersected but did not necessarily connect.

Lacking a church to attend out in the wilderness, she went to a prayer circle for her communal Catholic performances, leaving Ytzak alone to his solitary Jewish meditations. No menorah was ever lit in their house again, publicly or privately, no candle lit at all unless it was to the Virgin of Charity. Ytzak brooded and anxiously limped about on his peg leg but said nothing, not even when Leah brought a half dozen criolla women to the house to recite the Roman rosary on Mondays while he fasted. (Afterward, the women would retreat to their homes, where, for insurance, they'd blow cigar smoke, drink rum, and light candles for Elegguá.)

What the two of them shared was a kind of awkwardness and embarrassment. Water was boiled until half of it steamed away, laundry was pressed stiff with starch, and vegetables were rubbed raw in the kitchen. All the while, Leah's practical speech was accented with a flourish of may I's, thank you's, and por favor's that were both unnatural and vaguely threatening.

Ytzak, who couldn't bear to return to the grinder or any other job at the sugar mill, made a living for a while fashioning shoes for the nearby campesinos and writing letters for those who were illiterate. If he signed his own name, he'd follow it with samech tet, or True Sephardim, which nobody but other Jews—and not even most of them—ever understood.

In the years after "the dance of the millions"—the late twenties and early thirties—when world sugar prices dropped, chaos came to Cuba, particularly Oriente, where the mills were virtually the only industry. During that time Ytzak often served as an interpreter— he'd learned a bit of English from the Corwens—for the U.S. businessmen his Havana friends would send his way. These were invariably speculators, investors in sugar, cattle, or lumber, men who saw Cuba as the wild west, a new frontier to be conquered and attached to the mainland, one way or another.

"Statehood for Cuba's not important to me, not at all," a wily Virginian confided once after several glasses of rum while languishing in a rocking chair on Ytzak and Leah's porch. "You know why? 'Cause Cubans are going to become Americans anyway. Heck, man, you're crazy to buy everything we bring down here. Let me tell you, trade will make you an American faster than statehood, taxes, or that Platt Amendment."

The Moor, Ytzak's old friend from Havana, was still working as a traveling salesman now and then—he was successful enough that he had set up his own store on Muralla Street in Old Havana but had been stung, like everyone else, by the Great Depression. Though he was an undistilled capitalist in his own business dealings, in the intervening years he'd become friends in Havana with radical Jewish refugees from Palestine and Poland. They had brought with them pamphlets and books on Zionism, Marxism, and the Russian revolution that he found compelling.

Sometimes, late at night, The Moor and Ytzak would discuss these ideas behind screens of cigar smoke while rocking on the porch. Oriente, cradleland of all of Cuba's uprisings, was in anarchy then. With alarming frequency, the campesinos would set fire to the sugarcane fields. When hunger got especially sharp and distorted their reasoning, they'd turn on each other, their machetes sharp and murderous.

The Moor said Havana was no better; in fact, just a few years after the dictator Gerardo Machado came to power, the city was choking with panhandlers and thieves, workers' strikes paralyzed commerce, and there were frequent and armed insurrections. The Moor was sure anybody in his right mind could look out at the port of Havana and see the Americans sitting there in their impenetrable steel ships, directing the madness, ready to invade.

But Ytzak resisted The Moor's vision; it was the only way he could stand the misery around him in Oriente, the violence and the suffering of his neighbors, who appeared to him thinner and ghostlier by the day. Indeed, as time went by, the city took on a rosier and rosier tint in his mind: The Americans in Havana had always treated him well. There was a community of Jews, he had helped found the first Sephardic synagogue in Cuba. He remembered the way the fog lifted in the morning, the bright yellow globes of the gaslights extinguished one by one by lively boys with long poles that reached up to cap them. The city was wonderfully noisy, full of gaiety and beautiful women. He was sure it was comparable to Rome, Alexandria, or Hollywood.

On subsequent trips to Ytzak's house, The Moor brought him articles and books by Fernando Ortiz and Jorge Mañach that argued for a sense of cubanismo, and which Ytzak, of course, ardently supported. "Why do you think I went to war?" he'd ask. "Why do you think I gladly sacrificed my leg?"

Later, The Moor delivered issues of *Cuba Contemporánea* and other magazines critical of Cuba's growing dependency on sugar and the U.S. market. They were dog-eared and worn, but still capable of causing tense talks on Ytzak and Leah's porch. The only way out of

the morass, declared The Moor, was to free Cuba of all foreign influence, especially that of the United States. The only way, retorted
Ytzak, was for Cubans to act more like Americans, who struck him
as civilized and smart. All the while, Enrique and Moisés would roll
around between the rocking chairs and the tired extremities of the
passionate men, indifferent to it all.

When The Moor came to Oriente, he'd also leave goods at
Ytzak's for the campesinos to pick up. One time, a visiting American inquired about the vast collection of obviously new kitchen
pots stored on the back porch, and when Ytzak explained that they
belonged to some of The Moor's clients, the American offered to
bring him carving knives, cheap, on his next trip from the United
States.

That's how, slowly, without his even noticing it, Ytzak's house
developed into a little trading post, and eventually into a dry-goods
store. In its heyday, it carried everything from soap to oil lamps, underwear to pine nuts, and even reading glasses. Ytzak kept the political pamphlets and books The Moor brought him in his room, in
a box under the bed he reluctantly shared with Leah.

For Ytzak, those years were all a waiting game.

The focus of his patience was Enrique, who ran naked around
Luis and Sima's garden and played with Moisés, the roly-poly
charcoal-colored son of the only openly Jewish family they knew.
Ytzak had been heartened by the fact that Enrique had been naturally drawn to Moisés, although the Menachs' religious practices,
while out in the open, seemed to him as disinterested as Sima and
Luis's. No one seemed to know or care much about praying or the
Sabbath, much less anything more complicated, like tefillin. Moreover, the Menachs struck Ytzak as occasionally pretentious. Since
Haim had studied in French schools in Turkey, they seasoned their
already fractured judeo-español with the language of Napoleon and
added cream to all their sauces, constantly mixing meat and milk.

(Not that Ytzak understood or kept kosher very well—in Oriente it was virtually impossible—but he always hoped to find in other Jews examples for all the ways he aspired to be.)

After Enrique's brit milah, Luis and Sima's observances had dropped to a bare minimum, offering prayers, just like the Menachs, only on the High Holidays. Like their ancestors before them, they kept young Enrique away from their rituals. They understood that he might recognize elements from the Menachs' worship, or perhaps overhear something from the Lithuanian and Russian Jews who were streaming into Oriente to work on the railroad, but both Luis and Sima insisted on waiting until he was older before burdening him with the meaning of his Jewishness.

If Enrique ever questioned anything that seemed to separate his family from the natives around him, Luis and Sima assured him with what would eventually become his own refrain: "We are Spanish, descended from nobility, that is all," they'd say in their own unconvincing open-mouthed Cuban way. Not even they believed it.

Ytzak would roll his eyes and mutter under his breath: "We are Cubans—that is why we had a war of independence from Spain—and we are Jews." He refused to link up to the mother country, refused to claim any blood but that of Abraham and what he'd spilled on the island.

Most of the time, Ytzak simply observed Enrique from afar. Sometimes Leah would spend time with the two of them, undoubtedly out of grandmotherly love but also to supervise the untrustworthy grandfather. After the circumcision episode, the entire family was on the lookout for Ytzak. Luis and Sima had made him promise not to say anything without their permission, threatening to ban him forever if he went back on his word.

But Ytzak needn't have worried. As he grew older, Enrique began to drift toward him on his own, as if he instinctively recognized something that inevitably linked them together. He'd stroll from Luis and Sima's little home deep in the woods over to Ytzak and Leah's busy store and loiter about the place, reading, napping, just hanging around. Ytzak would sometimes give him and Moisés errands to run in exchange for candy.

"Goral," a proud Ytzak whispered to himself (he'd learned a little bit of secular Hebrew, and Yiddish, too, from his time in Havana) as he told stories to his grandson and Moisés. His heroes included José Martí and Antonio Maceo, Abraham Lincoln and the Indian Hatuey, who preferred to die at the stake than share a heaven with his Spanish oppressors.

But Ytzak also snuck in Jewish stories, like the one about David and his mighty slingshot, how he was just a boy like them once, tending sheep out in the wilderness. Ytzak was particularly fond of the account of David and Jonathan, of the remarkable friendship that surpassed women and war. As a result, he looked on Moisés as a sacred gift, a sign that Enrique's soul would not be lost to Israel.

That Ytzak could see his grandson in any kind of intrepid role— undoubtedly, in Ytzak's mind, my father was David, Moisés merely Jonathan, his loyal adjunct—was somewhat of a miracle of faith in itself.

Although Enrique was an excellent student, he dropped out of the mill-run school after the fourth grade. An exasperated Luis tried to teach him a few jobs at the sugar mill—hauling cane, helping to run Ytzak's old grinder, simply cleaning the machinery—but Enrique, whose exquisite hands would split and bleed with the slightest effort, was a disaster at everything.

In truth, my father was masterful in the garden, but it was not a talent that could be cultivated. What Enrique did was touch things, just touch them, and they would grow spectacularly. He could spit on the ground, out of spite even, and in days huge white tubulars would sprout, thick tentacles pushing anxiously out of the dirt. He'd pat a hen on the head and she'd deliver egg after egg, each one with a perfect yolk and plenty of white for meringue.

But Enrique had no interest in his special endowment. It baffled and frustrated him. Everything had to be coaxed, forced out of him, so that nothing in the end could be appreciated. People said he was spoiled, lazy, even cursed.

Left to his own devices, Enrique would throw himself in his hammock or rock away on the porch at Ytzak and Leah's and read and reread everything he had discovered in the box behind the mosquito netting and under his grandparents' bed. My father found that he loved Martí—the poetry most of all, tolerating the essays just enough to contextualize the verses.

When Enrique turned twelve, he tried to teach the kids who didn't attend the mill school how to read, a task most everyone considered useless, since many of the campesinos saw literacy as an affectation. The lessons were always interrupted by the more urgent needs of families and cane. Eventually, one of his students, a pale skinny boy with wild hair named Celestino, began writing poems on tree trunks, but the campesinos taunted and beat him. Sometime later, a stunned Enrique found Celestino hanging lifeless from a branch.

Traumatized and scared, Enrique stopped his lessons. He wound up working in Ytzak's store, taking orders from across the counter his grandfather had installed, dully discussing spices for meat and Mexican lace with the women who made up the majority of the clientele. While at the store, he often thought about Celestino, imagined him with scribbled bark stuffed in his mouth.

When he had to walk home at night, Enrique worried about every snapping twig, every flutter and tweet in the darkness. He envisioned killer shadows and his own legs dangling above the ground. He wondered if Ytzak felt the same way in Oriente, if that was why he'd developed his vision of Havana as a fairy-tale city—a city in which men were free—free to be themselves in every sense. In his heart, Enrique knew that this paradise could not possibly exist, that everyone he encountered who'd actually been to Havana reported constant mayhem. But in the thick black of the tangled woods, he'd close his eyes and visualize Ytzak's paradise: The mighty ships on the shore, the noise of the vendors, the tang of sea salt. At the time, he'd never even seen the ocean, and he was dying to taste it.

In the end, Ytzak's visions proved to be a kind of training ground: Listening to his grandfather talk about Havana, Enrique learned how to construct a dream of perfection, how to conjure heaven so as to live on earth.

XVII

For Leah, watching Enrique grow up was a trial of patience, too, but for different reasons. While Ytzak watched him anticipating freedom, Leah couldn't help but see an inevitable disgrace coming upon her. Twice Ytzak had left her, and she knew the third and final time would be with Enrique. She'd look at him and mutter, "Goral, goral."

Ytzak, who was known as Antonio then and hadn't yet decided he wanted to use his Jewish name, first disappeared in the summer of 1897, shortly after they married. Leah had been a beautiful, black-haired fourteen-year-old bride, supposedly lucky to have snared a husband from Santiago instead of one of the cruder campesinos. But after reading treatises by José Martí (illegally smuggled into Cuba from Tampa and New York, where they were published), sixteen-year-old Antonio and all four of his older brothers left to fight for Cuba's independence from Spain.

For months, there would be no news from him except maybe a report from a friend saying that he was okay, a hero in General Máximo Gómez's regiment; or that he was dead, buried with honors on a hill somewhere in Las Villas or in the fields of Pinar del Río. A few times she heard he'd been interned in Spanish concentration camps (a generation later, Adolf Hitler would tell a journalist he knew about the camps in Cuba, and thought they were a great idea).

Four times young Leah thought she was widowed, only to learn later that the dead boy was not Antonio, but one of his brothers, each one a martyr for liberation. (With each death, she aged a little, so that by the time they were in their late twenties, she already had a few gray hairs and lines around her mouth, while Antonio, in spite of the horrors of war, remained sunny and youthful—their disparity was such that, years later, he'd often be confused for her ward.)

A few times during the war, Antonio appeared to her in the night—always a stranger, his downy beard dirty, his muscles flaccid, dressed only in rags—and they'd fall on each other, making love, holding on for as long as possible. He'd conclude his visit with an extraordinary feast in which he would forget his manners and gnaw like a wild dog at whatever meat was left on a salty chicken leg. He'd fall asleep, greasy and exhausted, snoring like a beast.

But as soon as Leah surrendered to the exhaustion of his whirlwind visit, she'd be startled by the sudden emptiness of his departure. She never saw the dawn with him, only the soft outline, the streaks of dirt left by his body on the sheets. Outside, the thick blanket of fog that covers Oriente each and every morning erased all trace of him.

Then for a long time there'd be no word, no touch, nothing. Leah heard from the men who came by that the yanquis were coming, lustful for the island. She heard about the *Maine*, about the black American soldiers who took San Juan Hill and the portly white colonel who stole their story and fame.

When Leah went to Mayarí searching for news about her husband, she saw for herself how the Americans had set themselves up to govern. Taller, thicker, and better dressed, they would push the Cubans around as if they had been the enemy. At one military camp she saw hundreds of Spanish cadavers being burned by the U.S. occupation forces and wondered if the wives and lovers who were waiting for those men back in Spain would ever know the real fate of their loved ones. Vultures circled above the crackling fires and stench, quietly waiting their turn.

———

Antonio didn't turn up until several years later, after the U.S. in-
vaders had left. He limped up to the house, balancing his weight on
his new peg leg, claiming to have been a victim of cannon fire, am-
nesia, and politics, a virtual prisoner in a Havana hospital. Never
having been convinced of his death, a gleeful Leah took him back
on the spot, wiping his brow, boiling soup from lamb bones, bits of
yuca, plantains, and wild basil.

In 1904, two years after the Cuban republic was established, she
bore Sima, blue-gray–eyed like Antonio, a fountain of sweetness, a
child who barely cried, just looked around as if in shock at the
wasteland into which she had been brought to the world. She
would grow up with neither her mother's severe beauty nor her father's brio, but with her own healthy radiance, prudent and reliable.

For Sima's naming ceremony Antonio and Leah couldn't find a
Jewish virgin (there was only one other anusim family immediately
nearby, and none of its members were young women) to be Sima's
godmother, so they resorted to recruiting a black girl named Lucía,
who assumed the wholly improvised rite was just the Garazis' own
style of orisha worship. It was performed in utter secrecy, of course,
with the windows closed in spite of the suffocating heat (they still
put out saucers of milk and honey for the visiting hadas). They
dipped the baby girl in a basin of warm water and tossed coins and
gold into it for good luck. In the end, Lucía left there no longer sure
about what she had seen, not sure at all if Antonio and Leah's
strange rites and prayers weren't all devil's play.

Two years later, when he was twenty-five years old and Leah
was twenty-three, Antonio met The Moor. He came home from
Mayarí in a tizzy, talking nonstop about the salesman's brazen admission. "He just said it! He just said, 'I'm a Jew!,' just like that," he
exclaimed, amazed the man hadn't been consumed on the spot by
the native anti-Semitism.

Leah winced. She knew from Antonio's stories about the hospital in Havana that he'd met American Jews, doctors and soldiers
who let him know about their common faith. Since their arrival,

there were even public worship services in Havana. But she considered that their ability to function as public Jews had more to do with their U.S. citizenship than with any new tolerance. Now here was this Lebanese man, brown as mahogany, stirring things up. She remembered The Moor's effortless smile, the easy credit terms she was sure could bankrupt them, the neckties and Catholic icons in his wooden peddler's box.

"Since when are you so religious anyway?" Leah asked her husband, who usually had to be reminded to come pray as she lit candles on Fridays.

What Leah didn't realize was how badly Antonio wanted to leave Oriente, to go to the city. He argued with her at every turn, ridiculing her paranoia when strangers came by and noticed the mezuzah awkwardly hidden inside the elaborate branches and leaves that served as decorations on the door frame, or wondered why their candles were braided and how it could be possible that everyone in the family should have an aversion to pork, Cuba's most abundant meat.

It took Antonio six years to work up his nerve, six years to put a few pennies together, and to realize Leah would forever be a crypto-Jew, trapped by tradition, habit, and fear. One day, he came home from the mill, black with dirt, his skin covered with the usual cuts from the cane stalks, and told her he wanted to be called Ytzak—the Spanish spelling deliberately jagged, the same way Hebrew letters might seem to the unknowing, so as to provoke questions—that he was leaving, that he would walk back to Havana on his peg leg if he had to.

"There has to be another way," he said. "I can't be pretending I'm only half of who I am."

"But this *is* who we are," Leah said between sobs.

Two years later, in 1914, Ytzak posed for a photo with the founders of Chevet Ahim and sent a copy to Oriente with The Moor (with whom he also occasionally would send some money). Sima, the daughter he missed growing up, pinned it on the wall next to her mother's bed, where she slept now that her father was gone. She wouldn't see him again until many years later, after she'd married Luis San José, the son of the only other anusim family they knew, and news reached Ytzak that she was pregnant with his grandchild.

At that, Ytzak immediately packed all of his belongings, said good-bye to the Corwens, and headed back to Oriente.

One steamy day many years later, Ytzak struggled up the path to the house he shared with Leah, shaking his head in disgust. Not far away, the earth was scorched, the sweet smell of blood and sugar rising in spirals from the cane fields. It was 1932. He was fifty-one years old, his hair a soft white haze. His grandson, for whom he had left Havana and come back to the countryside, was nearly twelve, practically a man by rural standards. Ytzak steadied himself on the painful prosthetic that left the soft flap of skin on his knee red, often bleeding from sores.

"What's going on?" Leah asked, gazing at the increasingly black sky. She had not grayed quite like her husband, yet the sternness of her expression made her seem like a schoolmarm always ready to impose detention.

Ytzak collapsed in a rocking chair, grimacing at the sharp ache from his war wound. "The foreman at the mill, Morales, accused the campesinos of being Communists, tried to get them all fired," he said. "That's their response." He pointed with a nod at the fire in the distance, clearly visible through the bush. "Then they killed him." He sighed.

"They killed him?" She drew her arms across her chest.

Ytzak nodded. "Slashed his throat," he said, "then cut him into pieces with their machetes and let the dogs at him. It's enough for me, Leah," he said. "It's enough."

She didn't need an interpreter. "What about the store?"

"Do with it what you please," he said. "I'm not taking anything with me."

"Except Enrique," she added bitterly. The corners of her mouth dropped like little steel clamps, harsh and cold.

"If he wants to come," Ytzak said. All he could dare to do was hope.

In a few days, Ytzak and Enrique were packed, saying good-bye to Sima, who wept, and Luis, who paced in dismay, knowing that it was useless to stop Ytzak, and now convinced that there was no place in Oriente for a delicate boy like his son.

"Perhaps," he had told his wife the night before their departure, "he will find his destiny in the city." Lovely, sweet Sima cried into his shoulder; she had never counted on losing Enrique so soon.

As they prepared to leave, steely Leah gave her grandson a formal, chilly embrace and wished him well. Then she turned away, walking back to her house with her head held stiffly, never once looking back on her husband.

"Write us, Enrique, write us—promise that you will write," Sima pleaded with her boy, who promised he would do so every week as he buried his nose in her hair (perfumed with the tangy scent of lemons)—a pledge he kept until she died.

Ytzak and Enrique climbed into a horse-drawn cart and galloped off to Santiago, from which they took the train to the capital, repeating what had once been another fateful journey. Ytzak waved his straw hat while Enrique beamed and laughed from nervousness and joy.

Sima held on to her husband's arm with both hands, her flawless peasant's face red and wet from crying.

After her husband left, Leah kept her house sealed, letting no one in but Sima, who resented the drama of her father's abandonment and its fallout. Sima wanted things to be normal—whatever that was—to stabilize, to calm down. But her mother insisted on bleakness, on hibernation and shame.

During this time, the store remained closed, too, the plank of the counter leaning against a wall. The neighbors all knew Ytzak had left Leah, although not his motivations, and they stayed away. The situation was embarrassing, after all. Moreover, of the couple, it was the eccentric Ytzak the locals had liked, with his war stories and warm smile, not Leah, who frowned and always kept to herself, almost as if she considered herself better than them.

Occasionally, an unwitting salesman would come by, hawking linen guayaberas or bottles of fancy perfume. Leah wouldn't answer his knocks, preferring to stay inside in her darkness until he gave up, bewildered by the lack of hospitality, and went off to Mayarí to find out what happened from the gossips who hung out on their front porches, rocking and twittering.

One day, a particularly incessant peddler appeared hauling two huge wooden crates of women's underwear. He rapped on the door and cooed in a language she didn't understand. When Leah didn't answer, he took residence on the porch, swinging in what had been Ytzak's chair and slicing a juicy mango with a pearl-handled knife. The fruit smeared his chin and dripped between his legs. When he was finished, the man leaned back on the rocker, put his feet up on the railing, and pulled his hat over his head.

Leah stayed up all night, pacing, worried about the stranger on her porch. When dawn came, she peeked out into the thick morning mist only to find him urinating just off the wooden deck, not at all worried about whether anyone could see him. He aimed his piss in an yellow arch and laughed. She drew back in amazement.

By noon, the man was conducting business off the porch, yelling at passersby with his gravelly Germanic accent. He would draw a few folks forward, rattle off his pitch in his native tongue, which caused the natives to laugh and snicker, and barter by holding up his fingers for the price he wanted in one hand, a pair of panties in the other.

Later that evening, still ensconced inside the house, Leah heard another pair of footsteps on the porch. These were heavier, blunt. Then she heard a voice she recognized—Tatán, a local fruit and vegetable vendor, a huge black man—ordering the stranger off the porch. When the peddler laughed at Tatán, Leah heard a growling like an animal—a tiger or leopard perhaps—a scratching on the wood, then a clatter, the stranger's bloodcurdling scream, and the fast clip of running feet.

That was how handsome Tatán began to court my great-grandmother. When she opened the door to see what had happened, he pulled off his hat, bowed his head, and asked her forgiveness for intruding in her life uninvited.

"I think a woman like you deserves more respect than that man was offering," a gallant Tatán said.

"Gracias, gracias," Leah said, blushing. Her rigidity just melted away then, the lines around her mouth suddenly seeming almost like dimples.

Leah couldn't invite Tatán inside—it wouldn't have looked right under any circumstances—but she did ask him to come by the next day, to help her reopen the store. Because he worked for her—an arrangement that satisfied them both—they could see each other nearly every day, spend hours on end talking and laughing, without drawing too much suspicion.

Whatever actually happened between them, whether in fact they ever became lovers, is a mystery. I heard the story from Moisés. My father refused to discuss it, telling me he was not in Oriente at the time, that he was busy in Havana, unaware of his family's daily lives.

But what Moisés told me is that at some point, Tatán became the object of Lucía's affection. When he tried to rebuff her, Lucía told him about the Garazis' rituals and accused him of having fallen under the devil's spell, that Leah was in fact a bride of Satan. For proof, she suggested he look in the tiny canister tacked to the inside of her door, hidden behind the dried branches on the frame.

Though he dismissed Lucía's taunts at first, eventually Tatán took notice of the mezuzah. One day when Leah was in Mayarí conducting business, he pried it from the door, emptying its contents. Tatán was illiterate, so the parchment was utterly meaningless to him but he ran with it to Lucía, who took him and the paper to one of the local santeros.

"You are very lucky, m'hijo," the holy man told him. "You've arrived right in time, we can still save you." He compared the Hebrew script with a page from a Cuban newspaper. "See? See the difference?"

A frightened, perspiring Tatán pressed the santero: "What does it mean?"

"It means you have been consorting with Lucifer himself," the santero said, "and you need to cleanse your spirit or you will burn for all eternity in the fires of hell. Had you stayed any longer, Tatán, you would have been consumed by demons who taunt humans with their perversity."

A wide-eyed Tatán never returned to Leah's store. Indeed, when she went looking for him, thinking something awful had happened— an accident, an illness—he ran from her, making the same clattering and screaming sounds as the peddler that night on her front porch.

Leah was baffled and heartsick. "What did I do to you?" she called after him, but he just ran, fast and away from her. Her face turned frigid again, this time pale and veiny like marble itself.

When Leah vanished, Sima and Luis scoured the woods between her house and theirs. A frantic Luis went to Mayarí and asked a million questions, but no one had seen her. Days later, when Sima had begun to imagine her mother had gone to Havana to confront her father after all these years, Leah's bloated body floated up on the shores of the river.

The official cause of death was drowning. But many people disagreed. In Mayarí, they said she was kidnapped by a güije, a spirit who lives in rivers, a mischievous male phantom who steals stray children and lonely women.

XVIII

Moisés's first letter to me arrived on a cold December day in late 1987 in the trembling hand of a shivering Cuban standing at my door who spoke virtually no English. I wasn't home when he knocked but a surprised and gentle Seth let him in, gave him some hot chocolate, and explained the theory of scarves and layers and contained body heat. The poor Cuban, his teeth rattling, was still barely able to speak when I arrived an hour or so later.

"My name is Félix García," he said, gloveless and hatless, fishing the blue-lined envelope from the inside pocket of his worn wool jacket. He would later tell us the coat was inherited from his father, who had come to the United States once in the fifties and kept it with the sure knowledge that someone in his family would eventually need it again, even if it was thirty years later.

I was so worried by Félix's icy condition that I barely glanced at the envelope, though I know now I must have been aware all along it was from Moisés. Who else, after all, would be writing to me from Cuba? It's not as if I'd made friends with anyone. But with Félix wheezing and standing frigid in front of the fireplace in his soaked socks, I was totally distracted. He was thin and ill at ease, his sparse hair plastered against his hard little head.

As it turned out, Félix was the lighting technician for a Cuban theater group that was spending a week at the University of Illinois's Chicago campus, part of a six-week tour through the United States that had also become a mail route. At every stop, Félix ran around the city delivering mail, most of the time unable to announce his visit because he didn't have anybody's phone number. When I asked him why he didn't simply stamp and drop the letters in a mailbox now that he was in the United States, he seemed taken aback, as if to do so would somehow be a betrayal to his friends to make sure their messages arrived safely.

"I'm Celina's brother," he said, trying to explain to us who he was.

"Celina?" I asked, drawing an absolute blank.

"Yes, yes, Celina," he said. "She was there when you were visiting the Menachs. The girl with very long hair, very wavy—like yours. Orlando's friend."

Celina! The girl I had tasted on Orlando's mouth—that was her name! My god!

I instantly noted that Félix did not say Deborah or Yosemí or even Rafa's friend, and I examined him for clues about how much he might know about his sister's relationship with Orlando. But his expression was more expectant than complicit.

"You remember her now?" he asked, all hopeful.

"Yes, yes, of course," I said. Then I immediately tried to change the subject. "The letter is from the Menachs, then?"

"Yes, from Moisés," Félix said, still shivering in front of the fire. He was staring out the living room window, at the utter blackness of four o'clock in the afternoon during winter in Chicago. His shoes, leather loafers completely unsuitable for snow, were curling stiffly as they dried in front of the fire.

"Who's Celina?" asked Seth, my amiable and boyish lover, having realized that she did not figure in any way in my Cuba stories. He was trying his unsteady but increasingly fluent Spanish on us.

"She's a young girl—"

"Well, she's fourteen, a young woman, really," interrupted Félix, who—with his unshaven, nearly sunken cheeks, ashen skin, and brittle bones—didn't seem at all related.

I smiled at him indulgently. "Yes. But here, in the States, that's more of a girl, really."

"¿Quién es?" Seth persisted.

"She's a neighbor of the Menachs, right?" I said, looking to Félix for confirmation.

"Yes, a friend of Orlando's," he said again without any guile whatsoever. "She lives next door, in your old building."

"Really?" I said.

"Yes, downstairs," he added.

"Orlando is the teenage boy?" a confused Seth continued, trying to pull the family tree together.

"Orlando is Moisés's son-in-law," said Félix.

"So how old is Orlando?" Seth asked, now amused.

Félix looked at him and then at me and shrugged. "I don't know. In his forties, I think. They are friends, Orlando and my sister, because he is who drives her to visit my father in prison. The prison is on the outskirts of town. Not everyone would do this favor."

"I'm . . . I'm sorry," Seth stuttered, embarrassed.

Suddenly, I couldn't breathe. I had deliberately put the entire episode with Orlando out of my mind, refusing to consider what I had seen with my own eyes or experienced in the flesh, choosing instead to view it as a fantasy almost, as a possibility rather than a reality. Now I was being forced to deal with the garish and vulgar truth. And I was horrified: Orlando existed, as a man, a man to whom I'd given something of myself, quite possibly a monstrous man.

"Are you okay?" Seth asked, touching my elbow with his hand. I nodded. Félix, indifferent, reached down to pinch his frozen toes.

"What is your father in prison for?" I ventured cautiously. I figured he could add murder to his charges if he ever knew the price of his daughter's visits.

Félix straightened and shrugged again. "For activities against the state, of course. What do most people in Cuba go to prison for?" he asked rhetorically. "The official charge, I think, is sedition or something like that. It's been very hard on my sister because, since her mother died a year ago—we are only half-siblings—she had become close to our father, and then this happened."

"You mean she lives alone now?" I asked. My stomach acids

churned; my disgust with Orlando became even greater. "You don't have other siblings?"

"No, no, that is why," Félix added with a smile, "I say she is a young woman, because she is older than her years."

"Your father, how long will he be . . ." Seth began to ask in his hesitant Spanish.

"About twenty-five years," Félix said. "It's about what they sentence everyone for those sorts of activities. Maybe he'll be out sooner. I don't know. There's a group in Miami that has him on their prisoner of conscience list, but I'm not sure how much that helps in Havana. And Moisés has promised to see what he can do, but so far, nothing." The more Félix talked—about his father's troubles, about his sister's lonesomeness and his own sense of impotence—the more Seth and I felt sorry for him.

But I had the extra burden of guilt: I could have stopped his sister's exploitation, I could have let the Menachs find Orlando with his head between her legs, but instead I'd chosen to make time for him, to serve as an accomplice. And to make love with him.

In my mind's eye I could see a weeping Celina in Orlando's brown arms, struggling to escape his grip. Her legs, long and tapered, kicking (though, curiously, not at him) as he leaned toward her for a kiss, which she avoided by vigorously shaking her head. I told myself this happened every day.

As I engaged in my own inner torture, Seth sat Félix down on the couch and brought a small blanket for his blue feet. We invited him to dinner—Seth made a delicious tortellini that Félix gobbled up in huge forkfuls. We opened a bottle of Havana Club and toasted to the future.

All night long I wondered when it would all explode, when someone would catch Orlando and kill him, or when Celina would become pregnant, or when he'd beat her out of frustration. I was convinced it had to end badly, no matter what moral lessons could be salvaged from the wreckage.

Although Seth and Félix drank wildly, chatting about politics and music for hours, I watched my own intake, fearful the rum would serve as a truth serum and I'd find myself talking too much, asking too many questions, giving myself away with too much interest. Seth, his dark golden hair flopping around his ears, his smile all pearly, seemed the very picture of health and goodness.

By the time we realized it was one o'clock in the morning, a warmed-up, sleepy Félix protested only out of courtesy when we invited him to stay in our guest room (which was really the sofa-bed in my office). We pulled out the mattress, gave him a pair of Seth's pajamas, indicated the bathroom and broke out a new toothbrush for him. He was grateful and a little embarrassed.

It was when we were in the bathroom, stripping the cellophane from the new brush, that I first saw a resemblance between Félix and his sister. It was in the intensity of his gaze, reflected there in the bathroom mirror as he stared at me, at my small breasts, without regard to Seth's naive presence. His eyes betrayed a lazy confidence, a certain arrogance as they lingered. I remembered Celina, her swan's neck leaning back as she met my eyes.

From the very beginning, Seth had been supportive of my first trip back to Cuba. In fact, in some ways, he'd been more excited than me—not because he had viewed it as any kind of return to my roots, or because he considered my connection to the island as something particular and special (although, of course, he did—my birthday was too much for him to ignore), but because he was an admirer of the Cuban revolution. (This was not a problem with my parents: Seth just kept quiet around them and, whatever their suspicions about his political affinities, they played their protocol roles perfectly, too.)

When I returned to Chicago, he peppered me with questions, thrilled at the snapshots I brought back of the Pioneros, the exercising seniors, and the doctors, and despaired at the sight of buildings beginning to crumble. When I pointed out the obvious poverty, he'd nod thoughtfully, reminding me that it was not abject, that people in the Mexican countryside were certainly far worse.

"The Cubans look healthy," he said. "The rural Mexicans, you can see, are skinny and malnourished. It's worse in places like Bolivia. There you can see the void in people's eyes. They have no idea at all why they are alive."

The truth is, I admired Seth, I envied the easy way he assumed his humanitarianism. In my mind, he was wholly noble, intuitively just.

"Whoa, the secret life of Orlando!" Seth whispered as we crawled into bed the night of Félix's visit. His skin was toasty, the little hairs on his chest like cornsilk.

"What do you mean?" I asked, defensive and guilty.

"What do I mean? Ale, you don't believe he's just friends with this totally vulnerable fourteen-year-old girl, do you? I mean, he sounded like an asshole when you described him giving his wife orders. But this . . . this is so evil!" said Seth. He stretched his arms around me, drawing me against him. "Imagine that girl—he probably has her completely intimidated."

But in my heart I knew better: Whatever was happening between them wasn't coerced, no more than what had happened between Orlando and me. I had scaled that wall of my own volition, I had gotten in the car with him of my own free will, exultant and aroused long before he touched me. My body had opened to him with a quake.

"I mean, not that I think fourteen-year-old girls these days are virgins or innocents," Seth prattled on.

To my surprise, his penis stirred against the small of my back. "Oh, really, what do you think of fourteen-year-old girls today?" I said, turning on him. I threw my leg over his, pressed his chest with my palm. "Hmm?"

My pure and virtuous lover blushed. "Well . . ." he said uneasily, unsure about where we were going.

"It sounds to me, Seth, like you're getting turned on by the idea of this middle-aged man making it with this nubile fourteen-year-old girl. . . ." I circled his naked nipple with my index finger.

"Who said anything about her being nubile?" he asked, grinning.

"What fourteen-year-old isn't nubile?" I continued, pinching his nipple, pulling it.

"I think it's turning you on. . . ." He was splayed on the bed, his arms and legs apart, waiting to be taken.

"Oh, not as much as it's turning you on," I said, reaching down to his penis, which had grown heavy.

Seth moaned. His arms stretched under the cascade of pillows, his toes cracked. I kissed his chest, his ribs, his hips, then slowly turned him on his tummy and pushed him down, my hand still on his member. I crushed my pubic bone into him from behind. He pushed his perfectly round little butt back at me. As he turned around to look at me, I could see the slope of his lip shimmering red. His legs were trembling.

We were playing, me on top but losing my balance, when Seth, his eyes shiny, flipped me over, dropping my head over the side of the bed. I was imagining the exquisite pleasure of his hardness inside me when Seth and I both saw Félix: a snide ghoul watching and enjoying the show, his pose relaxed against our bedroom door.

"¿Qué qué?" I blurted, grabbing the sheet to cover my nakedness.

"What the fuck . . . ?" Seth translated, angrily leaping from the bed, his penis bopping and gleaming.

By the time I was up, it was too late: Félix had gone bounding out our front door in his dry shoes, laughing and dancing on the freshly fallen snow, while an exposed Seth stood impotently at the entranceway, cursing at him.

XIX

4 December 1987

My dear Alejandra,

It's a beautiful dawn here, after a run of rain all last week. I awoke minutes ago and there was light already pouring in the windows. It fills the house and reminds me of your great-grandfather, Ytzak. I can still see him, his long white hair combed back, rocking on the porch at his house, explaining the concept of colors to your father, who sat on his lap, awed: "Blue is the sky on a clear day, yellow is the yolk of an egg." A generation later, he did the same with you, out on the balcony of your parents' apartment, and you gazed up at him, as enthralled as your father had once been.

This morning, I wish you were here, wish you could see this house when it is quiet and peaceful, and not just when it is in convulsions.

Much love from the entire family,

Moisés

Moisés's letter was on onionskin, thin as a whisper, with lettering that rose and fell with exquisite loops. It looked exactly like my father's script—so much so that I had to recheck the envelope, not for a postmark but to verify the flimsy construction, the par avion logo to remind myself it came from abroad.

"That's all? 'It's a beautiful morning'? That's it?" asked an angry and resentful Seth. He kept hitting his fist into his palm, pacing in our bedroom. The light on his skin was blue. He looked pale, frostbitten.

When I told my father I had received correspondence from Moisés, he lowered his eyes in that regal way they both have and savored the information for a second before opening them back up and smiling.

"That's wonderful," he said. We were in my mother's kitchen, soaking in the rich aroma of a pot of lentils simmering with garlic, carrots, and a huge soup bone.

"Don't you want to know what he said?" I asked, put off by his lack of curiosity.

My father shrugged, his big shoulders barely twitching under the thick wool of his sweater. "If you want to tell me, yes, of course, but the letter is to you, no? It is not to me."

I had shared with him and my mother all the photographs I'd taken in Cuba, including the ones of our old apartment and of Moisés and his family. My parents had gasped at the conditions of the buildings but had been so overjoyed to see Moisés's healthy brood and the utter light that came off his face in every shot that it was not until later that they shook their heads and sighed, noting that he also looked aged, fatigued.

"He is your friend," I told my father, as if that should give him permission, or perhaps more precisely, imply obligation.

"No," he said, his finger in the air as if he were in the middle of one of his lectures, "he is not my friend—friend is not the right word. He is my brother, if not in the literal filial meaning certainly in spirit."

"Well then."

"Yes," he said, almost smug now.

We were at a standstill, my father silently stirring the lentils, me watching him. His fingers barely touched the wooden spoon, creating a slow vortex in the middle.

"Then, do you want to know, or not, what he had to say?" I asked.

"Like I said, I'd happily listen if you choose to tell."

20 February 1988

My dear Alejandra,

Your letter brought much joy to this house. Your friend Estrella, the interpreter, delivered it the day after she got back to Havana. She had many wonderful stories to tell about her visit to Chicago and about working with you again. (The world is so small—who would have thought you two would run into each other like that?) She said Seth is very handsome—and that he is so much in love with you, he is learning to speak Spanish!

I was particularly happy to hear that he is a Jewish boy, although in the end, it is really only love that matters; that is what I tell my children, that is why I was so happy when Angela married Orlando, because that he is not Jewish could not be a criteria when what is really important is that he is a good person and loves my daughter. (Some members of my community used to protest his not being Jewish to cover up their real objection—that he is mulato—but having felt the sting of that kind of racism myself, however erroneously, I find the whole idea of judging a person this way simply repulsive. It's what's in the heart that counts.)

We had already heard from Félix, Celina's brother, about what a terrific time he had with you and Seth. It helped me imagine you in your own space, instead of just here with us, and made me feel closer to you.

I loved the photograph of your parents that you sent. It has been a long time since I have laid eyes on them and their faces were both new and familiar. Your mother, of course, is as radiant as ever. She looks energetic, just like in her youth. But your father! He was always big-boned, but I can hardly believe that he has become such a large, robust man. He looks Russian, with that beard and that hair and that long black coat!

Everything here is going well. We appreciate the vitamins and the jeans for Deborah and Yosemí but, honestly, we do not need anything. Save your pennies and come visit us instead. We are well taken care of.

Un abrazo,

Moisés

"Why don't you write Moisés?" I asked my father. I was slumped on the couch in front of his big mahogany desk, reading up on some new immigration cases, preparing for a series of hearings the following week, and my father always had the best, most complete dictionaries and reference books.

"I did write him," he said, his stare fixed on the yellow notebook in front of him.

"One letter, that's all," I said.

He said nothing, just sighed and continued to bend into his work. I watched as he scribbled a few more notes, scratched out whole lines. His reading glasses hugged the tip of his nose.

"Why not write him again?" I implored. "He's your brother, after all."

"Alejandra," he said, gazing at me over his glasses with a vaguely condescending air, "he did not write back to me, but to you."

"So?"

"So you write to him. It's as good as if I wrote to him. Better, probably. You have more to say. All I could tell him is that I spend all my time here, amid books and papers."

"I can't imagine that he's all that interested in the particulars of my life either, Papi. He has his own children, he doesn't know or care about life in the United States. He's a revolutionary, remember?"

My father laughed and finally sat back in his desk chair, relaxed. He lit a cigar, one of those sweet, stubby ones from Cuba that made their way to him via his writer friends. "Yes, yes, he is, from way back," he said. He savored the smoke, let it ease out of his mouth on its own. "He was a Communist before anybody else was a Communist. He was a Communist before Fidel, that's for sure."

"And you?" I knew the answer, I just wanted to keep the conversation going.

"I could care less about politics, really." He leaned back into his desk, stared at the yellow tablet again.

"But Moisés says he first read all that Communist stuff with you."

He nodded. "Yes, but we responded differently. I just wanted to keep reading, to enjoy the words. He wanted to go to Spain and fight against Franco."

I knew this story already; how, on one of Moisés's visits as a young man to see his uncle in Havana, he and my father argued so heatedly a crowd formed around them at the café where they'd been sharing a soda. They were both so alarmed that they ran, leaving the throng screaming and fighting among itself. As they turned the corner, squad cars pulled up, ready to beat and jail the agitators.

"A man like that, what can I tell him? That I spend all my time by myself scrutinizing letters, doing exactly what I've always done? He likes action, gestures even if they're small. Besides, we haven't talked in a very long time. Better you write, Alejandra. Your voice is fresher."

As my father returned to his writing, I burrowed deeper into the couch. The window from which I'd spied on him as a child was just above me, now completely covered in impenetrable black plastic. Somewhere in this room, I knew, were the well-worn ancient leather straps, the tiny boxes containing prayers. I was sure they were cherished, expertly hidden but easily accessible.

"Can you imagine," my father said suddenly, as if coming out of a trance, "wanting to go to Spain to *fight*? As if there wasn't enough of that in Cuba. . . ."

13 August 1988

My dear Alejandra,

It's El Comandante's birthday, and your father's, too. I think of this and chuckle. Certainly there can be no truth to astrology, otherwise how could two such different men share the same day of birth?

The best gift for El Comandante, I believe, was the victory two days ago of our Olympic baseball team over the Americans. For your father, it is hard to say, perhaps a book of poetry, one he does not already own, which would be, I suppose, very difficult now that he is a literature professor.

You could, however, write him a poem. It would be a great family tradition: It is what he did as a child to honor his parents, whether on birthdays or anniversaries or any other important occasion. His were always very short, just a few lines, often borrowing from other writers, much too sentimental, and very bad. I used to change the lines now and again, to make them funny, but he stopped showing them to me because I made fun of him. He was always very defensive. Perhaps that has changed now that he is older, and presumably wiser.

There is a lot of talk here about negotiations between El Comandante and an American Catholic cardinal. I listen but it doesn't bother me. People say Cuba is antireligion, but I have found that it is simply wary of Christians, especially Catholics. El Comandante, as you surely know, attended Catholic schools; I suspect he knows something the rest of us may not.

In any case, it is not like you've been told. And as a Jew, I can't complain. It's true there's not much of a community here, that almost everyone left in those first few years after the revolution, but I firmly believe that was hysteria, nothing more.

The truth is that Jews were allowed to leave freely after the revolution if they were making aliyah; permitted, in fact, to take their furnishings and money. The truth is that, although property was nationalized, it was not just the Jews' that was nationalized but everyone's, and that no one was forced to leave. We've always had a kosher butcher in Havana (it's where I'm assigned in my ration book). We have religious classes at the Sephardic Center, small, yes, but that is no one's fault but our own.

In one of your last letters you asked how I could reconcile being a Jew and a revolutionary. For me, there is no contradiction. Jews are revolutionaries, the very first real revolutionaries. Jews—who have always been a small nation—changed the world, just like we are doing here, on our little island. For me, as a Jew, justice is the highest calling. Because of that, it is my duty to be here, nowhere else.

Besides, have you noticed the parallels between Marxism and Judaism? In both, there is first a state of innocence, then a fall into a period of social chaos (I think we can agree this is where we are now), and then, finally, harmony. I don't believe this is a coincidence. (Remember that Karl Marx himself was Jewish, however lax.)

Cuba is not a perfect place. Ours is not a perfect revolution. But if everyone left, who would stay to keep it on course? The world is changing so dramatically, so unpredictably. How would I know what to do anywhere else? Who would I be anywhere else? I was born here.

Un fuerte abrazo,

Moisés

P.S. Do you ever talk to your father about any of this?

XX

It came out of the blue one fall day, it seemed, after a long, torturous summer: The Berlin wall—that hideous stretch of murderous concrete between the German people, the line in the Cold War sand—emerged as a riser for dancers, a wailing wall, a fortune for those with a pick and a shopping bag, gold nuggets strewn on the cobblestones on a cold autumn night.

It appeared the whole planet was watching Berlin in November 1989, when harmony and goodwill seemed to reign. In Chicago, as everywhere, coverage dominated every channel, every station, every solitary conversation. It was a world away from the summer's news about Arnaldo Ochoa, the Cuban general executed in Havana over drug trafficking charges that no one could believe; those headlines had been buried, wire stories on the inside pages, or ignored.

"Remember, Ale, what you do tonight," a friendly lawyer told me after we finished a deposition early, eager to rush home and turn on the tube to watch the drunken, jubilant revelers in Berlin. We already knew how even the border guards, those notorious Stasi wanna-bes who'd been cold-blooded assassins just the day before, were now happily unified Germans, carried away by the wave of emotions. "This is history. You'll want to be able to tell your children where you were when the Berlin Wall fell," my client said all misty-eyed. "It's a nice little Christmas present, don't you think?"

By that time, the city was already flushed with holiday decor, twinkling lights, plastic reindeer, and swarms of shoppers that seemed to suck all the air out of the sky. We stood on a corner waving aimlessly for a cab for him. I was feeling proletarian and wanted to take the train, but I'd driven in and would have to face the solitude of driving out.

"It is kind of marvelous," I said, allowing myself to be awed by the wall's fall.

A taxi pulled up to the curb, its braking tires tossing slush at our shoes. "Yes, imagine the lawsuits!" my client said, laughing as he got in. "My god, as soon as those West Germans start claiming all their lost property in the East, it'll be a gold mine!"

They had the wall's collapse on the tiny black-and-white TV behind the cash register at Cachita's, a barren little Cuban bodega up on Berwyn that I thought looked an awful lot like the empty-shelf groceries on the island. The old man who owned the place, an exile named Santiago with thick glasses held together with white tape, had been talking for months about selling it, thinking about moving down to Miami with his daughter and her new Puerto Rican husband. He was sure with Ochoa's execution, an uprising was bubbling right under the surface in Cuba, and he wanted to be as close as possible when all hell broke loose. There was a huge sign outside Cachita's door, right under the Cuban and Puerto Rican flags, which advertised the Realtor's name.

Every time I stopped by—it was usually on the drive up to my parents to pick up a last-minute can of guava shells and a packet of cream cheese for my father—Santiago would joke around with me about taking it over.

"You have come to give me money!" he'd yell whenever I stepped through the door. There was usually a handful of Cuban men loitering around the cash register, talking politics and trash, smoking cigars and thinking up new combinations for lottery tickets. I knew a few of their faces from my father's domino games. They'd welcome me with huge smiles and say, "Ah, the new owner!" It was all a big, sweet joke.

"Alejandra, isn't this incredible?" Santiago said, pointing at the

TV, his eyes like huge freak house distortions behind the thick lenses of his glasses. His face was inches from the too loud screen behind the register. The crowd of men nodded and murmured.

"It's unbelievable," I concurred, setting my father's can of guava shells and a slab of cream cheese on the counter. I had refused to let my client's comments about lawsuits and property depress me; I had kept Ochoa's ghost at bay.

"You know who's next, don't you?" one of the men around Santiago's cash register asked.

When I didn't answer right away, another guy piped in: "Fidel!"

"Oh, he's a goner, a real goner!" exuded Santiago, rocking back on his heels, rubbing his hands together.

"They're on their way down—finally!—those Russians!" exclaimed still another.

"And then Fidel, and then Fidel!"

"You know how much money he takes in from those Russians? A million dollars a day! He can't survive! He'll come down!" cheered Santiago.

"Abajo Fidel!"

I finally grinned at them, shaking my head. How long had they had that cry in their throats? How many times had their hopes been raised like millions of festive balloons, only to deflate within days? Maybe this time, with Solidarity raising the ante in Poland and Vaclav Havel drawing the spotlight to Czechoslovakia, Fidel might finally stumble—so many people thought the stage had been set by Ochoa's execution.

Then one of the men, a man I didn't know, turned to me. "Are you Cuban?" he asked.

"Of course she's Cuban!" Santiago shouted.

"Well, I don't know, I can't tell," the man said.

"She's Enrique San José's daughter!" Santiago exclaimed, as if that were obvious—or as if my father, the Cuban called down so patriotically at that moment, could testify to any love but for Spain.

"Oh, my, yes, Enrique San José," the man said, stepping back, genuinely impressed. "He's brilliant, very decent. You must be very proud."

"Of course she is," Santiago chimed in as he collected the can of guava shells and the cream cheese and put them in a little sack. "She's a translator, too—she's following in his footsteps."

"Well, not exactly . . ." I tried to explain. Up on the TV screen, a young woman danced with a soldier, the wall's vulgar graffiti in the background, but transformed: Even in black-and-white, it looked fluorescent, psychedelic, like paisleys now.

"No, no, Enrique San José's a genius," the man said. "With all due respect, you can't possibly touch the sole of his shoe, but it is a noble thing to follow in your father's footsteps. Do you have a brother?"

I fixed my eyes on the man, who was exactly my height, balding, and dull-skinned. "Excuse me?" I snapped, in English, deliberately, and with a sharp, cold edge to my voice.

A flustered Santiago waved his hand in the man's face. "What do you know, huh? What do you know? She is the pride and joy of Enrique San José—even he says she is a better translator than he is, okay?" He turned to me with the little sack of groceries. "Give this to your father as a gift. In honor of a free Germany, you don't pay tonight."

I protested. "Santiago, you don't need to . . ."

"And a free Cuba—that's what's important . . . a free Cuba," added the man who had questioned me, his lecturing finger in the air just like Fidel—and my father.

"Next year in Havana!" Santiago shouted, making a tense power salute.

"Next year in Havana!" echoed his chorus of cronies, who stood at anxious attention looking at me.

"Yes . . . next year," I responded, then quickly exited Cachita's into the bitter cold of Chicago.

At my parents' house we sat in front of the television, little portable TV dinner tables before us. I spread out on the couch with my mother while my father sat a few feet away in one of his Cuban-style rocking chairs. My mother, her hair up in a glorious bun of black and sparkling silver, nervously switched channels with the remote control while my father stared dumbfounded, his guava shells drowned in their own syrup, the cream cheese covered with beads of perspiration.

"Why don't they say something about Cuba? Why don't they say something about Cuba?" my mother asked, overwrought, her hands rolling the channels up and down in futility. Since Ochoa's execution in Havana, she'd been obsessed with the island, checking the temperature every day in the *Tribune*'s weather page, spending hours on end with her ear up to the undulating sounds of short-wave transmissions. "Don't any one of these newscasters think something's going to happen in Cuba? Why don't they have correspondents there?"

I cleared my throat. "Journalists need Fidel's permission to report from Cuba, Mami, you know that," I said.

"Even at a time like this, when he might be falling, just like the wall?" She clicked and clicked, the TV a smear of color and light.

My father sat motionless, his hands beached on his thighs, heavy and useless. He stared, just stared, his eyes red, his skin flushed. Every now and then I'd see his Adam's apple bob as he swallowed.

"Papi, are you all right?" I had asked already several times.

"Yes, yes, of course, quite fine," he had responded, never taking his eyes off the screen as the images of celebration—grown men weeping, families reuniting, the barbed wire like confetti at their feet—continued scrolling with my mother's wild channel flipping.

"Stop! Stop there!" my father finally cried, his hands covering his mouth in an instant, his eyes widening.

My mother and I quickly glanced at the screen: A group of young toughs, their swagger luxurious in leather and chains, curled their lips in front of a newsman's microphone. Their leader's head was hairless, hard as a cue ball and nearly as shiny. His features were sharp and delicate all at once, and he spoke with a venom that came through even without the translation that was being offered by his sidekick, a little crew-cutted thug with a pin in his nose.

"They're just punks," I said, turning back to my father.

"No, they're not," he said, pointing now to the screen. The camera had focused close enough to the group's leader that his forehead took up more than half the camera's view. And there, in a fleshy cross of scars, was a swastika, just like Charlie Manson's, its crooked legs jerking in the light of my parents' den.

"Enrique . . ." my mother said, her hand now on his knee, the remote on the floor.

"They're just punks, Papi," I said again.

"They are German punks," he said, his voice no longer frightened but patronizing, as if I'd missed the most conspicuous observation of the night.

"Yes, well, Berlin *is* in Germany; it's only logical that the soldiers will be German, and the party-goers will be German, and yes, even the punks will be German," I hissed. "What did you expect? And what do you care, huh?"

"Alejandra!" This was my mother.

"A little racial memory, Papi? A little trouble with the family secret?" I continued as I got up from my seat and started to turn. I had every intention of making a grand exit, of leaving at the point of high drama in which I knew my father—the reluctant shame-faced Jew—would collapse like the wall into my mother's arms.

But I didn't get a chance.

"How dare you!" he boomed, shooting up from his chair and grabbing my arm, turning me around so fast that I fell back flat onto the couch. "You don't know!" he shouted. "You don't know!"

And then he caught his breath, straightened his shirt and sweater as if he were off to an appointment, and walked out of the room as regal and composed as the crown prince of a northern kingdom.

I glared at my mother, who by then was quietly picking up the room as if I wasn't there: turning off the TV, gathering the bowl of discarded guava shells and festering cheese.

"What don't I know . . . that he's a Jew? That even though he's in some sort of historical denial, when the neo-Nazis come, he and I will both be tossed into the ovens no matter how much he explains that we're Spanish nobility?"

31 December 1989

Dear Alejandra,

Greetings for the New Year. I hope it is good to you, that it brings you all the things you need and hope for. I certainly hope it brings you this letter, which I'm sending through the regular mail as a test.

Here, we are grateful for the blessings we have. Our biggest news is that Ernesto and Olguita appear to be reconciling, which makes us all very happy. They are seeing each other regularly and she has returned to our table for dinner.

But we have other news, too: Angela has begun a new job with the Spanish embassy. She is working as an office assistant, mostly processing permits and visas, and, though it is not within the scope of the diplomatic career she'd once hoped to study, she is very happy. I wish that her job were not necessary, that the lines of Cubans wishing to leave the country would disappear, but it seems that they are inevitable, especially now, as the world twitches and shakes.

There is much anxiety here, and I confess I, too, share it. I am not worried, like many people here (and there, too, perhaps even more so), that our system will collapse or fall apart. I know that we will prevail, we have worked too hard and too long, and we have already survived too many things, for it to be destroyed now. But I am worried about what else we may have to endure, and what sacrifices—not of the material kind, although that, too—but of the spiritual kind—we will have to live through.

I know that there are people in Miami, and perhaps Chicago, too, who looked upon the fall of the Berlin Wall and wished those rocks would fall here, wished they'd created a bridge from Mariel or Cojímar straight to Key West so that they could rush back, like the West Germans did into East Berlin.

I know you probably saw the other invasion, the needy Easterners staring at washers and dryers, color TVs and sausages hanging in store windows on the Western side, but there was another flow as well, a stream of West Germans and their allies looking at the forbidden zone, at the spartan cool of the east and imagining hamburger palaces, multi-level department stores, and car dealerships.

I have no problem with any of that, not on principle; what I fear is what will happen to the East Germans, whether Communist or not, whether in solidarity with America or not, while their streets are being paved with dollars and gold.

I know in Miami, and perhaps in Chicago, too, they are hoping that the fall of the wall will inspire spontaneous celebration here, and then, in turn, a horrible crackdown. But there won't be a civil war here, or the kinds of demonstrations they dream about in Miami. Our walls are all of our own making—all of us—and none of them are real.

In the long run, we will survive here, and there, too, with all our mutual yearning, and we will find our own way back to each other, and it need not be with war, cold or otherwise, or with dollars.

In the meantime, I remember that I'm a Jew, and I look at the fall of the wall in Berlin and know that it is more than just a pile of bricks, and I worry about what unification will mean, and what will happen next.

Please let your father know I'm thinking of him.

We haven't had a minyan in years here, but we pray and pray anyway.

Un fuerte abrazo,

Moisés

P.S. I was sorry to hear that you and Seth are no longer together. Though I had not met him, he seemed, both from what Estrella and Félix said, as well as from your own letters, to be quite a fine young man.

XXI

I'd like to say that at some point before we separated I fell in love with Seth, that my heart burst, that it overflowed its borders with passion, that we consumed each other. But it never came, that intensity, that painful yearning. At least not with him.

If I've ever been absolutely naked, numb from the absolute need of another person, it was when I met Leni Bergman, with her spiky hair and dirty green vest, standing in the cavernous front hall of the Art Institute of Chicago. She was a friend of Seth's, a pal from school who occasionally took photography classes to augment her video studies. When we saw each other at the museum entrance, for a minute I forgot her name.

"Ah, Jewish," I noted when she told me again.

"I'm not Jewish," she said, rolling her intense umber eyes in disgust. "My parents are."

"Oh," I said sarcastically, "you're one of *those*."

I was thinking of Seth, whose Jewishness consisted of bagels in the morning and a deep offense at anything anti-Semitic—not because he took it personally but because he thought Jews (in his mind, Hasidim, Orthodox, any Jew who outwardly manifested her or his Jewishness) should be protected from prejudice in the same way that blacks, Asians, and other racial groups should be free of discrimination.

"What? What? What do you mean?" Leni demanded, unable to take in the tidal force of Van Gogh's strokes, the way the paint seemed to lap up off the canvas, because she was too preoccupied with my dismissive tone. (We'd ended up strolling through the museum together for no apparent reason.) "I mean, what makes a Jew, huh? Seeing all those horrible bodies in those awful films they showed us in Hebrew school? I don't go to temple, you know, and I don't believe in all that matrilineal shit, and I'm with the Palestinians on their right to the West Bank and Gaza, okay?"

Leni had stubby little fingers, wrists jangling with her own crafted silver—heavy, highly textured bracelets with her individualized hieroglyphics. I understood their message was more complicated than Seth's, who offered me warm domesticity, fidelity, and armchair revolution; Leni was the rebellion itself, with all its anarchy and senselessness. When we got in bed, she would bury her hand inside me and I'd feel the coolness of the metal against my thighs. Her arms would ripple with tight tendons and lush veins, like mountains and waterways on the map of a faraway, magical country.

I trembled and imagined that I would always want her as much as that time when, in a state of uncontrolled rage about all the lovers she might have had, I pushed her against the wall and knelt before her in a urine-soaked subway stairwell. Pinning her hips with my hands, I used my mouth, my teeth, to get at those other pungent lips, at the soft core of her where I staked all my unsteady claims of conquest.

She called me her Latin Lover, reminded me that Dorothy Parker had humiliated us as lousy in a famed *New Yorker* piece, and prodded me into displays of adolescent paranoia I'd never known even when they were age appropriate. If she didn't call, I'd dial her number and let it toll endlessly, torturing myself with visions of her ignoring the relentless rings or clicks on the answering machine, too busy with her bracelets clanging between somebody else's legs. I'd show up breathless at her door, only to find her smirking and alone, surrounded by notes and storyboard drawings for her videos.

"I'm just helping you be Cuban," she'd say about my addiction to her, my insane jealousies, "bringing out that torrid Latin soul buried in all that Midwestern equanimity you work at so much."

Though her methods became predictable, and her scenarios eventually involved an elastic-limbed girl from a tai chi class and the husband of one her professors at the School of the Art Institute, there was something to her theory: I've never been more Cuban than when I was with her.

Between the two of us, I was the expert dancer, the gourmet, the one who related the history of Columbus and the island's geno-cidal Indians; I was the one who translated Ricky Ricardo's benign curses, explained why salsa is Cuban music without soul, and cleared up any doubts about how Latinos fit into the multicultural scheme in the United States. With Leni, I was closer than ever to all the dark peoples for whom I interpreted and to whom I repre-sented a system and established order that I never felt a part of. With her, I relished my own darkness.

With Leni I could be as free as I wanted to be about my cubani-dad because she never challenged my authenticity. I could use any stereotype I wanted in any way I wanted without fear or embarrass-ment. Leni listened, deferred; her very distance from Havana con-firmed my proximity. When I confessed my collapse into Orlando's arms in Cuba, Leni relished every detail, naughtily bringing a saucer of milk to bed that night.

But what Leni and I really shared was a certain shame about be-longing to oppressed minorities that had their own paradoxical privileges in the world. Because while I could talk eloquently about how negative Latino media images affected us all, I could also—with my white Cuban skin, my perfect English—enter any retail store with the assurance that I could wander the aisles at liberty, sure to be perceived as the descendant of an Italian dancer or, per-haps, a French winemaker, if I had any ethnicity at all.

Ironically, Leni—who, like Seth, insists there's no Jewish "race," no Jewish type, only stereotypes—had a harder time finding that no-ethnic-fly-zone. With her big dark eyes, full lips, and cinna-mon skin, she was always mistaken for Moroccan or Greek, some-times Brazilian or even Cuban. In a way, she loved the confusion, the way the stereotypes worked to cast her as beautiful and exotic.

She loved to defend herself against any latent racism by telling me how flattered she was by these mistakes.

But I was militant in my responses, always reminding her how easy it was to bask in such flattery when she could give her good Jewish name for restaurant reservations that were always affordable and available to her, or when car rentals always hinged on her less than exemplary credit over my own immaculate records.

Like Seth, Leni was remarkably alienated from her Jewish roots, her ethnicity nothing more than a name tag most of the time. Her parents had sent her to Hebrew school as a little kid, but never celebrated Shabbat or the High Holidays. Her first adult Pesaj was with me, with my friends, back in the old Rogers Park neighborhood of my childhood. While I knew every step, every syllable of every prayer in the haggadah, Leni fidgeted at the table, flipped the pages ahead of the reading, and made snide comments about how only Jews could turn Egypt's resounding and fatal rejection into some kind of celebration. (Later I would note that Cubans had converted a similar disaster—the attack on the Moncada barracks, which Fidel's men lost miserably—as the ceremonial centerpiece of revolutionary mythology.)

"The height of denial," Leni huffed, all twisted in her chair, her arms across her chest.

But the real denial was mine.

One December, Leni and I found ourselves riding home on a CTA bus in the midst of the Christmas gift-buying crunch. We lived in a little loft on the near west side then, in a neighborhood that was rapidly gentrifying—the city's premier producers of performance art had just relocated a few blocks away.

On the bus, everyone was balancing packages, some already gift-wrapped but most still in manufacturer's boxes or swathed in plastic. There was a strange smell: a combination of dry, acrid winter sweat and virgin vinyl, like a new car on the very first day. We were all too crowded. Leni's head seemed to fit into the armpit of the man who was holding on to the bar above her.

Then, as we crossed the river, as the bus strained over the bridge, a very large woman with honey-yellow skin positioned herself right up front, next to the driver, and began to sing Christmas carols. She had a lovely voice, low and gritty like Mavis Staples at her apogee, and gave even something as hackneyed as "Jingle Bells" a kind of gospel flavor. Whenever the bus stopped and a few folks got out, she'd stop her serenade long enough to say, "Merry Christmas! Jesus loves you!"

As we began to get closer to our stop, I realized no one would be spared. I looked over at Leni, who was already cranky over the whole ride.

"Merry Christmas! Jesus loves you!" shouted the sister.

Finally, the bus slid into our neat little triangle at Milwaukee, Chicago, and Ogden Avenues. "Merry Christmas!" the large woman said to me as I stepped down and into the blustery wind outside.

I turned around to help Leni, who was carrying a backpack stacked with videos for study and a gym bag with a sensitive new camera she'd borrowed from Seth, who'd remained a friend.

"And happy Hanukkah to you, little sister!" the big woman bellowed, her fat fingers touching Leni's shoulder as if she were claiming her for herself. "Jesus loves you, too!"

Taken aback, Leni stumbled, sending the gym bag to the ground with a distinct metallic crash. Hundreds of dollars of equipment shattered, the top of the bag crumbled like a slow-motion disaster scene in a Japanese monster movie.

"What the fuck . . . ?" Leni groused, her body splayed out on the sidewalk, everything too heavy and scattered all over.

Quickly, I put my hand around her arm but she shook me off, standing up in a flash, angrily grabbing the gym bag and readjusting her backpack with a little hop. She rearranged her bracelets, too, some of which were now bent.

"Let's just go," she said, "let's just go." She was so agitated, so hard.

We didn't talk about what happened, not then, not ever. But what I realized was that, for all the mistaken ethnicities with which Leni gets tagged, she's also pegged right a lot of times. It makes her uncomfortable because Leni wants to disappear into the storm, into the dusting of clean, fuzzy stuff. Leni wants to be anonymously American, unfettered and free.

What I can't tell her, even to this day—what I can barely admit to myself—is how much I secretly envy the inevitability of her Jewishness. Until I open my mouth and jabber or poke my tongue in some unholy tangle into another's mouth, until somebody gets close enough to taste the bittersweet traces of Havana on my blue-veined skin, I'm this blank space, unconnected to history, bloodless.

XXII

31 July 1990

My dear Alejandra,

Here's hoping that you are well. We are fine, given the circumstances. I'll admit everyone's a little jumpy, a little nervous about what will happen next.

Here in Cuba, we are feeling our isolation and the boundaries of the island. I can tell, from his speeches, from the frustration on his face, that El Comandante is also worried, however much it may feel like a betrayal to say that. I think that the defeat—at American hands, I have no doubt—of the Sandinistas is a big blow to us as well. We are the only ones left standing, it seems.

The rumors that you are hearing—the ones you wrote about—they are true. In the city, everyone is allotted three-quarters of a pound of chicken twice a month and that much beef once a month. At the Jewish butcher, where there are 650 of us assigned by our ration books, we get three-quarters of a pound of kosher beef three times a month. I am sad to report that, suddenly, there is a lot of interest in Judaism, both from Jews who never practiced and from regular people inquiring about conversion. Egg prices jumped from 10 to 15 cents. Bread rationing began this month in some areas.

It is also true, yes, that some young hooligans have doctored some of the signs on the roadways to read "Socialism

Is Death." Recently, some graffiti appeared near the university which said "¿Hasta cuándo Fidel?"—all of which depresses me terribly. Orlando and I joined the volunteers that helped wash away the offending words. They did it again the next night, but we got up at 4 a.m. and managed to have the walls clean before morning, so only a handful of people saw it.

I don't know anything about the incident you described—about the man who rose from the audience during the World Cup boxing match here and shouted "¡Abajo Fidel!" Rafa says he saw something on TV for an instant during the match but he couldn't tell what it was, or what happened. The TV just went blank.

That has been happening a lot lately. We're experiencing unexpected blackouts. There is nothing to do then, nothing to say. Ester gets very tired very quickly when that happens. She tends to just go to the bed (then she gets up at the crack of dawn, with the roosters that you can now hear all over the city).

But I can't sleep no matter what I do. I have taken to walking around the neighborhood. I walk slowly because I'm suddenly very tired, too, but I can't sleep anyway. In the early evening hours, people just hang out outside, playing dominoes by moonlight, reading the numbers with their fingertips like blind men. Citizens sit on their stoops, staring at nothing. There are also a lot of lovers who, with nowhere to go, must resign themselves to that same stoop. I see them all entangled, rather shamelessly actually, their dark faces melting one into the other. Havana is suddenly a city of shadows.

I'm sure you heard about everything that happened at the Spanish embassy. Poor Angela, she had to stay there through the entire crisis, until Spain recalled its ambassador. It was very hard on the entire family. Nobody knew what was going to happen. Angela said the people seeking asylum were all men, all very desperate it seems, and they wouldn't talk to her, even though she was in charge of the paperwork for their requests—the asylum-seekers wouldn't talk to any of the Cubans who work at the embassy, insisting they were all spies for El Comandante—and ended up threatening the Spanish employees there, although I don't know how, since they weren't armed. Thank god nobody was taken hostage, as happened at the Czechoslovakian embassy. It is all very delicate.

What I still don't understand—perhaps you can explain it to me—is why these people want to leave. I know life is hard here—it will get harder before it gets better, I can feel it in my bones—but it is our country, after all. Who will defend it if not us? How can they want to go the U.S. when it is the source of all our problems?

Please don't read this as a recrimination. I am not judging you in any way. I know you were just a baby when you left and had no input in that decision. I also know some of the machinations of that decision and I do understand—your father was never entirely comfortable in Cuba. He suffered a lot here, he felt very alone (until he met your mother).

Has it been better for him there? I suspect from your letters that he has finally found a place where he is comfortable, although I confess I marvel at your description of your parents' neighborhood as Jewish. Here your father didn't want to be around anything or anyone Jewish. When he was young, he had to be, because of Ytzak, but he never chose it of his own volition.

It's getting dark here so I have to finish this letter. Again today we have no electricity. Please take care of yourself, Alejandra.

Un fuerte abrazo,
Moisés

P.S. Thank you for the vitamins. We are saving them for Paulina, who will need them most. We are also taking solace in the Goodwill Games, where we won over the Americans so spectacularly that the mercy rules had to be put into effect!

25 November 1990

My dear Alejandra,

I think you are too hard on your father. Just like you did not choose to go to the United States and be an American, he did not choose to be a Jew. Yet he's stuck with it, with all that knowledge, all that anguish in his blood. It's not unlike your situation as a Cuban in the U.S.: Even if you wanted to assimilate, to become one of them, you would still know in your heart that you are Cuban. You could not deny the experience of your mother's saints, of this revolution. It has affected your life in a way that no American could possibly know.

So it is with your father and his very reluctant Jewishness. It is not a product of being in the U.S., it's the way he's always been, except for a very brief awkward but still golden moment back in the thirties. When he hastened back to his shame, I fought with him all the way, but it was a battle I couldn't win. His demons are more than 500 years old, his experiences very different from mine: I have known all along who I am; he found out later in life and had to accommodate to that new and harsh reality. Imagine his dismay when he discovered who Saint Esterika really was!

Perhaps it has made it so that he is now always anticipating that what he knows as truth will mutate, maybe he is simply that much more fragile and believes the world can change in the blink of an eye. I always think of him as a man more capable of seeing the flaw on the baby's cheek than its exuberance at being alive. There was always a sadness about him. Has that changed? I hope so.

Things here are both hectic and slow. On the one hand, change is constant—there are new laws, new regulations for everything every day. But the process of change itself is slow. Nobody really knows what's going on, and they're afraid everything will change again soon, so every step is taken very cautiously. Moreover, sometimes—with no electricity and no water or fuel—slow is the only speed available to us.

We are doing better here at home. We recently got bicycles for everyone—Orlando's car is no longer working, as there is no fuel—and this has been a good thing. Everyone is getting plenty of exercise, even Ester, who initially refused to ride. Deborah, who is in art school now, has gotten very creative and is making drawings from coffee grounds and (I don't approve but it doesn't seem to matter), of all things, menstrual blood. Everyone assures me this is a phase, just like the Special Period itself.

Angela continues to work at the Spanish embassy, where things have calmed down considerably. She got Orlando an interview with a Spanish investment firm, Grupo Sol, which is planning some businesses on the island. I don't know much about any of this, but after all these years and so many achievements, Orlando says he is sick of being an economist. I worry about foreigners in Cuba and about members of my own family working for them, but what can I do?

My problem is that I want Cuba for Cubans, not to the exclusion of others but so that we are not under anyone's boot. I often wonder how much of this desire comes from being Jewish and my generation's understanding of the Holocaust. I look at everything going on in Israel, with the intifada and the killings, and I think sometimes those are the consequences of our fears run amok.

Sometimes, I confess, I worry about my own capacity for extremes. Recently, some food concessions were opened in Havana, fast food, just like in the U.S., and people here were delighted, calling the sandwiches "McCastro's," and just the reference to the U.S. made it impossible for me to eat them. They were very popular for a while, then everybody found out they were made, at least in part, with soy, and Cubans—you know, carnivores that we are—rejected them fast. I suspect they'll all be closed by the end of the year.

I'm rambling now. Thank you for the new supply of vitamins. I promise we will all take them this time, not just Paulina.

Un fuerte abrazo,

Moisés

P.S. I know the Vatican announced the pope will be here by the end of next year, but I'll convert before that happens!

2 January 1991

My dear Alejandra,

We finally met Seth when he brought your letter. What a fine young man indeed! We were happy to see that you have remained friends, that because of you he is concerned about us, too.

Aside from the medicines and the art supplies for Deborah that you sent (she's still using the coffee grounds, too, but, to my relief, has stopped painting with blood), he brought us jeans for Rafa and the girls, which pleased them tremendously, and small goodies like soap and perfume for the women. Orlando refused his gift of a shirt but accepted Seth's offer to work for him as a chauffeur while he and his crew were here. Seth had a rented car and it was all very official, although terribly bureaucratic. Orlando earned dollar coupons that we were able to use at the diplo-tienda, which made Ester very happy.

Orlando, however, is not in very good spirits these days. He did not get the job with Grupo Sol after all. They are building a big new hotel in Varadero and will use some Cuban workers. They needed management consultants with a knowledge of finance better acquired in capitalist countries, and construction crews. But Orlando is neither as young nor as strong as other men who applied. I was relieved but he was distraught. He feels responsible for us—he thinks we cannot survive on the ration books because of the scarcities. As you know, there are lines everywhere these days. Sometimes it takes eight hours to buy onions, or a pair of shoes. Just recently Orlando was fined for being a colero—somebody who holds places in line for others, an act that is illegal when you charge for it. Then his frustration simply turned into shame.

I don't know what to say to him. I know we will be okay, but I don't know how to convince him that the revolution will take care of us, and so we both suffer. It reminded me of when your great-grandmother died, how your father blamed being Jewish for her death, and all I could do was put my arm around him and pat his shoulder. I was as inexplicably silent then as now.

In your last letter you asked me to tell you about a time when your father was glad to be a Jew. There was a period, I believe, when being a Jew symbolized both community and hope for him. But that same moment turned catastrophic and is what made him turn away most dramatically. To this day, I am not allowed to speak about it. I promised him this many years ago, in 1939, and time does not diminish that commitment.

I must confess, Alejandra, that I find it most extraordinary that he still prays on Friday nights. In Chicago, even surrounded by Jews, there is no obligation for him. I suspect there must be something in those moments of faith that makes him glad to be Jewish. Ask him. Perhaps he will surprise you.

Un fuerte abrazo,

Moisés

P.S. To answer your question, Saint Esterika is a purely marrano invention: They Christianized Purim by making Ester a saint. When your father found out nobody else in the world did that, he reacted the way Christian kids do when they discover the Three Kings are just their parents delivering presents on the Epiphany. He was miserable, defrauded, for weeks.

XXIII

Talk to me.

That's what I always wanted to say to my father.

Talk to me, tell me everything. Tell me about those days of confusion when your family finally revealed its true self—and yours—like a glass onion, each of its layers splintering, by accident and on purpose.

Had you wondered why your family lit eight candles on Christmas? Why linens were changed every Friday without fail? Or why, when a piece of bread fell on the floor, you were required to kiss its grainy face before biting into it?

"You are a child of Abraham, of Moses and the patriarchs . . ." somebody finally said to you, perhaps Ytzak, tears shiny on his beaming face, free at last to tell the truth; or maybe it was Luis, with a less poetic pronouncement, certainly, but with a voice as resonant as the shofar. (It would not have been Sima, with her timidity, nor Leah, with her resentments.) Or perhaps you realized, in the hazy hues of candlelight at the Menachs' home, that certain pieces of your personal puzzle had been haphazardly hidden from you.

Discovering god, I think, must be as mysterious and frightening as sex. Not the rituals, the methodology, but the purpose—the capricious responsibility of life, the strange and wonderful discovery of bliss. Fear of god, I think, must be something like fear of our own selves, of our bodies, of the pleasurable fluids and the latent illnesses that abide within. God, like sex, reflects our morality and mortality:

In their own timeless ways, we use them in the present to relieve us of the past, to conceive a future. We use them to get beyond death.

I imagine you as a boy with a heart as pure as spring water, winding through your paradisiacal wonderland of hardwoods and opulent flowers, silky vines framing every scene, each one more beautiful than the one before: a hollow log filled with luscious honey; blue, red, and yellow-striped snails climbing impossible heights with their sticky feet; a wild lamb and her still wet ewe murmuring under a shady tree.

I can see you awed—your senses at their peak—the way you could not understand the connection you knew to be true between the lamb and the hatchet in your father's hand.

Talk to me, Papi.

Tell me how you thought you were Isaac—Ytzak!—a prince and heir to the kingdom, and discovered instead that you were the bastard son Ishmael, spared by god but erased as the legitimate firstborn by the very circumstances of your birth.

Who am I in all this?

I'm a stranger, as out of place as a whale whimpering on the shore, a lute, a hairless native pretending to live free.

I'm my father's daughter, mindful of both the mystery and the exodus, but I am also heir to my mother. I ask the requisite four questions at Pesaj (always at a friend's house, never in our family home), but I also lay sunflowers and roses at the feet of the Virgin of Charity and arrange for fruit to ripen at her altar, peaches and bananas that turn black and viscous.

Like him, I'm a child of Amos, forever critical and self-critical; like her, I am a consequence of events beyond my control—and utterly practical, capable of creating god out of matchsticks, if necessary.

Like both of them, I believe god is everywhere, so I am constantly on the lookout, constantly glancing over my shoulder (like those Cuban TV announcers), under my bed and in the rearview mirror. But unlike them, I am ill at ease with all this vigilance and eavesdropping, with the idea that I might need to be protected. I always keep a light on, whether a candle with a saint's elaborate and kitschy image or the overhead lamp in another room.

The problem is that when I stand alone before the mirror—that's me there, the one with the blue-gray eyes just like my great-grandfather, my mother's pouty pillows for lips—I know everything and nothing at all, and I am overwhelmed, unable to look myself in the eye, struggling to swallow and to breathe, thinking always: Like the emperor, I have no clothes, no clothes.

Who will see my naked beauty, who will love me now?

Whenever I watched my father as he descended to his subterranean kingdom on Friday nights, his shoulders heavy with the weight of history and surrender, I wanted to run after him, grab him by the arm, and shake him.

Why? Why do it? I wanted to ask. Why not let it all go? What was the power that held him so even after whatever tore his soul in 1939? Why couldn't he put it all away and decide it was all fanciful mythology?

I watched him go down, step by step, just like the sun outside the windows of our house, all orange and yellow blazes. My mother and I would then go our own ways—she to the den for TV or downstairs to her own mysteries; me to my bedroom to sulk and ponder the riddles of life, then later, out, out of the house, to the joys of dancing, the tingle and fear of a mouth wet on my nipple and the heat of another's body, mortal and beautiful, hovering above mine.

In truth, I already knew the answers to my father's Friday night obligations. Like every ancient human who ever wrote on a clay tablet or cave wall, we both understood the cosmic sympathies between our guts and the moon's cycles, our brains and the scattered constellations, the rhythm of our earthly hearts and the eclipses of the sun and the moon.

When my father prayed, he pondered this: Perhaps god is a construct, but perhaps not. Perhaps light is a metaphor, simply what happens when we think we've found an explanation for what frightens us; but perhaps, too, it stands outside of us. Maybe the first sentient being to discover light did so not by the magic of internal illumination but by opening her eyes, seeing what was already there. The dark, perhaps, was not ignorance but the mere back side of an eyelid. (My father would take no chances.)

And heaven?

This is where he and my mother traded theologies, sitting there in the den—he in one of his rocking chairs, she on the couch, surrounded by the billowy, dizzying clouds of tobacco from the puro in my father's immaculate hands and perfect mouth.

"There must be something to that word," he would say aloud, "or it would not even exist." He would gaze at my mother through the brushstrokes of white in the air.

"Heaven is here," my mother would reply, smiling in her own knowing way, "right here, right now."

XXIV

When I was with Leni, I thought a lot about my parents.

I thought about the way they laughed together, the way they sat comfortably in silence as my father stared at his letters and my mother paid the bills, how he'd find her in the kitchen with his scribblings in his hand and read them to her for approval, sometimes so absorbed in his own words and the sounds of his voice that he never looked up, never made eye contact with her, but just listened and nodded when she finally talked, listened and nodded until he was swaying, lost in his difficult and particular paradise.

She'd say it wasn't quite right yet, or she'd suggest another word, or she'd say "almost, almost" in the most indulgent tones, the most soothing and satisfying of whispers. He'd hear her like the wind in the mountains, naked to the eye but irresistible.

"Yes, yes," he'd respond, "of course"—as if it were all as obvious as uprooted trees and rippling waters.

Then he'd rush back down to the imperturbable confines of his basement office and scratch and peck again until she said, "Oh, yes, that's beautiful, Enrique!" And with that, he'd lean back and straighten his shoulders, sigh, as if he had known what he was doing all along during the arduous scale to the top.

When I was with Leni, I thought about them because I wanted what I had with her to last, to mark me the way I knew love had shaped my parents. I wanted to breathe the same fresh air, to survey the world from the same heights.

It's not that I had my parents idealized. In fact, as a young woman, I was embarrassed by their togetherness, by what I thought was my mother's submission and my father's helpless vulnerability. They had often seemed stuck—together, yes, but trapped by their needs and desire for warmth. My parents, I thought, had never been hot, had never felt the discomfort of their own fires.

How, I wondered, could she have chosen him, this awkward and shy man, when she obviously could have had so many other options? And why had he—so much older and lonelier—waited so long for love? How did they know?

I'd look at Leni as she slept at night, searching for clues. She'd cuddle up into a ball on the very precipice of the bed as I followed the line of her curling spine and wingless shoulders with my kisses.

Then she'd open her eyes, startled. "What? What?" Her bracelets tinkled.

"Do . . . do you love me?" I'd ask, pleading, teasing, unsure of my own intentions.

My father was my mother's first love, but not her first boyfriend.

Before she met Enrique my mother was attached for a while to a young man named Jorge Ortega, whose university career consisted of paying people to take his exams while he raised hell out on the streets. Jorge came from a wealthy family, with country club membership and the means to rush him out of the island whenever his political activities became too dangerous.

My mother did not love Jorge Ortega. I don't believe this out of any particular loyalty to my father but because I absolutely trust my mother would admit it, the same way she freely confessed he was her lover, and playful as a kitten in bed. In fact, given my mother's age and status in Cuba, it would be easier and make much more sense to say she had loved Jorge and never confess they'd slept together, much less that she had enjoyed it so much.

I've seen pictures of the two of them. Jorge is a tall man, even by American standards, robust and bright-eyed, always at ease, his arm around my mother's waist. He looks fascinated with her in every photograph, ready to drop to his knees at her request.

My mother, on the other hand, is merely amused in these photos, biding her time, already waiting for her somber prince.

Curiously, though my mother was my father's first real relationship, the first person with whom he enjoyed the protocols of passion, she was not his first love.

Before he saw his destiny with my mother, my father glimpsed love with another woman, a dark girl, a doomed girl.

He never spoke about her, never even said her name aloud.

It would be on his deathbed, fifty-eight years after his singular meeting with her, that my father would instruct me to find a blurry black-and-white photograph of a girl on a ship's deck—she's sixteen or seventeen perhaps, with black curls and Anne Frank eyes, dressed in winter clothes while looking out at sunny Havana harbor—and ask me to give it to Moisés Menach.

In the photograph, the girl is clearly posing for the camera, for the man whose loving eye is capturing her beauty and glee. She is waving with one hand, her knobby knee jutting out between the railings.

To this day, I have a hard time imagining that the object of her mild flirtation is my father.

My parents met as if in a tacky Hollywood movie at the Hotel Nacional in Havana, poolside as my mother lolled with a frisky Jorge Ortega. She was sitting on a stretched-out towel, taking in the sun; Jorge was splashing in the water before her.

My father, who was waiting tables there, bumped into her by accident, nearly spilling the drinks he was taking to a group of American tourists sitting with their feet in the blue chlorine. But the drinks—mojitos the way Hemingway would have liked them—did not overturn. My father balanced the tray expertly, dancing around my mother in a rare moment of grace, as if there was an exquisite bolero for a soundtrack. When they realized they'd averted disaster, they both laughed, flushed and relieved.

My father thought Nena was beautiful, like so many of the girls who came with their rich dates to the Nacional's pool and bar.

My mother instantly recognized that Enrique was the end of her waiting, the end of shuttling back and forth between relatives and living with strangers. How did she know? She can't say, even to this day, laughing and shaking her head at the mystery. What is certain is that she left a frowning Jorge Ortega sitting in wet swimming trunks on the edge of the pool and followed Enrique inside to the bar, where the rest of the wait staff looked on in surprise that someone so young and stunning should be drawn to Enrique San José.

"Don't I know you?" she asked him.

And he said—delighted, radiant with confidence—"Shouldn't that be my line?"

When I reached my twenties my mother told me the rest, how she pulled him into a kiss the other waiters celebrated with cheers and applause. Enrique's knees wobbled, his eyes wide as she led him away by the hand, out of the hotel, down to the miraculous reef off the Malecón, where they sat out of view, touching and kissing wordlessly until the sun set.

My father's amazing hands, she has since told me, were designed by god for making love.

My mother's life is an open book, a story without missing pages. To every school year, there is a corresponding grammar book, an adolescent uniform. For every summer, there is a new chapter about Barbarita and Wang Francisco, a garden full of roses.

There is never a story about my mother's life for which there is no evidence. In each case, there's always an image, a ticket stub, a pressed flower, or a chorus of witnesses.

Nena married my father only weeks after meeting him, a giddy bride in a simple white lace dress hanging off his arm outside the notary public's office just off the majestic Prado. In the few photographs, they're at the front door, on the steps, and her hair is tossed back with abandon, her arms clasped around his neck and shoulders with a feverish possession. The dates printed on the white borders of the photos indicate that virtually no time elapsed between the poses with Jorge Ortega and these ecstatic moments with my father.

Enrique, however, looks traumatized—his eyes glassy and wide, his elegant hands a smear. He is wearing a crisp linen suit and his face is shiny from sweat.

The only witnesses to the wedding are my mother's cousin Gladys and Moisés Menach. She looks puzzled, her smile lopsided. He is tickled pink, both of his eyes bright with delight.

It's different with my father.

Though he seemed the picture of coherence—it is hard to imagine him, really, outside of his study, even when photographs suggest he'd been elsewhere, younger and leaner—there were huge black holes in his life. When he finally and reluctantly talked about himself, my father skipped over whole decades sometimes, hoping that no one would notice.

I asked, time and time again, about those blank years before he met my mother, about the time when he first arrived in Havana as Ytzak's young ward, and his answer was always the same.

"Nothing ever happened to me," he'd say, shrugging. "Everything was happening to everybody else, with the war in Europe and all that. I was just a bystander. I read the papers every day and, sometimes, I prayed."

At this point I'd always indicate that there was a vast expanse of time, a little more than a dozen years, between the war and that fateful afternoon at the Hotel Nacional, but he'd just shake his head.

"Nothing happened, honest," he'd say, smiling shyly. "I was a young man in Havana, doing what young men do. It was a very ordinary life."

There are a few favorite anecdotes, about seeing Fidel's name in the papers after the Moncada attack and realizing this was the same brash boy from the river, about the first and only time he went to the Tropicana, that luxurious and decadent outdoor venue, to hear Nat King Cole sing and how it had drizzled just enough to make it seem like snow falling.

"In my youth, there was a favorite street corner, San Rafael and Galiano in Havana, which was known as La Esquina Del Pecado," he'd recall, settling into one of his comfy rocking chairs, lighting a sumptuous and trimmed cigar. "On one side there was the Fin de Siglo department store and on the other, El Ten Cents. Across the street there was El Encanto and a Florsheim shoe store."

With Havana in my head, I'd be instantly distracted: I'd quickly color in the storefronts, imagine the glass windows, the advertisements for specials, and the crowded sidewalk.

"The afternoons were marvelous because all the shop girls would parade by, beautifully dressed and trailing the most rare perfume," he'd continue, smoke gathering around him like gentle ghosts. "They were perfect, but with an air as if they didn't care, as if they didn't know about their own perfection. And we—the boys—we'd gather on the corner to render tribute. We had a constant commentary, a rhyme, a riddle, a compliment, for every young woman who walked by. Of course, they ignored us, ignored us almost completely, but when one of them liked what one of us said, she'd smile a little shyly, and we knew, we knew right away."

In Rogers Park, where the dialogue on the streets was rougher and more direct, where there were so many languages at my schools it was hard to conceive the possibility of subtlety, I was intrigued by the codes my father talked about. "So what would you say, what kinds of things?" I'd inevitably ask, and my father would just as predictably jump back, startled at the question.

"Well, no, I didn't actually say anything, but my friends did," he'd say, then smile again as he drifted back to his cloudy, pastel memories. "If you had a girlfriend or you were meeting a girl you liked, you always met her there, at San Rafael and Galiano. You could go to the movies from there, or for a stroll. Or maybe to a dance at the Centro Gallego or Centro Asturiano, or to the Parisian cabaret in the Hotel Nacional. Everybody would end up in the wee hours at the Plaza del Vapor, to warm up on a little bowl of soup before going home."

It wouldn't be until much later, when I was tucked in between warm blankets in my room, that I'd realize my father only made cameos in his own stories. Instead of memories, his recollections were photo captions for tourists, snapshots of an idyllic and faraway moment in time.

When Leni and I broke up, it was sudden but calm.

"I don't know you," she said to me one day after five years of coupling. "It's not as if I don't know you anymore. It's as if I've never known you."

I wasn't startled or hurt by this. I had absolutely no defense: I stood before the mirror and saw a thirty-five-year-old woman with just a dash of gray in her hair, slender but with round balled muscles for calves—and hips, of course. My eyes turned dark then—black, black pools, just like my father's. My hands, however, were totally unlike his—nails jagged, the cuticles bitten and bloody.

During our time together, Leni and I had developed routines for work and play, hours of the day in which we knew to stay away from each other, and others in which we touched without even thinking about it.

There were weeks when Leni vanished, off on video shoots, business trips, or lectures, and though she called needy and girlish from her hotel rooms, she came back glowing each time.

I had my leaves, too, though not as frequent, and always draining: to Nicaragua after an earthquake, with aid workers who didn't speak Spanish; to Puerto Rico after hurricanes; to Indianapolis for a custody hearing. I always came back jaundiced and ill-tempered, unable to speak about what I'd seen, my hands trembling.

Most of the time I locked myself in my office at home, put

Ernesto Lecuona or Antonio María Romeu on the stereo at such a low volume I could hear them only when I looked up and away from my work, more and more of it on videotapes (while I was with Leni I got into subtitling for industrial and educational films as a respite between catastrophes), all of which I left in tidy piles next to my computer at the end of the day.

When Seth and I broke up, it had been a hideous, violent day of argument, recriminations, and the occasional slammed door and tossed shoe. But when Leni and I finally decided to separate in 1994 after five years, there was a stillness, as if the earth had ceased rotating.

We spent the day making love, touching with uncommon tenderness.

XXV

One day, three years before we parted, Leni answered the phone and found herself talking to an officious Cuban operator who asked her in fractured English if she would accept a collect call. I wasn't home but Leni said yes anyway. The caller, it turned out, was a young woman in some sort of panic, and where and how she got our number was a mystery to both of us. She spoke only Spanish, and Leni not a word, so the questions lingered.

I don't know why but at first I thought it might have been Estrella, the Cuban interpreter with whom I'd remained friendly in an official sort of way, but it didn't make sense that Estrella wouldn't speak in English; she was, after all, flawlessly fluent. We considered, more logically, that it might have been Deborah or Yosemí, Moisés's granddaughters, but I was certain if there had been a family emergency it would have been Moisés himself, or Ester, who called. I imagined it would be Angela, with her job at the Spanish embassy, who would have the best chance of getting through.

After much debate, we decided I'd place a call to Moisés's house in Havana, friendly, just in case the call had had nothing to do with them, but open enough so that if a crisis was at hand we could help. It took hours to get through, even with patient and sympathetic operators—at first the line wouldn't connect, then the call would crash instantly, or we found that even screaming into the phone, they couldn't hear me. We'd stand there helpless, listening to their faraway, echoing voices asking who was calling, debating among themselves who could be calling.

At some point, Ester and I finally heard well enough to recognize each other, but after some awkward greetings and exclamations of surprise, she offered nothing dramatic enough to have justified a call, and Leni and I, now more confused than ever, sat on the couch dumbfounded after it was all over.

"She did sound sad," I said to Leni.

"How could you tell—you were both screaming," Leni said. "And besides, everybody in Cuba sounds sad."

"Not everybody—"

"Oh, please!" Leni said, exasperated.

In good Cuban fashion, I contemplated extremes—that the call had been some sort of test from state security, that perhaps it had been designed to tap my phone by the CIA, or that maybe even Moisés himself might be a part of some larger conspiracy and had placed the call as a way to acknowledge contact with me to someone else.

"You are nuts," Leni said, incredulous. "Maybe, just maybe, I didn't understand and the call wasn't from Cuba at all." Her bracelets rattled with her quick, jerky gestures. I think she wanted to slap me, like in the movies, to bring me back to my senses.

But I was convinced the call was from Cuba—Cuba calling, if not Estrella, Deborah, Yosemí, or Moisés, then the island itself, a chorus of ghosts in limbo.

In March of 1991, as Cubans reached a kind of numb nadir, *Playboy* magazine did a spread of women on the island (amazingly enough, apparently with the cooperation of Cuban authorities), that would ultimately serve as a portent of things to come. Leni and I sat on the couch reading the article, convinced all the models would be out of the country in a matter of months, courtesy of marriages—arranged, willed, or bought—with foreigners.

"This is at the pool at the Hotel Nacional, where my parents met," I explained to Leni, ignoring the desperate, leggy girl strewn on the chaise longue in the photo. "And this, obviously, is a rooftop in Miramar, what was once the poshest neighborhood and where a lot of the embassies are now." On the page, a young woman raised her arms in the air, exposing beautiful, natural breasts, firm and brown, through an open shirt.

"This is so twisted," Leni commented. "It's like they're officially advertising sex tourism."

One particular photo caught my eye and it was not because of the cityscape. In it was a young, caramel-colored beauty, her hair long, lush, and wavy, naturally streaked with a rainbow of browns and reds, and an irresistibly sensual but melancholy gaze. She was not entirely nude, managing to show just a few curls of bristly black above a casually draped towel. Her breasts were ripe buds, the aureoles like drops of butterscotch. The caption identified her as Marísol and said she was an engineering student but she seemed too young to me to be in college.

"This is the girl," I said, astonished.

Leni understood my meaning immediately. She sat up right away and examined the picture up close. "Really? Do you think? My god, she could be at the *Playboy* mansion as we speak, swapping blow jobs for freedom!"

I cut the photo out—just around the face, so that no one would ever suspect her nudity or the source—and found a simple frame for it on my desk. For days afterward, I contemplated her while I worked: the smoothness of her skin, my memory of her marine essence. I'd close my eyes and try to focus, imagining that moment when she leaned back with Orlando between her legs, the way her eyes sparkled and welcomed me. But every time I tried to configure her face—its actual color and tone, the shape of her nose—my mind would become a wash of intense white light and I'd lose her.

"Are you sure it's her?" Leni asked, amused as much as anything else. "I mean, you know, beautiful fourteen-year-old girls don't necessarily grow up to be beautiful seventeen-year-olds. The real Celina might have gotten acne, or needed glasses, or maybe her teeth rotted."

I didn't mind Leni's gentle teasing, perhaps because in my heart

I wasn't entirely sure it was Celina at all, but also because, in a way, the banter kept Celina fresh for me in a way I had never expected. As if to seal our bond, I bought a small bouquet of yellow roses and put the vase by the picture frame, an offering to Ochún, the Virgin of Charity, patron saint of Cuba, and of love.

By the winter of 1992, we were used to hearing about the hardships described by Moisés: the never-ending lines, the blackouts, the food shortages, the daily debacles, even the new emerging blindness and immobility some Cubans were experiencing.

At the Menachs', it was Rafa who was afflicted. We got updates with each letter about his condition: a debilitating weakness, swollen joints, extraordinarily painful and too frequent bowel movements. "It's as if he's atrophied," wrote Moisés. "Not his body so much, but his heart and mind, his experiences."

Rafa spent weeks on end paralyzed, a younger, sickly version of Rodolfo, the mummified TV-watching old man who seemed immune to the conditions, so bad by then that even Fidel allowed that Cubans would have to "create miracles" to survive. Leni and I sent medicines whenever we could, vitamins and foodstuffs, especially powdered milk and eggs. We consulted with American doctors about Rafa's symptoms, offering advice whenever medicines weren't available.

Then one day, in a letter with a typical listing of tragedies but still imbued with Moisés's unshakable faith in the revolution's ability to come through, we got the news: Félix, Celina's brother, had killed himself sometime the previous summer, as the entire island was celebrating another brilliant baseball victory during the Pan American Games. He had been accused of a political infraction, told he would be forbidden to leave the country, perhaps forever, and he'd become despondent.

But the manner of Félix's death was something else entirely: Unable to find a length of rope, he had wrapped his neck in one of his father's ties and, while sitting on the floor, forcibly hung himself from a doorknob. I could have never imagined him capable of such an act. It was Celina who had found him, framed by the door, a trauma serious enough to have caused her to be hospitalized until just recently.

"That means your pinup girl can't be her," Leni said immediately. "I don't know which is worse, though, really . . . "

All I could think about was how badly Félix must have wanted to kill himself to do it in so willful a way.

I didn't take down the framed photo of the semi-nude girl in Havana. Instead, I bought more flowers and added a clear glass of water for good measure.

Though I'd resented Félix terribly when he had spied on Seth and me, his was the first death in Cuba I had to deal with as an adult. It caused an overflowing and restless anxiety. Not only was there the surreality of the circumstances, but time and detachment had distorted Félix, too. Suddenly he was not some sadistic voyeur but a funny, almost pathetic fellow, someone I could feel for and mourn.

I knew even then that what was most unsettling was the question that Félix's death provoked: What would happen to Celina now? Though I already knew she lived alone, I began to imagine Félix as her guardian angel, as the brother who bridged the distances to bring her news, food, and affection. (I put aside the question of Orlando, understanding too well that her brother's death might make her even more dependent, more vulnerable to him.)

In response to the news about Félix, I wrote Celina a short note in care of the Menachs, bought her some blue jeans and a green pullover (with the pinup girl as a guide to what her size might be), packed some pens and soaps and tampons in a box and sent them down with a Catholic delegation working against the blockade.

"Let me get this straight: All this for someone you didn't even talk to?" asked Leni, adjusting and readjusting the metal bands on her wrists. "I think your little fantasy's getting out of control here. . . ."

———

In the meantime, I tried to get Félix out of my mind. For months on end, all I could see was his body, hanging lifeless from the doorknob of the bedroom I'd once shared with Seth. In these terrible night-mares, whenever I approached him to undo the tie, he'd wake up, cackling madly just like when we discovered him snooping on us. I'd shoot up screaming, the sheets scrambled about the bed, my skin cold from sweat.

"Sweetie pie," Leni would whisper each night, her body stretched over mine as if to protect me, "you need some closure, you need some closure."

Sometime after that I found a picture of Félix and us that Seth had taken the night of his visit. He was so skinny, so brittle. In the frame, he's looking at the two of us instead of at the camera. Seth is beautiful and in love. My eyes are downcast and ashamed.

I pulled open my desk drawer, took out a pair of scissors and clipped Félix out of the scene, propping his figure like a cut-out doll against the glass of water I'd set for his sister. Then I went rummag-ing through my bookshelves, the ones way above head level, until I found what I knew was the answer: "Y'hey sh'lama raba min sh'ma-ya . . ."

XXVI

Death in Cuba—as aloof as this may sound—is a literary phenomenon, at least for those of us who are not there. They do not really occur as events, but as narratives, each one with its own complicated unfolding, its cast of characters and subtle plots.

What informs us are the details related by others: "Félix," wrote Moisés, "hung himself with a silk tie, black with a white stripe down the center, a little blue apostrophe somewhere in the middle."

I couldn't imagine the temperature of the room; Félix's cool, hard skin; or whatever bitter bile had leaked from him. I never saw the tie undone (by whom?—Celina, a paramedic, Orlando?), or whether his eyes were open or shut, if they covered him immediately or if he stayed that way, the red streak across his neck exposed for a minute or two, or longer.

But even when I couldn't quite picture his body dangling limp from the doorknob, I could see the little blue apostrophe on the tie, signaling a contraction, the swallowed vowel stuck in his throat, and Félix taking possession of his fate. There was a hush to Moisés's voice on the page, the kind of reverence for the event that comes much later, after the shock and hysterics and denial of real life.

Death in Cuba is sometimes foreshadowed, as in most good stories, although the metaphors in real life tend to be mixed, not quite as orderly as literature. That was the case with my grandmother Sima.

The first sign of her death came early, in 1970, when my mother rushed home one day almost in a panic, convinced she had seen a vulture—"There are no vultures in the U.S., Enrique!"—and that this was an omen of some sort. The creature, its mighty wings still and silent, had circled my mother as she lay back on the little pier at Jarvis Avenue, coming within only a few feet of her, so that she felt the force of the wind rushing under it and the heat from its breast. She was sure the bird, with its awful, militaristic shadow, had come with a warning for her, not about death exactly, because that would have been too obvious, but certainly to prompt her into a spiritual evaluation or cleansing.

My father, had he been anyone else, perhaps might have raised an eyebrow at my mother's reaction, or concerned himself with the way her hands shook over the bathroom sink as she washed her face and neck over and over, hoping in that manner to get rid of the vulture's terrible sensation. But instead he listened intently to her every word, to her divinations, and then suggested something else entirely, though the way he arrived at his particular meaning had nothing to do with his own beliefs but rather with his perception of hers, and what she might find plausible.

"The vulture is not just necrophilic, it's nurturing, too; a martyr in its own way," he said, rubbing his beard as he watched my mother soaping up yet again.

"Nurturing? A vulture? Enrique, are you crazy?" my mother protested.

"No, I remember seeing them in Oriente, swarms of them, sometimes the sky was black with them," he said. "Anytime anyone died, especially unexpectedly, or when animals were slaughtered, especially sacrifices . . . But I also remember when there was hunger, when there was nothing for them to eat, how the mother vulture would offer her own blood to her nestlings that they might survive."

"You saw this?" my mother, the urban child, asked.

"Yes, with my own eyes: I watched a nest of vultures survive that way," he said. "The mother eventually died but the baby birds lived, as if the mother understood the difference between the present and the future, and the importance of continuity."

My mother dried her hands—all the while considering this—kissed my father's cheek, and disappeared into her room to move glasses of water about.

Later, when the ten-million-ton Cuban sugar harvest failed, my father asked my mother if she thought perhaps that that had been the vulture's real message, and maybe it was possible the revolution was waning. My mother weighed his question but decided against that interpretation—she, too, is a translator, in her way—convinced the vulture had meaning, but that it was personal, and that she was still missing vital elements in order to decipher it.

That same summer, my great-grandfather Ytzak, who was then eighty-nine years old, became very ill. We got word via Moisés, who sent a Western Union telegram to my father, saying the old man seemed to be going under. I remember my father sitting by the phone, jotting down every word from the wire service as it was read to him, his usually graceful hands suffering a horrible case of the shakes. When I peeked later at the notepad on which he'd been scribbling, it contained nothing legible, only the kinds of scraggly lines found on medical charts.

"What can I do?" he asked my mother, who stood above him, kneading the tense and unfortunate muscles of his shoulders. My father's face was darkly molded into an expression of utter impotence.

"Nothing," my mother said, "nothing," kissing the top of his head, her hands at work on him as if he were the earth she had learned to soothe and manipulate so expertly.

But my father felt incapable of simply sitting there, waiting for the next morbid wire. So he spent a week attached to the phone, trying to place a call to Mayarí, where my grandparents now lived, so he could talk to his mother.

It was all instinct on his part because Sima had very little contact with her father; his final desertion of Leah had made it virtually impossible for her to even look at him. Ytzak's behavior at the funeral had been the last straw for Sima, his comportment a kind of madness from which she had willfully distanced herself.

What my father hoped to accomplish with this call to his mother was a puzzle to both Nena and me. To tell her the news? Surely Moisés or someone else had done that already. To commiserate with her? That was, at best, a tricky proposition, as there was no guarantee that Sima hadn't already sat shiva for Ytzak long ago, in her own way.

What was certainly unexpected was the reception my father got when his father, Luis, by then hard of hearing and retired, came to the communal phone at the neighborhood pharmacy in Mayarí.

"Sima? Why, she's in Havana, with your grandfather," Luis lisped through his toothless gums.

Enrique just about dropped the phone: "¿Qué qué?"

"Yes, he's very ill," Luis continued, his voice grave but still strong, even through the static and unmanageability of his own flaccid lips.

I was only eleven then, with barely a memory of my grandfather's stout little self, but I clung to my father's shoulder just like my mother, trying to listen in. It would have never occurred to us then to eavesdrop on another extension: The idea, although unspoken, was to be as physically together as possible, especially during those times when it was clearest that we were separated from others we loved. Up close, climbing all over the mountain that was my father, I could hear not just my faraway grandfather but my father's intimate breathing, the way his body jerked when he learned his mother—not exactly sprightly at sixty-six—had taken the arduous, almost impossible train ride through the rugged countryside from Oriente to Havana.

"Oh my god, oh my god!" my father exclaimed, his hands so sweaty that the phone slid right through them and my mother had to clasp her own fingers over his to hold it in place.

For days after that call, my father paced nervously from one end of the house to the other, addled, as if he might run into walls, muttering to himself. He was pale and cold all the time. He could barely eat; whatever food he ingested came up. I noticed that by the end of the week his clothes were looser, especially his pants. He tried calling Moisés, but the Menachs didn't have a phone then and so it entailed calling a neighbor who wasn't always home, and who didn't even seem to know who Moisés was sometimes.

"Ah, ¿el turco? Sí, sí como no," he'd say, then rush out to find Moisés, leaving my father hanging on for fifteen, twenty minutes (at about two dollars a minute in those pre–direct dial days) only to return to the phone and say he didn't see him anywhere and he couldn't go down to the Menachs' house because he couldn't leave his own mother alone, and besides, didn't they have two houses? Which one did my father want him to go to? Was he sure the Menachs still even lived in Havana?

At about this time, my father began to have dreams about a wounded angel. It would begin in Havana, on our balcony on the dawn of the invasion of Playa Girón, as a black shadow dropped from the sky. In the dream, my father thought it was a bomb of some sort, except that, like the vulture that had visited my mother, it left a residue of sensation, like a rush of feathers fanning his face.

When he looked over the balcony, however, it was not a bird, not a crow as he had imagined, but a badly battered angel that lay on the ground. The seraphim, neither male nor female by his estimation, had bloodlessly torn a wing, its clean white bones protruding from its shoulders. In my father's dream, the Havana street kids—orphans and tiny hustlers, neighborhood kids who played baseball between cars all day—stuffed the bone back in and patched the wing by tearing pieces of their own clothing. When the angel finally came to, cradled in the arms of the urchins, its face was as dirty and innocent as theirs.

In his dream, my father threw the angel a rope down from our balcony, but when the creature finally reached our apartment and tried to fly from there, its wings sputtered and it fell into the panicky crowds. The angel then picked itself back up, wiped its face with an arm that now sported a wristwatch, and disappeared into the tumult, where the cops were swatting people with billy clubs and the street kids were back to playing ball.

My father did not have this dream once but many times, with slight variations but always the same general format. Once, he saw his mother in the crowd, but both he and my mother dismissed it, convinced she was imposed on the divine message because of his worries about her, not because she was actually an organic part of the vision.

They pondered my father's dream for weeks and weeks, each consulting their own gods, my father rummaging through book after book while my mother played with her water glasses, until they finally determined the dream was a sign of approbation.

"The angel is us, irreparably wounded because we left our country, of course," said my mother. "We threw ourselves into the sea like the angel threw itself into the air."

"And it disappears into the unruly crowd—which is the United States, that's clear—the way we are also becoming a part of the fabric here, in spite of our injuries," my father quickly added.

Even then, I thought they'd skipped something, and in one of my first and last excursions into their realm of prophesies, I posed a question: "But doesn't the angel disappear into Cuba, into a Cuban crowd?"

"Well, yes," said my father, clearing his throat, "but it is important, Alejandra, not to translate things too literally."

"The angel comes from the crowd and then disappears into it," said my mother.

"No, it falls from the sky," I said, all adolescence.

"Yes, yes, but then it's with the children, who are part of the crowd, and it returns to the crowd," my mother insisted, annoyed with me. "So it can't be that the crowd is Cuban because, though we are Cuban, we can't return, even if we wanted to."

About two months later—and long after Sima's death—an exultant letter arrived from my great-grandfather Ytzak, his florid script practically dancing off the page. He was much better; his daughter Sima had come to Havana and they had gone to the synagogue together!

Of course, my parents didn't share this with me at the time, instead they told me that Sima had revitalized the old man with her presence, that he'd gotten well enough that they were able to go for walks through Old Havana and visit friends of his to whom he had proudly introduced her.

"Una guajirita en la capital," my father sighed, happy and sad and amazed at all of it.

I imagined Ytzak using a cane and, like a tropical Colonel Sanders, waving to the neighbors as he strolled through the district, my grandmother Sima like a Southern belle on his arm, her skirts wide, her demeanor shy, even a little embarrassed.

Years later, after my father's death, I would find Ytzak's letter among his personal papers and read about the reconciliation not just of father and daughter but of Sima and her ancestral faith.

"It was the proudest of days!" wrote Ytzak. "My daughter and I at temple together. I sat as close as I could to the women. I wanted to look at my daughter. I hope god forgives my lack of concentration—it was a dream come true for this old man to see his baby (no matter how old she may be), there, finally, in the House of David."

It was hard to tell which synagogue they had gone to—in Cuba, they are all orthodox or conservative. I guessed it was Chevet Ahim or Adath Israel, a more recently constructed orthodox temple in Old Havana, because Ytzak preferred always to stay in the colonial district, even if it meant attending services that were more emphatically Ashkenazi (he may have even preferred them, it's hard to tell with him).

Sima's visit had lifted him right up out of his sickbed, made him strong again, satisfied and busy. He took Sima to museums and parks (shopping was pretty much out of the question, since after the zafra's failure, even the little that was rationed had become even scarcer, and more precious), to dinner in Chinatown, to free classical music concerts, and to a rare and splendid poetry reading by Eliseo Diego. (Another poet, Nicolás Guillén, was in the audience and this seemed to thrill Ytzak just as much.)

Years later, Ester would tell me how Ytzak completely overwhelmed his daughter, how she would come home with aching, swollen feet and pounding headaches and collapse on his bed while he, still energized, still infused with the miracle of their reconciliation, would stay up for hours, reading Torah, working himself up into ecstatic frenzies of prayer. Sima would hear him from the bedroom, buzzing like a swarm of bees.

What Ytzak never saw was that while Sima surprised even herself by being delighted with the fact of the temple—she, too, had cried at her first public service; she, too, had shivered upon hearing aloud the barely recognizable prayers she had said in whispers all her life—she was also aghast at the way the handful of old women in the female section chatted and gossiped through the prayer service, or that while he flitted about excitedly, she still recoiled from acknowledgment outside of the synagogue walls. Nearly five hundred years of shame and fear lingered in her soul and would not be exorcised so easily.

The trip back to Oriente proved both dramatic and fatal for Sima. It took more than a week of riding in trains that slowed to a crawl due to lack of fuel, trains packed with campesinos and brigades of surly urban workers heading to the interior, skinny chickens and pigs on their way to slaughter, men snoring and pissing on the rails between cars. Her traveling dress soaked through with her own perspiration, causing her chills; it became infused with cigarette and cigar smoke, the stench of diapers and vomit, and of rotting meat. The heat was like a weight around her head and neck, like a big sticky pillow that shed cotton and feathers and refused to let her breathe. Once, against her better judgment, she accepted a glass of

water from a peasant woman who insisted she have some, her lips
having cracked dry by then.

Sima came home to Luis with a burning fever that turned her
skin red like a Russian tourist. He put compresses on her head, fed
her chicken broth, injected her with the free medicines the local
doctor prescribed, but nothing worked. She came in and out of consciousness, sometimes not recognizing where she was at all, other
times chatting away as if she was a young woman again and they
could steal some private moments rolling around the aromatic tobacco that Luis had once tended behind their tiny home. Amid the
babbling, she told him something about her trip to Havana, about
the way her heart leapt when she first heard the Amidah murmured
by so many voices.

When Sima finally died and a heartbroken Luis called to tell
Ytzak, who despaired knowing he would not be able to attend her
funeral, the old man insisted his daughter had renounced all her
pretensions to Christianity in Havana and that she should be given
a proper Jewish burial. For Luis, this was a nightmare—Sima never
told him this, although it was also clear to him that something had
happened in Havana, that perhaps a change had occurred in her.
But what was that change? And if she had in fact come out of her
long imposed religious exile, what, exactly, was a proper Jewish funeral? The last living marrano in the world, lonely Luis had no idea.

In the end, he did the best he could: He had one of the few re-
maining priests in Oriente give a blessing at the burial site (just in
case Ytzak was wrong) and then, later, when no one was around but
the cemetery keeper—a drunken old fool given to visions no one
believed anyway—he draped himself in a threadbare prayer shawl
and, in the full light of day, recited the kaddish.

On Sima's simple headstone he had her name and the dates of
her life engraved, bookended by a Christian cross on the right and a
tiny Star of David on the left. It never occurred to him to look
around, that the odd pairing was already echoing through the graveyard, especially in the older, decrepit tombstones from the eighteenth

and nineteenth centuries, in which Christian trinities and crucifixes were often accompanied by six-pointed stars, now-faded engravings of Torah scrolls, and artfully disguised tetragrammatons.

In Chicago, my parents grieved as much for Sima, who was not just my father's mother but suddenly the symbol of all things maternal, as for their lack of clairvoyance.

"The vulture meant Sima after all," said my mother between sniffles.

"It was literal then?" I asked, remembering the lesson they had tried to impart to me.

I wanted to mourn with them, but at twelve—the revolution and I had had a birthday since Moisés's first telegram about Ytzak's illness—death itself was too far away, and Sima, my grandmother, was a figure I could only reconstruct from photographs and stories. Since both the photo albums and my parents were still there to re-create her, it was nearly impossible for me to conceive something had happened to her. I knew that if I went to my father's desk and looked, she'd still be there, framed with my grandfather Luis on the porch of their simple home in Oriente: modest, unadorned Sima, with her hair in a bun, her eyes as clear as the sky, just like Ytzak's and mine, but without our intensity.

"Yes, yes," muttered my father, his large body imposing again, now laid out on the couch as if it were ready for internment. I remember he still had on his dark business suit when my mother told him about the wire from Luis, how she'd led him to the couch where he lay stiff and still as she sobbed beside him.

"And the angel?" I asked. "The angel was Abuela Sima disappearing into Cuba, right?"

My father scowled. "No, it was—" then he stopped himself and exchanged a quick, cautious glance with my mother. "Yes," he said, "that's exactly what it was. You were right." There were centuries of denial in that look.

A week later, Luis died in his sleep without warning. The news reached us through Moisés. No one said the kaddish for him until many, many years later, when Ernesto, Moisés's oldest son, found himself on a work brigade in Oriente, constructing homes for the campesinos. He said he had no trouble finding my grandfather's grave in the cemetery outside Mayarí—it was next to Sima's, with an identically marked tombstone, the work of a laborer who, without specific instruction, simply copied the wife's iconography for the husband.

XXVII

On my first trip to Cuba, after the first few minutes of confusion and tumult upon my arrival at Moisés's family home, his son, Ernesto, and I sat outside on the stoop for a bit, sipping from glasses of rum that melted the ice he had beaten to pieces for me. He nodded next door to the building where my family and I had once lived.

"It's funny that you came back," he said, one of the few times I heard something less than sweet in his voice. "It seems that everybody who's ever lived in your apartment leaves, like there's a curse or something up there."

I looked up at the balcony, chewed up by rain and wear. "Well, your father says that the man who lives there now—David—is just in Trinidad visiting his girlfriend," I said. "I didn't get the impression he was going anywhere else."

Ernesto shrugged. "He wanted to leave but he can't," he said. Even though he was thirty years old, his cafe au lait skin was smooth as a baby's, as if he were incapable of growing a beard of any kind.

"What do you mean?"

"I mean, he wanted to leave the country," Ernesto said again. He looked at me with his big raccoon eyes, perhaps a little condescendingly. "Oh, don't get me wrong. I think if people want to leave they should be able to leave. I've thought about it, too, except it would kill my father. Everybody here thinks about it, at least once. It's normal for islanders. And if something's forbidden or made nearly impossible, then it becomes that much more enticing, don't you think? But David did more than think about it."

According to Ernesto, when he was just a young man, David—big, blondish, and easygoing—had made a request to leave the country, claiming an aunt in New Jersey would sponsor him in the United States. The aunt was certainly willing but her husband died before David's paperwork was finished, and after they finally figured it all out, the aunt wound up on public assistance and unable to help him.

That petition for asylum proved costly for David: Even after he'd resigned himself to staying in Cuba, it followed him like the stench of his uncle's rotting corpse. "Compañero," a sour-faced bureaucrat said to him when he tried to get an athletic scholarship, his index on the petition in David's files. The bureaucrat shook his head from side to side without saying another word, just "compañero" over and over.

And so, in spite of his speed and strength, David was kept away from any possibility of developing whatever athletic potential he had. "What would be the point?" Ernesto said sarcastically. "If David became a great baseball player or javelin thrower or whatever, who would he compete against? No one was going to let him go to the Pan American Games, much less the Olympics."

When David tried to study medicine, an academic counselor showed up with the file under his arm and claimed that, because of that petition, it was unclear whether David really understood his debt to the revolution. Frightened by the visit, David set out to prove his commitment, volunteering to take on additional patients at the neighborhood clinic, joining cane cutting brigades, staying up all night for neighborhood watch, often taking on extra turns to relieve his elderly neighbors. Soon, David was falling asleep from exhaustion in his classes, unable to focus and read the Latin script on the medicines he was supposed to prescribe. He began having nightmares about making mistakes, his patients purple with poison in their systems.

It wasn't long before David tried to leave the country again—this time much more dramatically, on a raft constructed from inflatable tubes and a carved-out tree log. He was caught just off the coast of Cojímar and sentenced to three years in prison. Due to Moisés's intervention on his behalf with Johnny Suro, who was then married to a woman whose brother was a colonel in the Ministry of the Interior, David only served two years. But within days of his release in late summer of 1980, he was scrambling down to Mariel harbor, desperately trying to find a boat that would take him during that chaotic and explosive exodus.

"I tell you, though, he's cursed," said Ernesto with a bitter laugh. "I mean, he's just not meant to go, you know?"

During the Mariel crisis, Ernesto had been a committed young Communist who'd riled a bunch of compatriots to go taunt those who were leaving. "¡Qué se vayan! ¡Qué se vayan!" they screamed, their throats sore from the litany, their arms numb from flaying in the air and throwing things, skin burned from exposure.

"The thing is," Ernesto said, "you get caught up in it, in the moment. You don't even know why you're doing it anymore, but you can't get away from the noise in your own head and you forget you're yelling at people you know, people who were your classmates, your girlfriends. I had an ex-girlfriend leave via Mariel and it was like a stake in my heart, like a betrayal, like she was fucking Uncle Sam in his vilest most disgusting guise right there in front of me, just to humiliate me—it was personal, you know?—and suddenly I'm yelling at David . . . like it had to be David, it couldn't be somebody else. I'm saying things like 'maricón'—imagine how embarrassed I am about this now—I'm yelling 'traidor,' 'escoria,' you name it, like I hate David when, in fact, he's my neighbor, he's this guy who always had a big crush on my sister and we all sort of felt sorry for him 'cause he was a nice guy, but my sister, well, my sister wasn't going to go out with just anybody, you know."

That's when David, who had always been something of a gentle giant, suddenly stepped out of the boat he'd finally climbed into, grabbed Ernesto by the throat, and, without saying a word, began to pummel him right on the beach. Two lost teeth and a shattered rib cage later, Ernesto was saved by a pair of soldiers who put a gun to David's head and threatened to blow his brains out.

"He served a few months for that," Ernesto said, sighing. "My father talked to Johnny Suro again—I think my dad knows him through your father. Anyway, they decided he'd been punished enough. He'd missed his boat, he couldn't really get a decent job. My ribs never healed right, they hurt when I run or swim." He touched his torso with his fingers, as if checking the dressing on a wound. "But that's okay, I deserved it."

I looked at him, unsure how sincere he was.

"Really," he said, as if he'd read my mind. "Now I just feel sorry for the guy. You know the only thing they've let him do? Sign up for an army tour in Angola, that's what. The poor motherfucker figured he'd seek asylum in South Africa or something, but just before he left, he fell in love with this girl from Trinidad. That fucked everything up; he had to come back because she was pregnant. Then she lost the baby. And then he began to have all these strange pains in his joints. It turned out he'd picked up some horrible parasite or virus; I'm not really sure, but something awful. Cuban medicine's fantastic but they don't quite know what's wrong with him, and there are days he's as stiff as a piece of wood, he can hardly walk down those stairs. And now he really can't leave; he's not going to get free doctors like these anywhere else in the world."

It would be years before I could appreciate the ironies in Ernesto's story. Back then I just listened to him talk, with his self-deprecating manner, the way he would incriminate himself then shake his head and look off to the now darkening skies. At different intervals during the story I wanted to ask him questions, but each time I'd open my mouth, he would wave his hand in the air, begging me to let him finish, his eyes glistening.

"Hey, I'm sorry, I'm sorry," he said, swallowing hard, "it's kind of selfish of me to indulge like this when you've got your own Mariel tragedy, which is so much worse, really."

The Mariel crisis began on April Fool's Day in 1980, far from the harbors, outside the secured walls of the placid peach-colored

Peruvian embassy on Fifth Avenue in Miramar, when an exasperated bus driver crashed his minivan through the front gates, scatter-
ing the guards with his screaming pleas for asylum. To everyone's
amazement, the Andean ambassador acquiesced to the driver's request and, in a pique, Fidel removed his sentries from the embassy,
leaving the stately, terraced mansion vulnerable to the desperation
of the more than ten thousand Cubans who quickly filled its yards.
(The house was later turned into a museum about revolutionary triumphs, and later still, razed.)

"¡Qué se vayan! ¡Qué se vayan!" yelled many of those standing
outside who were staying behind. Their faces were red with rage,
veins throbbing, fists bloodless. They exercised their limbs by pitching things over the walls, especially the identity cards the refugees
had tossed away in disdain.

Inside the embassy compound, a constant fusillade of rocks and
bottles, eggs and feces came over the fence. Those inside—packed
face to face, shoulder to shoulder, buttock to buttock—laughed gid-
dily as their bodies became covered with sticky egg whites and
runny yolks, rotting food and gooey excrement. They stunk from
the garbage, from their own joyful and acrid sweat and the need to
take care of their bodily functions in the very spot in which they
were standing. They talked standing up, prayed standing up, slept
standing up, ate what little came over the walls standing up.

Outside, others stood beyond the barred gates, reaching over
with their hearts if not their still and empty hands, too frightened to
move forward, too anxious to return to their Havana homes. They
just stared and imagined themselves hopping over the fence—it
wasn't even five feet high—saw their own ghosts leaping, vaulting
over the multitudes.

On the second day of the siege, Cuban soldiers surrounded the
embassy, a heavily armed cordon of menace and might. If someone
outside tried to hand over a bowl of rice and beans to someone inside, the deadly police batons would come down hard, bones breaking, bowl flying, rice in the air. Eventually, it was the soldiers
themselves who were forced to feed the thousands in the Peruvian

pen, passing out trays of drippy beans and barely steamed potatoes that never made it past the first few hands extending out from the gates. Among the future exiles, fights would break out over a piece of bread, knives were shaped from rocks and belts, men—and women, too—became scarred, both inside and out.

It rained sometimes during the siege, and some of the interned Cubans would reach up to the clouds with outstretched arms, to get as much of the refreshing water as they could. Others would simply turn their faces toward heaven and let the rain wash them clean, slowly soaking through to their skins, making them new.

For nearly two months, the Peruvian embassy housed the ten thousand as they slowly trickled out with safe-passes, some of them refusing to leave altogether, convinced they'd be arrested, torn to pieces the minute they set foot off the sacred grounds. These men— it was mostly men, young men—had to be convinced, some forcibly dragged away.

When it was all over and done with, when the last of the refugees got their visas and were finally escorted out of the compound (even as Mariel harbor leaked thousands and thousands more exiles into the sea, all headed north or to their watery graves), the embassy grounds had been trampled flat. Not a live blade remained, not a flower survived. It was all brown mud and debris.

And there, amid the shredded papers, the discarded chicken bones and plastic bottles, the torn rags, loose and unmatched shoes, coconut shells, putrid eggs, dried shit, and broken glass, were the crumpled remains of my great-grandfather Ytzak, his eyes open as if in perpetual shock, just like Olinsky's, his face turned to the embassy wall.

No one recognized him at first. His body had shrunk to the size of a tote bag, all rolled up and flat. Against the wall, with his back to the thousands, his white hair and dirty Dril 100 suit merged together so that he looked like discarded linen, somebody's lost shirt or jacket, not a person at all. He was a light, little thing. The only reason it took more than one paramedic to remove him was because his body had been broken in so many different places that his limbs and torso went every which way, like a loose bag of stones. His peg leg was missing, the blood glazed black on his stump.

No one knows how Ytzak got there, whether he made the unlikely decision to seek asylum in a moment of clear-eyed logic, whether age and fear conspired to panic him, or whether he simply got lost in the crowds, a frail ninety-nine-year-old man swept up by a wave of desperation and desire, the fleshy tide of ten thousand of his brethren pulling him under until he couldn't breathe.

In Chicago, a slow-motion volcano gushed from my father when he heard the news: All that was in him came spilling out, a thick lava fetid and sick. For days, he lingered in his bathroom, his giant body in a continual aftermath and eruption, upturned and ominous. During this period of mourning and mortification, my mother would occasionally push in buckets of ice, fresh towels, glasses of mango juice. Outside the bathroom door, we'd hear him wail and whimper, like some great injured animal.

In August of 1994, after Leni and I separated, I took a vacation by myself to St. Maarten, a tiny Caribbean island, thirty-seven square miles of hearty hills and tourist traps divided between Dutch and French authorities.

The French side was picturesque, its architecture echoing for me the kind of quaint colonial style I had seen in Havana: two-story homes with balconies from which people peered out all day, their poverty evident regardless of the past grandeur of their homes (now divided into many, many homes) or the defiant dignity in their eyes. The French islanders were not friendly. They made no effort at all to speak English but were occasionally willing to have an exchange in Spanish, thinking I was—depending on the situation, my dress, and my attitude—either an oil heiress from Venezuela or another undocumented Dominican come to clean hotel rooms and steal a job.

I stayed on the Dutch side, in one of many luxury time shares (a lawyer friend had loaned it to me for my getaway), nestled among the casinos and sugar white beaches, in a suite with a living room, a terrace, and a Jacuzzi that could have hosted a half dozen guests. The bedroom had two overwhelming king-sized beds covered with blue bedspreads that undulated with my weight as endlessly as the turquoise water outside my patio. My view was clear: white plastic beach furniture, New Yorkers burning brown while reading Stephen King, a few red-roasted children making sand castles, and a handful of charcoal-skinned natives, all peddling palm frond hats and cheap jewelry, or dressed in cabin boy whites and happy to replenish towels and drinks.

At first, I tried desperately to engage with my surroundings—parasailing, scuba diving, window shopping, playing endless blackjack. I didn't want to think about Leni, all snappy somewhere by now, drawing admirers like moths to a flame, and perhaps as deadly. I wanted to warn them all, to explain that to love so completely is to perish. I wanted to wave flags and caution everyone—the girls who were too good to die so young, the boys who didn't understand and didn't deserve so ecstatic a finale—that they were better off going about their business, having fun, just like me. But then the limber young woman who tugged on the pulleys of the parasail would wink at me, just like Leni, and I'd plunge, not into the sea or the sky, but back to my last descent into Leni's lushness, the way she could make time stand still with a kiss.

I got plenty of attention, attention I didn't care about in the least—from the taxi driver, a Saudi businessman, the Canadian flight attendant, and everybody, it seemed, in the casinos. But like the young man who backed up his car at the entrance to the timeshare complex and punctured his tires on the steel prods designed precisely to stop that sort of thing—he was yelling at me, "Take me with you, oh my princess, please"—I found it all too crude or ridiculous or both. I wanted to get away from Leni, but her jangly wrists were always playing somewhere nearby, causing my thighs and pelvis to ache.

Then one afternoon, leaning against the bar while ordering my third Havana Club (legal in St. Maarten), I forgot all about Leni: There on the big screen TV behind the counter, surrounded by twinkling bottles of spirits as if they were altar pieces, the azure of Cuba's shoreline appeared, shattered by hundreds and hundreds of bobbing brown bodies floating on the surface.

"What's going on?" I asked no one in particular.

"It's Mariel all over again," said the bartender, a handsome, serious man who was efficient in his job and rarely spoke. "Fidel has given them permission to leave." He wiped wet tumblers, setting them in a tower on the bar counter.

I squinted at the tube. I hadn't been paying attention to the news. All I had been obsessed with had been my own pain, my own singularly smashed little heart, so Cuba had been far, far away—like a dream I once had, or a bill I had forgotten to pay. Now I plopped down on a bar stool, recognizing the stubby grass of Cojímar just off the emerald sea, and I felt overwhelmed, guilty, and suddenly very afraid.

"How long has this been going on? I mean, what happened?"

But the bartender didn't get a chance to answer me.

"It just started a few days ago, but it's picking up now," a young man across the way said in a fractured English. If his accent hadn't told me he was Cuban—all open-mouthed and cocky—surely his posture would have: He had come-on written all over him, languid and insolent. His dark good looks weren't as dreamy as he imagined, and the body he was showing off with his Speedos and fishnet top was flabby in places he would have never acknowledged, but he was, all of a sudden, a terrific distraction.

"¿Qué pasó?" I asked, switching to Spanish.

He was so delighted—"¡Ay, pero si hablas español!"—he came right over (he would have anyway) and stood next to me, his hand on the back of my stool and giving me one of those burning Cuban gazes. I gazed right back, a little drunk and much amused.

His name was Roberto. "Well, what do you know about Cuba?" he asked, sipping his drink with the same hand with which he held a cigarette between his fingers, his lids lowered so that I might imag-

ine him in a more vulnerable state. "Just so I know how much I
have to explain," he added, trying really hard to sound sincere.

"I'm Cuban," I said with a laugh.

"Nooo . . . ! You're not Cuban! You're Cuban? Really? But you
were born in the U.S., no? Really, you're Cuban? From where?"

I explained and then he explained: That he was right off the island, on a mission in St. Maarten with a colleague from the Ministry of Tourism, sent to look at time shares to try to develop new
ideas for Varadero. I laughed, he laughed. All the while, his hand
was traveling: from the back of the stool to my shoulder, then to tip
my chin, then to pat my exposed thigh.

We were in my room in record time, with him stroking above me
like an Olympic swimmer destined for a record. When he finished—
with a grimace and a high whistle—he rolled over, his upper lip covered with beads of sweat, patted me on my naked butt and flipped the
TV on with the remote. The room was instantly filled with balseros,
up close this time, paddling and waving their arms at the cameras
while the water splashed about them.

"What are you doing?" I asked.

"Just taking a break," he said, grinning.

"A break?" I couldn't believe it; it had taken him—what?—a
minute and a half?

"Well, and also . . ." He was immensely pleased with himself.
"I'm checking in with those poor sons of bitches. I mean, I'm here,
with a beautiful girl—with you—and two days from now, I'm flying
to Miami."

"What?" I was thoroughly confused.

"Yeah," Roberto said, even cockier now, stroking the soft dark
curls on his chest with his gluttonous hand. "I'm, like . . . defecting!" He cracked himself up, laughing with his tongue hanging out.
He and his colleague had it all set up with the French consulate on
the other side of the island. They'd fly to Miami, disembark, and
plead for asylum. "What do you think now, huh?"

"I think you owe me," I said, reaching down to the wet, limp
worm between his legs.

"¿Te gustó, eh?" he asked, leering, getting hard from the idea that he was such a stud.

"No, I didn't like it," I said, climbing on top and guiding him, "so now you're going to make sure I do."

Then I tugged at him hard, as if he were an unreliable, rebellious sloop while, on the TV screen behind my back, Havana continued to overflow into the sea.

"There you are!" a woman's voice exclaimed behind us. It was many hours later.

My Cuban lover turned around slowly from the bar, his lids and lips droopy, a mug of coffee steaming in his hands. He said, "God, am I . . ."

I blinked.

"Alejandra?" the woman said, ignoring him. She was my mirror, only darker, beautiful.

"You know each other?" Roberto asked, astounded.

We hugged like long-lost relatives, kissed each other's faces and necks, even cried. It was Estrella, years later, her body toasty and warm like bread.

"I can't believe it," I said, holding her by the hands as we stepped back to appraise each other.

"You look exactly the same!"

"No . . . look . . . gray hairs!"

"It makes you look interesting, debonair," said Estrella, laughing.

"You know each other?" Roberto asked again, slurry as if he were drunk from the coffee.

We sat down, Estrella and I, our hands locked together, one on top of each other, amazed. "What are you doing here?" I asked.

"So . . . eh?" Roberto said, this time his voice trailing off as he threw himself into a comfy cushioned chair. The mug managed to slide onto a little side table before his eyes dropped shut.

"I'm with him."

"You mean . . ."

"Oh, god no, on a business trip," she said laughing. "I work for the Ministry of Tourism now."

"You're his colleague! My god, and you're defecting, is that true?"

"What?" Estrella yanked her hands away, her eyes quick daggers at Roberto, now slumped in the chair, snoring. "Is that what he told you?"

"It's not true?"

"Ay, Ale, life is so complicated," she said with a sigh. "No es fácil."

We left Roberto in his slumber and walked outside. The night was balmy and clear, stars glittering overhead. She did not want to leave but she had allowed things to move along, to see how far fate would take her in another kind of test, one that had nothing to do with politics and which I understood completely: She was in love with her boss, a much older and very married man.

"I thought it would be just fun at first," she confessed, her eyes glossy. "But then I found out I could barely breathe without him, I needed him far more than I ever imagined." She hid her shame by turning her face to the darkness.

But he would not leave his wife, would not even entertain the possibility, and she couldn't bear to continue as his mistress. As soon as she arrived in St. Maarten, she called him and told him that unless they could be together, she was staying—asylum would force her to live without him. When he didn't respond, Estrella let Roberto—who was crazy to leave Cuba—make all the arrangements.

"But I can't really fathom Miami," she said. "The last time I was there on business everyone kept offering me steak—no matter the time of day or the circumstances. It was all, 'Let's talk about it over filet mignon,' 'Here, let me buy you a sirloin,' 'Come over, I just put two juicy slabs on the grill.' I was nauseous the whole time. But to go back . . . especially now, after telling him . . ." Her voice trailed off. The water whispered along the shore, its black surface lined with light.

"You still have a couple of days to think about it," I said, taking her hand like schoolgirls and leading her back to the bar. "I think, though, right now we need to rescue Roberto. We really can't abandon him like that, you know."

She let herself laugh. "What's the story there, huh?" she asked, jabbing me in the ribs as we pushed open the door. "Something's up, no?"

But it wasn't what either of us imagined: In the lounge, a very alert Roberto greeted us sitting up in the chair where we'd left him, nervously wringing his hands. Another man was sitting with him, broad-shouldered, his back to us. They were both watching the exodus from Cojímar, which continued to stream from TV screens everywhere.

"Muchachas . . ." Roberto said, shooting out of his seat the instant he spotted us. He seemed to be waving us away but it was too late. The other man stood up, too, a handsome silver-haired gentleman in a crisp linen guayabera. As he turned to us with an almost embarrassed smile, Estrella gasped.

"Ay dios," she said, tears free flowing, her hands covering her face as she buried herself in the man's shoulder.

He kissed her as if she were a child, on her hair, her shoulders, all the while gently stroking her arms and back. "Mi negra, everything will be fine, and just as you want," he said, his clear eyes reflecting the truth of his promise. "Let's go home, okay?"

The years, I noticed, had not diminished Johnny Suro's charms, or his compassion.

When I got back to Chicago, there was a message from Moisés in the voice of a Cuban operator on my answering machine. It was the very first time he had ever called me and, though it surprised me, I didn't return the call right away.

Instead I grabbed my mail and the pile of newspapers—all bannered with news about Cuba's flood of rafters—and sat down before the TV, its sound a drone, its images all familiar now. I opened my bills one at a time and perused the math on each as if it mattered. I prepared for the worst, though I couldn't fathom what that was, and dialed Havana. It took hours, then the line beeped, as it always does to signal an international call.

Orlando answered. "¿Oigo?"

"It's Alejandra. Hello."

"Hello."

"Is Moisés there?"

"Yes . . . just a minute . . ." There was din and confusion, the blur of Orlando's hand trying to cover the phone. "He can't come to the phone."

"I got a call from him, a message from an operator."

"No, that was me."

Silence.

"Just a minute," Orlando said.

I could hear him conferring with Ester, who was saying, "Just tell her, just tell her."

"Is everything okay?" I called out.

Orlando came back. "Yes, just a minute." Then more hazy noises.

"Orlando . . ." I said into the receiver. "Orlando!" I was yelling. I was imagining Moisés dead—that was the worst, yes.

"Excuse me, Alejandra . . ." he said, embarrassed and apologetic. "It was my father-in-law who asked that I call but now he won't come to the phone."

"What's wrong?" I demanded.

"Nothing's wrong, we're all fine," Orlando insisted. "But Ernesto . . ."

"What?" I loved Ernesto; after Moisés, I may have loved Ernesto most of all.

"Well, Ernesto is on his way to the United States."

"¿Comó?" I was stunned.

"Yes," said Orlando, letting out a deep sigh. "He left yesterday from Cojímar. He has your phone number. But if you could check, you know . . . it would be helpful, a favor to all of us."

The waves from Cojímar brought about thirty thousand more

Cubans to the United States, but Ernesto Menach wasn't among them. I checked with the INS, with Cuban refugee organizations, with the Red Cross almost daily for a month. Nor was he among those forced into resettlement camps at Guantánamo or the Bahamas.

"He went on a raft, with some friends," Orlando told me. "He is wearing a T-shirt that says, 'Cuba sí'. I don't know if that helps. It's a yellow raft, a real raft, the inflatable kind. They bought it from a British tourist. It was hidden here at the house for months; we didn't know. We don't know anything."

In November 1994, Cuba and the United States established direct-dial long-distance calling. On New Year's Eve, the biggest holiday in Cuba, I called Moisés's home and a man whose voice I didn't recognize answered the phone. I considered I might have dialed wrong because he had a distinct Iberian accent. There was a great deal of noise behind him, as if there was a party going on.

Then Orlando came to the phone.

"Who was that?" I asked, perhaps jealous that an unknown foreigner might be making himself cozy in my Cuban home.

"That was Francisco," Orlando said dryly.

"I don't know him."

"No."

"Who is he?" I ventured.

"He is Angela's new husband," said Orlando. "We are all saying farewell to them now, it's a going away party. She is moving with him, to Spain."

For thou did cast me into the deep, into the heart of the seas . . .

Orlando and I were silent a long time, the static like boiling water. "Will you write to me?" I asked him.

"Yes," he said, and I knew he would.

. . . and the flood was round about me; all thy waves and thy billows passed over me . . .

"You are staying there?"

"It's my home," he said. "My children live here. This is my family."

The waters closed in over me, the deep was round about me . . .

"I called to wish Moisés a good new year, and to give him my condolences for Ernesto," I said.

. . . weeds were wrapped around my head, at the roots of the mountains.

"He won't accept your condolences," said Orlando. "He won't sit shiva. Ernesto is not dead to him but like Jonah, in the belly of some great fish, just waiting to be vomited out."

Oh Lord . . .

"Ale . . ."

"Yes?"

"Tomorrow . . . happy birthday."

XXVIII

Water has its own language.

It talks, hums, ripples, and giggles through brooks and fountains while the wind plays on the clear skin of tidal pools, their treasures alive, busy, crawling. Water groans—the deep of the sea can pull back and hurl forth a fierce tsunami, unstoppable and orgasmic. It exalts, heals, and kills. Afterward, water sighs, retreats with a siren song.

Havana is surrounded by water. The blue whispers from every corner—a severe blue, then a greenish blue, cobalt, azure, sky blue, sea blue. This is a blue, blue city, even the night has the plush density of blue velvet, the stars rain down in staccato, leaving a bluish sheen on the grimiest street, the most forgotten of stoops or doorways. The blue swivels, dips, disappears into rivers deep underground, gurgles, and purrs.

There is no way to leave Cuba without traversing water, without paying it tribute with promises and prayers, without talking back to it. This is the island's constant intercourse. Even the leap into U.S. territory at Guantánamo requires crossing a brackish moat.

"Were you born in Cuba?"

I'm inevitably asked this when I say I'm Cuban, as if my identity depended entirely on being birthed on the island, the fragile pouch of my mother's water breaking, its flow rushing, returning to its own mysterious source and writing my name indelibly with indigo ink on the firmament.

My passports—both of them—say I am Cuban: an American citizen but not American, Cuban, cubana, born in Cuba.

This is the part that never changes.

I can be, of my own free will, a woman or a man, an engineer or a chef. I can live anywhere, declare whatever allegiances I want. I can love anyone anytime in any way that I choose, and it changes nothing about that fixed moment in time: The first of January 1959, and my first gasp of air outside the womb, in Havana.

This is what's both inevitable and inscrutable: That moment of first light, Cuban copen, one in the afternoon, the waters already arguing among themselves, and dividing, blue and red and black.

At Moisés's house in 1987, one of his lingering neighbors, in a gesture without any ill intent, asked me casually when I'd left Cuba.

"She didn't leave!" Moisés bellowed from the kitchen. He came rushing out, a brown-edged plastic spatula in his hand, sprinkling grains of yellow rice in the air. "They took her! She was just a child, she had no say. ¡Se la llevaron!"

I was bundled up, I was precious cargo.

"You were saved," whispered the same neighbor as soon as Moisés ducked back in the kitchen. "When you get back to the U.S., my god, tell your parents how grateful you are."

Ernesto laughed.

"No, really, Ernestico," the neighbor insisted, one eye on the kitchen door in case Moisés should leap back in the room to a swashbuckling defense of his revolution.

A grinning Ernesto just shook his head. "You realize what the real lesson is here, don't you, Alejandra?"

"What's that?" I asked, poised coolly against the stairs to the barbacoa. I knew everyone was watching me.

"You are absolved, my friend, you may live guilt-free among

the bourgeoisie, the enemy, because you had no say in your predicament," he said. "You can come back and we will help you cry about your lost, lost Cuba because none of this is your fault. It may be ours, perhaps, or the kidnappers—except that would be your parents and it's complicated then—but not yours, not ever. ¡Te llevaron! Now remember that. It's a story you will need. And it will be even more convincing if you believe it."

One day, on that first trip to Cuba, a man followed me out of the Habana Libre all the way to the university, where I was working a series of meetings. At the time, I thought nothing of it. I figured he was another one of those guys who hung around the hotels clandestinely, hoping to get a foreigner to buy something for them at the diplo-tienda or take a letter to the United States or maybe just engage in some conversation and get a free meal or sex with a natural blonde (a Swedish tourist perhaps, or an East German).

But when I saw him again during the lunch break, leaning against the wall and nervously smoking a cigarette, I began to worry. At the end of the workday, he was still there. I considered my parents might have been right: that I was being followed, manipulated, spied upon. When I stepped off campus, I could feel him behind me, a jittery shadow.

Out on the street, I shifted gears and turned, then turned again, snaking through the busy sidewalks jammed in late afternoon with old women carrying bags of goods, young men idling in packs like eager puppies, couples in transit, bloated antique cars and honking buses on the thoroughfare.

Whenever I paused to see if he was still there, the man would shift, too—he had a swimmer's build, lean but strong, with a kind of curve to his shoulders. Whenever I spotted him, he would screech to a halt and pretend to be waiting for the bus, or suddenly lean into the window of a car at a traffic stop and ask for a light.

I finally led him out of the labyrinth, past the stifling crowds whose sweat seemed to stick to my body like smoke, out to the open air of the Malecón. The blue beckoned, breathed a promise of relief.

I didn't look back. I knew he was there, behind me, strutting probably, preparing a fantastic line or an indictment. I could almost see him, slowly swaggering across the street to the seawall, mission accomplished, victory in a long drag on his cigarette.

But when I finally turned to face him up close, my stalker was all nerves and shakes. He had a day-old beard and a web of tiny lines like scars around his coal-fired eyes. His shirt was worn, with loose threads at the seams.

"Señorita," he said anxiously, looking in all directions before finishing his sentence, "will you marry me?"

"¿Qué qué?" I wasn't sure I'd heard right; the sea behind us, with its constant agitation, must have altered his voice.

"Oh, no, not like that!" he exclaimed, even more horrified at my reaction than I was at his proposal. "No, look, you're a foreigner, right? Where are you from? Canada? Look, my girlfriend is in Canada and I can't get a visa. I'll do anything, I'll pay you whatever you need—I can work, I can get the money once I'm there, I swear—just marry me, please. Get me out of here."

When I return to Cuba for the second time in 1997, I have Orlando— who now drives a carefully preserved 1985 blue Moskvitch with which he earns a living chauffeuring tourists—take me to Varadero to see Barbarita, my mother's cousin.

Ten years after my first trip to Cuba, my mother wants to know everything about what's happening on the island, to hear from old friends, even visit. With me, she sends Barbarita one thousand U.S. dollars, which I have carefully stowed in a money belt strapped under my shirt and across my chest. The cash is meant to help her with repairs to the house, necessary after the last hurricane tore her roof, and for day-to-day survival.

Technically, Varadero is part of Cuba, just about an hour or so outside of Havana. The highways there follow the northern coasts, where empty snack stands offer false enticements, and huge cranes like pterodactyls peck at the shore for oil. All along, the greenery on the south side is thick with pines and palms, hills sloping into the mists.

But, in fact, while it may be found on the island, Varadero exists through a space portal into another dimension. It's Cuba but a kind of neofuturist Cuba, hysterical and hallucinatory. Everything in Varadero seems new and has a price tag, everything in Varadero feels urgent and expendable.

The hotels loom like Atlantis, effulgent and alien, one after the other, rising out of the raw shore. They are all painted in inoffensive Euro-friendly pastels, with tiled roofs and tinted windows, real (and ghastly) hamburgers on the menus, and working air-conditioning. There are no pesos anywhere; in fact, clerks sniff at the national currency as if it were Monopoly money. There's a golf course, with perfectly manicured sod, reserved for the exclusive use of Italians and Spaniards who want to teach mellow mulato girls how to play. "Fore!" they say, and laugh while drinking their mojitos.

There are no blackouts here, the roads are smooth, the telephones always work. The discos—and there are plenty—play Madonna and Gloria Estefán without apologies. When the floor shows come to life, the dancers are always black as night, with hard round buttocks, wild plumes, and overly ripe breasts that vibrate in accompaniment to hand drums and congas. The girls are all beautiful, witty but sweet, and so easy to talk to . . . Here, even the street signs speak English: "mini-market," says one; "USD only," says another.

Because she is Cuban, Barbarita lives in the underbelly of Varadero, with the rest of the natives. These are the neighborhoods to the sides, away from the main avenues, the lights and the hustle. These are the places that never appear on postcards and tourist brochures.

Here an occasional hen, skinny and riddled with some sort of blue mold on its feathers, rests comfortably on the front stoop of a weathered, gray, clapboard house, its shutterless windows open to a kitchen with a snoring old man on a cot next to the stove, his middle-aged daughter fixed to a rocking chair, her hands folded as if in prayer, just like Rodolfo back at Moisés's, static before the TV set.

There are domino games under the shade of massive ceibas, the men slapping the pieces on a flat scrap of wood resting on their bent knees, a kind of human-held table. Cigar smoke whirls, children with dirty faces run across the dusty road, mischievously pull the laundry from the line, and ask anybody they think is a lost tourist for money.

When we get near Barbarita's street, neither Orlando nor I can figure out the exact address on the letter she sent my mother. Finally, Orlando parks the car. "Who are you looking for?" asks an old black woman across the way. She's large, bubbling almost, and as she makes her way to us her whole body seems to percolate. She talks to Orlando because she thinks I'm a tourist and don't understand. "I've lived here all my life; I know everybody," she says, offering her credentials.

"We're looking for Barbarita Abravanel," I say in perfect Cuban Spanish, all attitude and style, although here in this hovel in the shadows of Varadero, where the ocean's misty perfume can't mask the stink from the nearby hotels' garbage dumps, nothing will shroud my privilege either.

"¿La china?" she asks, surprised but unembarrassed about looking me over from head to toe, her upraised eyebrow indicating her continuing doubts.

I nod, which catches Orlando by surprise. He knows nothing about my mother's side of the family.

"I'm Alejandra San José. She's my aunt," I say, using another kind of license—the Cuban custom of rearranging and renaming relatives and others we love according to need, not bloodlines.

The old woman grins. Her eyes turn from dead dirt brown to a warm, swirling chocolate. "You're Nena's daughter?"

I nod again.

She points the way, down a path that seems hardly there—even at high noon, it's murky, covered with a thick canopy of vines and branches. Orlando takes my hand and reluctantly leads the way, pushing the strings of what appear to be kudzu from our faces.

In ten years, he has changed dramatically. His hair has a patina of slate to it, its roots still remarkably black, but all his running around in the sun with tourists has given his skin a browner varnish. His hands, which were once as delicate as satin, are now calloused and rough from so much driving, maneuvering steering wheels that feel like they're on fire, and carrying luggage in and out of hotels. His palms are distinctly outlined in copper and faded yellow. He is slimmer, too, not muscular, but conscious of his weight and looks in a tender way. He is fifty years old now, the age at which men become aware of death, and everything about him is vulnerable.

When we arrive at Barbarita's we know it's her house because there's nothing else, only brambles and bush. It is a large home, long like a train; we see it disappear back into the wilderness. The last hurricane not only tore the roof but the walls, too, opening the front room completely to the skies and the elements. Amazingly, the front door is intact—its frame a hard mahogany, with roses carved into its face, a knocker, and a doorbell with tricolor wires like the Cuban flag that leak out and down, along the exposed and weathered blue-and-white living room tiles. The door and the frame hang as if suspended in the air.

"Oh my god." It's Orlando. Even he's a bit shocked.

Beyond the door are two rockers, their termite-eaten arms practically disintegrating before our eyes. On the floor are worn strips from other, long ago chairs, the more preserved blue tiles where a table or wardrobe might have once been.

We look at each other, confused. Do we ring the bell? Knock? Do we dare pass through the door to the other side, where another door installed on a wall to the rest of the house waits?

"What the hell," I say, in English, and ring the bell. I feel a surge in my fingers and a buzz echoes from the house. Nothing happens.

"I'll wait here," Orlando says. "Why don't you try that other door?" He points past the vast emptiness of the floor tiles.

In a gesture to the fact of the door, I turn the knob, step inside, though I could just as easily have gone around it. As I walk across the naked living room, I feel like a thief, a trespasser, and I call Barbarita's name. There is no sound, though, except the briny breeze ruffling the trees just beyond the borders of the house, the ocean's faraway roll, and the hum of traffic in the distance. I knock on the second door, the one that's attached to a wall that threatens to crumble at my touch. But there's no answer again. I look back at Orlando. He waves me on.

"Buenas," I say to the penumbra inside. My eyes need a second to adjust, but my nose takes in the dust and mildew. There is furniture stacked to the ceiling, I can see its outlines. It leaves only a thin passage of light to a patio just beyond, where the sun illuminates a clothesline, a stack of wood, and what appear to be hundreds of glass bottles.

"Sí?" says a tiny spectral figure with extraordinarily long arms, a little prune of a woman whose tone betrays fear at the sight of me. She steps into the center of the patio and walks tentatively toward me, her shoulders back.

"Barbarita . . . Barbarita Abravanel?" I say.

"I'm Barbarita Abravanel," she says, and her face, which has been in the dark until now, comes into focus: an elegant face, round, with high, fat cheeks and little gleaming almonds for eyes, someone not Chinese by birth but perhaps by osmosis.

"I'm Alejandra," I say, but she doesn't recognize me.

Her small, moist mouth starts to form my name, to repeat it, but because I know it will end with an ellipsis and a question mark, I anticipate her—I can't bear the idea that she doesn't know me.

"Nena's daughter," I add, and whatever it was inside her that was ready to confront me, to defend herself before the intruder she thought I was, collapses, her long arms trembling as they close around my neck. She is so small, I have to bend from the waist to hold her. She makes little chirping sounds in my ear, giggles and kisses every part of me that's exposed.

In the afternoon that Orlando and I spend with Barbarita, we are entertained by about a half dozen other elderly women, all of whom come in and out of her kitchen with ease and familiarity. We are served pumpkin soup, fried chicken, and regaled with hilarious stories about how the chicken came to the table, and how the hurricane stole the living room, and the absurd things that happen on the buses to and from Havana. I notice Barbarita has little buddhas everywhere in the house, rosebushes in the back.

On our return to the city, I'm exhausted and settle into the passenger's seat, toss off my sandals and sigh. "They're not so bad," I say.

"What?"

"Their lives—I mean, I get it, there are ways in which they are cursed: by the scarcities, the poverty, the limits of their mobility, but they're old now, too, so maybe that's less important," I say as the wind whips in the windows. "And yet, still, there is something oddly paradisiacal about their existence."

"Are you crazy?" asks Orlando.

"No, really, even the house, with its front room blown away, it's really quite comfortable, quite large, it's kind of amazing that it's all still there," I say. "In the States, that would never happen, you know, it would have been picked apart by looters, somebody would have killed her by now. I mean, she's surrounded by friends and people who love her, she's taken care of."

"Don't romanticize this, Alejandra—you'd never live here," he says, his eyes intent, almost angry, as he looks past the windshield. "Not like us, not ever. If your parents hadn't taken you, you'd have left on your own." The muscles on his arms twitch, his brow darkens.

"Please . . ." I say, reaching to him over the vast gulf, kissing his shoulder, "don't hate me so much."

"The problem," he says, still annoyed but less so, "is that you think you've missed something."

"I did," I say. "I know I did."

I'm not an expert swimmer.

My blue-veined strokes are asymmetrical, often messy. My feet kick as if I were resisting being dragged somewhere, as if I were always trying to escape from my captors, to go back rather than advance.

When I'm submerged completely, moving as if in slow motion in all that gloom, I am always aware of the water talking. It's a low, low sound, like a moan, a rolling tenor from somewhere deep, horrible and dazzling. It trills in my chest, my throat. It's the last sound we make with our mouths wide open—it's a longing to belong.

In the water, I turn over, my face to the surface. The colors burn, flicker, just beyond the skin of the sea. Without moving a muscle, the blue washes away and my body rises to the whitest, most lucid light. When I emerge, slick like a newborn, my first sighting is always, always Cuba.

XXIX

In March of 1995, I was spending all my time at Illinois Masonic Hospital, watching over Leni, who'd managed to shatter her body in a sensational car accident that killed an Uruguayan doctoral student in economics at the University of Chicago. An angry, whiskey-fueled Leni had plowed head-on into his midget Italian sports car on Lake Shore Drive, tossing him over the embankment and into the tumultuous and icy lake. It took divers several days to recover the boy's body, by which time his family—including his father, a former colonel who had participated in some of the army's less decorous activities during the country's bleak years—had arrived, threatening a lawsuit, then a bloody revenge, then crumbling.

I found out about the accident not because I'd been called as Leni's emergency contact person, but because the distinguished Uruguayans needed an interpreter. It wasn't until we were right smack in the gleaming hallways of Illinois Masonic, after I'd heard the dreadful story from the grieving parents who were themselves in need of medical care because of the trauma, that I was handed a copy of the police report and almost choked when I saw Leni's name.

I ran to her room only to find her bandaged and blind, hooked up as if to the thousand albuminous tentacles of a giant jellyfish, lying there in the bluish light of the hospital. I approached her as if she were an extraterrestrial on view in a laboratory, not recognizing anything as familiar, but with my heart pounding as if I, too, were possessed by an alien creature trying desperately to escape from my throat and chest.

"Leni . . ." I touched her hand, all purple and bloated, her wrist bracelet-free and riddled with scratches and cuts. Leni just lay there, breathing through a clear plastic tube that ran in a tangle among all the others, as peaceful as I'd ever seen her.

When she finally awoke, days later, she remembered nothing but having an argument with her new girlfriend, going off in a huff to hear a jazz singer on the South Side, and coming home happy because she'd scored a phone number from the pianist, a girl as stately as a Nubian princess. When the visiting police officers told her what had transpired, Leni blinked and said nothing. Later, when we were alone and she was able to take the tube out of her mouth for a bit, she began to mutter that it was an accident, that it wasn't like she was trying to kill him.

"And, you know, one less little fascist Friedman economist won't exactly hurt your part of the world . . ." she said, sarcastic and hurt and unable to grasp exactly what had happened.

If someone had foreseen and warned me about Leni's accident, I would have imagined myself devotedly back at her side in a flash, taking care of her, trying at whatever cost to salvage her limbs and spirit and maybe some hope for us. But though I went to see her nightly during her weeks in the hospital, and even took on the task of accompanying her to physical therapy and court once she was released, I was pulled from Leni's vortex by the most unimaginable of champions: Orlando.

His letters began arriving the very day of her hospitalization, like Moisés's, in those gossamer blue envelopes. But unlike Moisés's long, eloquent epistles, Orlando's were more like notes, quick scribbles, always written on scrap paper while sitting in his car or at a cafeteria or bar waiting for somebody. Sometimes I swore I could smell the sea, or coffee, or stale beer on them; other times I was convinced there were spicy traces of cologne.

Because Orlando insisted out of some weird pride on mailing the letters through regular post—in spite of his easy access to scores of foreigners—they took weeks, sometimes months to arrive. When they landed in my box, they'd come out of order, sometimes in bunches. He'd often repeat himself, telling me the same story two or three times, unsure whether the previous letter had made it, or whether he'd already told me. The versions were often slightly different, sometimes informed by some critical new detail, other times just abbreviated accounts.

That first note he sent was about the longest I ever received, a full page, his script in awkward blocks, and to my amazement, full of grammatical errors. Everything suggested he was rushed: Instead of Alejandra, it was just "A"; instead of que, just "q." He wrote in pencil, on paper that he'd obviously carried around bunched up in his pocket, and the lead had gotten shiny and soft, arriving in Chicago as faded and mysterious as the cave drawings at Lauscaux.

"My wife is not my wife," he wrote. "She is someone else's wife. She was always someone else's wife except we didn't know who he was. She's my sister, really, and we lived in our father's house. I know you thought she was my wife—everyone did—even we did—we were confused—everyone was confused—I think everyone might still be confused—but she is not my wife. Yes, it's true, we were married for years, and there are even pictures to prove it, not just of the wedding but of us—husband and wife, you can see it in our faces— but it was more something we were trying to be. We love each other, certainly—that is not in doubt—but a few years back—when no one was looking—we talked it through and got a divorce. We didn't tell anybody. Why would we tell anybody? Nothing changed, except we changed, but maybe not. I think we knew all along."

Over time there were literally hundreds of notes, some of them with a list of activities: "Today: Take Rafa to the hospital, take my father-in-law to temple, fix shoes." Other times, quick sketches: "Went by the piquera near Central Park. I was walking around, checking the car. A man came over to me and without prompting started telling me my future. It's too horrible to tell you." Or, "Deborah has won a prize for one of her sculptures (it was made of mud and none of us understood it, but everyone at the state art council says it is brilliant). In the meantime, Yosemí has taken to hanging around the cathedral plaza, singing with a group of young people who all seem too earnest. She came home wearing a crucifix around her neck. No one has said anything. My father-in-law stares at it with his good eye—which is not so good anymore. We say nothing—no one here ever says anything."

Orlando's feverish pitches kept me awake—I knew something was stirring inside me, something ancient and wistful. I'd write back immediately, short letters like his but loaded with questions and doubts, sometimes two or three or four messages a day, whenever I got inspired, that were often more like journal entries, conversations with my own confused self about everything from the most mundane and sappy song lyric to the importance of rain and my father's obsessions with heaven.

I had never, ever, talked with anyone about these things, never confessed these tiny torments directly to another soul, and I would find myself exhilarated with our exchanges one day, terrified the next.

Leni's accident cost her not just a degree of motor skills but her lover at the time, who couldn't endure the antiseptic medical center or the tediousness of physical therapy and left her while she was still held together by wires in her hospital bed.

I stuck around, not because I'm any more decent, but because I wanted to be perceived that way. We were well beyond the possibility of jealousy or reconciliation, but onto some other plane where we acknowledged the inevitability of our intimacy but no longer found desire between us convincing or worthwhile.

"Get out of here! Get out of here!" Leni screamed red-faced when I came through the door one day at the hospital.

I got only a glimpse of her: rolled on her side, the hospital gown damp and twisted about her like a straitjacket, her white arms still stuck with tubes, and the wires suspended above her. Behind her, a nurse bent between her legs, parting the half moons of her slender bottom with gloved hands and wiping at something that exhumed a dreadful stench.

"Get the fuck out of here!" Leni shrieked, crying, her lips swollen.

She managed to somehow upset the night table, sending a lamp and the phone smashing to the floor. A small box of juice with a straw sticking out of it tumbled to my feet. I stepped back, practically pushed out by the strength of her will. I stood outside her hospital door, flat against the wall, listening to my own heart and Leni sobbing, berating the nurse all the while.

I tried to imagine Leni needing help but just as I was conjuring her leaning on my arm to get in and out of the bathtub, or maybe rolling into bed at night, the image of her in my head would leap up, absolutely defiant, and throw javelins, lift two-ton trucks, and run.

Yet knowing that in real life Leni would soon be propped up on a bar stool making wisecracks during salsa night at some dance club made all my conclusions too benign. I realized how easy it had been for me all along, because we didn't have any expectations, to come to the hospital bearing flowers and smiles, knowing at night I'd be in my own bed, certain of both its solitude and abundance.

Maybe, I thought, Leni's treasonous lover, with her brutal, immaculate honesty, had done the right thing after all. In her place, I might have thought twice, too, about how we could fit together, if there might not be new, endless cavities in Leni's body in which I might just drown from pain and eventual regret.

Years ago, when I was a kid, the women in my family—my aunt, all my cousins, and I (my mother refused to participate, skipping the beach altogether)—would sit on the shore in Miami Beach during vacations and comment derisively about the elderly Jewish women who wore two-piece bathing suits and swam a mile or two every day. Their skins would sag along the elbows and knees, collecting freckles and dark patches on their shoulders and backs. This, I imagined years later, is what Leni would look like when she retired, how she would spend her time away from me.

"¡Qué ridículas!" my tía Gladys would say about the Jewish women, forgetting her mother-in-law and her own daughters' destinies. (I always imagined there was a twisted jealousy to all this, as if she knew they were the women Mike Kauf would have been with if fate hadn't intervened and introduced her to him.)

We'd spread out on lounge chairs and beach towels, all copious thighs and generous bellies, and watch the Jewish women stroking the water. We'd pretend to pity them, preferring to think they were abandoned by heartless families back in New York and Arizona instead of so obviously independent.

I'd join the fun, too, but after everyone had lost interest, I'd still be watching the Jewish women, their strong feet kicking up white foam as they neared the horizon. Their powerful arms arched flawlessly over the water, cutting through the air like strategic missiles.

"Tell me you love me," Leni whispered to me one morning during her recovery as I helped her from the bed to the bathroom. She was back at her own place by then. Her arms sort of flopped around my neck. "Tell me you still love me, at least a little."

I kissed her cheek and hauled her up on her feet. "I love you," I said. Her girlfriend was gone, every bit of her obliterated from Leni's apartment. It was like the Russians in Cuba, erased without a trace.

"Okay," she said as we shuffled together down the hall to the bathroom, "now tell me in Spanish, for old times' sake."

"Te quiero," I said, smiling, because it was true still.

Leni pulled away. "That's not how you used to say it," she said, not with her usual sarcasm, but with her voice hushed and small, sore like her wounds.

"Sure I did," I said, plopping her down on the toilet. Her left leg jutted out, unable to bend, the pins a gift from Dr. Frankenstein.

"No, I remember: te amo," she said, her balance uneasy. I immediately wondered if she might be abusing any one of her many medications.

"It's te quiero now."

"What? Your Spanish Language Royal Dickhead Academy eliminated te amo?"

This is the beauty of Leni: At any given time, she retains just enough detail about what's important to make you feel like she's really listening.

"No, no, but you and I . . . you know, we're just te quiero, it was always te quiero underneath, that's why it works, that's why I'm here," I said.

Leni guffawed. "Oh please," she said. "You're here 'cause, let's face it, there's some sick kick in seeing me not so cute anymore. I bet you think if this had happened earlier, there wouldn't have been so many others, so much damage to us." She took a breath. "Aw, hell, you're all fucked up, you don't know what you want. . . ."

She didn't just mean me, but us—Latinos, probably cubanos in particular.

It's not just a prejudice on her part, although I wouldn't be surprised if Leni's bitterness had turned that way without her realizing it. What she meant was that we have a twisted way of expressing love: Te quiero, from the verb querer, doesn't mean love at all, but desire. Querer is to want, to yearn for.

But here's the madness: Querer is quotidian, what you say to parents and friends, cousins and children. Querer is love designed strictly for living things. You can't querer a movie the way you can love a film in English, you can't querer arroz con pollo or a bicycle or a particular and comfortable old pair of shoes (although, just to be confusing, you can querer arroz con pollo in the sense that you can have a taste for it and want some). Querer always implies an imperfect and human bond. Combine querer with any number of other words and its latent urgency shines through: como quiera, anyhow; cuando quiera, anytime; donde quiera, anywhere.

Amar is so much more precise: love, romantic love. It's the stuff of both the most lyrical poetry and the tackiest soap opera, making it virtually impossible—especially among Cubans, I think—to say with a straight face. Te amo practically requires that you recite a quick verse by Federico García Lorca and cut your veins. I said it to Leni in moments of complete adoration but more likely because there were no knowledgeable witnesses, no one to make me follow through on its real and complete usage.

"Te amo is so cold, don't you think?" my father once asked when we were discussing this very subject.

"Cold?" I was stunned. This was, I'd always thought, the most wildly intense and amorous thing you could say to a lover. How could that be cold?

"Well, it's so formal, so sharp, " he said, embarrassed. "It's nothing you could say to someone with whom you're ticklish or playful . . . I mean . . ."

"Don't you say it to Mami?"

"Oh my god no," he said, chortling. "She'd never take me seriously again!"

Like querer, you can't really amar a thing either; it's generally reserved for person-to-person application. In fact, you really can't love inanimate objects in Spanish; it's an emotion for warm bodies, sentient beings. A cat maybe, a parrot, perhaps a car if it's been anthropomorphed enough.

In Spanish, if you like something very, very much, if you love it the way you might love books or flowers in English, you are then enchanted by them (me encantan) or you like them (me gustan) and you use tone and context to convey your deep, deep affection that's awfully close to but never quite love.

But gustar is tricky, too. It's versatile, good for both people and things. But while you can gustar trains and postage stamps and music by Arsenio Rodríguez, you have to be careful when it applies to individuals. That's because gustar, like querer, is chock-full of lust. In other words, while you can gustar your lifeless leather jacket and no one will necessarily think you kinky, the minute that you gustar your mother-in-law, as opposed to just liking her, you have crossed all lines of propriety.

The safest thing to do in Spanish, it turns out, is to always be encantada—enchanted—perpetually caught in some kind of spell or trance, this way your actions are not necessarily entirely your own.

When I return to Cuba in 1997, Moisés and Orlando pick me up at the airport, which is as airless and hot as ever, except now it is full of happy Canadian and Spanish businessmen (no women) chattering on their cell phones. Although Havana has been rocked by a series of bombings—as many as ten explosions and at least one dead Italian tourist—there's a party atmosphere the whole way through customs, with the soldiers from the Ministry of the Interior now playing second fiddle to the young, blue-blazered hosts from Havanatur and the other agencies that facilitate the bureaucracy for foreigners. New TV monitors on the walls loop scenes from Cuban variety shows featuring salsa bands that play to American tastes.

On the way to their home—I couldn't fathom staying at a hotel this time—all Moisés can talk about is how the Florida Marlins will surely win the upcoming World Series because their pitcher, the young Liván Hernández, is a Cuban trained by the revolution. I understand it's a way to avoid more troubling topics so I just go along with him.

"But is it true what they say," I ask, "that his older brother, El Duque, is much better?"

"Oh yes, oh yes," gushes Moisés as Orlando looks on via the rearview mirror. He's driving. I'm sitting up front on the passenger side, half turned to talk to the old man, who leans forward, his chin on the back of my seat.

"Not that it matters," mutters Orlando. When I arrived, we kissed and hugged each other but awkwardly; it's as if we know one another too well yet not at all—both at once—as if we'd seen each other naked by accident.

"What do you mean?" I ask.

Moisés suddenly leans back in his seat.

"Oh, he doesn't like to talk about it," says Orlando, nodding at Moisés in the mirror. "It doesn't matter how good El Duque is because the government won't let him play, that's why. And even my father-in-law has a hard time explaining that."

Moisés looks at me, shrugs, and closes his eyes. He drops his chin on his chest like a petulant child. For the rest of the ride, it's impossible to tell if he's asleep or just pretending.

"No es fácil," says Orlando, resigned.

As we drive into the city I recognize the road as the place where Orlando and I pulled over. Although this is a sunny, sleepy afternoon, the highway doesn't look significantly different from ten years ago. There are thickets of palms, prickly green and yellowing bushes along the sides, clouds of mosquitos and massive blue flies visible even from the speeding car. The remains of an unlucky cane rat lie flat and bloody across the pavement.

Along the way, the houses are gray, grayer still, the wooden boards slicker, but—with the exception of a huge, almost ridiculous Benetton ad—the billboards boast revolutionary slogans just like before: "En Cuba, no habrá gobierno de transición." A huge, ocher-colored truck in front of us pulls a trailer with a hump; it's filled with people wearing the same cool, impertinent faces as a decade ago. Orlando passes it with a quick swerve.

"Tell me about Celina," I say.

He's a little startled. "She's doing well," he says, unsteadily.

"Still friends?" I ask, but I'm looking out, away from him. There are loose dogs, breathlessly watching from the dried patches of grass along the way. They stare at us, as if remembering a time when they chased cars with impunity. From a long line of black figures on the horizon, there's a constant, hollow barking.

"Still friends," he says, nodding for emphasis. He looks at me expectantly, raises his brow.

"Just friends?"

"Ah," he says, nodding more assertively, suddenly understanding my meaning. "I forgot that you knew . . . she told me. Yes, just friends. We were always just friends." He glances at the backseat, either to check on Moisés or out of paranoia. The old man's bowed head bounces along with the bumps in the road.

"She told you what?"

"You saw . . . right?"

"Right." We're silent for a bit. "You loved her, no?" (I'm using querer.)

"Always, still do. She is very special. To you, too, I think."

I'm a bit taken aback. "I don't even know her, Orlando," I say.

"Yes, well . . ."

"But did you love her?" I persist. (Now I'm using amar.)

Orlando laughs. "You mean, was I in love with her? Is that what you're asking me?"

He takes a turn, tosses me toward him, then shakes his head in amusement. In the backseat, Moisés rolls from side to side.

"What's so funny?" I ask, annoyed.

"What a question!" he says. He's grinning, as if I've just asked for the map to the fountain of youth.

"It's a real question," I insist.

"I'm sure," he says. We pass my parents' old apartment, which I note is green with mold and decay, boarded up as always. Downstairs, on the first floor of the same building, Celina's rooms open to the world with sheer white curtains on the windows, their hems dancing on the sills and reminding me of her feathery dress ten years ago, the way her sun-kissed skin simmered underneath.

"You're not going to answer, are you?" I ask Orlando. I'm suddenly cranky, restless. I scan the area in front of my family's old lodging, furtively surveying every window, every crack in every door for a glimpse of Celina, but I'm rewarded only with empty hallways, chipped walls, shadows.

Orlando pulls up to their house, which is weathered and looks lopsided now, but I hardly notice. I'm now taking him in: his crooked nose, the creases around his sad brown eyes, the papery blue shade of his lids, the tight coils of silver on his head.

"I know what you're thinking," he says, sitting there in the hot, bright stillness of the afternoon. There's not a peep from Moisés in the backseat, just a steady breathing. "Let me say this: I know what you saw and what it looks like," Orlando continues. "I don't think I can explain so you'll understand. My wife and I . . . we were not really married."

"You've explained that part already," I tell him.

Orlando nods in embarrassment. "Yes, yes, but I know what's going on in your head. "

"No, you don't."

"I do, I do . . ."

Orlando insists, though he can't possibly know. I'm imagining that night on the road, the way I made his lip bleed as he reached into me. I'm gazing at his once elegant, satiny hands now cracked and swollen on the steering wheel.

"I was lonely . . . it's not an excuse. And she and I were friends and there were things she wanted me to teach her . . . I was older . . . and willing, very willing."

I can't read him. I can't tell if this is a confession or a statement of facts or perhaps even a clever, subversive sort of boast. "She was fourteen," I finally say.

"So was your great-grandmother Leah when she married Ytzak," he says.

"That was, like, a hundred years ago . . ."

"Do you think they went through any more, or less, a hundred years ago than we have, here and now? Do you think—what?—they were more mature?"

"Do you think that's an excuse?"

"I never slept with her, I observed limits." This, finally, is his trump card, his final offer.

"You expect me to believe that?"

"Yes."

"Why should I?"

Then he smirks—I recognize the smirk—it's the same one he gave Angela when she only brought him a half glass of milk.

"Well, first," he says, "because you need to . . ." He takes a breath, looks faraway, finally smiles (in an almost forced and inevitable surrender), then turns to me. Just like a decade ago, he's lacking a sense of triumph at the most critical moment. Instead, his downcast eyes betray what is almost a plea. "And second," he continues in a barely audible and melancholy whisper, "because you love me."

He uses the verb querer.

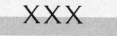

XXX

My father suffered his first heart attack in March of 1997. He was sitting at his desk in the basement, felt a jab in his chest, and hauled himself up the stairs, feeling every prickling inch of his huge mass, a thread of white froth following him until he dropped on my mother's kitchen floor like a porpoise twitching on the shore.

After that, my father began to spontaneously repeat lines from poems and books he'd translated. "Viento del Este: un farol y el puñal en el corazón," he'd whisper to nothing and no one, not even glancing at his yellow legal pads. "East wind: a torch, a dagger in the heart."

He'd wince and touch his chest, then place his palms down as if already retired, simply waiting to be treated to a final manicure. In the heart attack's aftermath, he seemed to constrict, so that suddenly he was not as tall or formidable. His shoulders slumped, his cheeks drooped and folded under his beard. In the shroud of light from his reading lamp next to the rocker, he appeared pious to the extreme, almost afraid. His hair, which had always been silky, was suddenly dry and brittle and his whiskers scratched when I kissed him.

"It's Cuba," said my mother, fingering the bluish mole on her face.

"Cuba?" I asked.

Actually, I wasn't surprised by her diagnosis—since the fall of the Berlin Wall years before, my mother had become engrossed in all things Cuban. She'd subscribed to various newspapers and newsletters from Miami-based exile groups, publications with screaming headlines about Communist infiltrations and Fidel's certain demise. In each room in the house, including the bathroom, my mother had placed a short-wave radio tuned to different stations throughout the hemisphere just to keep track of events and rumors back on the island. In this way, the whole house was constantly buzzing; the only space safe from the static was the cool quiet of my father's basement refuge.

In the last few years, my mother had also bought a computer and learned enough about the Internet so she could participate in chat room and newsgroup discussions about the island. (Her screen name: MamaChola, the name for Ochún in palo monte; her password: aché, Yoruba for grace, a blessing.) Because of all this, she was able to anticipate Fidel's announcement of the pope's visit, the commercialization of Ché on the thirtieth anniversary of his death, and the first breathless broadcast from CNN's brand-new bureau on the shores of Havana, as omnipotent and azure as ever. When Ernesto Menach disappeared, it was my mother I relied on for information and contacts about where to make inquiries.

Curiously, in spite of all this my mother did not stake out a political position. She had one, of course, but more than anything else, she had questions. On the Internet, she'd lurk and listen, popping in only when something intrigued her. No matter how much she was baited, she knew to extricate herself from the endless diatribes, from the polemics and posturings that always accompany such debates. She'd submit her query—always about Fidel's health, the weather on a particular day in Havana, the availability and price of certain items, and how things might be for people she cared about who had stayed behind—and then she'd sit back and wait.

But while Cuba was clearly her mania—the Elegguá was now a proud cultural artifact, evidence of nationality as much as spirituality, resting openly in a corner of the living room—it had never been my father's. As I well knew, for him Cuba was an endless dream, something he indulged in only for my mother, only as a part of his matrimonial promise.

Still, my mother insisted: "He's getting sicker, and it's because of Cuba."

We both watched him, diminishing before our eyes, the books thicker and graver in his hands. When he'd look up to try and catch our eyes, there was something vulnerable and desolate there and we'd look away quickly, all of us embarrassed.

She had a theory: "The problem with being born on an island," she said, "is that you get used to gazing at the horizon. You develop a longing for whatever's on the other side—the island always looks small and miserable compared to what you've imagined beyond. Then, one fine day, you leave the island, and you go out into the world and discover something terrible: You have not beaten the habit of looking at the horizon, of yearning for what's invisible to you. And so you find yourself consumed with nostalgia."

As she spoke, my father stacked CDs for his new pastime, swaying back and forth in his chair with his eyes closed, listening to María Teresa Vera, Bola de Nieve, and the Vieja Trova Santiaguera.

(Later, when I hear this soft, often melancholy music again in Havana, it doesn't recall an idyllic Cuba for me but, paradoxically, the cozy confines of my parents' home in Rogers Park, my father rocking, a knitted afghan about his lap.)

After his illness my father was slowed enough that he had to admit he couldn't do his work. Medication robbed him of his sharpness, a sense of fragility kept him from engaging with authors in the robust dialogues that he had so enjoyed before.

To my surprise, he didn't insist on martyrdom, didn't let pride exhort him to finish work that would ultimately be deemed mediocre, or at the very least, not his best. (My father loved to race himself, to hold up each subsequent job against the one just completed and measure the new distances his mind had traveled, the fresh meanings he'd extracted like rare gems from the deepest caves.)

So when he realized he could barely keep his eyes open for more than a few hours at a time, when the yellow Dixon Ticonderoga No. 2s he preferred fell through his beautiful fingers and rolled on the desktop, he called and asked me to please finish a few projects already begun, particularly a prison novel by a young Cuban Genet named José Farraluque. My father did not choke when he called me, did not express regret or distaste but rather sighed, resigned, explaining that it was a difficult assignment to which he could trust no one else. He said he would be there by my side, the angel Gabriel, if I needed him.

What astonished me most when my father asked me to complete the job for him, besides that he might actually delegate to me such an awesome responsibility, was the fact that Farraluque was not an exile flung to one of the far corners of the diaspora, but a Cuban sitting in Havana itself, bitching and moaning in his own way, but refusing to cross the blue borders of the Caribbean.

"Did you know?" I asked.

My father shrugged, the bones of his shoulders like the horizontal pole of a marionette.

I combed Farraluque's manuscript, stunned by the lurid sexuality and graphic violence my father had decided to tackle. It seemed a million miles from García Lorca's precise lyrics and the dazzling labyrinths he'd traversed to bring someone like, say, Octavio Paz into an easy, almost conversational English.

This was one of the great mysteries about my father's genius: Most translators work best into, not from, their native language, using instinct to access the vernacular, the familiar. But my father did it both forward and backward, into and from his native Caribbean Spanish into a pure, songlike American tongue, as serious or cheeky as necessary, with a New England clip, the airy haze of southern California, or the wholesomeness of Wisconsin.

There, among the notes for Farraluque's racy story, were words I'd never heard my father pronounce in any language: for pinga in Spanish he offered dick, cock, man-sword, worm of death, shlong in English (or Yiddish, as was the case of the latter). Where in heaven's name had he picked up this stuff? I couldn't fathom him skulking at the bus station or even glancing at the kind of pornography that would reveal these terms to him.

"Papi," I said laughing, "this is smut!" I'm not a prude, not at all above using these words myself in everyday conversation, but they seemed as unlikely out of my father's mouth as big sticky bubbles of gum.

"It's literature," he said, nodding, "brilliant, modern literature."

Even though he seemed to be joking, I knew he'd never have agreed to the project if he didn't believe in it.

"Shlong?" I said, holding up the page with his notes. "Where the heck did you learn shlong?"

"I have secret lives, don't you know that by now?" he said, using his toes to push himself back in the rocker, his lids trembling shut, a satisfied grin on his face.

It was Pesaj (not that my parents acknowledged this in any way) when my mother heard the news on the radio that rocked her and my father that spring.

The kitchen counter was a cornucopia of vegetables she intended to slice and chop for a hearty soup she hoped to present to my father. From her garden, the afternoon light shone through the windows, as resplendent as the breezy day blooming outside. While she cooked, my mother would gaze at her roses and the stiff-necked sunflowers stretching to the sky.

On the airwaves, excited announcers had been prattling on about the palestinos, not the Palestinians from the Middle East but the country folk in Cuba who'd migrated to Havana and were now being forcibly returned to their small towns and destitute farms in the interior. A dizzying smell of garlic and cumin, onions and green peppers swirled from the stove.

In the living room, my father rocked in his chair, his face pinned with a beatific smile as he listened to Ignacio Piñero: "Viandas, qué ricas son las viandas . . ." The singer rode on top of a soapy mix of

rhythms, the backup vocalists a nasally bunch who looped their refrain around the naughty improvisations. Between his fingers, my father let burn a Cuban puro, its ashes sprinkling my mother's floor.

Though I lived apart from them, I was spending more and more
time at their house, in part to help my mother take care of my father, but also because it made the Farraluque translation move faster
with my father nearby. Since I preferred working on a computer to
his method of pencil and paper, I had brought my laptop and set it
up in the den, making that my office by default. I told myself it was
easier for my father to pad his way around the first floor of the
house; it took me a while to admit I was also overwhelmed by the
idea of working at his desk, imagining myself filling up that immense and exacting throne.

For the first night of Pesaj that year I was joining friends, as I always did, right in the neighborhood. One of the seder regulars—the
freckled-face Latvian boy who'd spied my father davening in the
basement years before—had married an Iranian Jewish woman
who'd left Tehran only a few years ago and was still longing for her
homeland, insisting that if she could, she'd return. It had spun us all
into a whirl about exile, and we'd planned an evening of readings
around that rather obvious topic to supplement our usual haggadah.

For myself I had chosen (guilty, frustrated as always at my father's refusal to confirm what I already knew to be true) a small
snippet from Psalm 137: "By the rivers of Babylon, there we sat
down, yea, we wept, when we remembered Zion. We hanged our
harps among the willows in the midst thereof. For they that carried
us away captive required of us a song; and they that wasted us required of us mirth, saying, Sing us one of the songs of Zion. But how
shall we sing the Lord's song in a strange land?"

Almost by accident, our group had become increasingly Sephardic over the years. Even though there were still some Askenazis
among us—the Latvian boy, a few Poles—we'd been joined by the
sons and daughters of refugees from Iraq and Yemen, exiles from Ar-
gentina and Brazil. Our texts reflected this, with the Hebrew pronounced slightly different from what our Askenazi friends used. The

meal ignored gefilte fish and included rice, often with nuts and dates and other sweet things more reminiscent of Spain and the Middle East than the cool climes of Eastern Europe.

I'd just finished taking a shower in my old bathroom—the air was foggy and damp and infused with the smell of violets—when I heard my mother's voice downstairs.

"Enrique, did you . . . did you hear?" she asked, her voice wavering. From her volume, I knew the exact distance from her to me and that she was standing at the door between the kitchen and the living room, wiping her hands nervously with a dish towel. And for reasons I've never understood, at that moment I felt my gut twist. I grabbed my robe and rushed downstairs, hitting the last step just as my father was turning to her, a slow motion pivot during which his eyes opened quizzically, brows arching.

"Arturo Sandoval . . ." my mother said.

"Arturo Sandoval?" I asked, surprised and confused. The former horn player with Irakere? What could he have done? Had he committed a terrible crime? Had he died? And if so, why would my mother be so muddled? My parents were not jazz fans, and Sandoval, to my knowledge, was neither a relative nor friend.

"I heard it on the news . . ."

"¿Qué, Mami, qué?"

My father gazed at her. He had a kind of expectant halo about him, his thin frigate of bones tipped forward in the rocking chair, suspended in time.

"He was refused citizenship," said my mother, "American citizenship."

A black coarseness descended on my father's face. For a moment, he looked like an injured bird, a crow fallen from the skies.

"What?" I didn't understand.

She was flustered now. "They turned him down, Arturo, for U.S. citizenship," she said again, pronouncing each part separately. "Remember how he played at the president's inaugural?"

"But that doesn't make any sense," I said, convinced she'd misunderstood the report. "Cubans are always welcome here, always."

"No, no," my mother said, shaking her head, her hands wrapping themselves compulsively in and around the dish towel.

The news was peculiar, harsh, but their traumatized reactions seemed out of proportion to me. My father was motionless, his hands gripping the sides of the rocking chair. He stared into an abyss only he could see. I thought back to when the Berlin Wall fell, how he'd looked stricken and lost.

"Papi . . ." I said, brushing back the clumps of hair that had fallen on his forehead, casting dreadful shadows across his face. My mother continued nervously rolling the dish towel between her hands, the skin red on her fingers.

"He's a man without a country," my father whispered through dry, tender lips.

"I'm sure there's been some sort of mistake," I said.

They both shook their heads, surrendering to a terrible inevitability only they seemed to understand.

"This always happens to me," my father sighed, tears welling. His lashes were shiny and wet, dangling tiny diamonds from each lush tip.

"What? What always happens to you?" I asked, disconcerted, wondering what mystical message they were deriving from what I was sure was just a bureaucratic snafu with Sandoval.

"This, this," he said, as cryptically as ever, waving his hand like I imagined old man Olinsky had done at him so many years ago.

Less than a week later, we learned that Dulce María Loynaz, one of Cuba's greatest poets and a friend and favorite of my father's, had died in Havana at age ninety-four.

"I am the survivor of a generation of poets," she had told him in a letter years earlier. "I even outlived myself, which is the worst thing that can happen to a person."

My mother took to the Internet and printed out as many messages as she could about Dulce María to read to my father, including an eyewitness account of her internment at Colón Cemetery posted by a Costa Rican journalist.

But no matter what my mother did, whether she read him Dulce María's intense and intimate verse or rubbed the knots on his neck and shoulders with her sage hands, my father remained despondent, weeping uncontrollably at the most unexpected moments. He refused to eat, refused to take his medicines, refused to speak on the phone, dictate correspondence, or help me with Farraluque.

Then in May came the news that Gastón Baquero, a Cuban poet who wrote about memory and magic, had died of a cerebral hemorrhage. Since Fidel's rise to power in 1959, he had been in exile in Spain, quietly jotting down poems that arrived at our house in handwritten sheaths tucked into manila envelopes.

"Well," said my father with his labored breath, "Dulce María was wrong; clearly, going on now is what would be the very, very worst thing."

XXXI

After two days at Northwestern Memorial Hospital, my father came
home to die, in the dim and golden halo of my mother's votive candles. His lips were still soft and perfect but we all knew the life in
him was ebbing. Soon his fever would pass and the sheets on the
bed would be as velvety smooth as if they'd been airing out on a
winter night in Havana.

My mother and I made the decision to bring him home after the
doctor at the hospital shrugged her shoulders and sighed. She was
about my age, only grayer, certainly wiser-looking. My mother said
nothing, just stood there, her eyes wandering over the immaculate,
flowered wallpaper in the waiting room. She followed the design—
the sweep of a leaf, the graceful reach of the blooming buds—as if
looking for the telltale flaw of connection, the tiny leap from one
sheet of flowers to the other, the gap that inevitably exists no matter
the workman's care and trepidation.

There were no crucifixes on the wall, no sounds from outside coming in through the hermetically sealed windows and the
thick, rubbery curtains, no water to be spied twinkling on the horizon. It was all dry land, sour aftertastes. I stood there as well, my rib
cage imploding, my heart pierced by brittle, broken bones. All the
air left my body, just as it was slowly but inevitably leaving my
father's.

Finally, my mother blinked. The doctor peered at me, her eyes
wet but empty. When she unexpectedly took my hand, pointing
with her head back at the room with my father—what was left of

my father—I wanted to say, "That bundle of sticks under the covers? That's not my real father." I wanted to shake my hand out of hers and whirl like a dervish. I wanted to shout: "You should have seen my father! With his wide girth, his shy smile and shiny eyes."

But I just nodded numbly instead, more or less like I did later, as a local parish priest came through the front door of our Rogers Park home, his face even more tearful and meaningless than the doctor's back at the hospital. He glanced at the mezuzah I'd placed on the door frame a few weeks back—a little soft leather roll-up—then looked away, as if he'd decided it was something else, a shadow maybe, or a snail.

"Oh, Mrs. San José, I'm so . . ." he whispered to my mother, his voice trailing off. He was wiry and bent, in need of a haircut and anxious. He was the result of a sudden spurt of my mother's Catholicism, a last-ditch effort to keep my father alive. I stared at my mother in disbelief but she was a blank space, as hollow as the priest's condolences.

"Ale, por favor," said my tía Gladys, signaling something concerning the priest.

My mother and aunt sat him down in one of my father's chairs—the graceful Cuban-style rocker in the living room that still held the shape of his great body. My cousins aped their mother like ladies-in-waiting, each one a mirror reflection: round and buttery. The priest, catered to by the women in my family as if he were a prince or a groom, was a beehive fallen from a tree, surrounded by a barely contained panic. Mr. and Mrs. Choy floated like ghosts in the hall. She held a large metal bowl of rice, a gift no doubt, sprinkled with scallions and sprouts from her garden.

My aunt waved at me again. I was right outside the den, which had been turned from my office into my father's sick room. "Por dios," she said, exasperated. "Help us, Ale." She stomped over to me. "Get the father something to drink, please." My cousins, idle and indignant, shadowed her.

"No, no," I said, shaking my head. Mr. and Mrs. Choy glanced up, their eyebrows twitching on their otherwise flat satin foreheads.

"What do you mean 'no, no'?" Tía Gladys asked, incredulous, looking at me as if I'd lost my mind. The cousins gasped.

"I can't help you," I said.

"¿Qué qué?" Tía Gladys's face was all scrunched up, annoyed. She scanned the room for her husband, the weight-lifting dentist, but he was lost behind the cousins, the Choys, and a small group of my father's students who'd stopped by to pay a visit. "This is no time, Ale, for whatever is going on with you. We need to do this soon, before your father dies. The Last Rites don't count if he's already gone. Get the father some water, please, some Coca-Cola—his throat is dry."

"I can't, Tía, I'm sorry, I can't help with this. You guys didn't even discuss it with me!"

"With you? With *you*?" It was as if she'd been stung by a loose bee, her face distorted. "Why should we consult you?" In Gladys's world, my father was my mother's province. Even I was an intruder.

"I'm his daughter, remember?" I looked to my cousins for support but they seemed temporarily confused.

In my head, I was already plotting how I was going to sneak into my father's room after they were all gone, with their incense and oils, how I would have a private, final audience with my father's body. I'd clean his fingernails, buff them with cloth as he had done in life. It would be a small gesture, the tiniest symbolism, but it would be something.

Master of the Universe! Have compassion for Enrique Elías, son of Luis and Sima, for he is a descendant of Abraham, Isaac, and Jacob. . . . May he tread with righteous feet into the Garden of Eden, for that is the place of the upright, and god protects the pious.

I was deep in my reverie when my mother came up to me leading the black-garbed priest, the rosary dripping from his fingers. I was about to protest—about to repeat the whole business of not being consulted, about to tell my mother how inappropriate I thought it was to have this man here—when she leaned up and kissed my cheek with her moist lips.

"This is not for him, not for you," she said, meaning the priest.

"It's for me. We'll do something else, something for you and him, later. Isn't there something to be done later?"

The door opened to the den before I could answer. They disappeared, the priest mumbling. Incense wafted from inside, pungent and yellow in the candlelight. I listened to them praying on the other side of the closed door, a hive buzzing. And I remembered that the tropical variety—the only kind native to Cuba, the only bee on the island before the Spaniards arrived—is stingerless, capable of defending its territory only by distracting the enemy.

If my tía Gladys had asked, I wouldn't have been able to explain. Even though I stood by, in my own mind insisting on my and my father's Jewish souls, I fear if called to testify I might have breathed nothing but empty air, my mouth wide apart in an O, mute and cowardly.

Why? It's in my genes, just like my father's, a DNA string that carries scratched into its intricate binding sparks from broken vessels and ancient light. But unlike my father—whose anxieties are historical, whose worries are based on the knowledge that he could not hide his Jewishness even if he tried—mine is exactly the opposite: What I fear is discovery, not as a Jew but as a fraud.

I have only claimed to be Jewish once in my life: at the airport in Indianapolis, on my way home from deposing a Mexican farmhand in Martinsville, Indiana, home of the Ku Klux Klan. He had watched a piece of machinery completely swallow his teenage son, spitting him out in a completely unrecognizable and bloody mash. At the airport, I was minding my own business when two fresh-faced young white Hoosiers approached me with vinyl-bound Bibles.

"Have you found Jesus yet, ma'am?" asked the young man, well-scrubbed and plain, his shirt ironed stiff.

I was reading *Newsweek* behind dark glasses. I was sipping black coffee from a Styrofoam cup and thinking about that poor man back on the unyielding farm, where he and his grieving wife had lived for twenty years and owned nothing more than a tin trailer, a TV, and a hot plate.

"Ma'am?" asked the young man again.

I studied him over my sunglasses.

"We're here to talk to you about Jesus Christ, Our Lord," said his companion, a young woman in a yellow rayon dress.

"I thought you weren't allowed to peddle at the airport," I said.

"We're not selling nothing," the girl said with a strained smile. "We just want to talk to you."

"I'm a Jew," I said.

The boy stumbled; he quickly glanced at his partner, his mouth agape, unclear about what to do next, but the girl stood her ground. "That's okay," she said. "Jesus was a Jew, too."

I've never done that again, never used Judaism as a front or shield, no matter the temptation. The irony of it all didn't escape me even then—to tell the truth, the immediate truth, would have only encouraged the proselytizers. I knew as I stared them down that what I was seeking was protection, authenticity, weight. What I really wanted to say was that I belonged to something so powerful, so strong, that it would repel them.

And yet the reason I'm not a Jew—a real Jew, a public Jew—is because claiming that very same identity five hundred years ago before a vicious Spanish council would not have protected my ancestors. If they stood up to the Santo Oficio and said "I'm a Jew," they would have been tortured, perhaps killed, certainly mocked and ridiculed. Being Jews guaranteed their suffering. It is because they were Jews then, in that moment, at that time, choosing to embrace their Jewishness at all costs, even at the cost of lying and pretending to be something else, that I cannot be one now.

But when those kids approached me with their Bibles tucked under their arms, I was clear-voiced: "I am a Jew." It didn't stop them, of course, they continued their preaching, condescendingly telling me that there are many Jews who believe in Christ, that Judaism is just a beginning. They talked and talked, but when they finally walked away, exhausted, the pages of their Bible wilted, I had not been converted.

I'm a Jew.

It was for my father, for Luis and Sima, for Leah and Ytzak—and for me. In that moment, under siege in a sterile airport, I avenged the injustices of five hundred years ago, even if for only an instant, even if only in my own small way.

XXXII

When it came to translation, my father's method was always the same: use the clearest, most lucid language; the point is always and above all to communicate. Nothing was ever too complicated, too obtuse. Even when the original was deliberately vague, my father found ways to bring it into the light.

But on the topic of his own life, he retreated from his profession, preferred to talk as if what had happened was just beyond his grasp, a mystery so deep even his finely honed talent of investigating meaning was completely eluded. By the time my father died, I understood that well enough to know I'd always have a million unanswered questions. I'd have to be satisfied with reading signs, with looking at his life as parable or prophecy. I knew I was destined to be an acolyte at Delphi.

In spite of my mother's best efforts to save my father from extinction, to cut deals with African and Christian deities, he died with me as his only witness. It was not in the black of night but at dawn, with the sky painted in pastel ribbons, delicate fingers reaching in through the windows of the den. They seemed to cradle him, give him an olive tone, revive him for an instant. My father passed away wearing a halo of morning light.

Earlier, the strain of watching his life leak away had been too much for my mother, who at one point just collapsed and had to be given a sedative, convinced to rest upstairs in their vast and empty bed. My tía Gladys dozed on the living room couch, her husband

and daughters back in their own cozy home, waiting for the new day's vigil. I imagined their alarm clocks ringing, Mike Kauf buffing his biceps with a thirty-minute workout before calling in to cancel his appointments, my cousins all taking turns in the shower, pondering closets of inappropriately colorful clothing.

It had been a rough night. My father was ashen, sunken, often unrecognizable. His chest heaved, his purplish hands quivered like frightened starfish. Every breath was an effort. At about three in the morning, it was just him and me, my mother's candles, roses, and sunflowers. My father's prayer book—a gift from Ytzak, a sheath of powdery pages in Ladino published in Salonika shortly after the fall of the Ottoman Empire—was balanced on the blankets covering his spindly legs. We said nothing about it; it was understood, finally, that his secret was out.

I can't remember exactly what we were talking about—maybe it was the Farraluque translation, or the rumors swirling around Miami and Havana that Fidel had finally died because he didn't show up on the 26th of July to deliver his usual speech—but my father just looked up at me with stubborn tears, tears that wouldn't fall.

"Your mother . . ." he whispered, smiling, eyeing the makeshift altar she'd erected on top of the TV. It covered all her bases: flowers, rotting fruit, pieces of candy, novenas, a rosary coiled in a circle, and her Virgin of Charity. A small table held a handful of glasses of water (these would be stagnant, powerless) and a candle lit to Babalú-Ayé, the god of illnesses, depicted as an old white man on crutches on the label. All of this vanished whenever the parish priest arrived, shoved in the closet or under the bed, the candle trailing a silvery wisp that always prompted the cleric to ask if something was burning.

My father and I both laughed a little. He coughed, his body lifting off the bed each time, then falling back into it with a muffled thud. I knew both of us should have been elsewhere: Him, downstairs in his office, puffing on a puro, preparing notes for a lecture he'd deliver to a throng of adoring students somewhere in Mexico,

London, or New York; me, dancing somewhere, swiveling my hips like my mother, away from the usual heartache and boredom of my job, perhaps in the arms of someone sleek and sinewy.

"Alejandra . . ." my father said, his voice hoarse. No doubt there was pain there, effort, too. He rearranged his bones on the mattress, in the nest of pillows we'd built for him. "I need you . . ."

"I need you, too," I said, meaning it more than I could have ever imagined.

He closed his eyes in his kingly way—for a second, I confess, I held my breath, afraid they might not open again, and I made a million promises right then so that I might see myself reflected one more time in his deep, dark pools. "Yes," he said, smug, his lids rising in his usual condescendingly slow motion, "but, you see, I've always needed you." The tears still clung to the rims of his eyes, his lashes black and beautiful.

He could be infuriating even while dying, I thought.

"I . . . need a few things . . ." he said. He swallowed. "In my office . . ." Then he gave me instructions in his new elliptical style. And I understood that when I descended the stairs this time, I was breaking a seal, I was entering his Holiest of Holies.

In my father's office the light is different, clearer somehow, although there has always been less of it there than anywhere else in the house. It's a cave with an Amazonian waterfall, a bridge of bones, the secret passageway to another dimension. Whenever I stepped inside, I always felt my heart slow, its beat mute.

When I entered it on the night of his death, I breathed in the lingering sweetness of tobacco, the vague traces of cologne, the spice of his still living body. I stood there for a moment, on the threshold between the real world and his, trying to adjust my senses.

Through the play of light and gloom his desk appeared to me like a sailing ship, wooden and dark, Columbus's caravels—not imposing but efficient, sturdy, typical of Spain's conquering fleets. I could see him standing atop that smooth surface, like a captain

(Noah or Columbus, both a little mad), searching for land, for a white feathered bird to bring him a sign that somewhere there was a resting place, an Eden, a heaven.

I touched his desk chair, grand, padded like his own body had been once, and felt it like the pelt of an animal now surrendered to its own mortality. I might have heard a whimper, I might have heard a howl.

"You will be . . . returning to Cuba . . . no?" Every word my father spoke was a test balloon, an experiment in using a limited supply of oxygen.

"Yes," I said, "but I don't know when really. . . . I want to go, but I don't have much reason to, not really."

I opened the velvety white bags I'd brought up from his room, both relatively new, and pulled out his prayer shawl and the two little black boxes wrapped tight in their well-oiled leather laces. I don't know why I was surprised that my father's tefillin wasn't hundreds of years old. I suppose I had a romantic notion that they might have been passed down for centuries, that I'd inherit a relic infused with the spirits of many, many generations.

"Ytzak . . ." my father said, his chin pointing at the phylacteries, as if he'd read my mind. "A gift . . . bar mitzvah . . ."

"You were bar mitzvahed?" I was stunned.

He struggled with the prayer shawl, draping it over his head, then pulling it down around his shoulders like a scarf. "Not like here, no. No . . . my thirteenth birthday . . . that's bar mitzvah. No party."

"No Torah reading at the synagogue?"

He shook his head again, his Adam's apple twitched. "Not required . . . just birthday . . . then tefillin." For an instant, his eyes drifted back, as if he'd momentarily lost consciousness. "You will say kaddish for me?"

It was such an airy, hollow whisper I wasn't sure I'd heard right. I thought maybe I'd willed it, but then I saw him, his eyes drowning in tears. Mine were not as stubborn as his and as I nodded, they free-flowed down my cheeks, landing in huge circles on the sheet.

"Women . . . can say it . . . in private, it's okay. . . ."

As I stood there shivering, trying to pull myself together—*my father was dying, my father whom I absolutely adored, was dying*—I heard him pawing the blankets. I lifted the tefillin, one in each hand for him to see but he shook his head and kept searching like a blind man with his hand outstretched. I grabbed the bags but he waved them away, as annoyed as Olinsky had ever been.

"My siddur . . ." he croaked. His hair, which was now as wispy as cotton, was also extraordinarily long and fell in his face, further obscuring his view.

I put the tefillin in his hands and picked up his prayer book. The thin leather-bound volume shed a confetti of disintegrating pages as I lifted it into the air. Then my father motioned for me to open it. I lifted the cover. A black-and-white photograph dropped from it, zigzagging through the air until it landed on his thigh. When he bent his head down to look at it, his tears finally fell, one of them forming a ring of bloated moisture around the central figure.

"For Moisés," he mumbled.

I put down the prayer book and stared at the girl in the photo. "Who is she?" A swirl of script on the back said: "La Habana, 1939."

He opened his mouth and I could see his tongue gummy and white inside, struggling like Jonah trapped in the whale. "Moisés . . . can tell you. . . . Now, help me . . . help me with these. . . ." And he gestured at the boxes in his hands. "This one . . ."

I don't know where he got the strength but my father sat up for the binding. He held out his bony left arm while I moved the box up to what had once been his bicep and pulled on the strap. It was practically impossible to keep it from falling, and I feared that if it was knotted too tight there might be terrible consequences.

But my father, like an addict desperate to isolate a vein, yanked on the strap, breathing hard, his eyes bulging, then waved at me to help him wrap it around his forearm. I moved quickly, draping the leather ties over and over, watching the sweat form on his forehead even as the skin on his arm grew colder and colder. Knotting the straps to his hand and fingers was a complicated process, frustrating because I had no clue what I was doing and was trying to follow some sort of logic ("Ashkenazi . . ." he snorted at one of my efforts) and because I feared hurting him. His hand was puffy, bruised from where an IV had been.

"Baruch attah Adonai, elohainu melach ha olam," he mumbled, embarrassed.

When I reached for the other tefillin, he pushed me away, moved his legs to the side of the bed.

"You're going to stand?" I asked, horrified.

"I have to stand," he said with his typical condescension, as if it was all so obvious.

After a struggle, he managed to put his stockinged feet on the floor, his buckling knees locked as best they could, and he more or less sat on the edge of the bed, leaning forward.

Trembling, I lay the tefillin on his head, letting the box drop between his eyes—on a trip to Israel, I'd seen the old men at the Western Wall with them practically resting on the bridge of their noses—but my father cringed, aggravated. "Up! Up!" he practically shouted, as if he might throw a tantrum. I pushed it back, making his hair stand up in funny waves, white bursts like Olinsky's, but he reached up, felt the box with the tip of his swollen right hand and nodded approval.

He pulled the shawl up over his head. Then he picked up his prayer book, held it to his body, and actually tried to balance himself without help. I watched as he teetered, his eyes closed, the uneasy sway of his once magnificent and now emaciated torso creating a kind of natural although uneven davening.

At one point, he stumbled, as if his legs had given out for an instant. But I was standing in front of him and caught him. His body against mine felt like paper, the shawl a deflated kite, like something that could take flight if I gave it just enough of a push.

For a moment, I buried my nose in his shoulder, his hair smelling of tobacco now mixed with medicine and Vicks. As I stood him up, I didn't let go but maneuvered around him, so that I was standing behind him, my arms around his waist, my face against his wingless back. He was bony, his heart like a bird in a cage, each prayer sung sending powerful vibrations down his spine, into me.

I don't know how long we were rocking like that, only that it was until he finished and climbed into bed on his own, silently helping me remove the bindings. When I finished putting everything back where it belonged, he patted the bed and signaled me close to him. The August sun was washing in through the windows. I leaned in to him, waiting for his final words, but there was a quiet stillness instead.

XXXIII

"What?"

I sat stupefied in my parents' living room, unable to believe what my mother was telling me.

"Alejandra, please," she said. Her mouth was swollen from crying and biting, her eyes were red-rimmed. My tía Gladys sat on the couch with her arm around her, patting her shoulders and back to comfort and support her. My cousins and the undertaker were on their way, my father's body stiffening on his deathbed under Mike Kauf's watchful eye.

"I can't believe that," I said, tipping the rocking chair forward, bringing it as low as possible without slipping and falling.

"He wrote it out," my mother said, sniffling, her hand reaching out to my knee, turquoise twine underneath her pale skin. "Do you want to see it?"

"Nena!" my aunt protested. "You don't have to prove anything to her! If you say it's so, it's so! He was your husband!"

I turned away in disgust.

"Gladys, por favor," my mother pleaded. She shook her off, got up, and marched downstairs to my father's office.

My tía Gladys and I sat in silence. I stared at the floor and the wall and into the blackness. I felt my chest exposed, my bones seared by caustic winds. All the while, my aunt eyed me in disbelief and loathing.

My aunt, who wed Mike Kauf for love, always saw her marriage as some sort of spiritual battlefield. Early on, she convinced him that their children should be Catholic—strictly Roman, fully invested in the pope's infallibility—a decision I always thought he might have reconsidered if he'd realized her future fanaticism: Not just Catholic schooling for their primary and secondary education, but Catholic universities, too, DePaul and my father's beloved Loyola. (I graduated from Jesuit-run Loyola, too, with a degree in Spanish, but mostly because my father's position translated into free tuition.)

For my cousins, it was Catholic summer camps, church-approved movies, subscriptions to Catholic newspapers, antiabortion protests, passage on the cruise ship to see John Paul II in Cuba the following winter—the only reason to ever go back to the island, my aunt assured us, looking accusingly at me, while my father pondered aloud (but not in her presence) why, if seeing the pope was so vital, she hadn't traveled to Nicaragua or Nigeria during those papal trips, or why she'd settled for edge-of-the-park seats during his holiness's Chicago stops. . . .

Of course, in my aunt's eyes, my family had never set a particularly good example. My parents treated faith as an individual quest. I was baptized, certainly, but no great effort had ever been made to haul me off to church on Sundays or instill in me a particular vision. When I was a child my aunt had tried to include me in some of her family's hyper-Catholic activities, but my mother always asked me if I wanted to go, and when I saw that neither she nor my father were coming, I couldn't fathom why I should. My mother never forced me, even though my aunt tried to convince her I really wasn't old enough (ever) to decide these things, that I needed a stronger, firmer hand to guide me before I could make such decisions on my own.

Once, as a child, I'd asked my mother about the room in the basement reserved for her altar—next to my father's office, naturally—and she'd been good and patient and told me the story of the black women in her grandmother's kitchen. She told me, too, about how the Virgin of Charity had saved us on our escape from

Cuba, led us right into the warm waters of South Beach. The altar, which was modest by comparison to others I've seen since, was a way of giving back, my mother said. The Virgin was its center, surrounded by flowers, water, little gifts (always fruits and candies, never animals in the United States). The same room, however, had its practical purposes: This was where my mother kept the vacuum cleaner, where she accumulated clothing for charity that we'd outgrown or no longer favored, where she kept her photo albums and my old report cards.

A few times, I had helped my mother fill the glasses with water, scrubbing the rings formed from previous infusions, and I'd watch—she let me watch, unlike my father—as she prayed, sometimes silently, sometimes aloud. She'd ask la Virgen de la Caridad for my father's health, and to keep us both safe. "And help Alejandra find her own way," she'd say. She'd hug me afterward, and I'd feel warm and sleepy against her.

For my tía Gladys, my mother's animism was annoying but not terribly threatening. My aunt considered my mother's faith essentially superstition, tolerating it as a result of Nena's orphaned youth, a refuge the poor girl had found in her abandonment. In Cuba, Tía Gladys had seen the most educated of people put a glass of water under their beds to keep away evil spirits. And she knew it was possible to play these silly games and still be a good Catholic—that the imagery of the orishas depended so much on Roman iconography gave her, I think, a certain reassurance about Catholic inevitability. My aunt counted on last-minute enlightenment, deathbed repentance, and conversion.

In his later years, my father and I talked about how—though Gladys claimed to respect Mike Kauf's Judaism—we knew she had illusions of him coming to his senses in the end, her years of conviction repaid with a final whispered acceptance of Christ. We knew it was no accident that, as the years went by, Mike Kauf observed fewer and fewer Jewish rites, his family obligations on the High Holidays always too complicated to let him get away or make time. Not that Mike Kauf was that observant to begin with: Raised a

Conservative Jew, he rarely attended services, but each year during Yom Kippur and sometimes at Pesaj he'd pine a bit and my aunt would shrug, looking hurt as she let him know he was, of course, free to do whatever he needed, if only he could first help her clean the gutters, quickly before it got dark.

I know my aunt was less than thrilled when my mother explained my father's heritage. But I also know she assumed, since he was already publicly on the road to Christianity, however uneven the route, that his journey would be relatively quick, somewhat effortless. It never crossed her mind that my parents would find mystical coexistence, that they'd help each other—my father fixing my mother's icon, my mother learning to prepare holiday foods, even if the feast days themselves went unnamed at our table (among my favorites: her black-eyed peas with roasted fish head for Rosh Hashanah). That my parents allowed, even encouraged, my seder attendance at friends' homes bothered my aunt, but she was hard-pressed to criticize too much when, as young adults, my cousins began to go, too, although not regularly, and more out of curiosity and politeness than the need for connection that I felt so feverishly.

"Well, the Last Supper was a seder," my aunt would say, rationalizing. "It's part of our Judeo-Catholic tradition after all. I mean, it was Jesus who started it."

For the longest time, I know my tía Gladys thought my destiny was like that of souls in limbo—ignorant, impotent, at the mercy of prayers by the faithful still in the material world—until I grew old enough to start questioning my father, fascinated by his mysteries, and became more and more drawn to his private, anguished worship. The more my mother shared of her world, the more it underscored the forbidding gates at my father's kingdom, the more I wanted to see past the mist, listen for the murmur of prayers beyond the silence. And this intense curiosity about him and his ways seemed to tip the scales, sealed for my aunt my and my father's doomed fates.

Later, as he realized he was dying, he seemed to see me staring at him just outside Elysium, and at some point he let down his guard, allowing me a closer peek at his realm. We talked more openly, we touched and laughed together as if it had always been that way, sweet and easy. My mother was so relieved at our reconciliation that she celebrated my gift of the mezuzah, she placed a fragile copy of Judah Halevi's verses on the nightstand for me to read to my father: "It would be easy for me to abandon all the splendor of Sepharad / and beautiful simply to regard the ruins of our ravaged temple."*

But when it became clear my father was going under, that a gentle but all powerful tide would gather him and suck him down into the abyss, she panicked like a drowning woman. She lost all reason, twisting madly, grabbing at everything and nothing. She kicked and screamed; she fought with everything she could muster to keep him on her plain and sunny shore.

It's not just that my mother was dependent on my father in myriad ways, but that my mother had never, ever imagined life without him. Who was she without my father? What was there to anchor if not him? (Me, I'm a balloon, a bird in flight, already well beyond her reach.)

When she found me at my father's side after his last breath, she squinted as if trying to readjust the picture of her new life, held her heavy head in her hands then bent down to him and felt his chest for his heartbeat. When she failed to find it where it should have been, she began to look everywhere, as if he had hidden treasure in his body, checking the pulse on his arms, neck, throat, with a frenzy and desperation that flabbergasted me.

"Mami, Mami," I said, putting my arms around her, trying to hold her steady.

She hiccupped. "It wasn't supposed to be this way, Alejandra," she whispered.

* From *Poetas Hebreos de Al-Andalus (Siglos X-XII)*, *Antología*, edited by Angel Sáenz-Badillos and Judit Targarona Borrás (Córdoba, Spain: Ediciones El Almendro, 1990). Translation by A.O.

"He was fine, Mami, he was peaceful, it all happened very quickly," I tried to reassure her.

"No, no," she said, practically wrestling with me, "you don't understand, you don't understand."

I let her go. She put her forehead on my father's chest, caressing him through the sheet I'd pulled up to cover him. She cried like that for a long time while I stroked her back. As I watched her, I tried to imagine her in the aftermath of all this—wandering aimlessly from room to room, the kitchen cold and useless, letting her roses wilt and die, everything turning into mushy black like the fruits at her altar.

"I thought I'd be first," she said, fingering the bluish mole on her cheek.

I sighed. "Papi was older, Mami, it's logical he should go first," I said.

She shook her head like a petulant child. "No," she said in frustration, then pointed at her face. "See this? See this?" The mole was like a polished stone that morning, shiny and brazen. "I thought if I just let it go . . . you know, if I just left it alone . . ."

"Mami!" I gasped.

"It's true. I thought I could be first then," she said, awash in tears as she gazed at my father and placed his cool hand between hers, squeezing and patting it. "I thought . . . for sure . . ."

I put my hands on her shoulders and leaned into her, kissing the back of her neck, holding her to me, thinking the whole time: What will she do now? What will she do?

"See?"

My mother had handed me a short handwritten letter from my father that was to serve as his will; the taunt was not coming from her but my aunt.

"Your mother would not lie to you, Alejandra—my god, only you would even think it."

"Gladys! ¡Ya! ¡Por favor!" my mother exclaimed. She was genuinely irritated. She sat down next to me on the couch and leaned against me. Gladys made a face and plopped down in one of my father's rocking chairs, resigned.

I read over my father's words, through the blue ink loops and curlicues: "I know Alejandra will balk, but I also know she will honor my request. I know that she will think I've compromised. But what I know is that god is beyond my imagination, his power beyond my abilities to see, and that what is clear to me is that he said, 'Return to me and I shall return to you.' This is what I wish, nothing else: Not to be buried, but cremated, my ashes returned to Cuba and spread over the bay in Havana. That is all I want—no elaborate ceremony, no shiva, no mass, nothing but that. And I'd like to ask Alejandra, who is so precious to me, to be the person who takes me home."

XXXIV

Although my father had explicitly expressed a desire for anonymity, my mother ended up caving in to his friends and colleagues and allowing for a memorial service after all. Held at Loyola's breathtaking lakeside Madonna della Strada chapel, it was supposed to be ecumenical but managed, nonetheless, to exude Catholicism.

In the front row, mourners composed of older Cuban women stared at the space where the casket should have been: Among them the Morlote matriarch from the South Side, the Torres great-grandmother from Skokie, and the Pelaez's spinster aunt from Hyde Park. They eschewed the reforms of Vatican II—as if the pope's decrees were just well-intentioned nuisances—and decked themselves in black from head to toe, their heads covered with veils of old Spanish lace, laps filled with pools of rosary beads. Their lips moved furtively, in Spanish or Latin, or perhaps a combination of the two. Our next-door neighbors, the Polish-born Chmelowieczes, sat among them, vaguely confused.

To my surprise, my mother chose to put off the creepy priest she'd brought to the house on my father's last few days. He had called and called, like a spurned suitor, but she refused to pick up the phone and accept his condolences.

"It is not the priest's fault your father died," my tía Gladys told me. "It's as if your mother is blaming him, and it's not his fault. It's god's will!"

At the service, my mother tried to blend in to the front-row blackness, a lump of human flesh, pressing mourners' outstretched hands between her own palms. With each expression of grief, she retreated further and further. Almost as soon as we had begun, my mother had taken on a kind of glassy, faraway look, a mask that anyone who knew and loved her understood to be a projection of her inexhaustible pain.

All the while, my tía Gladys hung next to her, moaning as if it was she who was widowed, while a patient Mrs. Choy took up the other side, gently guiding friends and relatives. I was on the other side of my aunt, who would occasionally thump my back during her anguished throes or impatiently point and push me toward whoever was offering condolences. When a now thin-haired Seth showed up, it was Mrs. Choy who helped my mother stand up and accept his sympathies. He had to practically bat my aunt away to get to me, she was so busy crying into his neck.

"How are you holding up?" asked Seth.

"Okay," I lied. In spite of his genuine feelings for my father (and me), I knew it was too much to expect Seth to comfort me beyond his simple presence.

He nodded. "Good, good," he said, relieved. "If you need anything, let me know." But I knew better: Seth would be who I'd dial up in winter, when I didn't want to talk, but needed somebody to get me out of the house—to the movies, a lecture at Columbia College, a midnight show with some bluesy crooner at the Green Mill. He touched my elbow, just like old times, before he went and took a seat in one of the back pews, unobtrusive and safe.

"Nice mourners," said Leni, who'd flown in from her New York home for the occasion. Leni hadn't said anything when she arrived at my apartment earlier that day, just wrapped me up in her arms and wept with me, her bracelets sturdy and still. Now she eyed the black bundles at the front of the chapel. "I hear in parts of Asia some women make a living hiring out as professional mourners. Maybe a little vocational training could be useful here."

"Nah," I said, smiling in spite of everything, "they're not loud enough. I think one of the qualifiers for hired mourners is that you have to be able to wail on command. These women will only wail if it looks unintentional, as if they're just having a natural—"

"—exaggerated—"

"—well, yes, natural but somehow exaggerated response," I said as we both suppressed our indecorous laughter.

"I promise," Leni said, seriously and out of nowhere, "to be there for you, no matter what."

I watched as she moved gingerly across the muted carpet of the chapel, her bracelets jingling now as she offered condolences in her Berlitz Spanish to all my relatives. They jumped up when they saw her, surprised but delighted, even in their sadness. Because Leni walks with a slight limp, they took her hand for balance, hoping to steady her, and perhaps themselves, too.

Although we had pleaded with friends not to send flowers but to con-tribute to charity instead (a literacy program administered through Loyola), the blossoms piled up anyway—giant wreaths, bewildering arrangements two and three feet tall with notes from my father's writer friends, sent from Spain and Italy, Venezuela and Mexico.

To everyone's amazement, José Farraluque, the erotica writer from Cuba, relayed a long, surprisingly touching letter accompanied by a bouquet of Paul Neyron roses. In his note he talked about my father as a passionate man, a true Cuban whose soul knew the burn-ing flames of love. During the service, his words were read by Mario Vargas Llosa (in the United States for a Harvard residency), who choked from emotion before delivering his own rather humorous re-membrance of my father.

I sat in a state of dull grace, Leni next to me, occasionally touching my wrist as if discreetly checking for a pulse. The truth is, I didn't know the man Farraluque or Vargas Llosa described as my father.

"This is so incredible," my mother whispered to me across my aunt's heaving bosom. Did she recognize my father in these peoples' memories? "I . . . I don't know what your father would think," my mother continued. She dabbed at her dry mouth, her finger lightly touching the mole on her cheek.

"He'd be proud," I whispered back. It was the right thing to say, certainly—I recognized it as the words spilled from my mouth—but I had no idea, not really, whether they could also be true. I felt Leni's hand covering mine.

"I don't know," my mother said as my aunt shifted uncomfortably at being ignored. She sniffled and coughed. "He didn't like people talking about him . . . not even good things," my mother said. "You know, he blushed so easily . . ."

All his life, my father had been a quiet, private man, so there was little reason to think he would draw many people to his memorial, except perhaps his Loyola colleagues (which included a number of clergy), a few of his students, and maybe, if they just happened to be available, as was the case with Vargas Llosa, the writers for whom he'd been instrumental.

But to our amazement, the chapel filled with all sorts of folks: old men from the Cuban-American Chamber of Commerce who considered him an outstanding citizen, the ordinary guys from factories and security jobs with whom he'd played dominoes, immigrants from all over the neighborhood whom he'd helped with letters and legal papers (always for free), and even a representative from the mayor's office, who insisted on reading a proclamation honoring my father for his achievements. The service was ignored by English-language TV and radio, but cameras from the Spanish-language networks came and taped special reports.

There were plenty of people I didn't recognize, warm Cuban bodies who would, after a few words with my mother (and my sobbing aunt), turn to me and press me to them for a few seconds, whispering their sorrow in my ear, telling me how noble a man my father was. "A great patriot," more than one man told me, "the kind of Cuban that would make José Martí proud." I said nothing, just smiled weakly, always peeking back at my mother, who'd inevitably moved on to the next person.

There were plenty of non-Cubans in attendance, too: Jews and Mexicans, recently arrived Russians, the entire maintenance staff at Loyola (which was mostly Polish and African-American), people from a Puerto Rican cultural center I didn't know my father had helped start back in 1977, after the riots in Humboldt Park (another surprise). There was a little brown man who never said anything to anyone, just played with the brim of his worn blue golf cap. And, for almost the entire service, a fidgety old man, his chalky body disfigured, sitting in a wheelchair in the back, fussing and angrily mumbling to his attendant, a round African-American woman, who patiently moved up the blanket around his waist, pushed his heavy, dark glasses back up on his nose, and held his hand when he got weepy.

I don't know precisely when it was the old man exited, only that he was already gone when my mother and I, after many more greetings from friends and strangers, finally began to walk out of the chapel at the end of the service. When we got outside to the dazzling August light, she and I—we were holding hands, just the two of us—found ourselves momentarily jolted. As my own eyes cleared, I saw the old man through gray and orange flashes, his mouth downturned and sour, right next to a van with a lift that was obviously waiting for him.

"Oh my god!" my mother screamed, letting go of my fingers as if they were on fire and throwing me off balance for an instant.

As I tried to clear my own sun-stunned vision, I saw the cloudy smudge of my mother dashing across the walk, fuzzy arms in the air, her voice shrill, throwing herself in the old man's crippled lap and sobbing like I had never seen. I know I was not the only one paralyzed by the scene: My tía Gladys, Mrs. Choy, and Leni all stood, jaws dropped, eyes wide. As I focused I saw the old man staring ahead as if blind, his jittery hand attempting to stroke my mother's head.

"Ale!" my mother called to me, turning around and waving me over excitedly. "Ale! Come here, Ale!" Her face was wet and hot, the blood having rushed to her temples; veins shivered on the surface, blue-green like her mole, and feverish.

"Alejandra?" said the old man, his mouth working hard to pronounce my name. Tufts of white stood out from his head. Then he
laughed a little and I saw delicate streams of tears escaping from under
the tinted glasses that obscured the abyss of his blank, black pupils.

At my mother's house, while Mr. and Mrs. Choy helped serve a
Cuban-Chinese buffet (fried rice, black beans, pot stickers, and
tamales, among other things) for our guests, ninety-seven-year-old
Gregor Olinsky—blind, cathetered, and completely dependent on
his attendant, a woman named, appropriately enough, I thought,
Rose—held center stage. He told stories about the Holocaust, about
bribing his way into Cuba when the United States denied him a
visa, about the irony of coming to Miami after the revolution with
a passport stamped REPATRIATED all over it, and then becoming a
real estate tycoon in Detroit.

Mostly, though, he talked about the mystery of my father, who,
according to Olinsky, had denied his fate by ignoring the gift of his
hands, the way they caressed the earth and understood its secrets.

"I loved him, yes, it's true, but sometimes—and I don't mean to
be disrespectful, I don't mean this to be taken the wrong way,
okay?—he was not very smart, that Enrich," he said, to the horror of
the other guests, especially my tía Gladys, who gasped, put down
her plate, and walked out of the room, offended.

"The . . . the nerve!" she huffed in the kitchen as Mike Kauf
tried to calm her. "Where is his respect for the dead? A man that
old, doesn't he realize people could be talking about him that way
very soon?"

My mother, however, picked at her food with a fork in a con-
spiratorial fashion and giggled. To my disbelief, she seemed com-
forted by Olinsky and his outrageousness.

"Okay, he did well with the translations and the teachings, yes,
but can you imagine what he would have become if he'd surrendered to the destiny of his hands?" he continued. "They were beautiful, beautiful hands!"

My mother nodded in affirmation. When the old man started in on the story of our escape from Cuba, she howled, spilling her food from the exertion. Mrs. Choy appeared on cue with a Dustbuster and a paper towel, and Mr. Choy right behind her handed my mother a fresh plate with considerably smaller portions.

"I mean, who else but Enrich would plan to fly out of Cuba on the very day of Bay of Pigs, huh? Who else?" Olinsky said, a line of drool measuring the distance between his chin and lap. Rose wiped his face with a folded white cloth. "One of our shop's drivers was involved with the underground—with the CIA, really—so I had a pretty good idea of what was going to happen. I tried to tell him he'd never fly out of Cuba. I mean, *everybody* knew except Enrich—those Kennedy fools had practically run an ad in the *New York Times!*"

I was sitting on the living room sofa with usually shock-free Leni, who was now thoroughly astonished by the way the old man was carrying on—all to my mother's apparent delight. But after hearing about my father's futile attempts at going to school, at romance (prior to my mother), at dancing and dominoes (Olinsky was amazed he had regular partners in Rogers Park), I'd had just about enough.

I leaned forward from the couch, my shoulders stiff. Even before I opened my mouth, the room had grown tense. "Mr. Olinsky, if you thought my father was such a bumbler, what are you doing here?" I demanded.

The entire room—Leni, the Choys, my cousins, everyone—turned my way as Olinsky's sightless eyes swung from my mother to me. "I came to honor him," he said without hesitation, "because he had the purest heart of anyone I've ever known."

My mother nodded again, whimpering, barely looking up from her new plate of food.

My mother, Rose, and I helped take Olinsky down our front steps at the conclusion of the visit. A huffing Rose held the back of the wheelchair and led, tilting Olinsky, while my mother gripped his foot rests. I walked next to them, carrying his bag of medicines and supplies. "You don't like me, Alejandra," he said, but the bastard was smiling.

I glanced at my mother as she straightened up, searching for clues for a response. Did she expect me to deny it? To insist otherwise just to please him? But when she finally focused my way, she smiled weakly and shrugged.

"That's okay, I'm not very likable," muttered Olinsky as Rose swiveled the chair toward the waiting van on the curb. "Why would you like me, eh?"

Rose parked him on the sidewalk, took the bag from my hands and rushed to the car, setting its gears and the lift in motion. After the lift had dropped to the ground, she came around, positioned Olinsky in it, and locked the chair in place. My mother made a grand show of farewell, with a big hug and lots of kisses and promises to stay in touch. Then Rose pressed a magic button that boosted Olinsky into the air and pulled him back into the van. She unbuckled the chair and pushed him into the passenger's side.

"Vamos," my mother said, tapping me on the shoulder.

I had just started to turn around when I heard Olinsky call out to me. "Come here, young lady," he said from the car's open window. I cringed at his command. My mother gave me a nudge forward. "Hrrrmmmph," the old man said.

"What?" I answered, not moving, but he wouldn't speak again, just twitched and grimaced. My mother was getting annoyed so I gave in and stepped up to the van. "What?" I said again.

"You don't have to like me but you have no reason to be so angry with me," he said; it was a scolding. "I think you're just angry at your father." In the driver's seat now, Rose nodded.

"Fairly simple psychology," I said, exhausted.

"Yes, well, I'm a simple man," he said, clearly sarcastic. "I think you're mad at him not just for dying but for making you go back to Cuba, to have to spread his ashes, no?"

"I'm mad at him for dying, yes, and for getting cremated," I said, surprised by my own admission.

"His decision," snapped Olinsky. "He understood dirt better than you and me. What do we know? What do you care?"

What *did* I care? How many people did I know who'd stipulated cremation in their wills? I knew both Leni and Seth, Jews, too, had embraced that way for themselves, so why did it bother me so much that my father, a pseudo-Jew, had chosen it, too?

"Hmm . . . you know your father's Hebrew name, no?"

"Elías."

"Elijah, yes."

"So?"

My mother was nervously waiting on the walk back to the house, her arms across her chest. My aunt and Leni both stepped up now, my aunt draped along my mother's shoulders. Leni was waiting for disaster, I could tell.

"Elijah was swept up to heaven bodily by a whirlwind, if I remember correctly," said the old man. He coughed. "Maybe that's what your father wanted, to be lifted up by one of those powerful tropical gales down there."

When I return to Cuba in 1997, I decide to visit Ytzak's grave in Guanabacoa, just outside of Havana. Orlando takes me on a blue, cloudless day. Although he has been to the Jewish cemetery many times, he's unsure of where my great-grandfather is buried, and so he stops at a little office at the front gate and tries to get help. Across the street from the graveyard, a handful of schoolboys play ball in a gravelly, arid lot. They use a stick for a bat.

"There's no one here," Orlando says with a sigh as he steps back outside. "Maybe we can find it by ourselves, it's not that big a cemetery."

We walk past the tight rows of tombs, all cracked blue-veined marble and white pigeon splotches. The trees are few and scraggly, affording us little shade, but they smell green and sweet.

"Cohen, Shiller, Amado, Velázquez, Bello, Maldonado," Orlando reads from the headstones. He tries hard to pronounce each non-Spanish name correctly, looking over at me for approval.

I take his hand, feeling the rubbery skin of his palm between my fingers. "Is it true what they say about the prenda judía?" I ask.

"Is what true?"

"That it takes the skull of a Jew?" I look around at all the tombs, pieces scattered like broken pottery.

He shakes his head. "That's a lie," he says. "First of all, you don't ever need a whole skull for anything in palo monte, just a little bit of bone, so that its spirit can be evoked. But it can be any bone, any size, just a chip."

"But is it more powerful if it's from a Jew? That's what I've always heard."

He sighs again. "Look, Ale, where do you get this stuff?" He stops to explain. "That's an old Christian thing. For them, anybody who wasn't baptized was a Jew—I mean, I'd count as a Jew. They don't mean a Jew like the Menachs or your father or Ytzak."

We both stop talking at the same time. We hadn't realized it at first but we're right in front of Ytzak's grave. "Antonio Ytzak Garazi, 1881–1980" reads the headstone. There's a little Star of David underneath. I touch the marker and it's cool.

As I reach down to the warm earth for a pebble or two, a young man runs up to us. He's out of breath, his unshaven face smudged with chocolate, his plaid shirt open from missing buttons. "You were looking for me," he says to Orlando. We both notice he's carrying the remnants of an American candy bar in his left fist. Some of the ball-playing schoolboys linger behind him; it's impossible to tell if they're with him or on the chase. "I'm Rene, I'm the caretaker," he says by way of explanation. He's still chewing a bite of the chocolate, gasping a bit, too. He looks like something's not right about him, like he's slow or demented.

"It's okay," I say, waving him away. "We thought we needed help finding a grave but we found it ourselves. Thank you."

As Rene starts to go, he sees me put a little pile of rocks on

Ytzak's headstone. "Excuse me," he says, "do you know who that was?"

Orlando and I glance at each other. "Her great-grandfather," he says.

"Was he, you know, important?"

"Well, he was a veteran of the war of independence," I say, suddenly flushed with pride.

Orlando shades his eyes with his left hand. "Why do you ask?"

Rene laughs nervously. "Oh, nothing, really. Just curious. You wouldn't happen to know, would you, who here was, what do they call it, a rabbi?"

"Why a rabbi?" I ask.

Rene shrugs. "Rabbis, you know, aren't they the most powerful Jews?"

"So you're really gonna stay home for seven days and mourn?" Leni asked as we walked by the lake after Olinsky's departure. She wore her stylish black funeral dress, not making the slightest attempt to hide the scars on her legs.

The water opened up beside us, a blue slate. In the distance were sailboats, waterskiers, a few parasailers. Bikes whizzed by on the park trail my father had loved and strolled so many times.

For a moment, I imagined us—Leni and I—in Miami Beach. In this picture, her skin is the color of rust, her scars thick rivers of magenta. When we get in the ocean, Leni dives in, even though it's shallow, and disappears under the lather, emerging ahead of me like a seal pup, vigorously shaking the water from her head and laughing. In the dream, I just watch her, out of my element, depleted and doomed.

"Yeah, yeah," I said, back in reality, back overlooking the vast expanse of water. "I'm really gonna mourn for seven days, really."

As we approached my mother's house again, we noticed a group of mourners gathered like crows in the front yard, hands like claws around their rosaries, which dangled like entrails. It was at that moment I told myself I'd do it all: sit on boxes, say kaddish for eleven months, pray every day.

"Oh, Ale, you're such a good Jew," Leni said with a smirk and a little laugh, "you're even better than the real ones."

XXXV

After the memorial service, after the obligatory get-together, dispatching Olinsky and saying good-bye to Leni at O'Hare, I went home by myself for the first time in weeks. When I wearily stepped into my place—a third-floor two-bedroom in Uptown—it was a wreck. Dirty clothes littered the floor. Sourness leaked from the cups in the sink, lined with green moss around the rims. Spiders dropped spit from my office ceiling to the floor.

I took my backpack from around my shoulders and plopped myself down on the living room floor. My apartment seemed dark and cold and small. I could feel my heart in my chest, its steady and dumb beat; I could hear my own hollow breathing. My head felt heavy. This was it, this was life now, I thought to myself, surveying the emptiness.

To my surprise, after my father's death, my tía Gladys had suggested I move in with my mother—there was certainly enough room and, with the Farraluque translation still outstanding, I'd be spending time there over the next few weeks anyway. Years before I would have automatically sniffed at such an idea—I had a life, after all, with an edgy rhythm that would be unsettling to my mother—but now I found myself considering the possibilities. We could be roommates of a sort, my mother and I; we could certainly respect each other's space, live openly with one another yet with discretion, too.

But when I mentioned it to her, my mother laughed. "I'm not ill, I'm not so old," she said. "I don't have to be taken care of."

I stopped in my tracks. "Well, what about me? Maybe I need to be taken care of," I said, hurt and offended and sarcastic all at once. I must have sounded like Leni, though I knew even then it was my pride that was injured.

Wisely, my mother decided not to take me too seriously, joking instead about what a nice gesture it was on my part, how sweet but unnecessary. "I can manage," she said. Then she looked serious, determined. "And if I can't, I need to learn how."

The summer my father died, Fidel disappeared from the world stage. For weeks, no one saw him, there were no traces of his slow black Mercedes-Benz limos slithering through the streets of Havana, no marathon speeches on television, no coy commentaries from the maximum leader as he strolled through a hospital or sports stadium. In Miami, rumors swirled about his demise.

My mother listened to her maddening cacophony with even more ardor than usual. "If it's true, what a gift!" she said, the radio in each room tuned louder and louder. She imagined herself returning with me to a Fidel-free Cuba, suddenly resurgent and glittery, just like in the vintage postcards sold in thrift shops all over the world. On the Internet, she began engaging in chat room discussions, tentative at first but then more confidently. "I don't think Jorge Más Canosa's plan is the answer," she posted in one of her messages. "I don't think exchanging Soviet influence for American influence is the way to go. We've done that before; it's a lesson we should have learned by now."

She told me she knew she'd experience shock on first sight of Havana—she had read and heard so many other reports of first trips back—but she was just as convinced she could acclimate. "I read in one newsgroup," she told me, "that there are exile retirees who spend almost the whole year there already, their pensions and Social Security checks routed through Mexico or Canada."

"Mami, we're just going for a visit," I reminded her, "not to stay."

"Oh, I know, I know, but someday—just you wait!—someday . . ."

"Someday what? You always said it was this life, events here, that mattered."

"Yes, but . . ." And she would drift off.

As the days passed, her basement altar became more and more elaborate: wild yellow bouquets lined the walls, water vessels—jars and clear-glass pots, goblets, vases of all sizes—covered the floor. The plaster-cast Ochún my father had pieced back together so many years before reigned mightily on her throne, dried peaches turned to stone on an offering plate, shriveled pumpkin slices and petrified pieces of cakes giving testimony to my mother's devotion. A cigar burned continuously. The room had a vaguely nautical feel, sea smells and tobacco, an imaginary breeze that gently kissed the water and made it sway.

As my mother dreamed of her return, I tried to get our papers in order to fulfill my father's last wishes. Her Cuban passport (required by the Cuban government) posed a major bureaucratic problem. In a moment of defiance after her U.S. citizenship hearing, my mother had burned all the paperwork tying her back to the island. Gone were her original birth certificate, her University of Havana I.D., and her passport. Holding on to my father, she had severed Cuba from her life like a rotten limb, then catherized the joint. I was just a child then—just twelve years old—but I'd argued with her before she set the Cuban papers ablaze, begging her to keep the documents as a kind of patrimony for me.

"You will have your own connections, your own memories," she had said, "you don't need mine—you're an American now, that's who you are."

Now, as I called the Cuban Special Interests Section in Washington, D.C., and travel agencies in Miami that specialized in Cuba trips, I helped my mother fill out the many forms required for reinstatement into her native land. I thought of my father back then, how he smiled wanly when they toasted their new status, how I found him sobbing in his office the next day. When I asked him what was wrong I noticed the papers on his desk—his rescued Cuban passport, his spared Havana driver's license—his smooth hands passing over them as if they were written in Braille.

Trying to piece my mother's Cuban life together, I had those same papers before me as I filled out the questionnaire from the island authorities. To my astonishment, my father had not updated his passport after marriage; it still said he was single and claimed an Old Havana address.

"Mami," I called out to my mother, crouching next to one of her transmitters, "your last official address in Havana . . . that was the apartment you rented from the Menachs, no?"

"No, no—San Miguel 1112," she said without hesitation. She underscored the number by holding her fingers above the noise—one, one, one, two. "That was our first apartment together, just before Moisés bought his building."

Her fingers lingered in the air long after I copied her, as if she were trying to locate something to hold on to.

When I find San Miguel 1112 on my return to Cuba—Orlando convincing the current tenant that mine is a visit of reconciliation, not reclamation—a young mother with two small toddlers clinging to the hem of her robe lets me in, following me curiously as I look around my first home on earth. It smells of boiled plantains here, of rancid butter.

"This is Centro Habana," Orlando says, "not Vedado."

I understand what he's telling me between the lines: This housing is older, smaller, more practical, nothing as elaborate as the sculpted fantasy mansions to the west. But it isn't quite the bland Soviet bunkers either.

As I enter what was my parents' first bedroom together (and where I was most likely conceived), I notice the window's astounding view: the spire of the Church of Our Lady of Mount Carmel at Infanta and Neptuno. There, framed by the window and slashed by faded wooden slats, floats a bronze messiah, brown as mud, and from here it looks like a man walking across the heavens.

———

When my father died, my mother left it up to me to call the Men-achs, to tell them what had happened. Later, when I return with my father's ashes, Ester and I sit alone one sticky night on the front steps of their house. She's just finished explaining how her family sat shiva for my father, all of them except Rafa, who doesn't care about anything, and Yosemí, who has become an evangelical Christian—although she never quite says that in so many words.

"Yosemí prayed in her own way," Ester tells me. She is silver-streaked now, rounder than when I first met her, her face still beau-tiful but marked with an infinite sadness. "What matters, I think, are the prayers, their intention and intensity. And Yosemí prays with all her heart." When Ester swallows, I can't tell if her discom-fort is because of my father or her own losses. Her enormous bosom trembles.

"The last time I was here," I say, almost in a whisper, "I sat on these same steps with Ernesto . . ."

She sniffles. We have never spoken about her son's disappear-ance—with the exception of Orlando, the entire family avoids the topic to the exclusion of Ernesto's name.

"He liked you very much," Ester says (meaning he was en-chanted with me, the way Cubans delight in each other's company).

"I liked him, too," I say, using the same construction. "By the time I left, I felt that I cared about him."

"The day he left," she continues, entering a kind of trance, "the balsero crisis had been going on for days. I had to have a tooth pulled—I'm sure you've noticed, in spite of what everyone says, everything here is very, very behind. It's not our fault, of course, but the Americans—If the blockade were lifted, everything would be different."

"Yes, yes," I say. (In Cuba, this is not a political position, but an assertion of reality, like saying that the island is surrounded by water.)

"I went to the dentist that day," Ester remembers. "It was so hot we could barely breathe but they couldn't turn on the air conditioner because it was prohibited, we had to save electricity."

Sitting outside the house tonight, our only light is the moon, a slice of tangerine in the hazy skies above.

"When the doctor was about halfway extracting my tooth, the lights went out and the old fan they'd had going sputtered to a stop," Ester recalls. "Suddenly the dentist couldn't see what he was doing. He asked the nurse to use a hand mirror to catch a ray of light coming in through the window, and to direct it into my mouth. Just imagine! Then he asked her to please mop his brow. He was perspiring so profusely, his sweat was dripping on me, into my open mouth."

She stops, gazes at me intensely. "Do you understand what I'm saying?" she asks. I look away, shift my bones on the steps. *Do I understand?*

"I thought it would taste like salt—the sweat, I mean. I've kissed my children, my husband, when they're perspiring. I've even licked them, like a cat," she says. "I always thought sweat was made from the same thing as tears. But the dentist's perspiration was sweet, like sugarcane juice. At first, it was too intimate, too urgent. But then it was okay, like we were at a crucial moment in saving a life, and we were both part of the effort."

I imagine the nervous nurse, the light fluttering in the cavern of Ester's mouth.

"The nurse, she was barely paying attention to him, to the dentist," Ester continues as if she can read my mind. "She was busy being horrified, telling us what had happened on her way to the clinic that morning, when she'd gone by the Malecón, where they were dragging in the remains of a human torso, the clear arch of shark's teeth on its skin."

Suddenly, Ester stands up with one quick, unexpected motion. She holds her arm out to balance herself against the door frame, as if she's dizzy or numb.

"That's when I knew," she says, her voice level and hard.

She goes back in the house without saying another word, but I

can't move. I sit out on the stoop for what seems forever, watching the shadows stir, trying to decipher the difference between angels and ghosts.

In the days after my father's memorial service, after the promise I made to myself to say kaddish for the next eleven months, I tried to find a temple that seemed appropriate for my task. For a couple of days, I attended morning prayers at a well-appointed synagogue on Lake Shore Drive. The rabbi was kind—I'd called ahead—but I found myself among a group of elderly Yiddish and Russian-speaking Jews who seemed as distant to me as those first Askenazis in Havana must have appeared to Ytzak. It's not that I didn't recognize their ruddy faces and customs, it's just that I didn't see myself or my father in any of them.

I tried a reconstructionist congregation up in the suburbs, where the rabbi fingered my father's tefillin before I could put them on, but their earnestness overwhelmed me—they touched me too much, seemed too eager to include Ladino prayers just for me, to talk about Cuba.

At the recommendation of my old neighborhood friend—the Latvian boy—I finally tried a tiny Tunisian storefront temple up on Devon Avenue, just west of Rogers Park, situated near a bunch of Russian émigré bookstores, Pakistani and Asian Indian groceries, and Chinese restaurants bearing kosher seals on their menus. I'd get up at the crack of dawn and drive up there without the radio or tape player, remembering how my father always said silence was like a cleansing fast for the linguist. In the early hours, Devon was invariably deserted, debris skipping across the pavement, the security gates still crisscrossing the facades all along the avenue.

Inside the temple, the men looked like my father and his domino partners: Yemenites, Lebanese, Portuguese chanting a softer Hebrew, sprinkling in a little Ladino; they could have all been Cubans claiming Spanish ancestors. Their hair and beards were lush, jet, unruly; their eyes pools of Indian ink. They would nod at me, a little embarrassed, just as if I were their lost daughter.

"Hallowed and honored, extolled and exalted, adored and acclaimed be the name of the Holy One," I prayed silently. Each morning I went, I was the only woman there, relegated behind a plywood partition with see-through lace curtains at the top. "Let us say amen," I continued in prayer, knowing no one would join me in that amen, no one would count me in the minyan, preferring to go without one before including me.

One day when ten men showed up almost by accident and the low gurgle of prayer became more pitched and ecstatic, I pulled my father's velvety bag from my backpack and began to strap his phylacteries on my arm. There was an instant commotion on the other side of the partition, a desperate whispering and ruffling of shawls and prayer books. Finally, one of the men undid his straps and, with his head exposed, walked back to my section.

"Excuse me," he said apologetically, "but you . . . you can't do that here." His English was rushed but imperfect, too open-mouthed to be natural to him.

I stared at him, dumbfounded. *"Levi?"* I said. It was Karen Kilberg's bionic-armed client.

"Excuse me . . . ? Oh my god," he stammered, wide-eyed. "Alejandra?"

We laughed nervously and he hugged me with his robot arm, which caused a major rustling in the congregation—someone slammed a book down somewhere—then, after undoing my phylacteries and putting them away, we stepped outside where we could talk. I heard the door close behind us, then the click of a lock turned by hand.

"My god, Levi!" I said.

He flexed his mechanical fingers like an octopus showing off its tentacles for tourists at the aquarium. "So good to see you, so good," he said, then squeezed my hand too hard with his, "but you can't do that, Alejandra, you can't wear tefillin."

"Nothing says that, you know. It's just tradition, not law," I said in my own defense.

He shook his head. "No, no, you can't do that, not here. Don't come back if you're going to do that."

The first day of September 1997, after a three-week blackout, Fidel popped up in Havana, laughing and joking about how his brief disappearance had Miami television and radio stations actually declaring he was dead.

"Dream on!" shouted Fidel at a school opening ceremony. When the skies turned gray and it began to drizzle, the old lion was defiant: "Those of you with colds, those of you with delicate conditions should go home," he intoned, pointedly holding his ground against the heavenly downpour. His olive cap drooped, his military fatigues darkened to an algae of navy blue, but he continued.

My mother and I watched him on the Spanish-language news in my parents' den, all traces of my father's last few days there now removed. Both of us sat on the couch, as always, his rocking chair like a monument neither one of us could consider defiling with our own weight. It was on a bookshelf here that we kept my father's ashes in a small, innocuous cardboard container. It was our equivalent of a pine box, plain and humble. I peeked inside once, finding the powdery white ashes, the little chips I took for bits of bone.

"He thinks he's fooling us," my mother said of Fidel on the tube, "but look at him—he's shaking, he's old. He thinks he's so tough but he stands out there long enough and he'll catch pneumonia—wouldn't that be something, if he died like that just because he's so full of himself that he thinks he can defy the elements?"

I looked closely at Fidel: Every exile I know is constantly seeing age spots, signs of Parkinson's, dribble, an addled response to a question, a maniac's gleam. But the truth is that, as usual, he looked the same to me: a man typical of his age, his hair and beard dashed with salt, his tired but handsome face coursed with lines, a moment of confusion now and again.

Within a few days of his resurrection, it was almost as if Fidel had personally answered my mother's taunts: A note from the Cuban Special Interests Section came, announcing that Havana had refused to grant her a visa.

"But why? *Why?*" she pleaded between moans. "This destierro will kill me!"

I held her and cried with her and, when her breathing had returned to normal, I called the Interests Section myself, begging the bureaucrats there for an explanation.

"My mother is an old woman," I said. "She's a housewife, a widow. Her only desire in returning is to scatter her husband's ashes."

But the clerks held their silence, refusing to be tempted by any of my exhortations. As I hung up the phone I watched my mother as if from an impossibly increasing elevation: an ever-shrinking black dot in a vast wasteland. Soon she'd vanish completely, from black to gray to dust.

There are words, I know from my old talks with my father, which never quite translate. In English, destierro always converts to exile. But it is not quite the same thing. Exile is exilio, a state of asylum. But destierro is something else entirely: It's banishment, with all its accompanying and impotent anguish. Literally, it means to be uprooted, to be violently torn from the earth.

XXXVI

When I return to Cuba with my father's ashes, the Menachs have cleared the barbacoa for me as a guest room. When I stand up in it, I can feel the ceiling just above my head, and though there is a window—the one where I first glimpsed Orlando ten years before—the loft has a stifling, airless feeling. The walls are margarine yellow, stained with sticky bluish leaks from the roof. There's a poster of a young Madonna on a gondola in Venice, and another of Enrique Iglesias dressed in white like a santero. When Orlando hands my bag up the ladder to me (I refuse to let him play valet with me), it lands with a thud next to the thin mattress that will serve as my bed. The floor, made of warped pressed wood, quivers.

Ten years after my initial visit, it's as if time has stood still here—yet nothing is the same. The panorama decays while struggling to retain its shape. Everything and everyone has been weathered and patched a thousand times. The Menachs' house is itself held up by dozens of wooden beams tied together and pressed against an outside wall. They are round like telephone poles, cracks revealing a chalky white inside that looks like bones. Grass grows in stiff bursts all around the upright logs. "We . . . we had a problem after the last hurricane," Orlando says, embarrassed as he grabs my things from the car's trunk. At the front door, I notice the mezuzah is chipped now, the bottom of it completely gone, the prayer scroll missing.

I want to talk to Moisés about the photo my father gave me in his last moments, but as I begin to explain that I have something for him, the old man just walks away, his gaze blank, chicken legs uneasy. Moisés is seventy-seven now, my father's age if he were still alive, but he is tentative about everything. His eyes swim in a milky pond, surrounded by rings so ashen they look like burnt charcoal. At one point during the ride from the airport he stares at me as if trying to find me through the haze of a house on fire. "Ah, Alejandra!" he finally says, slapping his forehead. "Yes, yes, it's you."

This time around, the grand Menach front room is as empty and cool as a tomb. A new wall made of flimsy cardboard and uneven plaster divides it in two, separating it from where the dining table used to be. The cracks shimmer like tiny sapphires. The room is more of a box now, a vestibule, where Rodolfo, the patriarchal zombie, sits under a flimsy white sheet with the dead TV set. The only sign of his breathing is the soft, intermittent billowing of the fabric around the wet circle where his mouth should be. Still framed up on the wall, the numbers on Moisés's lottery ticket are obscured by ancient mold.

Was it always this dank, this dim? I ask myself as I climb the ladder to the barbacoa. My own vision is blurred, smudged by emotions. Was it always this way?

During my stay, the Menachs have rearranged their lives. The loft is normally where Yosemí, now a pudgy young woman with round rolls of flesh cushioning every joint, and baby Paulina, grown to a buoyant, skinny adolescent with caterpillar eyebrows, sleep. Yosemí is as serious as ever, only now her features have a strange serenity about them. The two of them have been parceled out during my stay—Yosemí downstairs, to what is now Rafa's room (and used to be Ernesto's), while Paulina stays nights with Deborah, who has grown up to be an artist and lives with her boyfriend in a small converted warehouse on Muralla Street.

Rafa, I'm told, spends most of his time with his girlfriend, although he's around—eating and drinking, taking up space at the kitchen table but not helping with the preparations for the night's meal. Due to hassles with my visa and flights, I've managed to arrive on Rosh Hashanah and the family is gathered here, readying dinner. Ester lumbers from one end of the room to the other, watching pots of boiling water, stirring the skillet with a mangled piece of plastic that might at one time have been a spatula.

No one says anything but it is clear when I finally see Rafa that he and Orlando, his father, barely speak. Instead of the beautiful teenage boy I once met, Rafa is now a sullen young man with yellowed half moons under his eyes, as if he's never quite recovered from his childhood illnesses. When we meet this time, he is monosyllabic and unenthusiastic, kissing me hello out of obligation and quickly shooting his father an accusatory glance.

"Listen, I really don't need that much room," I protest to Moisés and Ester about the loft. "There's no reason why Yosemí and Paulina can't also stay up there." I haven't finished speaking before Moisés washes his hands and leaves the kitchen.

"Oh, please, Alejandra," says Yosemí with a blissful smile. "I'm happy to give you my room."

"That's because that way she doesn't have to haul her fat ass up the ladder!" says a sulky Paulina.

"Hey!" Orlando's head spins toward his twelve-year-old, who runs out of the kitchen, disappearing behind the new wall. Yosemí shrugs, smiles again.

"What is it with her? Why is she so mean?" Orlando says to no one in particular.

"It's her age," Yosemí says with an understanding so earnest it sounds false. She's carefully cutting an onion on a scratched wooden board, her eyes watering freely. The white bits look like dozens of little teeth swimming in clear saliva. Above breasts as ample and soft as her mother's, I spy the gold crucifix around Yosemí's neck that Orlando has told me about. Is her new faith what keeps her here, so righteously? Or will it serve as a passport out?

A tired Ester shakes her head. Rafa, who's straddling a chair and leaning his chin on its back, snickers. He's so scruffy: unshaven, in a dirty T-shirt and expensive Prada pants, turquoise and soft as velvet. They must have cost about $700—I can't begin to fathom how he got them.

"Listen, Alejandra, why don't you get some fresh air, go for a walk?" says Ester. Then to Orlando: "Go on, take her to the Malecón. This will be a while yet."

I swallow, struggling with unexpected shame. I may be visiting the Menachs but in this moment what becomes clear is that I'm Orlando's friend, his charge, his project.

At the Malecón, the craggy lip around the city, we scratch the skin on the crumbling bulkhead and pitch pieces of gravel into the fetid waters. They gurgle below us, green and black. With the tide low and the coral naked, bare-chested children play in oily pools, skip stones on the surface and chase the elusive shadows slithering underneath. An old man leans against the wall as if he's been there forever, intoning his unchanging litany: "Por el amor de dios, por el amor de dios." In the distance, a ship's horn wails mournful and long.

"You don't know what happened here—how empty bowls became units of currency . . ." says Orlando, out of the blue. "You don't know . . ."

He tells me how his son has learned to split his brain in half: one side convinces him he is in love and is loved by a wonderful young woman who works long, arduous hours as a tour guide to help support both her family and him; the other half twinges each time she comes home with a gift from a Spanish or German friend, exceedingly generous gentlemen who buy her clothes and appliances or just give her money to ease her hardship.

"With each new item she brings home, Rafa loses a function," says Orlando. "For example, he can no longer multiply. He says this is okay, that zero times zero is still zero for all of infinity. But for a while, he couldn't keep his eyes open. This was after his girlfriend received a stereo system. He was perfectly awake, but his lids would drop like steel doors. He had no control over them, couldn't blink, couldn't cry. Deborah devised these tiny clothespins and pinned them back, but his eyes got dry and infected from all the things that flew into them and Rafa almost went blind. A new shirt will cost him the use of his hands for a week, $300 in currency will constipate him. Those pants he has on? He was deaf for days because of them. The only thing that restores the lost function is when the men who give his girlfriend these things leave, when he can see that Iberia or Lufthansa flight arching across the sky."

To make matters worse, Orlando explains, Rafa is crazy about his little sister Paulina and quite often his girlfriend will pass on perfumes and athletic shoes, dresses and compact discs, making Rafa a momentary hero, and making it even harder for him to resist temptation, to see the situation for what it is.

"Rafa is mentally twelve, like Paulina, and she likes American things," Orlando says, "much to her grandfather's chagrin." There are Barbie dolls, and Levi 501s; there are those posters up in the loft. "She thinks Rafa is a magician, she thinks he is Superman. But he is nobody, he is nothing."

"But what does the girlfriend get from having Rafa around?" I ask, confused.

Orlando takes my hands in his. They are warm, meaty. Our fingers dance around each other and my heart rises in my throat. Then he slumps against the seawall, looks north to the orange and amber mists of sunset.

"What does she get besides a foolish boy who really loves her? Two things . . ." he says with a sigh. "One, because he has applied for aliyah, and because he is a Menach, I suppose, and might actually get it, she sees the possibility of leaving the country. They'd have to marry—he'd marry her now if she said yes, but she is leaving that option open, that's clear. And the second thing . . . is me."

"*You?*" I yank my hands away with a gasp, step back, and tuck them under my pits, which are suddenly damp and tart. What is he saying? Is he going to try to tell me another Celina story? How twisted can this man be? "What the fuck do you mean *you*?"

"*Me,*" he says again, emphatically. "Me, the chauffeur. Who the hell do you think drives her on her tours? Who the hell do you think chaperons her dates?"

For the rest of the evening, I have a headache—a thunder-clapping, medieval vise of a headache. I barely talk at dinner, barely touch the food though it is plentiful and fills the house with a salty smoke. Everyone else chatters and grunts. It isn't like ten years ago, when the babble was high-pitched and energetic; this time, it's the tired, low mumble of old men at prayers. At one point, I finally excuse myself—the throbbing is so awful I can barely keep my eyes open from the pain. I throw myself into the black front room, stumbling for the ladder to the barbacoa. No one protests, no one tries to stop me except Orlando.

"Alejandra," he says. Even if my emotions weren't swirling, I wouldn't be able to see him: He is standing in shadows, his voice coming at me from the bottom of a well.

I start up the ladder, one step at a time.

"Alejandra, I'm so sorry," he says in a hoarse whisper. He reaches for my hand—his own palm is moist and warm—but I snatch it away.

I think my eyes are closed, I can't tell. I grope for the floor above me.

"You don't understand," he says. His hand is on my lower back now, supporting my weight, helping me up.

"You're right," I manage to say.

"Rafa doesn't know about the girl," he says in explanation. "He doesn't want to know. And she would never stay with him . . . if I stopped helping. He's my son, my idiot son. And she's the only woman in his life. It's that simple."

315

I shake my head, I rattle my skull. It's that simple? Is he kidding me? "How the fuck do you get yourself into these incredible situations?" I ask through gritted teeth.

"I live in Cuba, Alejandra, I live in Cuba," Orlando says. Then he steps back into the darkness, leaving me in the air.

Hours later, Moisés steps on the ladder of the barbacoa to let me know they're headed for evening services at the temple. "Are you coming?" he asks.

I crawl over to the hole in the floor and lean down—they're in a tenebrous ether, just their faces floating above the murk. Ester is exhausted; Rafa is restless and embarrassed; Paulina, listlessly hanging off her brother's arm. But Moisés gazes up like a holy man, his aimless eyes shiny beacons in an infinite sea.

"I . . . I think I'm beat from the trip," I say. Every joint aches, my forehead is heavy and greasy from sweat.

"Well then . . ." he says, clearly disappointed, his lifeless eyes dropping to the floor.

"But tomorrow . . . can we spend some time together tomorrow? I have some things for you, including a photo from my father—it's of a girl on a boat . . ." but before I finish Moisés's hand is flapping through the air like a silvery fish on a hook, not just dismissing me the way Olinsky might have, but trying desperately to get away. I never have the chance to tell him about the simple box filled with my father's ashes and covered in plastic that I've got permanently tucked into my backpack.

"May you be inscribed and sealed in the book of life!" he says as he disappears, but it sounds more like a rebuke than a wish.

I hear the rest of the family shuffling after him. In the kitchen, water runs for the dishes and I assume the newly evangelized Yosemí has stayed behind. Outside, Orlando fires up the car's engine. Doors open and slam shut. As the tires turn on the loose gravel I hear Paulina's cruel cry from the car's backseat: "Next year in Miami, Abuelo, next year in Miami!"

Many hours later, I hear noises in the kitchen that now exceed the ordinary clang and splash of water on pots and pans. There's a lively stepping back and forth, as well as a honeyed female voice uttering a peculiar chant: "Qua qua—quack quack . . . Miao— meow . . . Au au—bow wow . . . Quiquiríqui—cock-a-doodle-doo." (Actually, she struggles with cock-a-doodle-doo; it sounds more like Co-ha-dudel-du.)

I glance quickly at my watch, its whaleskin numbers indicate I've been sleeping for an eternity: It's two A.M., the middle of the night. If the Menachs are back, I never heard the car drive up, never heard their footsteps, the sound of chairs moving, of teeth being brushed, of the refrigerator opening, of water flushing or being spit back out before sleeping. I heard nothing.

I scramble down, scratching my elbow in the process, and scan the room with feline eyes. Rodolfo, the ghoulish elder, is a white shadow in his rocking chair, which squeaks as he tips forward, then back. It is not a free-flowing movement but careful calculation: Even in the unremitting night of the room I can see him pitching forward just enough to squeeze out his trebly peep, then inching back with satisfaction.

I peer past the jagged caulk of the new wall to the kitchen only to be blinded by the naked bulb in the overhead fixture. It's a floating white orb, a spinning planet, a free spirit. I snap back into the shadows, my head against the craggy plaster, fuzzy bursts of color playing before me. I don't know how long I'm standing here, like a criminal hiding from the law—I'm breathing like I just ran a terrified mile, I'm cold with sweat and fear—when I feel a scalding, rugged hand on my shoulder, then another on the back of my neck. I spasm against my will, I shiver.

"Alejandra?" It's a woman's voice, husky and sweet. I feel her breath on my face but the sound is coming from a distance—from a harbor, a pier, a splintered coral key in the middle of nowhere.

"Alejandra, are you all right? Can you hear me?"

Her Spanish is perfect, confidently Cuban, full of billowy vowels but with intact consonants.

"Water," she says.

And I hear water: It trickles, cascades, pulls at me with a moan. I feel its moist embrace, my own feverish spit merging into its cool stream.

XXXVII

In the English-speaking world, Yamim Nora'im—the time between Rosh Hashanah and Yom Kippur—is translated as the days of awe. But in Cuba, all element of wonder is erased, giving way to fatalism and terror. In Cuba, the holiest days in the Jewish calendar are called los días terribles—the terrible days.

When I return in 1997, there are barely any signs of the holidays. Life goes on: the roosters cackle and car horns blare at dawn, the neighborhoods explode with raucous music and argument by noon, and the sun blinds the eyes and scours the soul. At the city's Central Park, the debate rages about the merits of Marlins pitcher Liván Hernández and the tragic fate of his brother, El Duque.

Every stoop is occupied at all hours, there's always someone rapping at the door selling lightbulbs, overripe avocados, or slices of a wilting wedding cake. (Each time there's a knock, my heart jumps with the hope it'll be Celina come over to visit, but it's always a stranger.) When it rains, people worry about buildings crumbling, but after the downpours—cuando escampa—they run to see what can be scavenged from the rubble: doorknobs and lamp fixtures, a child's rattle, and bricks to patch other shaky walls.

In the evenings, a man across the street from the Menachs sings tangos until the wee hours, occasionally joined by his adolescent granddaughter, the two of them laughing and quarreling about the repertoire. Another neighbor attempts suicide nightly: "Bring me the alcohol!" she screams at her young son. "Bring me the matches!" Eventually, a man intervenes, tries to console her but it all ends in frustration and anger. "Go ahead, do it," he dares her, but she never does.

Some nights when it is excruciatingly hot and swatches of the city are black from government-ordered power outages, people sleep outside on their balconies or patios, hauling pillows and cushions to the open air. The red flares of scores of cigarettes simmer like tiny fires dotting railings and rooftops. No one really sleeps, they just rest their bare legs and arms on the cool metal or stone of the buildings, breathe the pungent air and make love. You can hear the murmuring, the groans, the slapping of wet flesh on wet flesh, and the laughter—both tender and cruel.

In my country, the sidereal clock is backward. "Two homelands have I, Cuba and the night," wrote José Martí. "Or are the two just one?"* Here, time measured by the stars is always longer than that measured by the sun. The nights are meant to be spent alert, traversed like a boiling Styx or a hallucinogenic Mardi Gras parade route, whiled away in the sopping womblike hold of an infinite lover, or in wait of—what?—a messiah, a sign, the dawn, more rain. In Cuba, to experience the night awake—out—aroused, is to *trasnochar*.

It is, of course, a regular verb.

When I come out of my heat-fueled stupor, it is Deborah's steady hands on my shoulders, guiding me to the kitchen table, bringing a glass of water and bits of ice to my mouth. She doesn't live here anymore but I've been told she stops by once every day or so, often helping around the house, sometimes staying the night.

"Are you okay?" she asks as she anxiously places her cool fingers on my forehead then on my cheek and neck. Her hands are rough like her father's, but from making art: hammering wood, moving stones, filtering through the lost and found of life.

*From the poem "Dos Patrias," originally published in *Flores del Destierro*, by José Martí (Havana: Molina y Cía, 1933). Translation by A.O.

I feel swathed, caramelized. "I'm sorry . . ."

"Sorry for what? Don't worry about it. You scared me, that's all. The weather's unbearable. You want more water?"

I tip back the clear glass, then hand it to her. She goes to the counter and plucks pieces of ice for me from the center of a towel that she must have banged against the hard surface to break up some big frozen clump. When I remember Ernesto doing the same thing ten years before, I can't help but chuckle a little.

"What?" says a tall, slender Deborah, turning around and smiling brightly as she pours water into my glass.

She is a young woman now, and her hair has darkened a bit; it flashes brown and reddish highlights among beaded braids and scattered dreadlocks. But if I didn't know better, I'd think we'd been transported to New York or Amsterdam: Black-garbed, punky Deborah—boots, jeans, and a loose-fitting T—also sports a dozen or so tiny silver hoops on her left earlobe and an elaborate, blue-black tattoo of the Hebrew alphabet's aleph on the top of her right hand.

"What the hell is that?" I ask, still a bit dazed, when she gives me the glass.

"Oh, this?" she says giggling as she glances down at the swirl on her brown hand.

"Yeah, that," I say again, joining her in laughter.

"This is evidence of my shame," she says in a mocking tone. She goes back to the kitchen sink and begins to fill an empty plastic bottle with water. "At least according to my grandfather."

"So what is it really?"

She shrugs. "It's body art," she says. "I liked the idea." She stretches her hand for me to see, flexes her fingers like Leví. "I designed it myself."

"Nice job," I say admiringly. The lines are crisp and clear and have a certain elegance. "Where'd you get it done?"

"In Old Havana," she says as she fills another empty bottle with water. "There's a guy there who runs a tattoo parlor. One day this artist from San Francisco came—and this guy was really amazing— so I had him do it. I told my grandfather it was actually a sign of pride, that this way I could never deny being Jewish, but he just scoffed. I mean, okay, they won't bury me in Guanabacoa, so what? Like, if there's a god, this'll matter more than what I've done in my life. . . . But I'm the black sheep of the family, you know."

I consider her siblings' current states and tell her I can't imagine that. So she explains that because much of her performance work is seen as politically ambiguous, she's constantly drawing official suspicion and thus embarrassing her grandfather. Her last piece— a collaboration with a U.S.-based Cuban-born artist named Pilar Puente—actually drew the attention of both Cuba's Ministry of the Interior and the *New York Times*.

"Didn't you see the article?" she asks with a mixture of pride and amazement. "It was in August, with a picture and everything."

"My father died in August," I say. "I wasn't paying attention to much of anything."

"I'm sorry, of course," she says, pausing respectfully from her task as the faucet gushes white.

"What's with the water?"

"Oh, these?" She scans the half dozen or so plastic bottles she's lined up next to the sink. "They'll get us through the next few days, while the water's shut off. Don't flush the toilets unless you have to. It'll be at least three or four days, maybe a week, before we can fill the water tanks again. It's so hot, everybody's going through their water really fast."

Deborah plucks a curl of hair from her face. She explains that her piece with Pilar involved simultaneous actions in Havana and Miami. They each wrapped themselves in a Cuban flag and hung by a wire from the apex of a historically important building. In Miami, Pilar dropped from the old Freedom Tower, where arriving refugees like my family and I were processed. In Havana, Deborah was lowered from the spire of the cathedral. When they touched ground, both women dropped the flags to reveal their naked bodies. Then they walked through the streets until each was arrested.

"That was the point," she explains.

"Getting arrested?"

"Confronting authority, confronting conformity, confronting the attitudes that say the truth—which is beauty—can only be defined by imposed order," she says, turning off the water to finish talking, her energy all intense. "The idea was to force another look at ourselves, to reconsider that all of our accomplishments—whether it's the revolution or the success of the Cubans in Miami or whatever—are all meaningless, all illusionary, unless we go back to our true origins, to our unmasked, vulnerable selves, the ones we see in the mirror when we're alone. We wanted to take this image, which is of such magnitude, and confront the institutions of our society, but not in a violent way, not in a disrespectful way, and not in a way that could possibly echo left-right politics, because then everything just gets lost. We wanted it to be universal, classic, but also fresh, also radical."

"And your grandfather . . . he got freaked out by the nudity?"

"Not so much, really," Deborah says getting back to filling more bottles. "He worried that it could be interpreted as antirevolutionary, which is ridiculous. It's about renewal, which, maybe in these stagnant times, is pretty revolutionary in its own way. In any event, the police didn't hold us long, either one of us. Just enough to try and scare us a little. Pilar and I, we're going to do another piece, about communication. We're trying to get animal sounds down in different languages. I'm learning the English ones now. She's learning the Spanish. I don't know how we're going to do it yet."

As Deborah talks, it becomes obvious to me: She will never leave. She's the one who will wear the legacy, the one for whom the future's a gift of awe. Then I feel a night breeze, a cool blue air snaking through the house. In the living room, a veiled Rodolfo squeaks in his rocking chair. My head is lighter, my vision clear.

"So what does your father think about all this?" I ask her.

Deborah turns around slowly from the sink and grins. "Who do you think snuck me into the cathedral?"

During Yamim Nora'im, Moisés goes to temple every day, morning, noon, and evening. Most of the time, he has Orlando drive him to the Sephardic Center, but sometimes he goes to the Askenazi synagogue in Vedado, the Patronato, the one with the silver arch at the door and the high, tattered ceiling where birds fly in and out during prayers. Chevet Ahim, Orlando tells me, is closed.

"The congregation was very old," he explains one day as he drives me to see José Farraluque, with whom I have to discuss the translation I worked on with my father in his last few months. "Everybody died or emigrated. The few old men who were left couldn't really keep it open by themselves. They eventually drifted off, some to Adath Israel—the Lubavitchers give them a free lunch, you know."

Every day, I try to catch Moisés, to talk to him about my father and the photograph he left behind, but he puts me off each time with a dismissive wave and a grunt. His foggy pupils roll away from me.

"Not a good time," says a weary Ester. "Los días terribles—he has so much on his mind."

"So much for which to ask to be forgiven," says a nasty Paulina as she gobbles a piece of buttered bread at the kitchen table. Rafa, sitting idly at the table, guffaws loudly. I remember what Orlando told me and immediately note Paulina's New Balance sneakers, the gold chain around her neck, and the midriff-revealing tube top above her tight, impossibly high denim shorts. She's thin and flat, a little girl cynical and bitter beyond her years. She sneers at me as she chews and I begin to wonder what Rafa's intentions really are, whether he's grooming his sister to take on his girlfriend's business if she should leave him.

(Later, Orlando will tell me that part of Moisés's stress these days comes from the Cuban Jewish community's new relationships with foreign Jews, how Cuban Jews are in desperate need of knowledge and materials about their own faith and need the foreigners to bring them, but how it also puts the Cubans in the strange position of trying to prove their worthiness as Jews, and even their Jewishness.)

"You must have so much to do here besides just, you know, your father's business," says Ester, sensing the tension. Her face is shiny from sweat. Here in the kitchen, the temperatures are even higher as she boils the water Deborah has hoarded. "That fellow Farraluque called."

"Yes, yes," I say, feeling like Ester's pushing me out the door, trying to get rid of me again.

I leave the kitchen and crawl back to the unlit, dank loft that is my refuge. In the darkness I pull out my father's plastic-swathed ashes and the photograph he gave me and stare at the girl on the ship in Havana harbor. She is olive-toned and comely but she isn't Cuban, this I know. I try to decipher the ship's coordinates, looking for clues in the photo's horizon, but I feel too lost to trust I'd know what to do at that water's edge.

Farraluque, it turns out, is a devilishly handsome man, his hair almost blue it's so black, his eyes clear like mine. His jaw is square and his nose slightly hooked, his upper body rippling with muscles. Rumors suggest he has an enormous penis and many lovers, but what no one has told me is that Farraluque uses a wheelchair in his home, his right foot a butchered stub from an accident during a sugarcane harvest. An elderly aunt and uncle live with him, making his meals, running his errands, and helping him about. His house, a two-story structure in Miramar, is equipped with ramps and a strangely rigged, homemade elevator on which the uncle pulls to get his famous nephew upstairs.

But because Havana's streets are so riddled with potholes and rubble, Farraluque leaves the chair at home and maneuvers on wooden crutches in public, swinging his body like Tarzan. I have to rush to keep up with him; Orlando follows along silently, his long strides effortless.

"The thing is, really, how do I know?" Farraluque says in reference to my work. "Forgive me but I have no choice but to take your word that the translation is what you say." He is wearing baggy brown pants that hide any possibility of taking his measure. When Orlando catches me looking, he chuckles and I blush a Russian red.

"That's ridiculous," I say, rattled. The heat continues, steam rises, everything is so bright there are no shadows anywhere. "You can have somebody read it whose English you trust, you have my references—"

"But you've never done a literary translation before," says Farraluque with a sly smile. He sucks on cigarette after cigarette, each gesture suggestive of other possibilities. "I mean, it's not the same thing as an immigration form or a legal writ."

"You have her father's recommendation," says Orlando, the first words he's spoken during my meeting with Farraluque, who insists on taking me to a friend's house. I'm going along because the exchange has been strained and when he suggests it, Orlando signals that it might be a good idea.

The weird thing is, Farraluque hasn't rejected the translation, hasn't commented on its merits. What he wanted, he says, was to see me with his own eyes, to ask me how I'd gone about the work. By hand or via computer? he asks. Do you read it aloud first, or later? Do you go silent during the violent or graphic scenes? Can you say singar, mamar, pinga, papaya above a whisper?

At first I think he's kidding. I want to say, Look, buddy, I was raised in the United States, what do you think? Then I remember Deborah and Paulina and the neighbors all around the Menachs—their loud, salty arguments, the constant innuendoes, the brazenness—and I want to grab him by the shoulders and ask him what kind of macho asshole is he that he thinks such language might unnerve me, or any Cuban woman anywhere.

An unflustered Farraluque lurches forward, his bad foot hanging back, working like a rudder. And suddenly I realize he isn't really asking me anything. He's simply talking, posing, winking at me between sentences.

"Come meet my friends," he says, "we'll have a drink, we'll

dance." He peeks down at his useless foot and lets loose a chilling laugh.

At his friend's house, a perspiring Farraluque waits patiently for the large wooden door to open. It's a lavish mansion on the shore in Miramar, like his own only two stories high, but much more expansive. All around it are foreign embassies or corporate headquarters for Cuba's collaborative ventures with European and Latin American partners. They are painted picture-perfect pastels, with manicured lawns and bent Cuban gardeners pruning orchids and hibiscus behind decorative steel fences. There are no wildflowers here, no uncontrolled bursts of tropical exuberance, no dusty patches.

At Farraluque's friend's, a gated driveway curls around to the back, disappears in a thicket of stout palms and lush evergreens. Through the windows we see immaculate pink walls, a whirling overhead fan with shiny new blades, and a large canvas of splattered colors buzzing with a devil-may-care energy.

"Aren't you just dying?" Farraluque asks, meaning the heat. He pulls his V-neck T from his chest, showing off wet hairs making squiggly lines on his skin. "We can swim here, there's a pool," he adds before I can answer. I feel as if the temperature will strangle me.

The door slides open and we are greeted by a smiling, older man, a starched white shirt on his black pear-shaped torso. "Señor," he says warmly in Farraluque's direction. "So good to see you. Come in, your friends, too."

I quickly look to Orlando: Can this be real? A butler? In Havana?

"Where are your friends from?" Orlando asks casually. He is amused, I can tell.

"From Havana," Farraluque says as we follow the butler through the modern living room—everything is made from imported blond woods and metal, the lamps scream of Scandinavia. In the background, the air conditioner's frosty breath hums. "I know what

you're thinking," he continues, "but they're Cubans, real Cubans—
in fact, revolutionaries of the best kind." Then he snickers.

As we near the sliding glass doors to the back patio, the view
comes into focus. There's a large kidney-shaped pool, a psychedelic
glare distorting its surface. The ocean sways just beyond, undulating
like a blue whale waiting to be petted. The men make a small hud-
dle, patting soft bellies. Shapely young women stretch on lounge
chairs and dangle off the diving board. They are cinnamon-toasted
Cubans (I'm relieved when I realize Celina isn't one of them), the
men mostly scorched Europeans, trembling blisters ready to burst.

"Wait a minute," I say as the butler, too much like a character
out of *Gone With the Wind* for my taste, tugs meekly at the door for
our passage. "What's going on here?"

"I can't believe it!" a startled voice says behind me.

I pivot. "Dios!" I swear. I've moved too fast and my head spins
into a momentary fog. In reality, I've been taken by surprise once
more by Estrella, my old interpreter friend. She's doughy now, almost round, but with all the elegance of the lady of the house. A
confused Orlando blinks; Farraluque, muscles relaxed on his
crutches, grins malevolently. I'm dizzy and unintentionally lean on
him, which makes Orlando edgy.

"Alejandra, I am always running into you unexpectedly!" Estrella's wearing a white linen dress, tastefully accessorized as if she
were hosting a business luncheon or diplomatic visit. "What are you
doing here?" she asks, her hands fidgety. But, like Farraluque, she
does not let me answer, kissing me and sliding her arm through
mine, leading me out to the heavy heat of the pool. "Johnny!
Johnny!" she calls out excitedly to the men, who turn around as if
in slow-motion. "Farraluque brought us a surprise! You're not going
to believe who's here!"

A dashing, satin-robed Johnny Suro, his Clark Gable mustache
snowy white now, excuses himself from the group. He's lean like a
movie star, a whiskey glass and cigar poised in the same hand. "Welcome to our home," he says, kissing both my cheeks, pulling me to
him so I feel the moist softness of his lips.

On the way home from Miramar, Orlando turns on the car radio.
It's the first time Fidel has appeared in public since early September
and he's been talking for hours now. There's nothing else on; when
Orlando skips stations, Fidel hops with him from frequency to frequency. Finally, Orlando clicks the knob off.

"Quite a day," he says with a sigh after a brief silence.

I can't talk. I'm too distressed, too flabbergasted by what I've
seen: Estrella and a now retired Johnny are running a private club
for foreigners out of their home. I'm taken aback by the way Johnny
has reverted to his old playboy persona, even if it's just on the surface, and that Estrella has surrendered. This, I keep asking myself, is
the same strong woman who was willing to sacrifice it all for principle? For love? These two people turning tricks for foreign currency
are the same two proud Cubans I used to know?

"Doesn't it upset you?" I ask Orlando, who understands what I
mean without my needing to explain. He shrugs. "I just don't get
it," I say, "I just don't get it."

"If you lived here, then maybe you'd get it," he says. "Maybe
you'd even be a part of it."

"I can't imagine that," I say, absolute, defiant. "Doesn't it turn
your stomach, the way they were catering to those foreigners—all
men, I might add? And these were people who never had it so bad."

Orlando nods as he drives, the night air crisp as it filters
through the car's open windows. "They were catering to you, too,"
he says softly.

"Yes," I admit, swallowing hard, "but it's different."

"Is it?" He fixes me in his gaze, letting the car drift on its own
for a second or two.

"Yes," I say with a startling confidence. (I have been surprising
myself all day.) "Whatever you may think of me, I was born here . . .
that means something. I was born here—like Martí, like you."

Orlando says nothing, just drives, taking in all that I'm saying but
refusing to engage with me. And suddenly, it's all maddening to me.

"Doesn't it enrage you that that club even exists?" I ask, goading him. "I mean, even if you had dollars, it's not as if you could go there . . . that club doesn't even exist officially, right? They still probably wouldn't let you in, just because you're Cuban—and those women . . . they could be your wife, your daughters."

Orlando nods again, this time with a sardonic smile. "It *is* my wife, remember?"

"I'm sorry, I'm sorry," I say, shaken, vanquished.

"Look, of course it's upsetting," he says, waving his hand in the air like his father-in-law, "but I'm way past that stage. You know what I think now? I think that if somebody's going to make money, if someone's going to live well in Miramar, I'd rather it be Cubans. And if it's going to be Cubans who profit from all this, I'd rather it be people like Johnny and Estrella—because they're essentially decent people—than others who were so much more revolutionary, or who were trying to leave the country until two minutes ago. Those girls are going to find a place to go with their Italians and Spaniards and I'd rather they go there, where they won't be beaten, where there's some privacy and cleanliness, than to some dark room in some creep's house, or to a hotel where the foreigner's always right, even when he's slapping a girl around just for fun."

"I can't believe you," I say, horrified. "You're saying it's okay!"

"No, no, no," he insists. "I'm saying this is not a perfect world, there are no good choices here, not now."

"Then why are you still here?" I ask, shocked by my own question. "You know so many foreigners. Why haven't you left?" I have to stop myself from telling him not to answer, I have to stop myself from apologizing for my audacity.

"Where would I go?" he asks. "To the U.S.? And what would I do? Look at me," he says, his eyes luminous. "I'm a socialist economist in a capitalist world, a fifty-year-old chauffeur for foreigners who was once a young patriot, convinced that we Cubans would change the world, that we would set the example. I'm now taking tips from the very people I thought we'd help. Isn't life ironic? I'm dependent on them now for the worst kind of charity."

"I . . . I'm sorry," I say, ashamed.

"This is the part I don't know that you'll understand: The truth is, I'll never leave," he says. "It's not a matter of belief, because I still believe. I still believe we needed to do everything we did, it's just that . . . look, look around . . . it didn't quite work out how we'd hoped. There are many reasons for it, many guilty parties, and not all of them are in Miami or Washington. And now, who will take care of my family? I can't do much, I'm no hero here, but what moral choice have I got?"

That night, Orlando and I finally make love.

He simply pulls off the road on the way home, dogs howling nearby, and our bodies cling to each other in a sea of absolution. His mouth is honeyed, his calloused hands sturdy, skin fragrant like apricots. His sex is ripe fruit splitting its skin and heavy with juice. (He never enters me with it, he never comes.)

He takes things slowly, even later, when we dance together in the airless and orgiastic moonlit pit at La Tropical, magnificent bodies writhing like eels in the deep, and his fingers dip down in the dark between my legs until I'm quivering, every inch of me drenched.

I am always breathless, awed, caught in the pitch of a heat stroke, suffocating. When I finally let go and air pops into my lungs again, I cry each time, just like a newborn covered with blood and brine.

XXXVIII

There are a few theories about when Jews first arrived in Cuba and the Americas.

The first proposes that the inhabitants of the continent whom we view as indigenous and call Native Americans or Indians are actually the descendants of the Ten Lost Tribes of Israel. According to this story, Jews somehow sailed across the blue from northern Africa and first populated this vast and sylvan continent. Disconnected from Judah and the Levites, they eventually lost their Jewish identity but retained certain rites and values, especially of the mystic variety. Symbols such as the Star of David still linger, although often hidden or distorted, in contemporary native pottery and talismans.

Subscribers to this line of thought often see these Jews through an ideal prism: Connected to the earth and the spirits, they lived collectively and naturally, their Eden interrupted only when the white men, with their viruses and criminality, upset the balance of their idyllic American environment.

This is what Moisés, who has never left Cuba in his life, prefers to believe. He cherishes the notion that the lost tribes might be found and likes to think that every man he meets is his brother, that every act of kindness on the island lifts them all closer to redemption. He doesn't believe all of Cuba's Indians perished but that they intermingled, that they spiked the general population with their blood, each Cuban, if not each Latin American, from the Rio Grande to Tierra del Fuego, an unwitting Jew, part of god's plan to save humankind through—what else?—the eventual triumph of Marxist revolution, the embodiment of Talmudic promise.

A second theory says it was with Columbus that Jews first came, men like Triana and de Torres and the first American San José, hiding behind baptisms and crucifixes but Jews nonetheless. In his seminal *Historia de una Pelea Cubana Contra los Demonios*, a book about an inquisitional exorcism, Fernando Ortiz in one of his many digressions suggests that even such quintessential Cubans as José Martí and Antonio Maceo probably came from a long line of forgotten crypto-Jews.

Those who buy this idea often paint anusim such as my relatives not as assimilationists but as part of an intrepid resistance. Against all odds, these men and women persevered in their Jewishness. In this way, it can be construed that it was Jewish thought—Jewish values—that underpinned the concepts of justice that men like Martí and Maceo first brought to Cuban independence.

Deborah, Orlando's artist daughter, is behind this one because she likes the idea of resistance, of subversion against the established order, of secret meetings and rituals. For Deborah, revolution is constant, meaningful precisely because its work is never done.

A third theory is vaguer, less heroic to Jews and their heirs, but perhaps more acceptable to historians and thus more common. This one claims Jews first came to Cuba in the twilight of the nineteenth century, along with all the other displaced Europeans who began landing on American shores. Later, as the Ottoman Empire crumpled, Turks—including, supposedly, Fidel's maternal grandfather, presumed to be a converso and the source of his discreet but particular sympathy for the Jewish community—arrived by the thousands in Havana harbor.

These Jews, however, do not provoke the same dewy-eyed fascination as the myths of the judeo-indigenous or the anusim because—though they really resisted wars and persecution in their home countries, survived the long transatlantic crossing, and the miserable poverty of life in the tropics—they were the great unwashed, the dark and disabled peddlers and cooks seen in the sepia-toned photos of a young and newly free Cuba.

Within a few decades they would be displaced in popular thinking and in their own community by a great wave of more sophisticated European refugees from Nazism—Romanian doctors, Belgian jewelers, and Austrian merchants—who'd arrive with enough money to pay Cuban immigration officials' exorbitant bribes, set up businesses, schools, and social groups.

Instead of the soft judeo-español of the Sephardim, these newly arrived Askenazis spoke Yiddish and, often, English instead of Spanish. They made quick connections with Americans in Cuba, and with power brokers such as Batista, and lived with the certainty that when the horrors of the Holocaust were over, they would return to Antwerp with their diamonds or sail north to New York where they would be welcomed. Cuba to them was nothing more than a pit stop.

It's late and black when we enter the city the night Orlando and I return from visiting Barbarita in Varadero. A power outage has erased all color except for the shimmering blue of the night sky, the stars blinking. I glance next door quickly, hoping for Celina, but her apartment is still and shadowy. Upstairs, my family's old place remains the same: shuttered and sealed. We pull up to the Menachs' house, all lopsided and crumbling, and hear laughter from inside.

"This is what happens when Deborah's here," Orlando says, love and pride mixed in his voice. "She always gets my father-in-law going, gets him telling stories and jokes. And then she turns it all around on him, using them in her performances and stuff. He protests but he's delighted, he really is."

"You, too," I note.

I'm relieved to hear him; he has been sullen during the entire trip, unable to forgive me for saying life in Cuba might be possible after all. Although my conclusion should have, on the surface, brought us closer together, in fact it's had the opposite effect.

"Yeah," he says with a sad smile and a sigh as he gets out of the car.

Inside the house, we find Moisés and Deborah in the glow of candlelight in the kitchen. Everyone else is asleep, put away for the night. Even the ghostly Rodolfo is missing from his usual post. In the warm hues, Deborah is a picture of brio and beauty: Her face has traces of Africa, from her father's side, and of Sepharad, from her mother's. And yet she is so classically Cuban, her hands flying as she talks, her posture bold and sensual.

"Hey!" she says, jumping up from her chair when she sees us.

Moisés doesn't share her excitement. As she hugs and kisses her father and me, the old man turns away, his face vanishing into the gloom.

"What do you think, Alejandra?" Deborah asks. She and her grandfather are in the middle of their tireless debate: judeo-indigenous or crypto-Jews?

"What do *you* think?" I repeat, aiming my question at Orlando.

"It doesn't matter what I think," Orlando says as he reaches in the murky refrigerator for a warm beer. "I'm not a Jew obsessed with Jews, like you all. I'm a Cuban, obsessed with Cubans."

"Oh, please," says Deborah, taking her seat again at the table. "Like you have to be a Jew to have an opinion? Like you're not practically a Jew anyway, huh? And like you can't be both?"

"We *are* both," Moisés declares, his voice low and flat. I watch him in the light, his pearly pupils luminous. And I think of Ytzak so many years ago and his insistence that he, too, was both: Cuban and Jew.

"Well?" asks Orlando, leaning on the kitchen counter and popping open his beer. He takes a huge, noisy sip of the foam as it spills out the opening.

They all look at me. " 'Well' what?"

"What do you think?" It's Deborah.

"I think," I say feeling clever, "that both are perfectly valid opinions."

"Oh no!" moans Deborah, and her father and grandfather join her in a chorus of dismay.

"What?" I protest. "What's wrong with that?"

"The question isn't about the validity of the options," says Orlando, laughing.

"Yeah," says Deborah, "it's about what you think. You have to pick one."

"Why? Why not both?" I say defensively. "You guys get to be both Cuban and Jewish. Why can't I like both stories?"

"It's not the same thing!" exclaims Deborah.

"Both can't be here first—they cancel each other out," explains Orlando. "It's one group or the other."

"You have to choose," Deborah insists.

"I don't have to," I say. "I can wonder, I can live with both possibilities."

Then suddenly Moisés reaches across the table. For an instant it's clear he can't see me very well so his fingers stretch out a bit awkwardly but eventually cover my hand with his warmth.

"It's okay, it's okay," he says, his eyes fixed on me through their milky gauze. "And you're right—why should you be forced to have only one opinion about this? Why not consider both? After all, we'll never know the answer. And there are other things to think about, things that are maybe more urgent."

Deborah leans back in her chair, as if she's considering the old man's words. Orlando stares at the foam dripping from his fingers and into the sink.

"Thank you," I finally say to Moisés.

"Yeah, you're right, Abuelo," Deborah says, abruptly dropping the chair back on the floor with a thud. "Alejandra's American, she has other things to think about."

Moisés and I bristle at the same time. "I didn't say that," he says quickly. "Don't misinterpret me."

"But it can't be denied either," says Orlando. "I mean, come on . . ."

"No, but neither can any other part of her, especially being born here, being born here on such a special and complicated day," says the old man. Then he reaches up, kisses my cheek, and says good night.

For a moment, Orlando, Deborah, and I sit listening to Moisés as he shuffles down the dark hallway to bed. We look warily at each other.

"He's pretty amazing," I whisper. "I mean, whether you agree with him or not, you have to tip your hat to him. His fidelity to the revolution is a real marvel."

Deborah shoots up from her chair, shakes her head. "Yes, yes, a real marvel," she says, chuckling, and quickly kisses both me and Orlando good night. "I have to go," she says, grabbing the car keys and waving them at her father. "I'll have it back by morning, okay?"

Orlando assents, still struggling with the web of suds flowing from the beer.

"What the heck was that about?" I ask, staring off at Deborah's trail.

He smirks. " 'A marvel'? Have you any idea what's been endured here?" he asks, taking his daughter's now emptied seat and wiping his hands on his pants.

"Look, I don't pretend to have a handle on the kind of day-to-day detail and dilemma you have, Orlando. But, you know, I look at Moisés and I can't help but think of Job—no matter what plague fell upon him, he endured, his faith unshaken."

Orlando laughs. "Oh, my father-in-law is biblical, all right," he says with a chortle, "but you have the wrong story. He's not Job, he's Abraham. Remember Abraham, who was so faithful to his cause that he was willing to make lechón out of Isaac, his only son? Well, that's my father-in-law, willing not just to sacrifice himself but everyone around him—always true to the revolution."

"Orlando, what are you saying?"

He waves his hand in a gesture that looks vaguely drunken, but I realize a few sips from a warm beer couldn't have had such a profound effect. "Ale, listen, my father-in-law . . . he's a great man, a really great man, I love him like, well, like more than a father, really," he says. "But he's fanatical—don't you see that yet? Or are you as blind as he and everybody else in this family?"

"Well, Deborah thinks I'm off the wall, so maybe you're not alone . . ."

"No, no, what rankles her is your . . . naïveté . . . she's one of my father-in-law's biggest fans, are you kidding? He's her example, her role model," says Orlando. "But there have been consequences to so much loyalty. Look, I'll give you an example, just one. You know how important being Jewish is to him, right?"

I nod.

"So, of course, his kids—Ernesto and my ex-wife—they're like, Cuban super-Jews. Temple, bar mitzvah for Ernesto, Hebrew for both of them, talk of Israel, at least a pilgrimage."

"Sure, of course."

"No!" Orlando says angrily. "Not 'of course,' let me finish, damn it."

He gets up, starts pacing. In the smoky blackness, he's a shadow, featureless.

"There was a time in this country, in my country—your country, too, since you're so eager to claim it—when being religious was not such a good idea. Not that long ago either. Not just Christian but religious in any sense. Muslim, whatever. Obviously, Jews, too, a little bit more complicated than for others because of Israel and Zionism and all that. And when you were found out to be religious, you were instantly suspect. And so there were certain jobs you couldn't get, certain careers you couldn't study."

"I've heard that, yes. It was awful."

"You don't know," he says, gritting his teeth, fists at his side as he paces, occasionally running an anxious hand through his hair with a quick, exasperated gesture. "Let me translate for you, Alejandra. Ernesto and Angela were Jews in Cuba in their youth, with all that implies. Do you know what my father-in-law said to them when his own children were denied the benefits of his boundless loyalty? He said that that attitude would pass, that the revolution would recognize its mistakes and they'd get their opportunities later."

"But you studied . . . you were an economist."

"I'm not a Jew," he hisses, bringing his fists down on the table in a controlled, silent pantomime of rage. He spreads his palms on the table. "But you know what, Alejandra? My father-in-law was right.

The time came and nobody cared anymore—right now, with the pope practically disembarking here—it's even kind of chic to be a Catholic Communist, to be religious. But you know what else? Ernesto's dead and Angela's in Spain, and the last thing you could call either one of them is a Jew or a revolutionary."

The next morning I wake up again with my head in a vise, my temples throbbing. The barbacoa is suffocating, claustrophobic. Immediately, I prop open the window and gasp for air, but the brilliant sunshine hits me like an anvil and I tumble back onto the mattress, nauseous and sick.

When I finally crawl downstairs, I find Moisés and Paulina at breakfast in the kitchen, drinking café con leches and eating buttered bread. The toast is a bit hard and it crumbles, the table underneath both their hands covered as if by snow. There is an oversized magnifying glass on the table next to Moisés, but he's not using it. Instead, he stares off through the kitchen window—the one that looks out at Celina's quiet apartment—as a petulant Paulina reads to him from the day's thin and smudged *Granma* newspaper, Fidel's official rag. When I enter, both of them stiffen but neither looks up.

"What's the good news?" I ask as I pry open the coffeemaker and prepare to make a couple of quick cups. The pot's pieces roll away from me, clanging against the sink.

"El Duque dumped his wife for a woman he fell in love with walking down the street," Paulina spurts. "Now he says he wants to leave for Miami."

"Paulina!" protests her grandfather, slamming his hand on the table. "Please!" The magnifying glass rattles, my head pounds and pounds.

"I take it that's an exclusive report," I say as I settle uneasily at the table with them. The girl rolls her eyes in disgust.

"My granddaughter was just reading the news to me," Moisés explains, his eyes spinning in their rheumy orbits. "The bones of Comandante Ché Guevara are being transported to Santa Clara for burial. Thousands have lined the route. My only regret is that I can't be there to join them."

Paulina huffs and puffs. "You want to read the rest of the paper to him?" she asks, desperate to leave. Every day she looks more and more like the girls who linger around the Malecón: painted-on blue jeans, frilly, flimsy top; and points of red on each fingertip and on her lips. I'm suddenly glad her grandfather can't really see her. Next year, will she be in Madrid or Milan? Or can she ride this out and find her own space here like Deborah?

"Sure," I tell her, willing to take over the chore, no matter how painful in my condition, because I want the time, finally, alone with Moisés.

"No, no," he protests, his face contorting into something of a grimace. But Paulina is gone before he can turn to argue with her. He has no choice but to come back to me, *Granma* in my hands, its ink leaving blotches on my fingers.

"How about this article here, the one on Ana Quirot, the track star . . . did Paulina read you that one yet?" I ask, trying to be casual, squinting at the tiny letters on the page.

He shakes his head.

"Let's see . . . she won some race then she says, 'At this time, I have no plans about my future, about records. I am just exhausted. It has been a season for devils'. Hmm, yes, well . . ." My eyes begin to water from the pain.

"The coffee," says Moisés as the pot bubbles on the stove.

When I rush to stop it from boiling over, he defiantly picks up his magnifying glass and scans the paper on his own, muttering under his breath. I decide not to waste the opportunity and by the time he glances up again, I'm sitting next to him nestling a cup in one hand and extending with the other the surviving black-and-white portrait of that curious girl my father handed to me in his final moments.

Moisés doesn't react at first. He merely clears his throat, acts distracted. When I finally let the photo drop onto the bed of bread crumbs on the table, he looks at it sideways, almost as if he were afraid of the image.

From my discreet distance, I examine it again: It's a girl, a young woman, dark-haired, with raccoon eyes like the Menachs but a stranger, her knees knobby, her smile tragic in its own way. She is on a ship in Havana bay, all the usual landmarks fuzzily outlined behind her. She is wearing a coat.

"On the back it says, 'La Habana, 1939,' " I say nervously, reaching to flip over the photo.

But Moisés doesn't let me. He takes my fingers in his hands and holds them up close to his blind eyes, stroking them with his own all the while. Slowly, a smile comes over his face.

"You have your father's hands," he says.

I laugh a little. "Now I know you can't see," I say. "My nails are bitten, I've never had a manicure in my life."

He nods. "Neither had your father before 1939, and his nails were bitten, too," he says. "He should have left them that way perhaps. Anyway, that's not what I was talking about. I meant the shape of your hands, your strength, your softness. Don't misunderstand: I'm not fortune telling, just telling you what I see."

XXXIX

The next day is surprisingly beautiful, not a cloud in the sky, the temperatures mild, the blue breeze from the ocean refreshing. I peer out the window of the barbacoa, wishing I was leaning out the balcony from my old family home instead. I glance up at it but its ledge is still troubled, the boards across its door still in place. From one floor down, I envy the panoramic view I know so well of Havana from there, alive with noise and sex, commerce and play.

In the distance, there's the sound of laughter and the drone of airplanes coming in from Ottawa and Madrid, Kingston and Miami. Toni Braxton and the gentle sway of an early version of Compay Segundo's "Chan Chan" compete for airtime from taxi-bound tape players and boom boxes placed on windowsills, entertaining the whole neighborhood. Laundry flaps from every window, white flags of worn cotton and the occasional pastels.

The man who sings tangos every night across the street from the Menachs emerges with his granddaughter from their home, each of them freshly showered and powdered. They look up, using their palms as protection against the sun, then wave in my direction. I motion back and watch them disappear down the lane, headed in the direction of the Malecón and its spicy spray.

On a sunny corner, a few adolescent boys approach anyone they don't recognize, slyly asking them the time as an opening line. When the foreigners bite, asking in their stunted Spanish what they said, the boys descend, suddenly English-fluent (or not), volunteering themselves as guides, quickly offering to take them to a nearby home restaurant out of sight of the authorities, or just outright begging.

After a bit, I turn my attention next door again, focusing on a beaten old van just arrived. From its passenger side, a large, brawny man appears, his gestures tentative, while a roly-poly rust-colored woman jumps from behind the wheel and, after much effort, produces a folded up wheelchair from the back. I know immediately that the man is David, the man living in my family's old apartment, and find my heart racing. He plops down in the wheelchair, smiling and gesturing to the neighbors who spill out to the street to welcome him from Trinidad. The rust-colored woman hovers shyly nearby, bunching the material of his shirt at the shoulders as she holds on to him. Everyone shakes her hand, kisses her cheek, or hugs her.

As bursts of light pop around the scene, I notice a young woman—Medusa-haired, caramel-kissed skin, her lips a perfect Cupid's bow—snapping at the happy scene with an Instamatic. At one point, she looks up, almost as if she recognizes me at the window, but just as she's about to wave—I'm stunned, I'm frozen in time—I hear behind me the impatient knocking of Moisés at the mouth of the barbacoa.

"Alejandra," he yells up, "we have to go."

"Go? Go where?" I ask, confused, rattled.

His hand reaches up, wraps itself around my wrist, and pulls until my face is positioned above him and Orlando, who is jangling a set of old and heavy keys.

"*Now,*" the old man says, his eyes as clear as I've ever seen.

In Cuba, there's never much of a chance that sunset will catch anyone by surprise. It's a long, poetic process, as if each hazy line of color on the horizon demands its own contemplation, its own verse. By the time night clamps down, it's already late, midnight around the corner, epic.

But on the way into Old Havana in Orlando's clean blue

Moskvitch—Moisés uncharacteristically taking the passenger seat next to his son-in-law and forcing me into the back—all he can talk about is how important time is today, and how so much is still before us before night falls. I try to catch Orlando's eye in the rearview mirror, but he avoids me, just the slightest smile drawing his generous lips.

When the car finally stops, no one needs to tell me where we are. I know instantly that the dilapidated storefront on the narrow old-world street of the colonial quarters is Chevet Ahim. We disembark and Orlando struggles with the set of keys at the rusty and giant shuttered door, then finally pushes it open with a shove from his shoulder.

In truth, Chevet Ahim is only the second floor. The first floor may have been a private residence once, it's hard to tell; it disappears behind the large, imposing stairway that leads up, above the high ceilings so typical of early-twentieth-century Spanish architecture. The walls were once whitewashed a blush of rose or yellow, but they're now streaked and chipped. When we reach the top—we climb with only a bit of small-talk, all of us suddenly afflicted with a curious timidity and embarrassment—we find ourselves in front of a long counter that looks suspiciously like a bar.

"It's exactly what it seems," says Moisés, reading my mind and spinning slowly to survey the area. "We used to sell cold beer here. There were also rocking chairs, and tables on which to play dominoes. Of course, it's a bit disagreeable, on your way to worship, to pass by people drinking. But it wasn't always like that, only later, when we needed to make a little money in order to keep up the place."

He continues down a narrow balcony on which the metal railing is green with mold and looks like it could fall apart with a breath. His pants legs flap against his bones as he walks, his steps uneven, threatening to miss and throw him from the balcony. Orlando and I follow him unsteadily, past a couple of doors that look like offices and an open-air kitchen, then finally we come to what was the first synagogue in Cuba.

"Look, no foreigners!" Moisés says with a certain bitterness. He turns to me. "Imagine, if you will, this space as a place of prayer. The bima was at the center, with wooden chairs all around, and an oil lamp above. The men would sit around the bima, the women to one side, raised a bit from the floor and separated by a little wooden banister. The ark would be here," he says, standing just off where the hazzan might have once stood, his voice soaring in ancient song. "There's no place else like it in Cuba. I suppose, in a way, that it echoes medieval times, maybe Spain, maybe Palestine. I don't know. Whenever I came here, I always felt transported."

As he speaks, the afternoon light streams through dusty stained-glass portals on the walls. Moisés turns his face to its warmth, letting it bathe his brown cheeks, the ashen pools under his eyes. Orlando looks at his shoes, then at the ceiling, everywhere but at us.

"Services here were in Hebrew," Moisés continues, remembering with a sad smile. "Although, of course, all the community bulletin announcements were in Spanish. A few ritual songs were occasionally sung in Ladino, but much less so after your great-grandfather Ytzak died."

"These songs . . . how did . . . they were passed down . . . ?" I ask, amazed at Ytzak's persistence, at the inheritance I might have lost. In the background, I hear Orlando now rummaging through one of the other rooms.

"Oh, no," Moisés says with a laugh. "He might have known maybe a couple growing up but, you see, after he found out . . . after he came to Havana, he went through everything. He read, he studied. He was voracious. He could have been a rabbi, he was so ardent about it all, but it was mostly new knowledge—indeed, I think that was part of his zeal. To be honest, Alejandra, I'm not sure he knew for a fact he was Jewish growing up, just different somehow. It all clicked for him here, when he met some American Jews."

About then, Orlando appears with a pair of wooden chairs and sets them up for us in the center of the room. "Here," he says humbly, then steps back and away. "I'll wait downstairs," he adds, raising the keys to show us he's still got them.

Moisés extends his hand in a gentlemanly fashion, suggesting I sit down. When I hesitate, he forgoes chivalry and settles himself in the other chair. He lowers his eyelids slowly, then raises them again with that regal patience.

"Sit, sit," he says in a whisper. "I've got a story to tell you."

According to Moisés Menach, when my great-grandfather Ytzak arrived in Havana in 1932 with my father in tow, it was a much changed city since his last stay. There was a dictatorship, there was an official brutality. Since most of the anti-Machado terrorism exploded in and near Old Havana, the traditionally Jewish neighborhood, repression there was especially savage. The American Jewish community tended to stay away, conducting their own services, concerned mostly with their own situation, embarrassed by the natives.

Hurt by their indifference but undaunted, Ytzak went about the process of Judaizing young Enrique. He enrolled him at the Teodoro Herzl school, and took him to see plays and recitals at the Kultur Farain. They not only went to Shabbat services but to morning prayers. Young Enrique, it turned out, became more versed in Jewish prayer and rite than the vast majority of Jews in Cuba.

"He had a pretty good working knowledge of Hebrew," Moisés says. "I don't know if you knew . . ."

"No, no," I answer from my haze, "he never said, I never knew."

Later, for fun, Ytzak signed him up for the Asociacíon Deportiva Macabí, a Sephardic sports club.

"My father?" I ask, surprised. "Moisés, my father hated athletics. Are you sure?"

"They had a chess club," he says with a chuckle. "He was on that team."

According to Moisés, these were the years of the Great Depression, a global economic crisis that seriously affected the island. In response, Cuba implemented a series of xenophobic labor laws that eventually served as a foundation for a fierce and increasingly dangerous anti-Semitic campaign.

"Wait a minute . . . what I've always heard is that Cuba has always been tolerant of Jews . . ." I say.

Moisés nods. "Sure, the average Cuban, yeah. But not in the thirties, not when your father was in Havana as a boy. I'm certain you never heard him say Cuba was tolerant. I'd be shocked if you had."

I think long and hard. I try to imagine him here, in this holy space where we're sitting, but I realize immediately this is another one of those long stretches in his life my father never talked about.

"In the thirties, just about every newspaper in town, except Ortiz's *Ultra*, was on an anti-Semitic campaign," says Moisés, "especially the *Diario de la Marina*. I don't know why, what prompted the gentleman who ran it to write the things he did, but he was adamantly against Jewish immigration, and he was constantly threatening that a Jewish presence in Cuba undermined national sovereignty and native culture. It was a nightmare."

It didn't help that when Jews established themselves in business, they were often competing in the same trades and neighborhoods as the old Spanish guard in Cuba, much of which had Fascist tendencies. In 1936, sympathizers of Spanish fascism founded the Cuban Falangist Party; two years later, the Cuban Nazi Party was born with the tacit approval of Batista, who held the reins of power extra-officially as head of the army. (The Cuban population as a whole, however, was much more impassioned about the other side, sending more than a thousand volunteers to fight in the anti-Franco ranks.)

"The Nazis had a daily radio show," remembers Moisés. "It was an hourly anti-Jewish tirade every single day, which would then get repeated in the papers. Every day you could find this idiot—his name was Juan Prohías—passing out anti-Jewish pamphlets by the

Malecón. There was lots of espionage in those days, too. Eventually, a German spy was uncovered, and because Batista had joined the war on the American side by then, he had him shot by a firing squad. You can imagine your father, though. I mean, I loved him but he was, you know, a timid sort, easily frightened."

For Ytzak, it was all too much. This was his city, his Zion, his place of salvation. And he had waited so long to return, to have a chance to discover and be himself. He had yearned for too many years to just back away now—just because of these ugly, ignorant thugs. He was determined to not let them stop him, not let them intimidate him.

He decided to answer the taunts by throwing his Jewishness in everyone's face, just in case anyone had any doubts. When invited to dinner, he would loudly explain why he couldn't eat so that even the neighbors heard about kosher laws. When asked out on Friday nights, he would submit his friends to long, overwrought explanations of Shabbat celebrations and their importance. On the streets, he didn't just respond to insults, he could also be alarmingly provocative. He matched every jeer by Nazi sympathizers, who were growing quite bold in the city in those days. After a while, he wore a yarmulke and tried to get Enrique to do the same, but the boy resisted.

One day, walking in Vedado, they walked past a house displaying a red-and-black Nazi flag, and to my father's horror, the old man pulled it down off the pole and had just begun to unhook it when the residents of the house—burly German immigrants with ham hocks for arms—proceeded to beat the living daylights out of him.

"And my father?" I ask, dreading his answer.

"They got him, too," Moisés says. "He was sixteen or seventeen then, I don't remember. They were just punks, really, but there were so many of them. Your father ended up in a coma in the hospital. I know this because he almost died. Ytzak had no choice but to send word to Oriente. I came with your grandparents to the city, because they were just falling apart and couldn't really do anything for themselves."

Suddenly I remember my father's face the day the Berlin Wall fell, how the young neo-Nazis had caused him to tremble in fear. My own hands are shaking now. I tell Moisés I can't hear any more, I can't process the information.

He reaches up to my cheeks, which are wet from tears, and cradles my face in his hands. "You have to," he says. "I don't have much time to tell you the rest before it gets dark."

As the light changes, the multicolored portals aim beams at the western walls of Chevet Ahim. Moisés plucks the photograph I gave him from his shirt pocket.

"Who is she?" I ask impatiently.

He shrugs. "I don't know," he says. "I don't think your father even knew her name."

"What . . . ?" I'm so confused, I get up, start pacing. My footsteps echo in this ancient place. "Then . . . ?"

He tells me that in 1939, after my father and Ytzak had recovered from the thrashing at the hands of the local Nazis, the Cuban Jewish community was undergoing a massive transformation. Hundreds of European refugees were landing almost weekly in Havana, jamming cruise ships from Hamburg and other German ports and using usually illegally acquired permits to gain entry to Cuba.

My great-grandfather Ytzak had become involved through his beloved American Jewish friends—finally awakened to the need to do something—in helping spring the interned refugees from Tiscornia, Cuba's answer to Ellis Island, and assisting them in finding housing and temporary, usually under the table, jobs (one of the conditions of their stay was that they couldn't work, potentially stealing a position from a native Cuban). Needless to say, he'd recruited a reluctant Enrique, then a strapping eighteen-year-old but shy and even a little slow in many ways, into the cause.

"You have to understand, Cuba was very corrupt then, but it was a corruption that was saving lives, so nobody said anything, everybody just went along," Moisés explains. "And then, well, then there was the *St. Louis*."

"Yeah, I've read about it," I tell him as I try sitting down again. "There's a book, *Voyage of the Damned*, and a movie, too, one of Orson Welles's last."

"So you know what happened—how Cuba refused to let the refugees disembark; how the Cubans suddenly couldn't be bribed, there wasn't enough money in America to satisfy these bastards; and how the ship had to wander from port to port, eventually being forced back to Europe. Many of the passengers ended up in concentration camps where most of them didn't survive the war."

I take the photo from his hand. "Is this girl from the *St. Louis?*"

Moisés nods. "When the ship was docked here—it was out on the bay for almost a week—your father was helping with mail and taking papers out there and stuff. He'd row a boat out and, with the passengers' relatives who were already here, he'd toss up cans of food, that sort of thing. One day he managed to get about a half dozen pineapples up to the ship, a real delicacy for the Europeans. He was very proud of himself. The girl was someone he saw there, someone, I think, who noticed him, someone he had a fantasy about. Maybe you could call it love; he did, he kept telling me he was in love. It was the first time I ever heard him say such a thing."

She might have been pretty, I think as I look at her in the blurry photograph. She might have been smart and funny, someone with whom he could laugh, with whom he could find comfort. "They never spoke?"

"Not that I know of," says Moisés.

A few passengers were able to get off the *St. Louis* in Havana—some had legal permits, others had mysterious connections (it's said that the influential crypto-Jewish Maduro family saved its relatives but that's never been proven)—but most were defenseless, waiting and waiting for help that never came. During the ship's stay in Havana, it became unbearable for many; at least two passengers tried to commit suicide. When the ship finally pulled up its anchor, a great wail came from the ocean liner as well as the shore.

"Your father followed the journey on the news, listening to the radio for every report," Moisés says. "When the ship got to Miami Beach—they said the refugees were so close they could see the beach, could wave to the sunbathers on Fourteenth Street—he thought for sure they were saved. He'd managed to get a copy of the passenger list and he sat patiently waiting for the Americans to announce who got to stay—he was sure maybe a couple of hundred of the nearly one thousand passengers would get in. But instead, the Americans sent out the Coast Guard to make sure nobody jumped overboard, and to keep the ship sailing along."

"This explains so much," I tell Moisés, recalling our own arrival. I imagine my father's young heart broken, his alienation, all his fears simmering on the surface. "Cuba was such an open wound to him . . ."

"Hmm . . ." says Moisés as he gets up and stretches. He's so thin, he seems like a brittle skeleton inside his clothes. "But there's something else. And this one's a little harder to tell."

He steps outside the worship area, breathes deeply, then leans on the balcony's railing for a second, but when it begins to give, he lets go. Pebbles echo as they land on the courtyard below. I sit and wait for him to come back, rubbing his palms together, running his fingers through what's left of his once raven hair.

"Please . . ." I say, "just tell me . . ."

After the St. Louis sailed back to Europe, my father was despondent. He was also enraged, feeling betrayed at every turn. Why had Ytzak brought him to Havana? How could he have thought that being a Jew could possibly be a good thing? If he loved him so much, how could he have exposed him to so much hatred and pain? Enrique and Ytzak fought constantly, arguments full of bitterness, nasty words, and recriminations. Maybe his parents, back in the blameless wilderness of Oriente, had had the better idea after all.

"Long after the St. Louis incident—long after the war—there was a lot of international condemnation, a lot of guilt, really,"

Moisés explains. "But the Cuban authorities never apologized, they never looked back. And that gave confidence to the Nazis, who began to appear in the *Diario de la Marina's* society pages, well-appointed men and women stupidly giving the Nazi salute for the cameras. I've always wondered how they imagined they fit into the Nazi plan . . . if they were so deluded they really didn't realize that, eventually, they'd be joining the Jews in the gas chambers."

One day in December in 1939, just six months after the *St. Louis* debacle, Enrique was wandering down Trocadero to just where it became Tejadillo at Prado, which was full of noise and people shouting. Distracted by the beautiful shimmering blue of the ocean nearby, he was swallowed by the mob, realizing much too late that the gathering was a demonstration by Cubans and Spaniards snapping their hands in the air to the rhythm of a sharp Nazi beat.

Bewildered and terrified, Enrique stumbled and fell, only to be yanked back on his feet by a flushed-faced young man who laughed good-naturedly at his clumsiness. Then a speaker boomed something through a megaphone that caused the young man who'd helped him to stiffen and hurl a salutation to the Führer. Like the others around them, he was wearing a swastika on his bicep. As soon as he relaxed his arm, he noticed Enrique's panicked expression.

"What's the matter with you?" the young man said, giving Enrique a light shove that thrust him against another young Nazi.

The second young man turned around, his face distorted and cruel as he looked down at the skittish Enrique, whom he shoved right back. "Weakling," he hissed. "As soft and gawky as a Jew!"

That was all the crowd needed to hear. Immediately, they began circling a shaking, sweat-drenched Enrique. "No, no," he protested in meek defense. "I . . . I'm not . . ."

But just then, the speaker spewed forth another forceful declaration and the Nazi boys turned away for just a second, their arms like javelins. "Heil Hitler!" they screamed, their mouths red, the veins on their heads threatening to burst.

And then my father, in a moment of complete desperation, threw his own arm toward the fiery tropical sun and joined in the chorus: "Heil Hitler!" he shrieked, then ran and ran through the streets of Old Havana, down Amargura and Luz and Inquisidor, his throat burning, hating himself, eventually swooning in the doorway of the kosher cafeteria on Muralla Street run by Moisés's uncle.

XL

It's sunset, the sky still kindling on the night of Kol Nidrei, and Moisés feels I should accompany him to the Sephardic Center.

"You might find it appropriate in some ways," he says, both his eyes spinning white.

Kol Nidrei is a haunting prayer in Aramaic chanted on the eve of Yom Kippur, an ancient supplication that goes back to medieval Spain and asks god to forgive and annul promises not kept. It was designed specifically to reconcile those Jews who converted to other faiths under threat of violence or death and, having survived, wished to return. It is a necessary preamble to atonement.

But standing outside the weathered facade of Chevet Ahim, I instantly understand there is another temple I have to visit and other vows to keep. As Orlando's blue Moskvitch disappears into the narrow labyrinth of the mysterious old city, Moisés gazing back at me through the rear window, I make my way slowly past the crumbling buildings. Fresh drops of rain fall on my skin, a light cool drizzle that makes me shiver.

From nearby, I hear the soft siren of ships in port, long wailings with a primeval timbre. Around the city, white breakers rim the shore with their effervescent froth. The sky rumbles, its groan a deep and faraway ache. The rain generates little streams around the cobblestones, dipping this way then that, taking everything with them. As I walk, I see people step out of their homes to empty a bucket or jar that's been catching the water coming in through cracks and fissures in their ceilings.

"Compañera, ¿qué hora es?" a young boy asks as he leans against the cathedral wall at the main plaza. He's undaunted by the rain, his body language already haughty, much more seasoned than his years.

I glance at my watch without thinking. "Las ocho," I say.

"Gracias," he mumbles, disappointed, signaling across the way for his home boys to stay put, not to venture from under the protective awning at a local cafe.

What does it mean for me to be here?

Like everyone else in Cuba—land of symbolism and rumors—I'm trying to remember the blessing and the curse, the burnt-out dream, the wellspring, our true country.

Finally, it begins to pour, one of those torrential rains so typical and yet fantastic in the tropics. Thunder blasts like the bombs of years before. Jacarandas and roses, hibiscus and the sweetest tobacco rise up, intoxicating me. I begin to run, splashing my way through the streets.

When I turn the corner to the Menachs', for the first time since I've returned, I spy the lights ablaze in my family's apartment. Dripping wet, I run into the building only to find David and his wife at dinner, the door to the first-floor apartment wide open. He waves me in and I look around for Celina, but there's no sign of her.

"This is Alejandra," David says to his wife. He introduces her then tells me he and Celina have traded apartments because he can't manage the stairs anymore.

But I'm a gazelle . . . I take the steps two at a time, defying their slickness. The bulb at the top of the hallway hangs naked on a wire as delicate as lace. When I reach the third floor, my heart in my hands, the door is ajar, a faint humming coming from inside.

I find Celina framed by the threshold: a luminous young woman in a loose beige housedress and blue plastic flip-flops, her prodigious hair swimming in the humid air. As I watch, she runs water at the kitchen sink, letting it splash into a large metal bucket.

"Hey," she says when she finally sees me, smiling and not at all surprised. "I was wondering when you'd show up."

I step inside and the storm intensifies, the lights flickering above and around us.

"You'd think with this downpour we wouldn't need to hoard water." She laughs, tossing her head back, her swan's neck elegant and fine. "C'mon," she says, "are you gonna help me or what?"

Together, we fill the bathtub, the bathroom sink, various buckets and other containers, each one to overflowing. When we run out of pots and plastic bottles, Celina points to a cabinet above the kitchen sink.

"There are some more up there—goblets, tumblers, that kind of thing," she says.

I open the cupboard and reach for my mother's old wine and champagne glasses, one for every imaginable libation. As I take each receptacle, I hand it to Celina, who fills and places it on the dining room table. There are scores of shiny crystals, twinkling with a gentle music that matches the rain.

When there's nothing left to fill, Celina steps back, sighs languidly, and runs both hands through her lush hair in relief. "Está escampando," she says walking out to the precarious balcony and its breathtaking view of Havana. The sky is clearing, the Caribbean shimmers in the distance.

But I remain at the table with its pure waters, its verdant streams flooding the tributaries through the floors, the beams, the stairs, to the very earth.

Hours later, at the Malecón, I pull from my backpack the sealed box with my father's ashes. I carry it in my wet hand like a talisman, the rain beading up on the plastic. I'm soaked to the spine, my clothes meaningless.

Out in the bay, lightning cuts through the sheer mist like jagged spears. It's low tide and the green and red coral is exposed, tidal pools rippling with rain. Somewhere out there the St. Louis once hovered, its passengers weary and innocent, the blue of the ocean the least of their perils. My father traversed that watery frontier twice—once to deliver his precious pineapples and other gifts, then again, on a longer journey to deliver my mother and me.

Por el amor de dios, por el amor de dios, por el amor de dios.

When the rain finally breaks, I tear the wrapping and unseal the box, the white powder sticking to my moist fingertips. I hold the treasure to my lips for a kiss but blow instead, my warm breath carrying my father's remains north. I watch them scatter, even the tiny chips, for a moment swirling into a smoky funnel, a figure that, in another place, another life, could have been Ochún, the Virgin of Charity. Then a fluttering of birds lifts out of the darkness from the rocks, their wings white lines as they soar.

It is on the edge of my city that I offer my father a different, more appropriate kaddish: "I say in the heart of the seas to the quaking heart / Fearing greatly because they lift up their waves / If you believe in God who made the sea / And whose name stands for eternity / The sea shall not frighten you when its waves rise up / For with you is one who has set a bound to the sea."[*]

Judah Halevi may or may not have made it to his Zion, but here, through me, my father is at rest in his.

[*] From "On the Sea," from *Selected Poems of Jehuda Halevi*, edited by Heinrich Brodey (1924; reprint, Philadelphia: Jewish Publication Society of America, 1974).

GLOSSARY

Words are in Spanish unless otherwise noted.

"¡Abajo Fidel!" "Down with Fidel!"

Abuelo Grandfather.

aché (Yoruba) Grace, a blessing.

"Adim chanath chouts Lilith." (Hebrew) "May Lilith keep her distance"—a reference to Lilith, often believed to be Adam's first, rebellious wife. In the kabala, she's the moon goddess and wife of the serpent who seduces Eve. In patriarchal Jewish lore, she devours newborn babies. In modern times, she is a feminist Jewish icon.

"Ah, ¿el turco? Sí, sí como no." "Ah, the Turk? Yes, yes, certainly."

aliyah (Hebrew) Immigration to Israel.

amar To love; romantic love.

anusim (Hebrew) The coerced ones, forcibly converted Jews. Both anusim and conversos profess Catholicism but practice Judaism covertly; the anusim are forced, the conversos may or may not be forced.

arroz con pollo Traditional Cuban chicken and yellow rice dish.

Bahía de Cochinos Bay of Pigs.

balseros Rafters; people who leave Cuba on anything that will float.

barbacoa Loft spaces, usually resulting from overcrowding in multigenerational homes. The Cuban housing situation is dire and has in recent years produced a surprising and embarrassing number of homeless people.

"Baruch attah Adonai, elohainu melach ha olam, ha motzi—" (Hebrew) "Blessed art thou, O Lord our God, king of the universe who brings forth—" First words of blessing said over bread.

bizcocho   (Judeo-español/Spanish) Cake.

bohíos   The thatched huts in which people in Cuba's rural and poor areas live.

brit milah   (Hebrew) Ritual circumcision.

brujería   Witchcraft, usually santería or palo monte.

buenas   Hello.

campesino   Peasant.

castellano   Castillian; the original Spanish of Castille.

ceiba   Silk-cotton trees, believed sacred in Afro-Cuban religions.

CDR   Comités de Defensa de la Revolución, or Committees in Defense of the Revolution: Set up like block clubs, these are the Cuban government cells that keep track of a neighborhood's activities, including the comings and goings of citizens. Generally reviled by Cubans, they're considered dangerous, as a bad report by the local CDR can ruin a person's chances for certain jobs, services, housing, or educational opportunities. On the other hand, they are an effective watch against crime.

Changó   In santería, the god of thunder. He is playful, sexual, and temperamental. In his Christianized form he appears as Santa Bárbara, a flaming-haired female warrior riding a stallion or standing next to a castle tower.

chinelas   (Judeo-español/Spanish) Slippers.

colero   Vernacular. During the Special Period, when lines were exceedingly long, these were persons who illegally charged others to hold their place in line while they ran around doing other errands.

"Compañera, ¿qué hora es?"   "Comrade, what time is it?"

converso   Converted, forcibly or voluntarily; the polite word, along with New Christian, for Christianized Jews who continued to privately practice their ancestral faith. Both anusim and conversos profess Catholicism but practice Judaism covertly; the anusim are forced, the conversos may or may not be forced.

criollo(a)   Literally, creole, but in fact it doesn't refer to race or racial mixing; what it means is Cuban-born, quintessentially Cuban.

Cuba Libre   "Free Cuba." A drink made from rum and Coke; also called mentirita, or "little lie," in many exile enclaves, meant as commentary on the revolution.

cubanismo   The essence of being Cuban.

cubanitas   Young Cuban girls; little female Cubans.

"Dios mío."   "My god."

diplo-tiendas   Diplo-stores; retail establishments in Cuba for diplomats, foreigners, and the extremely privileged. They were fixtures in the late eighties and early nineties but have become less elite after the legalization of the U.S. dollar in 1993.

el innombrable   The unnameable one.

Elegguá   One of the deities in santería; a god who opens and closes doors, creating opportunities; the messenger of the gods. Also refers to the figures or icons representing the god, usually made of clay or wood, shells, and other natural items, molded into a headlike shape. May be placed behind doors or on altars.

"En Cuba, no habrá gobierno de transición."   "In Cuba, there will be no transitional government."

"¿Es tu primera vez en Cuba?"   "Is this your first time in Cuba?"

facha   (Judeo-español/Spanish) Literally, face, but can also mean general makeup or dress.

flan   An egg custard made throughout Spain and Latin America, with regional variations.

goral   (Hebrew) Fate, destiny, the inevitable.

golem   (Hebrew) Literally, a lump of clay (or mud, tar, etc.), a mass crudely shaped like a human, sometimes gigantic in proportions. Also a mythical figure who was made from inanimate material but under a kabalistic spell has come to life. Can also mean a dummy, an idiot, the ignorant masses. In the Hebrew vernacular, it means fool.

guajíras Folk songs, usually associated with rural life.

guayabera A four-pocket shirt used in the tropics, which can be either casual or formal.

güije A spirit, usually associated with rivers. He is frequently accused of stealing children, but often also blamed for sexual raptures.

gusano A pejorative used to mean Cubans exiled from the revolutionary government; literally means "worms" but actually refers to the shape of the bags used by the first wave of refugees, who left by planes or ferries.

Habana Vieja Old Havana, the historic colonial district at the city's eastern end.

habaneros Natives, residents of Havana.

ha-motzi (Hebrew) Traditional blessing at mealtime.

hadas Fairies, supernatural beings.

haham (Ladino/judeo-español) Sephardic rabbi.

"¿Hasta cuándo, Fidel?" "Until when, Fidel?"

judeo-español The oral language of the Jews expelled from Spain at the end of the fifteenth century, a mix of Castillian Spanish, Ladino (which, in its pure form, was used mostly for liturgical purposes), and Hebrew. In the diaspora, judeo-español was deeply affected by Turkish, Greek, and French. It is now spoken mostly by elderly Sephardim.

judío Literally, Jew. Also refers to the straw figures torched during Holy Week in certain cities in Cuba, such as Santiago.

kabalat shabat (Hebrew) Friday night worship services.

kaparot (Ladino/Hebrew) A distinctly Sephardic ritual before Yom Kippur in which live chickens are used as absorbents of sin and evil. It parallels an Afro-Cuban ritual called a limpieza or despojo, in which chickens are used for the same reason. It is impossible to tell if the rituals occurred as a result of influence from one another, if it was brought to the Iberian peninsula from Africa, or brought to Cuba by Jews, hidden or otherwise, and adapted by the slaves, most of whom came from modern-day Benin and Nigeria.

"¿la china?" "The Chinese woman?"

la esquina del pecado The intersection of San Rafael and Galiano in downtown Havana, at the center of the business district. Literally means "Sin Corner," but in fact it was simply a favorite cruising area in the fifties.

la Virgen de la Caridad del Cobre The Virgin of Charity of El Cobre, a city on Cuba's far east coast. This virgin, who is said to have appeared as a small wooden icon that washed up on the shore and was found by a local, is the island's patron saint. She corresponds to Ochún in the Yoruba pantheon.

Ladino The liturgical language of the Sephardim, particularly those descended directly from Spain.

"Las ocho" Eight o'clock.

lechón Roast pork, Cuban-style.

m'hijo Vernacular version of mi hijo: my son.

malanga A root used widely in Cuban cuisine, it's steamed, fried, or boiled; also known as taro in Polynesian and other Asian cuisines.

Malecón The seawall around Havana, it also serves as a broad boulevard where locals stroll, particularly in the evening.

mamey A red, juicy Cuban fruit with a very hard seed in the middle; very sweet.

maricón Pejorative; faggot, homosexual. Female variant: mariconas, but not very common.

mariposas After Cuban exiles, who'd been pejoratively called gusanos, or worms, were welcomed back as visitors to the island in the 1980s, Cubans cynically referred to them as mariposas, or butterflies.

marrano Literally, pig. Pejorative term for crypto-Jews from the time of the Inquisition to the present. Until contemporary times and the popular acceptance of anusim it was often the only available descriptive for persons who were publicly Catholic and privately Jewish.

"Me muero, me muero" "I'm dying, I'm dying."

"Me muero por ti" "I'm dying for you."

mezuzot (Hebrew) Containers filled with a tiny prayer scroll, usually placed at the entrance to a room.

mi negra Literally, "my black one"; vernacular: an endearment.

mi vida Literally, "my life"; an endearment, along the lines of "my dear."

milicianos Cuban militia, particularly visible in the early years of the revolution.

minyan (Hebrew) The minimum of ten males needed for formal Orthodox prayer.

"Mir sind pleitim!" (Yiddish) "We're refugees!"

mohel (Hebrew) The person charged with performing ritual circumcision.

mojito A delicious Cuban drink made with rum, lime juice, and mint.

muchachas Girls; young women.

mulata(o) A person of mixed race, usually of African and European descent.

"Ner Adonai nishmat adam" (Hebrew) "The human spirit is the lamp of God."

"No es fácil" "It's not easy." Since the Special Period, this is the Cuban national creed. It is employed constantly, indiscriminately, for any reason whatsoever.

norteamericanos Technically, North Americans, but generally refers to U.S. citizens only, not Canadians and Mexicans. Most Cubans, like their Latin American counterparts, see themselves as Americans—natives of the Americas—and find the habit of those born in the United States to refer to themselves exclusively as American as arrogant.

ñángara (Yoruba) Vernacular, pejorative; Communist.

oriental Native of Oriente province, on Cuba's east end.

orishas   (Yoruba) African deities.

"Oye"   "Hey."

paleros   Practitioners of palo monte, an Afro-Cuban religion akin to santería, but more determined in its relationship with the dead and more assertive in its dealings with evil.

paredón   The thick wall against which firing squads shoot their victims.

Pesaj   The Spanish transliteration of the Hebrew word for Passover; Pesach.

Pioneros   In Cuba, a Scouts-like Communist organization, compulsory for all children up to fourteen years of age.

piquera   Vernacular: taxi stand.

piropos   Street flirtations, usually presented in exaggerated fashion.

Playa Girón   The Cuban name for Bay of Pigs.

"Por el amor de dios."   "For the love of god."

por favor   Please.

porvenir   A hopeful future, the hereafter.

prenda judía   Literally, Jewish jewel. But in palo monte, an Afro-Cuban spirituality known for its aggression, this is one of the most powerful altar pieces and has as its centerpiece a sliver from a human skull or bone that must come from a non-Christian person.

qué   What.

"¿Qué me está pasando?"   "What's happening to me?"

"¿Qué qué?"   "What?"

querer   To love, most common usage. Literally means to want, to desire.

"¿Quíen es?"   "Who is it?"

"¡Señores imperialistas, no les tenemos absolutamente ningún miedo!"   "Imperialist gentlemen, we have absolutely no fear of you!"

santería   A religious practice created out of necessity by African slaves in Cuba, who recast their gods in Christian forms to appease their masters and gain favor with the local priests. Sometimes the African deities correspond to existing Christian saints, such as the Virgin Mary, but other times they are invented out of whole cloth, such as Santa Bárbara.

santero A santería priest, a holy man, or shaman in Afro-Cuban religions.

santiagueros Natives of Santiago de Cuba.

Santo Oficio The Holy Office, a branch of the Spanish Inquisition.

"¡Se la llevaron!" "They took her!"

señorita Miss, a young woman; also, a virgin.

Sh'ma Ysra'el, Adonai eloheinu, Adonai ehad (Hebrew) Hear, O Israel, the Lord is our God, the Lord is one.

shiva (Hebrew) Jewish mourning period.

shofar (Hebrew) Ram's horn used to signal the start of the High Holidays.

sí Yes. Without the accent, it means "if."

siddur (Hebrew) Prayer book.

"Somos socialistas . . . pa'lante y pa'lante . . . y al que no le guste . . . que tome purgante!" "We're socialists . . . forward, forward . . . and whoever doesn't like it . . . can just stick it!"

te amo I love you (romantic).

"¡Te llevaron!" "They took you!"

te quiero I love you; common usage. Also means I want you, I desire you.

tefillin (Hebrew) Two small black boxes, biblical in origin, containing prayers, which Orthodox Jewish men are required to wear each weekday morning. These are held in place by black leather straps.

toques de santo In santería, feasts to honor particular orishas, or saints.

tostones Fried green plantains.

"Una guajirita en la capital." "A little hillbilly in the capital."

vaca frita Literally, fried cow; a dish of shredded, fried beef.

"Vamos" Let's go.

vaquita Little cow.

vega A tobacco field.

¡Ya!   Enough!

yanqui   A mispronunciation of "yankee(s)"; Cubans much prefer yanqui as a pejorative for North Americans to gringo, which is more Mexican—some say gringo comes from "green coat," in reference to the nineteenth-century uniforms worn by North American cavalry along the Texas/Mexico border.

yeudim   (Ladino/judeo-español) Jewish.

"Y'hey sh'lama raba min sh'ma-ya . . ."   (Hebrew/Aramaic) The closing lines of the Mourner's Kaddish: "May God grant abundant peace and life to us and to all Israel. Let us say: Amen . . ."

zafra   Sugarcane harvesting season.

SELECTED READINGS

Bejarano, Margalit. *La Comunidad Hebrea de Cuba*. Jerusalem: Avraham Harman Institute of Contemporary Jewry, 1996.

Betto, Frei. *Fidel and Religion*. New York: Simon & Schuster, 1987.

Bolívar Aróstegui, Natalia. *Los Orishas en Cuba*. Havana: PM Ediciones, 1994.

Fergusson, Erna. *Cuba*. New York: Knopf, 1946.

Garcia del Pino, César, and Carlos M. Díaz Gámez. *En Torno a un Criptojudío: Dos Enfoques*. Havana: Ediciones Unión, 1995.

Gatewood, Willard B., Jr. *Smoked Yankees and the Struggle for Empire: Letters from Negro Soldiers, 1898–1902*. Little Rock: University of Arkansas, 1987.

Gitlitz, David M. *Secrecy and Deceit: The Religion of the Crypto-Jews*. Philadelphia and Jerusalem: The Jewish Publication Society, 1996.

Levine, Robert M. *Tropical Diaspora: The Jewish Experience in Cuba*. Gainesville: University of Florida, 1993.

Ortiz, Fernando. *Historia de una Pelea Cubana Contra los Demonios*. Havana: Editorial Ciencias Sociales, 1959; reprint: Madrid: Ediciones ERRE, S.L., 1973.

Perera, Victor. *The Cross and the Pear Tree, a Sephardic Journey*. Berkeley: University of California Press, 1995.

Pérez, Louis A., Jr., ed. *Slaves, Sugar & Colonial Society: Travel Accounts of Cuba, 1801–1899*. Wilmington, Del.: SR Books, 1992.

Revah Donath, Renée Karina, and Héctor Manuel Enríquez Andrade. *Estudios Sobre el Judeo-Español en México*. Mexico City:

Colección Biblioteca del Instituto Nacional de Antropologia e Historia, 1998.

Rosshandler, Felicia. *Passing Through Havana.* New York: St. Martin's/Marek, 1984.

Sachar, Howard M. *Farewell España, the World of the Sephardim Remembered.* New York: Vintage, 1995.

Silva Lee, Alfonso. *Natural Cuba/ Cuba Natural.* Saint Paul, Minn.: Pangae Press, 1997.

Stavans, Ilan, ed. *Tropical Synagogues.* New York: Holmes & Meier, 1997.

Telushkin, Rabbi Joseph. *Jewish Literacy.* New York: William Morrow and Co., 1991.

Thomas, Hugh. *The Cuban Revolution.* New York: Harper & Row, 1971.

Wright, Irene A. *Cuba.* New York: MacMillan, 1910.

Days of Awe

ACHY OBEJAS

A Reader's Guide

A Conversation with Achy Obejas

Ilan Stavans is the Lewis-Sebring professor in Latin American and Latino Culture at Amherst College. This interview was first aired in November 2001, in a somewhat different form, on the program "Conversations with Ilan Stavans," on PBS-WGBH.

ILAN STAVANS: *Days of Awe*, it strikes me, is about the tension between public and private identities.

ACHY OBEJAS: Indeed. It runs from the fifteenth-century Jewish diaspora during the Spanish Inquisition to contemporary Midwest America. But it's not exactly a linear story. Told from the point of view of Alejandra San José, the daughter of Cuban exiles living in Chicago, it's her personal journey through the family's history—and Cuba's history, too—to reconcile her identity and her soul. So it plays something like memory does: It moves according to her needs rather than a traditional time line.

IS: Memory—individual memory, family memory, national collective memory—plays an essential role in your work. This is in tune, of course, with Jews and Cuban Americans, whose memory is highly charged.

AO: With Jews, of course, memory is fundamental: to remember the essential; and the recovery itself is a mission. With Jews memory is history and moral lesson. But memory is crucial among Cuban exiles, too, even though as a people we don't have a very long history. What makes this community a bit different from other Latinos in the United States—and similar to the biblical Jews—is that the relationship with the homeland is ruptured. This might be changing among Cubans now, since there is a great deal of travel to the island, especially for post-1980s immigrants and those who grew up away from their birthplace and want to see it again. The young generation is tremendously curious. It asks, What is there in Cuba for me? Is it at all like the Cuba of dreams and fantasy I was brought up with?

IS: A promised land, sort of . . .

AO: Exactly. But no place on earth is perfect. If so, Fidel Castro's revolution would not have been possible or necessary.

IS: Isn't that a natural response to exile—the attempt to survive the present by inventing or embellishing the past? Isn't exile the transformation of memory into a homeland?

AO: In a way it is. It also has to do with the need to find a reason for one's own misery—after all, one needs to justify being away, broken, separated from the source. Why here and not there? And why here you're one of many, whereas there you're unique, special, personalized. The biblical Jews had God to explain their condition, but for Cubans, it's more personal. It is common to hear Cuban exiles say "We gave everything up" and "We left our lives behind." While the biblical Jews were moving toward paradise, Cuban exiles often feel that they moved away from it. And so exiles imbue life in the diaspora and on the island with a great deal of meaning—mostly a certain nostalgic predisposition.

IS: Like a lot of your characters, you left Cuba on a boat at the age of six. Do you remember the departure and arrival? How has the scene played itself out in *your* memory? Has it changed?

AO: It has a fragmented, impressionistic texture. Obviously I could not imagine, at that tender age, the unfolding drama. So, as a child, it was just an adventure. There were a total of forty-four people in a twenty-eight-foot boat. Seventeen of us were kids. It was late at night. We were told we were going fishing. For me, the sequence of events is episodic. For instance, I remember the inky blackness of the water. I also remember a storm. And I remember that we got sprayed with salt water. Halfway through the trip, we were picked up by an American oil tanker. Our little wooden boat suddenly was at the side of this huge metal ship. It was gigantic. I couldn't see above it, to the sides, under it—it was tremendous. It was like a wall in the ocean and Cuba was on the other side. Rope ladders came down. The little ones like me were handed up to the sailors by our parents. My father pushed me up. I remember a hot, pink arm, completely hairless, and the sailor's smell. The sailor grabbed me and hauled me up—not in a violent fashion but gently. Then he put me down on the floor of the oil tanker. I remember looking up at him and thinking, Might I have landed on Mars?

IS: What happened during the first few years as a little *cubanita* in the United States—the process of arrival, assimilation, the process of becoming, slowly, through school, through family, *una americana*?

AO: My family was in Miami for about a year and a half. Then my parents signed up for a program designed to assimilate Cuban professionals into American society. It was in Terra Haute, Indiana. So the family got transported to the Midwest. The landscape changed dramatically. I found myself in fields of corn, surrounded by lots of people who didn't understand us, while we didn't understand them. I spent six to eight months not uttering a word because I was in a classroom where it was forbidden to speak Spanish, and, obviously, I couldn't yet speak English. I was afraid of being made fun of if I spoke *en inglés*. So I made a decision: I wouldn't speak English until I could do it without an accent.

IS: Was there at any point a mix-up of the two languages—a little of Spanish and a little of English?

AO: At home it was absolutely pure Spanish from the moment you walked in the door. My father was dictatorial. If you started a sentence in Spanish and ended in English, he would back it up and repeat it for you fully *en español*. It was impossible to get an answer from him unless everything was in Spanish.

IS: To a large extent, *Days of Awe* is a novel about identity, one in which language serves as a key to map out the past. Several of the characters are translators or interpreters: Alejandra, her father, Barbarita. How does the act of translating serve as a metaphor for crossing cultural boundaries?

AO: I think immigrants and, particularly, exiles are always translating, not just language but culture and circumstance. One of the most significant differences, I think, between an immigrant and an exile is that the immigrant, on some level, undertakes the possibility of a new identity with some willingness and transports herself emotionally to a new home. But for the exile, return to the native land—and the true self—is both essential and eventual. Translation for the immigrant is necessary in order to penetrate, integrate and, more often than not, assimilate. For the exile it may be all that as well, but there is, I think, a great desire to preserve. An exile holds on, I think, in ways that require translation to be constant, as much an act of resistance as of survival, because the exile—forbidden to return home—lives for that return, even if only symbolically. Native skills—including language, ritual, the way of tuning one's senses—can't ever be taken for granted or lost. Exiles,

I believe, live not just between cultures the way immigrants do, but also between realities: There's the mundane reality of everyday life, and there's the reality that might have been and, hopefully, will be again.

IS: Jewishness is prominent in *Days of Awe*, which to me appears to be autobiographical fiction. Alejandra San José, aka Ale, born on New Year's Day in 1959, comes from Cuba to Chicago and eventually returns. What are the roots of this interest of yours?

AO: Well, the novel isn't autobiographical per se. It borrows from my life, the way I think all fiction borrows from the author, but it's more in the details than in the narrative. What I mean is, for example, the address of the place where Ale was born is actually the address of the house where I first lived. But her relationship to the place is completely different from mine. I have no emotional ties to it; I went once and that was enough. But for her, it's a significant landmark, a place constantly on view. By the end of the book, she's with a potential lover in the very place where she was conceived. As to the notion of return, I think that is pretty fundamentally Jewish.

IS: How did the topic of the *anusim*—the Jews who survived the Inquisition by pretending to be Catholic—come to you?

AO: Growing up, we lived in a Jewish neighborhood, had Jewish friends, and went to seders. Then a friend told me my surname was Jewish. I asked my father about it and he was surprisingly evasive. Then I did a reading in Boston in 1994, and a bunch of Latin American Jewish women came up to me and asked if I was Jewish, and I said no. But they were pretty insistent, and they turned me on to the story of *anusim*, or crypto-Jews. I went back to my dad but got more or less the same fog. So I began to explore the situation on my own. And it turned out that my family was, in fact, descended from these people on my father's side, though our particular story is not especially glorious.

I did research in three different countries: United States, Cuba, and Spain. It was like learning a new language, because the iconography of the crypto-Jews is very particular. So it wasn't just about reading, so to speak, but also rereading: Ordinary life is filled with all sorts of clues about the *anusim* in Cuba and throughout Latin America, but the signs have been corrupted and often coopted, so it's not so easy. The story's sweet and brave and tragic, and I wanted to tell it—to retell it, and to imagine it aloud, and to name it so others can come along and do something else, take it a step further, enrich it.

IS: How does it feel to be called a Latina? Or are you a Cuban only?

AO: I often feel Latina, although my metabolism, I take it, is different from other people's. I live in Chicago, which has substantive, representative numbers of different Latino subgroups, none of which dominates the mix: a gazillion Mexicans, Puerto Ricans, Central Americans, and smaller components, such as the Cuban minority. No matter how segregated the city might be, everybody ends up knowing everybody else. In a Mexican restaurant, the jukebox will have Celia Cruz and Tito Puente. In a Cuban restaurant, the waitress—who is probably Nicaraguan—brings tortilla chips to the table. The collage is inescapable. It means that we are all over each other.

IS: Another essential element in your literature is sexuality.

AO: When it comes to sexuality, I'm not especially interested in assimilation but I am interested in normalization. What I mean is that there are different cultural imperatives for gay, bisexual, transgendered, and other people with alternative sexualities—whatever they might be—and I think it's important that those identities be recognized and celebrated. I think that can be accomplished without shock, without judgment, and certainly without the kinds of legal consequences that make queer people second-class citizens in most of the world. In *Days of Awe*, I tried to just let everybody be whatever they were going to be, to live and love according to their hearts rather than any particular label.

IS: On this issue, I'm interested in the comparative response to your work from readers in Cuba and the United States.

AO: In Cuba I'm in a privileged position, since I come in as an outsider, a newspaper writer, though I rarely go to Cuba as a journalist. Thus, I have access to people and places that the Cubans themselves, the native Cubans, don't necessarily have. So I'm tolerated in ways that perhaps others are not. But, also, keep in mind that an important number of the canonical authors on the island

(José Lezama Lima, Virgilio Piñera, Reinaldo Arenas, to name a few) have been homosexual, and have written explicitly about sexuality. However, Cuban literature that is experientially gay doesn't necessarily use the term "gay." Instead, it takes an organic approach to sexuality.

IS: How about the segment of the Cuban American population that sees this as a dangerous subject?

AO: The notion of the Cuban or Latino community as homophobic is curious. I, for one, don't buy it. It occurs because we look at notions of homophobia through an Anglo-Saxon prism. But I think it is easier to be queer in a Latino context than it is to be Latina in an American-queer context. The prejudices of racism are so pervasive, so inherently stronger than the prejudices about sexuality. Gay people are usually born into non-gay families, so the gay-straight divide is being negotiated from the get-go. Everyone has a gay neighbor, a gay brother, a gay teacher, or whatever—it isn't alien, really. Even in small Indiana towns, without a gay community per se, everybody knows a gay choir director or florist or somebody's uncle. But not everybody has a Latino brother or a Latino neighbor. Not every town has a native-speaking Spanish teacher or a Mexican restaurant other than Taco Bell. This interaction remains more alien.

IS: You are on staff at the *Chicago Tribune*. . . .

AO: Yes, and it gives me a license to talk to and get to know all sorts of people in all walks of life. As a reporter, I'm constantly in contact with folks who wouldn't ordinarily be in my life—from a U.S. senator to the guy who sells live bait out of a bucket on the docks. But writing journalism is very different from literature—journalism is very immediate, urgent, public; literature is more reflective and personal. I think, though, that both experiences feed and give balance to each other.

IS: *Days of Awe* is rich, yet its style isn't baroque. . . .

AO: It seems that in the United States, books by Latin American and Latino writers that have the slightest abstraction or surrealism frequently get tagged as "magic realist," whether they fit the bill or not. Cuban fiction isn't really like that, and neither is *Days of Awe*.

This is a story grounded not just in history, but in reality—in a reality that's astounding, but reality nonetheless. Alejo Carpentier, the Cuban author of *The Lost Steps* and an essayist of much influence in Latin America, called this phenomenon *lo real maravilloso*—the marvelously real, or the marvelous reality. The idea, to which I wholeheartedly subscribe, is that reality, real life, is already so awe-inspiring that we don't really need to invent much for it to be truly amazing.

IS: The novel pays homage to Cuban literature, doesn't it? There is a myriad of overt and hidden references to authors and characters.

AO: What I was trying to do was pay tribute to Cuban writers who have been influential or to whom I feel I owe a debt. Most readers will recognize the reference to Celestino, the boy who writes poems on tree trunks, as an allusion to Reinaldo Arenas's *Singing from the Well*, and Pilar Puentes, a Miami-based performance artist, as a possible grown-up version of the character invented by Cristina Garcia in *Dreaming in Cuban*. Other characters—they are cameos, really—echo Cuban writers: Farraluque, the well-endowed erotica writer, sprung from José Lezama Lima's *Paradiso*; René, the chocolate-smeared cemetery caretaker is a possible twist of fate—a woeful one—for the character Virgilio Piñera created in *Rene's Flesh*; Teresa Rodriguez, Alejandra's Cuban interpreter friend, is a nod to Guillermo Cabrera Infante, author of *Three Trapped Tigers*. There are also brief mentions of poets: Eliseo Diego, Nicolás Guillén, Dulce María Loynaz, and Gastón Baquero. For me, these writers are the cream of the Cuban crop. The idea was to have a kind of discourse with the canon. The only significant writer left out, I think, is Carpentier—but that's because he's rather overwhelming, and I may need more time and another vehicle for him.

Reading Group Questions and Topics for Discussion

1. *Days of Awe* deals with the tensions between public and private identities. What, specifically, are some of the characters' conflicts between their public and private lives—especially in the cases of Alejandra, Enrique, Nena, Ytzak, Sima, Barbarita, Olinsky, Moises, Orlando, Leni, and Celina?

2. Each of the San Joses—Ale, Enrique, and Nena have their own way of worshipping. How would you describe these ways? How do these characters find balance? What is the role of faith in the story?

3. Much of the story also deals with exile. Many of the characters—Alejandra and her family, Olinsky and Ytzak—flee in order to change and, sometimes, save their lives. But others—Sima, Moises, Orlando, and especially Deborah—choose to stay where they are, almost in defiance. What does exile mean to the different characters?

4. What is the role of memory in *Days of Awe*? How does individual memory mesh with collective memory? What happens when memory is confronted by contradictory or conflicting facts?

5. The *anusim*—the descendants of Jews who survived the Inquisition by pretending to be Catholic—have a mostly hidden history. How does this play out in the story? What is the role or impact of history?

6. Many of the characters are also confronted with the challenge of assimilation and the emergence of multiple identities. Is Alejandra Cuban or American or both? How does Judaism play into her identity? How does Enrique balance being both Cuban and Jewish? How does that compare with Moises or Olinsky? What about Barbarita's affinity for her Chinese lover's culture and language?

7. Alejandra says: "What Leni and I really shared was a certain shame about belonging to oppressed minorities that had their own paradoxical privileges in the world." What does she mean?

8. Language and its mysteries is an integral part of the novel, and several of the characters are either translators or interpreters of some kind. How does the act of translating or interpreting serve as a metaphor for crossing cultural boundaries?

9. When Celina first appears, she's so bored with Alejandra's conversation and so insolent that she leaves the room. But by the story's end, she has established an eerie intimacy with Alejandra. How did this happen? What changed?

10. In the end, both Ale and Enrique return to Cuba, one way or the other. But Nena, Ale's mother, does not. Why not? Why is return possible for some but not for others in the story?

© Ovie Carter

ABOUT THE AUTHOR

Like her heroine, ACHY OBEJAS was born in Havana and came to the United States as a young child. She is a cultural writer for the *Chicago Tribune* as well as the author of a novel, *Memory Mambo*, and a collection of short stories, *We Came All the Way from Cuba so You Could Dress Like This?*